THE SHAPES
OF
DOGS' EYES

*The Shapes of Dogs' Eyes is
Harry Gallon's debut novel.*

Dearest Big brother,
Happy Christmas &
a happier 2016!

Gxxx

THE SHAPES
OF
DOGS' EYES

HARRY GALLON

DEADINK

DEADINK

First published in Great Britain in 2015 by Dead Ink.
An imprint of Cinder House

ISBN 978-0-9576985-9-8

Cover art by Darren Hopes

*Printed and bound by CPI Group (UK) Ltd, Croydon,
CR0 4YY*

WWW.DEADINKBOOKS.COM

Made possible by support from Arts Council England.

LOTTERY FUNDED | Supported using public funding by
**ARTS COUNCIL
ENGLAND**

Acknowledgements

My brother, Aki, Jack, Tom, Ella and my parents.

Thank you.

I'd been running with Max the Bass Player. Since Christmas and sofas and working in bars. Since Molly. I gave Max the Bass Player my old bass guitar. It was dusty in my mother's spare room. My father told me, 'You're in a story about working in bars.' This story begins in three parts. And I suppose it was about when I stopped playing guitar that I began playing taps. Taps like nipples. Taps like dicks. Beer like piss and come and spit. I'd been running around Hackney with Max, chasing The Shapes of Dogs' Eyes. One.

The nights were my favourite. Long London nights wrapped up on the sofa. All sofas that lasted forever. I moved to Hackney a year ago, to endless nights of tired feet still humming a comedown far from sight, always a glass of water on the floor I kicked over, always a rainy police car siren moaning. A love song sung to all the bartenders of London. And I am wrapped in Ace's spare duvet, in Theo's thick old throw with a map of the world sewn on it, in a towel or an old grey bed sheet with Max on the Shacklewell Lane, house-sitting in the gloam of street lamps that part the bars welded over the window, from the days when that place was a motorcycle repair garage. Orange light always walking in through whichever window I'd most recently slipped through. Nowhere to call my own, except my body, and even that was being shared. The nights were my favourite. That's two.

Have you ever looked into a dog's eyes? The pupils are not round. I have astigmatism in my left eye, so I know. When I was thirteen I stuck my hand down a terrier's throat to remove a chicken bone she'd been choking on. My mother once stuck her hand down my brother's throat. He had eaten the skin of a kiwi fruit, and it had lodged itself in there good. He was a child at the time. His throat didn't like it. It's all coming back. The dog coughed up blood, but only a safe amount.

Back to me. When I was a baby, or maybe two or three, I tried eating a wasp I found lounging in a garden memory. Well, this is what I imagine. There was an apple tree right in the middle, ivy on the walls and the remains of a Thomas the Tank Engine bicycle that didn't belong to me. The wasp only managed to sting my lip. As you can see, my family has a strange oral tradition. It involves shouting. I stuck my hand down the throat of a little white and brown coated terrier, to remove a chicken bone I'd given her two minutes earlier. Dogs don't pace their consumption, or care what danger they're chewing, and I wanted to test the rumour that bird bones would shatter. The chicken had been marinated in barbecue sauce, so who can really blame her? All the flesh was gone. She was happy when I freed her, wagged her tail. But I was too ashamed to tell her, 'Hey, it's all my fault.' Of course she knew. I could tell by the look in her left eye. It had a corner. But that didn't stop her turning the other paw. Dogs will do it all for the love of their owner. That's three.

The Queen kept leering at me. Mocking. Cashing tills. Smashing bells. Smells of brewer's yeast, of bugs, their faeces and families and drugs. The Queen kept changing faces when I opened the drawers for change. Horizontal folds around her cheek and she looked like a deranged outpatient waiting for a bus. On a tenner. Green fiver, green wrinkles crunched enviously out of some regular's drunken pocket – half a barley wine. Bit early for barley wine? It's still warm outside. The Queen glows red like Beelzebub on a fifty pound note, conjuring, shining with skin less wet. Got to check each fifty we get. Some pretty good fakes kept turning up. But this time she wasn't mine. She was yawning. Seven-point-four-per-cent.

I'm a tap-puller. No student, artist or writer. No cause but to put bowls before paws and pint glasses on bank note coasters. That's why Boaz hired me. Because I was good. And I think Dee had a lot to do with it. Boaz was telling me about when he used to work at one of the company's other premises, The Crown, on Chapel Road. I got off a bus earlier and nearly fell over. My right leg was dead. It had been crossed for fifty minutes straight, 276 from Bow to Stoke Newington, first thing, 8am. Warm ventilators that spoke to me, made me calm for all the sleep I missed on the sofa, having spent the night with Molly, who had a real bed for six fifty a month. I said I couldn't see the appeal, but then perhaps she was more real than me. I wanted to cook for her, but I didn't have a kitchen either. I only had an unfoldable sofa, but the frame was bent and the mattress was stained and old.

Boaz was telling me about when he first worked for the company, years ago, when he was lower down on the employee scale. I was setting up the bar. It was a fifteen minute affair, if you move fast, get the glass washer on to warm up and the benches set down outside, pavement swept. That left forty-five minutes to convalesce before disengaging the anti-human bolt on the door.

I had my own set of keys then.

That meant they wanted me forever.

Boaz said, 'We had five ashtrays at the end of last week.'

I said, 'We still have four.'

He was flexing his Turkish muscles. I was flexing my bottle opener.

'Didn't you get any sleep?' he said. I shook my head. We went to Lisa's the night before and had a lock-in. 'When I worked at The Crown,' said Boaz, 'there was this guy wandering around the pub, looking like he'd lost someone. You know how it's set out over there, not much bigger than our place here, but with more corners. And I said, "You alright there mate?" And he said, "Just looking for my friend." He had those shifty eyes.'

I was smiling like an idiot.

'So I said, "You haven't got any friends here mate," and you know how a guy is definitely up to something? He acts all nice and charming, and fucks off without a warning, not even asking why. I said, "You better leave," all nice and caring. And he just said, "Okay." And he left with his coat hanging over his arm. Remember that part,' pointing at me. 'But the manager,' as I was looking over the opening checklist, ticking off all the boxes, filling washer and sink unit with slice-of-lime-or-lemon catcher, which was actually an old tub of mayonnaise some phantom bartender stuck a few holes in with a screwdriver. 'The manager,' said Boaz, 'because I wasn't the boss here yet, was downstairs with a woman whose bag had just been stolen. And they were checking the CCTV. And they're looking, and they're seeing this guy, the same guy who was talking to me, walking past her, not even lingering, coat over arm and slipping her handbag off the back of her chair where it was hanging and sticking it under his coat.'

'Uh huh.'

'And they're watching me walk up to the guy, and, like a total idiot, asking him to leave.'

'Shit.'

'But that's nothing,' said Boaz, as he inspected some guacamole the chef was making, 'because the next day I'm walking along the street from Clissold Park to start my shift. This was when I was training to be a manager, right? And I see this guy, the same guy, and I run into the pub and I shout for the boss and the boss comes out with me and we run at this guy and I get him pressed right up against the shutters of a shop. It was Boxing Day.'

I laughed. 'Stole her bag on Christmas?'

'Right. And I said to him, "If you move I'm gonna punch your face in." And Thomas, the boss, checked his bag. And you know what he found?'

'What?'

'A fucking ashtray.'

My left testicle was hurting again. Usual cancer stress. I'd seen the doctor three times in three months. I'd seen the doctor six times in one year. The doctor. A doctor. Every doctor the NHS had to offer. I'd been scanned and lubed and fingered and prescribed drugs that turned my lips blue. But nothing would mend. Call it bad posture, standing up all day at the bar. No private health care offered, no London Living Wage. Molly asked me if it was Gonorrhoea on a London telephone Thursday. 'Only, I've been speaking to my sister,' she said, 'and, mate, I'll probably want to have children some day, you know?'

We used condoms, anyway.

I was obsessed with The Shapes of Dogs' Eyes. My mother's chicken-bone terrier was going blind. She wrote a book about it, in an attempt to vent her canine frustration. The Shapes of Dogs' Eyes. Terrified of humiliation. Of incontinence. Which was becoming a problem. I am terrified of castration. And also ambition. It makes being a bartender so much more difficult. Molly was living with her sister, who didn't like me. I didn't know why she didn't like me. Molly said, 'You probably didn't make enough of an effort the first time you met.' We'd been walking along Roman Road. Molly paused to look at a dress hanging by a market stall. I needed socks. Her sister wanted to know if she could take a dog into her office. Her office had no windows. She had this theory that men can't shit as easily as women. Lack of natural pushing.

She wanted a whippet.

The terrier's eyes had a milky white incandescence that leant towards bottle green, as though she was a wine bottle washed up on a tropical shore by a sea of frosted glass, made dull by having her ovaries and uterus removed before she could have babies and see them produce. Now her eyes are tempered by heat pressure, held together with a thin coating of plastic film, so when they decide to shatter, they won't. They'll just crumble instead like pencil lead whenever they hit the floor. A crack on the inside made even more edges, while the outside was only more blurred.

'See those porn stars, man?'

'Hmm?'

'They're porn stars, I'm telling you.'

He means –

'Who?'

'Over there. Table 165,' nodding. 'Must be, if they're hanging out with that guy.'

'Couldn't they just be his friends?'

'Hmm.' Boaz smacked his hand on the back of the bar, near the till. He looked up at me and said, 'Cockroach.'

I wanted the meaning of The Shapes of Dogs' Eyes. So I could have it. So I could validate it and be sure that I knew it and could thus relay it to others. I wanted to write it down, not just make it, keep it created in some kind of personal truth my brain itself stated when I came to Hackney to begin with and first witnessed the situation: the dogs. They were running it. And only I seemed to be aware of this. And I wanted to share it. The despair of all the humans. Stuck in forlorn relationships. Projecting emotions on hopeless canines who got better treatment because of it.

And I'd thought that I'd never want it.

'Yes, dogs are allowed in our pub, in fact they are encouraged.'

The idea of children was merely tolerated. As long as they stayed on the lead. As long as they stay in the condom. As long they don't force us to talk.

Boredom.

The lady who ran the Turkish café on Church Street, by William Patten Primary, didn't see it. She gave me a Post-it when I asked for a pencil, a coffee instead of paper. It was okay though – I just supposed she didn't know that all the dogs' eyes were square. They'd been watching too much television. Sniffing too much coke with those big canine noses. The King Charles spaniel by the door was begging to differ. I tried telling her, the dog, about my own astigmatism, and how, secretly, I was one of them, but she was too busy sniffing grounds of coffee to bark or listen. The human by the door just kept one ear open, the other plugged into an iPad. I tried telling Molly, who was sitting beside me, 'Holy shit I'm inside another story.'

Molly said, 'Which one is it now?'

I said, 'I can't be sure. Either it's Life Behind Bars, if my father is right, or else it's The Shapes of Dogs' Eyes.'

Molly rolled hers.

I said, 'I didn't want this responsibility, Molly. I came to London for the beer industry, remember?'

I suppose it was too early to tell.

Carla the German Philanthropist walked towards us along Church Street. Buggies, push chairs, prams and dreams of tapas estate agencies. She saw me sitting with Molly, coffee just finished. She was on her way to take over the bar which was a five-and-a-half-minute-walk-away task. Something that'd no doubt ruin her day. It was sunny. She was going to help people by getting them drunk on craft beer. She helped me decide which story to be in like this: 'No one gives a fuck about the lives behind bars.' She said that, then stalked off, hunched, fading like the red dye in her hair, denim shorts cut off, to wait for a possible internship.

Molly looked grave. She put down her Lady Grey. She nodded her head. Molly said, 'Of course she's right. People round here just want to tweet about terrible landlords. Get back deposits. Walk their dogs. Flay their feet with sockless Doc Martens. At least they look cool. At least they think they deserve it. Who cares about anything else?' Somewhere, inside the café maybe, Stairway to Heaven was playing. Molly was an actor in training. And I was barely listening, but still I nodded and knew that what she was saying was right because she was always downward dogging.

Max the Bass Player walked up and down the Kingsland Road. Free bottle of Prosecco and girls he'd known. Trains to Lewisham via London Bridge, where his older brother, a plumber, lived. Studio in Stoke Newington, Hackney, where he spent most nights a week on the sofa (like me), teeth unbrushed, pants unchanged. Out for poached egg mornings of coffee and sausage substitute so thank you Linda McCartney, headphones with Band on the Run. Max said that Kingsland Road is the greatest road in London, and of course that was where I found him. On the corner where Cazenove meets Stoke Newington High Street, just before the Hasidic convoy of people carriers and young Muslim kids kicking footballs. Stamford Hill. This was before last Christmas, when I wasn't long one of Hackney's sofa residents. I had just left Ace and El Hell's house on Kyverdale Road, with Molly. Max was walking the same way, had been in the studio that day, he later told me, which it turned out was on Belfast Road, just a few slabs over from the house I didn't pay rent for. Max was rehearsing a set list for a gig in Thailand the following week. His band were recording an album. Someone invited them to headline a festival in Bangkok and they flew out that Friday. So they'd been busy rehearsing and packing London into several flight cases. It had been five years since I'd last seen him. I was working in bars outside of London. A sort of catering event management system. Too generic alcohol consumption, too London Pride, Smirnoff and Jaegermeister for my own single malt, dry-hopped liking. I don't remember how we lost touch. One of us likely took a wrong turn while in the throes of a young relationship. Max moved, at some point, to Shepherd's Bush, which was cool at the time but was done by the time I found him. The studio smelled like a bike shop. It was late. Max was smashing strings and volumes.

He had to get it all down by tomorrow.

I said, 'Shouldn't you turn the bass down?'

Max said, 'Its fine. The landlord's probably high. This place used to be a factory, if you'll believe it. Not sure what they made here, but the operation went bust and the place was still filled with these weird old machines when we took it over.' The band had decorated it with quarter-inch jack and five-pin XLR cables, funny posters and pictures for motivational visions and listeners who'd been hibernating, waiting, tweeting crescendo hashtags. Recording a new album. That's the sound of carpet insulation. The back wall held a collection of preamps and iMacs, speakers and D.I. boxes, the desk a settlement for baggies and tobacco shavings. To the side, guitars hung from brackets. I sat in the vocal booth – a group of rugs thrown over a metal frame built round the sofa. 'Very real vibe here,' Max said. 'Hey, do you think I should wash all my clothes before I go? They really stink of weed.'

I laughed.

He said, 'My mum came up for business today. We met for lunch in Central. She put it on her company. And she really freaked me out.'

I said, 'What about?'

He said, 'She's afraid I'll call her from some Thai jail, say, "Mum I'm in here for ten years." Drugs mule.'

'At least you can tell her the show went well.'

Max smiled. Artisan wrists of a Geisha draped over the dislocated limb of a guitar. Long greasy dark hair. Max said, 'I think I have an STD.'

I told him, 'You haven't gone yet. Just chill out, wait and see.'

Not long after we refound each other, I met Max at the bar he used to manage in Finsbury Park, back when he hadn't long been in London himself, was just Shacklewell Max on the Shacklewell Lane, and lived in the old converted motorcycle repair garage, walking dogs to pay part of the rent. All this before I found him. Max. Again. In that bar in Finsbury Park with all its filth on floors and walls, powder and strobe atmosphere sitting loud opposite the tube station, housing ripped jeans of Max, dealers and people queuing for a club night. Floral eighteen-year-old girls on the verge of hipsterhood, in fake flower headbands giggling over half-grams of never-done-it-before impulse coke. No men under twenty-five allowed in, unsurprisingly, but we blagged it because Max knew the owners, the bartenders, the bouncers. He knew the in-toilet coke offerers. The guy on the door said, 'Alright son, been a long time hasn't it?' Not a question but an accusation.

Max's friend Jonny sang in another band. The whole band were staffing the bar. It was a kind of band takeover. Max ordered two pale ales, which was a very broad thing to say. I was alarmed, handed a Camden Pale – so things could've been worse, but still. Max said, 'Stick it on my tab,' but his tab was invisible. Max said, 'It used to get really grimy in here, man,' adjusting his leather jacket and checking his leather hair. 'Some of the guys come in here could fuck you up if it wasn't for the man on the door.' He drank. 'Ah, I forget his name. And this guy,' putting his hand on the shoulder of a man with his back to us, which prompted a quick, 'Who the fuck—Max!' from the stranger.

'This guy used to chuck me a free gram all the time,' said Max.

The stranger shook my hand and said to me, 'He went missing one shift for about two hours. They found him rooting through the old boxes of CDs in the stock room, didn't they lad? High as fuck, you were.'

I think he was from Lancashire.

Max laughed. 'How're you doing, man?'

I shook the guy's hand and he started speaking about a legitimate illegitimate car tyre business he was running. He said, 'I'm not really dealing anymore, just keeping car tyres rolling instead. Really nice tyres, man. Imported. May as well be selling drugs, though, because I've still got the police asking me questions: where'd the tyres come from, all that. I keep telling them they're alright. I think they're hung up on memories of me from before.'

'Before what?' I said.

He said, 'Before I got a dog. It turned me around, man,, I swear.'
'Shit.'

I kept my hands in my pockets and thought about The Shapes of Dogs' Eyes.

The tyre man said, 'She's a great girl, such a good girl,' and started showing us pictures of a grey and white pit bull on his cracked iPhone. The dog was wearing a pink collar, was on a bed wrapped up in a duvet. The tyre man said, 'I came home the other night and my girlfriend was in bed with Lucy.'

'Lucy?'

'My dog. They were all wrapped up and cosy. Such a good girl, man. Maybe the police are scared she'll bite them, but she won't. She's lovely.'

'Your girlfriend or your dog?'

He laughed, grabbed my shoulder. I felt less like a twat in my pinstripe blazer after that. Max said, 'Let's have a fag.'

We went to the roof. It was a flat, sunken roof, a sort of lead-lined swimming pool without enough water. Just a puddle in a centre that was threatening to fall. The walls of a higher next door building surrounded the below-us ceiling, thump thump of the club night going on. Here, there were windows into London. And I hadn't been around Hackney that long, so I felt amazing, felt strong about my decision to leave the last town in which I was living, about my sofa, too, not to mention my soon-to-be-vision, exposed: The Shapes of Dogs' Eyes.

Max, dipping his shoe into the puddle, said, 'I can't remember that guy's name either,' looking around at the worlds above us. We'd come through a door in the bar where some k-holing girl was taking tokens for newcomers depositing their Finsbury Park coats, walked up uncarpeted, spiky stairs where my shoes caught on nails, through a tiny deserted commercial kitchen and out to the London stars.

'You think I can climb up this?' I said to Max, meaning one of the walls around the terrace. Didn't bother to wait for an answer, I was already up there, humming Hyacinth House by The Doors, ready to dive into the great puddle pool of shitty rainwater and moss in the middle of the roof below me. Max wasn't convinced. He said it didn't look deep enough. I said it looked perfectly cavernous, heavy with all the weight of this London, whatever the hell that meant. Max shook his head. 'I'm telling you man, it's about to cave in and drown all those club-nighters below us. Poor Lucy won't have an owner.' Max danced around the banks of the lake, singing.

There was a pause.

I was feeling pensive so I said it: 'I'm glad that you're back in my life. I'm glad we're both in London.'

Max said, 'Me too, man, so glad,' and started rolling another fag and playing demos to me on his phone.

We found Jonny back downstairs, sitting on the end of the bar, swinging his heels into the wood. The three of us took a bus back down into Dalston, to the old converted motorcycle repair garage on Shacklewell Lane. Max said it was free for a few nights and though he no longer lived there, his old housemate, a drummer, had asked him to keep an eye on it while he was snare drumming in America. The old converted motorcycle repair garage was all wooden floors and guitar walls. A big giant desk with amplifiers and iMacs and fags. Jonny said, 'So tell me about The Shapes of dogs' Eyes.' He was sifting through skateboard videos on YouTube. Max was rolling a joint. I told Jonny they are not round. I said, 'They're all kinds of shapes. Shapes with angles. Just never proper circles.'

He said, 'How do you know?'

I said, 'I've looked. Plus, I have astigmatism in one of mine, so I can see when things aren't right.'

Max inhaled, said, 'Who says they're not right,' then blew out the smoke, 'just because they're not round?'

I said, 'Exactly.'

Jonny said, 'So what does it all mean? Is it supposed to tell us something?'

'He thinks dogs are controlling all people,' said Max. 'Boyfriends and girlfriends are too scared to break up, so they get a dog and pretend that they're happy.'

There was a pause.

THE SHAPES OF DOGS' EYES

'Bam Margera was never that good,' said Jonny, and clicked on.

I was twenty-four in the alleyway with El Hell and Ace skateboarding like alley cats with condom hats and can't-do-it kickflip rage. Scrape of grip tape in the London evening, sunny, pleased, which I am trying to express is the saddest time of lonely day to be sitting on a stranger's wall. Hood rats – children from several next doors – scampered in awe of the box Ace and I had built. Coping rail, nails sunk in, flush. He bought a cheap drill for the task, but it didn't have a strong enough choke. The kids were felt-tipping the sides, to Ace's chagrin, getting under the feet of both of them until Ace snapped and chased them all down the alleyway with a big mad grin on his face.

An apple melted gingerly beside me. He'd lived with El Hell for years and things were tense. And hungry. An infestation of flour mites made the purchase of all new personal ingredients prohibited. When I'd arrived they had given me a whole shelf to myself in the corner cupboard, but soon we had resolved ourselves to simply quelling the population growth of Royal Galas that were accumulating, reproducing, building civilisation and eventually softening, in the very bottom tray of the watery fridge. I don't think those apples had seen natural light since maybe March. Was it April or June by this time? I was afraid that they would oxidise and crumble, turn into cyanide capsules and become an easy way out for each of us – Ace, in despair of El Hell's canine troupe: the ambiguous terrier, Noodles, and Hedwig, the clumsy collie-cross. Not to mention Bernie the gay poodle, scared of new people, and some French Bulldogs who'd often stay for the weekends. They belonged to El Hell's clientele. El Hell, sad with politics and lovelorn for an ex, shied away from miserable bank statements because looking after Hackney dogs for a living did not pay particularly well, though the customer count kept growing. And Nanna, who slept in the room closest to the street and drew pictures of dreams in pencil and sketched a mural of pumpkin seeds and dried cranberries on the coffee table every night.

Apples ageing like gold London sky. Nanna tried cooking chicken drumsticks on a tiny barbecue outside the house on the pavement because they had no garden or terrace. But the hood rats kept flicking elastic bands into the coals. The chicken tasted like rubber. The boys had got bored and started playing with an old car tyre they'd found in the Bermuda Triangle, that void between Windus Walk and Kyverdale Road where unwanted possessions vanished, and had begun squabbling over colloquial possessions until the tyre got away and escaped down the street I didn't really live on.

I was an imposter.

Ace said, 'It's cool with the others,' when I asked about staying with them, about what life was like living in London, before The Shapes of Dogs' Eyes had meaning or had even made itself known. Ace said, 'Stay for as long as you want.' He met me at Stoke Newington Station on an October evening which was grey, a short walk from the house on Kyverdale Road. Ace pointed out the best corner shop, the one next to The Birdcage, and also the way into town. The first thing I did when I got into the flat was get locked in the upstairs toilet. I broke out with force to face Nanna, just met her: she was smiling and had four pairs of sunglasses on her head. Then we went and sat down on the grim green sofa that became my bed, discussing ways of employment. Nanna said, 'The pub on the High Street has a HELP WANTED sign in the window.'

Noodles climbed onto the sofa beside me and started licking herself.

When I first moved in the voice was sunshine and concrete it was heat it was hell it was the smell of rain on the awnings of chicken shop estates, of grease and THC on fingers inserted for gums. I used to stand on the Lee Bridge roundabout at five-thirty in the afternoon, unused, unavailable, unattainable, lost, looking East. I used to listen to the tower block and the palm trees outside the townhouse terraces on Kenninghall Road which shouted at me and threw chicken bones all over the floor. I was sweating constantly, didn't know this was the voice of a very old child. In March, in an attempt to temporarily escape the flour mites of Ace's house, I took a trip to Brittany, France, with Molly. We had been seeing each other casually for a few months and had decided to rent a small house there in the off-season. We had five days of lounging fireplace nudism and, 'Won't you come and look at the stars with me?' fantasies of the night. She had Easter off from training. The middle-of-countryside stars were something else. Stars and sex and real beds and emptiness. When we came back to Britain we took a coach to Victoria Station then the Central Line to Mile End where we walked back to her house, and on that walk Molly said, 'The chicken bones are welcoming us home.' We walked with our heads lowered, stepping round the bones like old condoms I'd thrown on the floor. I looked up at the expensive houses and the shitty towers and felt known. A few weeks later I went to Theo's house on Goulton Road, Clapton, and said, 'Have you got any space left in amongst your books? I don't think I can live with Ace for much longer.'

Theo, a new friend I'd met through beer, said, 'Why not?'

I said, 'I was only meant to stay for a month. It's been almost five.'

There was a sticker on the panelling behind the staff toilet. I used to read the sticker every time I went for a piss. I knew the sticker off by heart. The sticker said: refer to addendum sheet for wiring instructions as product may fail to function if wired incorrectly. I'd read it and wonder why my left testicle kept hurting.

I went to the pub on the High Street the day after my London arrival and got a job. My CV was perfectly catered towards the service industry. No three year degree to weigh me down. Just eyes set for selling craft beer, liquor, wine. I worked in a theatre bar for several years in an old hometown, where the only ales on offer were bottles of London Pride and Old Speckled Hen. It was awful. I'd done pubs before. I worked in one that was on a deserted four-way intersection. Back roads. No custom. The landlady closed early every night, bought me chips with battered sausage. That pub was tied to Wadworth. The first pint of ale I poured had no head. Too slow on the hand pump. Only gas assisted but I was young and unaware that beer didn't have to be fizzy. Mistakenly called it flat, but flat does not compliment. 'Still cider or sparkling?' Better. New staff – those with no previous bar experience or much knowledge of bars – always put customers off when they called cask ale and box cider flat. Flat and warm. Shake my head. Nanna and Ace, sitting on the sofa, which folded out into the bed I didn't use. I preferred the sofa cushions because they hurt my back so I got up earlier, early enough to think about pouring beer. Nanna and Ace gave me the idea. Dee was the supervisor when I began, when I started to exist. Dee lived in Stamford Hill then. Timbo, from Hertfordshire, was the oldest serving bartender, always on the floor on Sundays. He wore a purple bandana and was on acid during my first day shift. He knew how to play it. It was raining. Timbo showed me round the cellar in a daze, took me into the cold room and dry store. Showed me how the empty casks were plugged with spiles and corks in the keystone and shive. The keystone is where you knock in the tap. The shive is for venting the gas. Timbo took his shirt off in the rain, walked off down the street waving it at all the 106 buses going to Finsbury Park. Bobby, a part-timer, filmed it on his phone and said, 'Fucking Timbo,' shaking his head as Timbo got lost in the drench.

His shirt was bright red.

Boaz said, 'As it's your trial, we'll have you shadowing Bobby,' who didn't look too pleased about it. Bobby told me, 'Don't touch the till screens yet and don't pour anything from the pumps.' But it got busy quickly. The pub was always busier back then. I had initiative and impatience so I poured and took the money, using someone else's name on the till, got the job and finished at ten.

That's early. Boaz sent Timbo home then too, to recover and face a disciplinary jury of amateur porn stars and men with ammunition tattoos around their thighs. He was chasing the dream of a lost girlfriend. Done with plots, snorting lines in the toilets with whichever head chef the company was employing at whichever time he felt down. But that night Timbo just sat at the end of the bar, near the glass washer and the waiters' station, looking wet, drab, solemn and drinking his wages. He was quiet. He sniffed his clothes and said, 'Not even the Hackney rain can destroy the stench of cooking oil.'

The extractor wasn't working.

Boaz nudged me as he was cashing Timbo's tab. 'Free labour,' he said. And I didn't get paid for that shift, either.

The secret to treating mouth ulcers is whisky. It works best first thing in the morning. After months on a diet of dry pasta, chicken breast and oil-drenched fries from Ghulam, the sous chef who didn't know the colour green, you could easily get run down. There was no space on Ace's sofa to be ill. Too many dogs. Boaz squeezed my shoulder and said, 'You'll be happy, young man. I've ordered Talisker instead of Glenfiddich with the next delivery.' He took me downstairs and showed me the boss's chair. It was black, leather. It swivelled. But if you swivelled with your legs out your knees hit the wall. The Office was very small. It was narrow. It smelled like sweat. A monitor in the corner showed all the cameras that watched us. So I knew where to stand and be free. Steal crisps. Shot a drink with Timbo before finish. Not allowed. Boaz said, 'We need more female staff.' He wanted men for heavy lifting in the cellar and women for heavy flirting on the bar. Push up sales, push up bra. He said, 'When you're a manager like me some day, you'll have the same mind for business.' That idea made me nervous, so I went into the staff toilet which was dark, the light bulb non-existent, pretending to piss while I texted Max about what life was like outside.

He said, 'Hungover.'

I began shutting myself off. This was before The Shapes of Dogs' Eyes grabbed hold. I was still concerned with humans. One morning, after staying at Molly's, I walked home with a stranger's bag that I'd picked up the night before, slung around my neck. There was a crack in Molly's ceiling. When it rained it rained on her bed. I got up in the morning first thing to walk back to sofa home. Back through Victoria Park Village, through Clapton to Stoke Newington and Cazenove, then Ace's place on Kyverdale Road. Chicken bones of Roman Road replaced by Lauriston pizza ovens and autumnal memories of St John in Hackney churchyard, sweating. The stranger whose bag I had lived up Murder Mile, well past the Lee Bridge Roundabout, in a large old block of flats. I gave the bag to some children who answered the door and identified the guy on the Guatemalan driving licence I'd found in the inside pocket. He was their father. I remembered him: nice, drunk, alone. A smell like cats took the bag inside. The children said thank you. I said, 'Tell your father he owes me a drink.'

On Molly's birthday she had friends round for pre-drinks and pizza. It was a house full of actors. Her older sister didn't look at me. She had the room next to Molly's and left the house later than us each morning. Molly's house was a bed respite, even if the ceiling leaked occasionally. The first time it happened we were having sex. Something dripped onto Molly's back. I said, 'It wasn't me,' and how could it have been? I was lying on mine. She started laughing. Next day they called the landlord but he did nothing. So we put old inner tubes and worn brake pads between the slats of her bed and its legs to stop it squeaking. Forget the rain.

Molly's birthday: I went round before everyone else, found Molly partially drunk and reasonably high from the excess ibuprofen and paracetamol she'd taken to relieve some period cramps. Someone was getting married in the flat block across the road and had decorated the front door of their house with a sort of glowing blue trellis. It was a Zone Two fairytale. I began to catch up with corner shop lager while talking to a tall French actress who thought I was a poet. I said, 'No that's not me,' but she didn't get it. Molly was gliding around like socks on polished floorboards, more codeine, ibu, alcohol.

Molly was a cocktail.

She said, 'I've been wheezing terribly, tearfully, all the way from the theatre in Highgate. It just won't fucking stop.' And she was wheezing on the street in Soho after we left the bar, pole dancing with seven quid vodka coke, not even drunk anymore so the night quickly lost all its appeal (should never leave Hackney. That's the rule). Still, I was happy. Poor Molly clutching me and we stumbling out at three in the morning, tried eating plastic forkfuls of late night beef chow mein, couldn't, stood waiting for our Uber and for the nurse I'd call much later when the cramps became weird phantom contractions and we were up all night on the sofa, waiting for the nurse to tell her, via me, panicky, calling, think my girlfriend needs a doctor: 'No you shouldn't take anti-inflammatories, they'll only make it worse.'

Four o'clock. The door across the street was still glowing blue.

That was February.

Apart from my mother's and father's, the only other dogs who had so far come into my acquaintance were El Hell's, and they were always tired. The pub changed all of that. A timid boxer-bulldog cross came sloping inside one day, clinking on a chain lead and looking depressed, conscious that the people I'd just served bloody Marys to, who were watching Vice News on a hungover iPad by the standing lampshade in the corner, intermittently stroking his head, offering him water from our only dog bowl and talking to him like people who're in denial about their loneliness do, were the same people who cut off his testicles.

That dog had dark eyebrows.

Pale fur, beige, brown.

He had a look of perpetually perplexed self-loathing because he enjoyed the stroking, the doting his people gave him, in spite of his reduced libido. There was little to no interest given when herein walked a pretty rescued poodle who wagged her tail in pleasant grin of sunshine pupils, biggest bulging balls of eyes I'd ever seen. It was the ever-hope of canine conversation, muted into a subsonic whine.

The dog looked on. His chin was back on the floor. And when I walked past his people's table (140), I stroked his head, collected their dregs and filled up his water bowl.

That's when I began to feel uneasy about the redevelopment of Hackney dogs. Dogs that trotted along in front of bikes five times their size. Dogs that slithered with ears that dragged and eyes that spied dogs' arseholes. 'The Shapes of Dogs' Arseholes,' said Max, whose shirt had relaxed on his shoulders. My shirt. The one with bulldogs on it. 'Thanks for the loan,' said Max, and invited me to his sofa, wherever it was, whenever. 'No problem,' I said. 'Arseholes?'

'That's right. Has a nice resonance to it. You may as well look at The Shapes of Dogs' Arseholes. The smells. It's more edgy, makes people think you're really on to something. Really, though, you're just talking crap.'

'What do you think I'm on to?'

'I don't know. You're worrying about dogs, but have you considered that that's exactly what they want? That that's their game?'

'Hmm.'

'Can I have another beer?'

Max was at the bar. The pub was empty. 'Sure,' I said, keeping eyes out for Boaz, boss, office on CCTV, handing Max a half of the breakfast stout. 'Tastes like espresso,' he said. 'Reminds me of my Italian friends.'

He needed a comeup.

I was looking around. The pub was dead. I began chalking the beer boards, drawing brewery logos denoting which ales were on tap that day. 'Allyn says I'm the best,' I told Max. Allyn was the assistant manager, the beer wizard, the brains. I hung up the sign that said, "Kent Session Pale". I drew a horse like a white horse hillside for the label. 'Which I think you've captured perfectly,' said Max.

I told him, 'I still prefer eyes.'

He said, 'Well who the hell doesn't? What I'm saying is, dogs will always appear to be more interested in their arseholes, regardless of their bicycle surroundings or woollen jumpers or dog knickers or whatever dog idiots get their creatures for Christmas. Stop worrying about them. They're trying to confuse you.'

'Why?' I said.

'Because they know you know what they're up to.'

'Would you sacrifice your nuts for a plan to go smoothly?'

'I'd give my left one for a blowjob,' said Max. 'Do you think I should have asked out that girl at the café this morning?'

'But you only got one soy latte.'

'Didn't you see the heart she made in my milk? She wanted me, man, I'm telling you.'

'Must have been the chlorine in your hair.'

'First bath I've had in three days,' he said. 'Ah man, I want a girlfriend.'

We'd been at Clissold Park Leisure Centre earlier that day for a swim. We accidentally got changed in the family area. I dropped fifty pence out of my trouser pocket when I took them off and it rolled under the cubicle door and threw up a primary school cry of MONEY MONEY MONEY.

We had the adult pool to ourselves.

Max said, 'How long have you got to be here?'

I said, 'I'm training new staff at three. Everyone keeps leaving me.'

Max sighed. I heard the door to the office go, the click of the shitty deadbolt lock, the rustle of empty Whole Foods sushi trays crunched into non-recyclable waste. Boaz came up the stairs just as his ex came in. She approached him by the entrance to the kitchen. He flexed his biceps, eyes fixed on a cockroach sniffing round the base of an empty weissbier glass, using a mug of tea to muffle the sound of his voice as he said, 'Let's sit down and discuss us,' then waited for her to turn around before swooping down to crush it. He followed her to 190 and winked at me on the way. Max was watching in mute hysterics. He said, 'What's there to discuss about fucking?'

A pause.

'You need to get writing, man,' he said.

'About the smells of dogs' arseholes?'

'This place is a mine, and you don't even need to dig. Shit, you think songs could be about working in pubs?'

I said, 'Probably.'

'Maybe you should go travelling round the country,' he said, 'work as a freelance beer board chalker.'

This idea intrigued me.

'I could be a beer art celebrity. Not such a bad idea, Max.' Ghulam, poised between bar and kitchen, asked for a glass of water and struggled to understand why I wasn't in church on a Sunday. Instead I was filling up ramekins with apple sauce and horseradish, hoping the floor stayed as empty as it was when I arrived. 'I'm nothing, man,' I told Ghulam.

Ghulam said, 'What, no religion?'

'He's just a vision,' said Max, winking, as a timid whippet came creeping in, bored. Probably wanted to roll in marshland fox shit. We watched it take a seat, look at the Sunday menu: roast chicken, pork and beef. Veggie option negotiable but suspect. The whippet sighed. Something, some loud, bearded, sunglassed thing, tugged at its lead demanding attention.

Max said, 'I can see what you mean when you say that you're worried, but your feelings are misplaced. I'd be concerned for that idiot, not the dog. The dog gets everything from him. It's like wiping old buildings from the map, building something more enjoyable, more controllable for yourself.'

'Did you know they're building a Sainsbury's where the old textiles warehouse is? In that car park round the back of Whole Foods?'

'Jesus,' said Max.

Our school friend Sam had been in Moorgate, interviewing the City for work. Sam and I used to play guitar together, drink lager and Four X from his Simpsons mini fridge and smoke weed in my mother's kitchen when she was at her boyfriend's. That's how we met Max. Now, we don't really speak. I think we have vanished. I was waiting at The Euston Tap with suits of beer, train whisperers and a bus stop I couldn't take my eyes off. The bartender's blacks were flecked with silver fish of sweat. The lines were wriggling.

An old Manchester drunk was asking for change. I told him I was empty and looked at my phone: 'Get me to London.' Sam's comment on a photo of Max. I liked it, which was the extent of my relationship with Sam those days. A little red Instagram heart. We were remote controlled, as though by liking the photo I had triggered his appearance: he came grinning across the grass outside the train station, wagging his tale and looking mad.

'You're in a suit,' I said, blithely.

'I know. Dad gave it to me.' He started rolling a fag. 'Worth more than I am to my bank,' he said.

'Nice tie.' That was a lie. It was red and white and stripy. Very rigid. I got up and we hugged, back slapped, my ripped old cotton trousers barking at his brogues. 'You smell like bread,' he said. 'You smell like unwashed sex.'

'How's your mum?' I asked. His mum had tonsil cancer. Maybe she doesn't anymore. She was a heavy smoker.

'She's going to be okay,' said Sam. 'Thanks for asking. Hey, how did you know about that?'

'We spoke for forty minutes the other day. You tried telling me on Facebook messenger, but I called you. I was on the bus. I missed my stop.'

'Maybe I was high,' he said.

'You were definitely high.'

'You want a rollie?' he said. The old Manchester drunk shouted, 'THERE'S ONLY ONE MAN UNITED.'

Sam laughed and said, 'But they've gone to shit.'

The drunk didn't hear.

Parked buses reflected the sun. I blinked and the light imprinted the vision. My eyes had become a memory foam delusion. A sodden mattress. 'It was a shit couple of days, I'm telling you,' said Sam. 'The diagnosis, the tests. She was up in Reading, at hospital, all weekend.'

He took a drag.

'I took, like, twelve valiums and said something racist to a taxi driver. It was meant in a friendly way, I swear. They arrested me anyway. He wasn't even black.' He shook his head. Sam in a suit, silhouetted in the light that was reflecting off a bus's window, cigarette, pint of some farmhouse saison. Herby English take on a re-popularised Belgian traditional. 6.5%. I was in the haze of afternoon booze. Smoke. Eyes incised with streaks of soon-to-be-working UV flashes. A tiny dog in a lady's handbag. Sam, undoing his half-windsor, relaxed. 'How was the interview?' I asked him.

He said, 'I fucked it.'

My ears were frozen. The bus was reflecting. I was back in the studio with Max, listening to the slips of his fingers over the frets and along the neck, the swishing of his hair on floral shirt, eyelids closed in lonesome research, the SHHH of his £3.00 plimsolls on the carpet, which, once, was Persian. This was research of the soul.

I said, 'Don't think you'll get it?'

'No. I stuttered. I think I'll probably just get something back home. Stay with my folks and be closer to mum.'

'Fuck off,' I said. 'Come to London.'

'I want to. I want to see Max. Where was that photo taken?'

'In his studio. His band's in Thailand, playing a show.'

'He was always going to do well,' said Sam, still loosening his tie. 'What about you?'

'I can't stay long. I've got work in less than an hour.'

'Still working in pubs?' said Sam. 'Fuck that, I just want to make money now.'

'You alright Ghulam?'

'Fine. I want to go home.'

'Kitchen closes in twelve minutes. You shouldn't cross your arms like that. It looks unprofessional.'

'Don't look at me like that. Why are you laughing?'

'I've got a degree in physics. I don't want to work in a kitchen.'

'When did you come to London, Ghulam?'

'2008 I came from Pakistan, to study. From a town just near Islamabad. You know it? I work to pay for my studies. I'm doing an MBA at Westminster. You know it? I'm getting married, too. We've been engaged for five years. In eight, I have only been back to Pakistan once.'

'Why?'

'My family, they don't know I work in the kitchen. They don't ever work. My family has a supply business. They supply pieces for, um, construction. It's very successful. None of them need to work in a kitchen. Look at my brother.'

'Nice sunglasses. Is that your mother?'

'No, my sister. Let me show you a picture of my wife, Afrah. She's a doctor. She doesn't know I work here either. When she comes over to England, she will be a doctor still. She said she can come now. I said wait. Next year, when we are marrying. Then I will have a better job. After my MBA, no more working in kitchens. Is very exciting.'

'Guys, shut up and do some work. There's a ticket waiting. Kitchen closes in four minutes.'

Boaz came to London when he was seventeen. His first job was as a kitchen porter in an Indian restaurant in Covent Garden. He said, 'I could tell you some stories about that. The shit. The wastage. The state of the outside bins.' Men would walk past our pub, waving. 'Another old friend of yours?' I'd ask him.

The explanation would be something like, 'He used to work in the market. He used to run the stall next to mine. I sold clothes with my brother. He sold shoes. That's how I'm so good with money. No need for tills when I was twenty.' Boaz had a restaurant with his brothers before he started working for the company. The restaurant started going under and he jumped. He said, 'I'm on the lookout for something else. Always keeping my eyes open for new opportunities. There is so much property here. And so many people to feed.' He wasn't much of a beer drinker. He ordered from larger suppliers. They supplied less interesting ales. Made Allyn shake with rage on delivery day when another pallet of King of Kent or Windsor & Eaton arrived. Allyn beaten. His self-catered order form saturated with eighteen cheaper casks for the chance of two for free. It's easy to manipulate the stock count with an extra one hundred and forty-three pints to account for all the wastage new bartenders make because I do not train them properly. Boaz would say, 'You've got to distance yourself from them when you're supervising. You can't be friends with everyone. The pub has got to run.'

Unaccustomed bartenders would pull hand pumps too quickly, launching golden foamy fireworks that fizzled in the backwash of drip trays then exploded all over their shoes. Boaz would say, 'The ones who pull them right, who stay here all night and drink, who know they're working well, learning something about themselves. They're the ones you want to stick around. We've got two new staff members starting tomorrow. Don't forget to set a proper example.' He'd be standing at the side of the bar, leaning on the counter, texting, waiting for the kitchen, who were always less than busy, to prepare his second meal of the evening. Rice, guacamole and beef, rare-medium.

I was five minutes late for Monday's training shift. Is today Monday? Today is Monday. You are five minutes late for today's training shift. I was five minutes late and Boaz took me downstairs to the office as soon as I arrived. You've got to set an example as supervisor. Dee's gone. You've got to be here before everyone else. And began surreptitiously berating me for not caring enough. Look, I'm sorry. This job is so important to me. They're both upstairs waiting, the new employees. I gave them their training packs and told them to memorise the paragraphs.

Listen.

I began listening, which is to say fiddling with a hole in my long-sleeve t-shirt, avoiding eye contact with his strange protruding crotch. 'You've got to buy new clothes too,' he said. 'Arthur is getting on at me about appearance.' Arthur was the operations manager. We'd report to him on all matters of money, banking targets and problems fixing holes in the kitchen porter's ceiling, as well as infestations, then wait and see how long it'd take for him to do nothing about it. He lived in the building, on the third floor, and flirted with God complexes by asserting his right to smoke outside the door when we'd been told to go round the corner. He enjoyed Lycra but never rode his bike. It just took up space in the cellar.

'You've got some money,' said Boaz, 'you're not paying rent. Still no address to send your payslips to, young man. By the way, you may not get paid this Friday. Something about tax codes. The accountant emailed me. I'll let you know.' Boaz grabbed a stapler and connected the holes of my long-sleeve t-shirt together. Two shores converging. Opposing sides of a civil war reunifying. And then I went back up the stairs. 'Remember to be on time – before your time, actually, bike downstairs in the cellar quick, and if I decide to leave early and leave you to cash up keep the noise down, okay?' That meant keep the fun down, the wind down after hours of misaligned adrenal glands minimal. 'Wait,' he said, 'before you go I need you to take this money.' He asked me to take some money. 'And collect the change for the tills.' Boaz told me to be quick with the training manuals. 'Give them twenty minutes maximum then set up the bar. Use your phone to time them.' I asked to see their CVs so I knew what to expect.

The bars were thickening. I could feel them. They gave me a fifty pound bonus for one particularly good game of bowling during the company party at Bloomsbury Lanes. They wanted me in. People would steal our ashtrays, our Belgian beer glasses. People liked to feel precious, but the bar, its growing wild yeast and bar fly intrusion, felt cheap. Yet CVs came rushing in through the double doors, bringing people rushing through their lives. People who didn't look you in the eye and say please give me something to do. Overqualified? Female? Blonde hair? Blue eyes? Nice. Perfect for the role. Irish too? Natural bartender. An inappropriate tweet requesting "Lady bar staff" had only recently been deleted by Allyn, who was forever despairing, drinking, growing further facial hair to cover the murk: 'That bloody Turk.'

I told the new pair, 'Sorry guys, I was five minutes late for your training shift.'

My trousers were damp with London. London clouds dropped people by the dozen.

They splashed.

I sighed. 'So what are you?' I said to them: blonde hair and Irish, yes. Topknot and penis, check.

'I'm studying at St Martins.'

'And you?'

'I'm an actor. Just graduated.'

'What are you studying at St Martins?'

'Well, I'm a sculptor.' She smiled.

'Do you like beer?'

'I like to drink it,' he said, laughing.

Lack of originality noted.

'I have a gluten intolerance,' she said.

'So you don't really drink?'

'Not beer. It makes me bloated.' She rubbed her stomach as if to show me.

I raised my eyebrows. Looked unimpressed and impatient. Standard practice. Keeps them anxious.

I whispered down the phone to Boaz in the office: 'Why do you hire these fucking people?'

'To sell beer,' he said, 'not drink it. Besides, I thought you'd like it.'

'Like what?'

'She's pretty, no?'

I hung up.

'Get back to work,' he shouted up the stairs.

The guy wore a sleeveless shirt and I was suspicious. I was recording my notes on a hidden sheet that no one would ever revise. 'E15.'

'Excuse me?'

'It's the school I went to.'

'Ah, Newham,' I said. 'I'm sorry,' reaching out a hand for his shoulder, shaking my head. 'Well, you're here now, thank fuck. You made it to N16. Right,' shuffling papers, 'these are the company objectives.'

Just then an expectant pause, looking down at the training sheet for day one, first line: Company Objectives.

'Um.'

Strange stares from – 'Who are you again?'

'Heather.'

'Ben.'

There was another pause.

'Usually they're musicians,' I said.

'Who?'

'Writers, artists, dark room technicians. People who want a halfway job.' They were both looking at me. 'But they get pulled onto the pub bench pavement, the booze circuit, the hand pump fame. We – everyone who works in the pubs around here – know each other, without really knowing each other, if you know what I mean.'

They didn't.

'People pop around to borrow gas, exchange notes for change, radio warnings about Irish travellers causing closing-time problems (no offence).'

'None taken,' said Heather.

'We spend everything we earn on staff drinks after hours and drugs from locally sourced dealers. Jukebox at Lisa's Bar until four in the morning. We're all a big incestuous family, sort of. Everyone crying in each other's pub toilet, staining all our clothes with ketchup and sugar and yeast. It keeps growing, you see.'

Ben and Heather were staring.

'Perplexed?' I said

There was a resounding, 'Yes.'

I sighed. I said, 'You know what the best drink I ever served was? I'll tell you. The best drink I ever served was water. It happened when I'd finished early one night, can't remember which, and some people had just come in with their dog and sat there, at 210. It was a Labrador I think. Craft legs like craft beers, eyes like beer cereals, fur as dry as cornfields. Black like roasted barley malts and the ears of a floppy goblin.'

'Um.'

'And I gave the dog a bowl of water, and I said to the owners, "That's the best drink I've served all day."'

'My mother has a German Shepherd,' said Heather.

Ben said, 'So what are the Company Objectives?' but I'd forgotten. There was nothing even written on my paper.

The Albion on Lauriston Road always looked derelict. It's closed now, but even before it was closed it still looked closed. The windows were covered and the sign was missing letters. I mostly existed in that part of Hackney in the mornings, after Molly left for training and I'd walk back through Victoria Park. It took an hour and ten minutes to walk to Stoke Newington. Blue plaque in the common where Marc Bolan lived. That Londis on the corner by the zebra crossing which stocked good beer for cheap. Once, as I walked past The Albion on the way to meet Molly in the park, one of its peeling green doors was open to the street. Out of curiosity, I went in. Or tried. But I was blocked in my stride by a shield, a force field of old men, their pints and a fruit machine. Don't see those much anymore. Last refuge of Hackney originals. Secrets. Partisans. Old boys would come into my pub and say, 'I used to come in here at the end of every night. It didn't use to look like this though.' They would point out the redness of everything, trying to see me through the bars of beer taps, not the faces printed on the wallpaper or the open kitchen which, 'Actually, that used to be the toilet, if I remember correctly.'

That explained a lot.

'And the bar was in the middle, yes?' I would add, having heard it all before. 'Around those four pillars that hold up the roof. Yeah, I've heard what it used to be called: The Killer. Stokey's. Wasn't it also an Irish bar?'

And they'd say, 'You'd only come here if you were desperate for a drink, a snog or a fight. Now what drinks have you got? Stella?'

'No.'

'Jesus.'

Next time I went to meet Molly in the park she was waiting on the grass near the fountain. She was doing yoga. Her phone was in her shoe. The Albion was all boarded up.

The wild dogs of Thailand held one side of the island. Max and the band held the other, tripping over, floating under the surface of Thai water on acid, strategising, creating plans to conquer, come back around at night and save a bitten woman whose thirty-year-old daughter Max was trying to sleep with. But she, high too, was swearing ('She's fucking dying!'), as the band planned how to beat the wild dogs and recapture the rest of the island. The mother was hysterical, screaming: 'I've got fucking rabies, I know it. I can see it in their eyes.' The dogs had shifting eyes. The pupils changed shapes like kaleidoscopes.

'I saw something in their eyes,' said Max, back from Thailand, unimprisoned, free, retelling his post-show story to me. 'Edges, like borders between countries, hedges between neighbours. And, like, someone was trying to cut the hedge down. And I saw what you were saying.'

'About The Shapes of Dogs' Eyes?'

'That's right. They're smart. They know something that we do not. Hey, maybe they were on acid too.'

'So did you fuck up much?' I said.

He said, 'No, the gig went well, man. Thanks for asking.' He put

his hand around my shoulder. 'Why do you always smell like beer?'
he said, frowning.

'Did she have the disease?'

'Who?'

'The woman who got bitten. Was it rabies?'

'Oh, no. Must have been the drugs. Dogs' eyes like clouds like
fluid like, um, druids on acid. Ah man, we saw the darkness,' said
Max, who claimed he would stay off it for a while. Drugs. Booze.
Meat. Keep clean. 'Stefan and I were lying on our backs in the water,
and then there was this massive black shadow swimming around us
and it really started to freak us out. But at first we sort of played
with it.'

'Yeah, we danced with it,' said Stefan, singer, guitarist, sitting
next to us. 'Because when we moved our arms and legs it sort of
moved with them. There were only eight or so people on the island.'

'Does your mum know you're not in jail?' I asked.

Max laughed. We were on the motorway. 'I don't like leaving
London,' said Stefan, who meant Stoke Newington and Dalston.

'At least your moustache will comfort you,' said Max. 'Does my
hair look really greasy?'

I said, 'I thought it was supposed to.'

He said, 'Is there a shower on the boat?'

'Probably,' said Stefan.

The two of them were sharing a birthday. To celebrate, we rented
a narrowboat in Shropshire and sailed it into Wales for the weekend.
'Anyone driven one before?' said Max, when we'd met the others at
the tour bus.

We all said, 'No.'

I spent a lot of time at the front of the narrowboat. I was reflecting in
the water, which moved like syrup, as though it was contemplating
The Shapes of Dogs' Eyes, or the crumbs of rich teas in the bow wave
our shared contemplations made. Biscuit wake by the rudder. Tea in
the country tasted more malty, made me miss all the micro-beer of
Hackney. I tried to keep it out of me. We made our acquaintance

with ducks en masse and little settlements of animals on the banks. A Labrador tried to board us from a passing boat. It had a handkerchief tied round its neck. There was a skull and crossbones on the handkerchief. The dog chickened out and Stefan suggested we make him walk the plank. He didn't know we didn't have a plank. I'm not sure what the Labrador was afraid of. The water was cleaner than the Regent's Canal, Hertford Union and the Lea Navigation. 'There was a boat moored down by Victoria Park named Stella,' I said. 'We should've brought that one instead.' We were rolling lazy cigarettes and dreaming of London while Max played a tiny guitar by the tiller, steering through the country drizzle our floating bar. We'd brought a lot of Foster's, cava and wine. I'd said, 'I don't mind slumming it with shit beer. It makes me feel more thrifty.'

I had an edge.

Max agreed. Not £8.40 for a pint of American smoked porter.

Everyone had bunks, but Max and I, being the youngest, were on fold-out mattresses halfway along the corridor by the galley. We stopped at a Tesco for the night in some obscure town, stocked up on tobacco and avocado, enjoying the novelty of being in the country. We went to a pub called The Red Lion for dinner, stayed until our clothing dried beside a fake fire, jukebox, bartender who thought we were The Kooks, which passed round the small town surprisingly fast.

'Fuck knows why,' said Max. 'They're shit.' But he didn't deny it.

We were shotting their dusty Jäger, stuffing the mixed grill and veggie lasagne down our throats, pinching lights outside in the smoking area by a mural of the canal someone painted on the toilet wall. 'Oh sing something, sing something,' said the landlady, who started dressing Mark, the sound engineer, in a nappy she kept in her pocket. 'Instagram that,' said too-drunk-Max with a camera, too-drunk-Mark too tied up to question what she was originally going to use the nappy for. Maybe her husband? He was slumped on the floor by a fruit machine near the gents'.

Back on the boat, three a.m. guitars vibrated against my hip and made me think my phone was chiming.

Our boat was sixty feet long and bright red. It was covered in scars and bruises from years of cruising idiots like us. Manoeuvres round tight Welsh bends and under overhanging trees and hedges. There was not much traffic on the way to Llangollen. That made it easier and filled us with desire to drive the boat back to London, which was someone's marijuana fuelled idea. Max suggested I open a pub barge, like the sweet shop that floated alongside Victoria Park, or the boat people who gave out cheap haircuts on Sunday afternoons.

They'd throw your hair into the water for moorhens and coots to use as bedding.

There are two enormous viaducts on the way to Llangollen. I stepped off the boat and walked along them, took photos so all London could know what was happening. It must. The viaducts were great grey stone things riding the greenest landscape I'd ever seen. No safety railings, barely three inches of steel plating to keep in the water and stop the barge we were riding from crashing over the side into nothing.

Crunch.

The bow kept on bumping, sending shivers down our spines in some collective emotional calling. A cheer went up when YOU ARE NOW ENTERING WALES approached on the other side of a long cold tunnel which echoed with another boat's horn.

We waited.

My testicle kept aching.

When we got to Llangollen we left the boat in the canal basin. It was a feat of manoeuvring by Dean, their tour manager and Stefan, though they did almost drown two kayakers. There was a path down the hill into town. We had to wait and let a large horse pass. It was dragging a boat of tourists behind it. When we found an old grey restaurant all eyes were on the food menu, the wooden table, the bottles of wine and, through the window, the shine of a damp Welsh steam engine farting loudly for show.

We went to a pub just down the road where a band was playing The Doors. The song was Hyacinth House, and I began dancing around with Max on top of a broken wall. We were trying to call a dealer whose number we acquired from a young guy working the bar. It was half-past two. A drunk guy stopped us on the bridge, asked for a lighter. It was half-past three and he said he was the train driver. He said he had to be up at five, at work before six to stoke the fire. We tried to convince him to light it now and take us for a ride but he was wasted, so we went back to the boat and listened to music through a bluetooth speaker. My phone went off sporadically. Madness of missing 3G. 'It's the dealer!' I shouted and everyone went quiet. 'It's a text. He says, "Never call this number again".'

I was dangling out of a porthole when something decided for me that I missed Molly. It was a liquid epiphany. A small sign above the porthole said DO NOT OPEN WHILE UNDERWAY. My hair was flirting with the water and the water kissed my scalp and my phone was a thousand miles away in the galley, lounging in the sun where the other iPhones lounge. Mark was cooking the tiniest Sunday roast, and that was almost ready, and there was no signal, anyway. There was only tobacco, a three-way charger and some empty bottles. Something was making my heart hurt. A sensation I may have mistaken for actually being upside down, with my hair in the water and my feet hooked round a bench. A picture of Molly in the bow waves and a confusing desire to return to London immediately, which took hold of me and in a fury had me vertical, ready for action at the stern and, grabbing the tiller, as though swinging it from side to side would move us faster, steering the boat into the bank, narrowly avoiding a cow that laughed because the impact made Max drop his toothbrush into the water.

After that we halted, moored and metamorphosed into rolling, smoking, dealing-Texas-Holdem throats that croaked like cancerous gulls. 'Guys, I keep bleeding through my nose,' I said, and was returned with concerned, uncomforting looks that amounted to silence. Did another line yet still felt lethargic, damp in the ever-rain of draining locks with every foot sodden in vegan Doc Martens which, though plastic, did nothing to keep out the weather. Max and Dean had been throwing lyrical theories across the pop-up table, feeling porous. I'd been cleaning up the poker game, but we weren't playing for cash because no one had any.

An old text from Molly found its way to me through a forest of NO SERVICE, GPRS and will-o'-the-wisp 3G:

iMessage
Come back and do yoga with me.

My left thumb became scarily discoloured, a single temple threatened to implode. My body was bloody. I strained to shit. I said to Max, 'Is this what love is?' It was confusing, and frightening. I could see the dogs approaching, with their colour coordinated leads and neuterings and nights in with Netflix and Instagram accounts dedicated to dogs.

He handed me a bottle of something I couldn't make out in the light. He said, 'Drink this.' It was beer. He said, 'I got it especially for you.' It was malty, with a hint of rye and a burp of smoke. I sighed. 'Smells like a cup of tea,' I said, and stroked the head of a dog who poked itself through our open porthole. A brown Staffordshire bull terrier. Stefan handed a half-drunk can of lager to the dog's wandering midnight owner, who waved. Dean said, 'Did you see the shape of her eyes?'

I licked the rim of my bottle.

Paragraphs of duck quacks smacked against the hull of a delayed hangover. There was a hunger now, to get back to N16, E5, E8. No one knew what was wrong. We'd been going through tunnels and, I suppose, everyone had stayed too long. Theo texted me, finally, in a rare moment of 3G, and said he'd spoken to Nemesia, his girlfriend, and that they'd both decided there was a sofa free in their flat, all for me.

Things were moving.

Slow, yes, like a narrowboat. But moving.

'Shall we ride it all the way back to London?'

The idea was floating again.

Theo said, 'How far did you guys go?'

I said, 'To a place called Llangollen and back.'

'It takes twenty minutes by car,' he said, 'according to Google Maps.'

The current head chef was called Isi. Puerto Rican, Portuguese or Dominican. I can't remember, but he was scatty as hell. He lived in one of the flats upstairs where company staff members were treated to low on-site (steadily rising) rent. Halfway through my second week he made a signal at me from the kitchen. I was standing behind the bar. I was leaning over the glass washer. I was always leaning over the glass washer. It stuck out so much you could rest your elbows on the empty tray. It gave off heat. This was good because there weren't that many places to lean. Isi made a signal to me with his hand. He was standing in front of the kitchen fridges, fiddling with his pockets. 'Look at this,' he said, and lifted the pocket of his chef's jacket. It was the same pocket he'd been lifting since before he lived in London, in a thousand different kitchens of the world. From that pocket he pulled a joint, coned, almost bulging with veins. He said, 'Can I go for a cigarette boss,' to Boaz, texting, who nodded yes without looking. Isi gave me a wink and I met him outside, pretending to collect non-existent glasses from the unused benches. We sat, smoking, reading TripAdvisor. "SHIT SUNDAY ROAST," said someone. Block Capitals. Caps lock. Someone really did not want to praise us.

'Well they should stop employing foreign chefs,' Isi said. 'Only the English can properly cook such awful food.'

Another reviewer said, "The manager was coked through the

roof." It was dated 2010. I said, 'That'll be Zamir then, the last manager. Did you know him? Me neither. Apparently Arthur came round and caught him watching porn on the office computer.'

I took a drag.

'Really?' said Isi. 'Who told you that?'

'Boaz. That's when they made him the manager.'

Isi started talking about The Wire and I drifted back inside for some water. I'd had the same glass for three days. It sat on the side of the bar by the window near the old front doors with the stained glass. The quieter end of the bar. Which was made of black granite. Next door taxi drivers waited around outside, leaning against the former front door window, smoking fags, dialling Nokia dealer phones and stretching ankle bone memories of nine-to-five clutch control and left foot braking. Old doorframes. The ghosts of that building. Strange weird historical tours took place on the Kingsland Road. Tourists or just curious locals following white haired guides who looked up at the painted tiles of our pub facade.

On the bar, tweeted, was Devil's Rest. Seven-point-eight percent. Punk IPA, that's 5.4. Brodie's Hackney Red is 6.1. Magic Rock. Brew By Numbers. Redemption were scheduled for a tap takeover. It had been a busy Saturday night. We had three members on including Boaz and myself. Carla and the kitchen gone home. Timbo was in at first, getting angry with exploding tumblers. New glass stock arrived while I was still in Wales. We washed them to get off the dust. Little tumblers, for spirits and tasters, tempered. They didn't respond well to sudden drops in temperature. Timbo was stacking them back on the shelves two high, but the bottom layer were already dry, cold, so when he put down the first hot glass and it came into contact with one below, it exploded. Squares and diamonds and sapphires drifted right into his face and eyes. They were glass grenades in the hands of drunken toddlers. Timbo cleaned up and carried on, handling the tumblers like tropical dynamite. It was later, when a customer put money for two gin and tonics not in his hand but on the bar in a boozy, beery puddle, that he cracked. Went completely wide-eyed and silent. When his shift was over he couldn't get out of there fast enough. It was nearing five-past midnight when I got the call from Molly, who had missed me too apparently, though I was back in London serving booze while she was busy consuming it. I was stuck three deep behind the hand pumps and there was a massive queue for the toilets, broken light bulbs in the gents' so piss went everywhere, and someone had just puked on the floor. Saturday mix of craft beer hipsters seeming quiet, forgiving, and weekending City wankers up for the thrill of Hackney. They were all the same when they didn't get out the way as you were passing with a new bowl of ice. Squeezed and exhausted, 'Excuse me guys,' for the fifth fucking time going to the cellar for more blue roll.

Molly phoned me from somewhere in Soho on a drunken gay bar crawl. And when I finished I went to her house and lay in her bed as Molly, still drunk, whispered something which sounded like, 'I love you,' but I couldn't be sure.

iMessage
Yesterday 16:53
Are you around later man? I want to play you a song my brother and I wrote together. It's called Sad Lonely Miserable Life. I was on a train to Hither Green last night, and I was sitting on this luggage rack because there were no seats available. I was feeling pretty high. And there was this guy looking at me, smiling. And I think to myself this guy's a killer. And he had this little black thing poking out of his pocket. And the little black thing was smiling at me. And the train had stopped and it was raining. And I felt alone even though the carriage

was heaving. Alone, like what a
perfect rainy London night to
die in. But this guy put his hand
into his pocket and pulled out
a tiny umbrella. And I thought
Max, you're so high. We wrote a
song about it, my brother and I.
It's called Sad Lonely Miserable
Life.

Call me x

Thursday's delivery was the best shift of the week. I was in for the
ten a.m. line clean, out by four, which is when the humans arrived.
Ten a.m. Didn't see this light of morning Hackney very often except
on a Thursday, and even that was a rare occasion. Boaz said only
the men could do the lifting, so Carla the German Philanthropist
was in a constant state of despair. If I stayed at Molly's I'd see Tower
Hamlets and Hackney at eight, and that was a London treat.

Wait.

Allyn was ten minutes late. He was hungover. He lived cheap
above one of the company's other premises, damp and riddled with
old stemware, no oven or washing machine, in Finsbury Park. He
had a fridge in his bedroom and a cracked toilet seat where the other
employee-tenants would continuously climb up through the roof in
an attempt to imagine they had a legitimate terrace garden.

When Allyn arrived and opened the door we walked into an oily
cloud. Faint damp in the air and leftover heat of previous night
humans sweating booze and sexual fluids. The floor rotted more
with each pair of feet we got drunker. Luke, a young Scottish kid
and our then KP, would be in shortly to clean the grease off the walls
of the kitchen and sweep the crumbs from behind the oven – those
not taken during the night by mother mice feeding their children,
who were equally unused to humans existing in our pub at ten in
the morning.

You could hear the building yawn.

'Someone keeps stealing my beer,' said Allyn. He was an intuitive home-brewer. 'And it can't be Isi anymore. Not since they made him move out.' He shook his head, put his hat back on and said, 'Keep an eye out for the next keg distributor. I'm going to buy a padlock.'

To clean your lines first disconnect the kegs, the casks, the boxes of cider and place all the hoses in a barrel of water. Connect the keg couplers to the cellar buoys. We used S Type and G Type couplers mainly. These were high quality chrome plated forged steel couplers with stainless probes (got to wash off the dried beer with hot water before). A Type couplers slide on and spurt, so you should face them away from you. The S Type spurts upwards so keep your head away from the top of the keg to avoid a face full. American S Types have a slightly wider probe and they need an adapter to be used. Allyn said, 'Leave the KeyKegs on.' There would be around a pint of wastage for each line, and the KeyKegs were expensive. We used them for guest ales. They have a small valve on the side of the coupler so when they're empty you can depressurise them and throw them away. Allyn said, 'Leave the infuser too.' When the infuser is full you cannot clean it until all of the product is sold. We had Anarchy Warhead, then – a 10% IPA. It took a month to get rid of because people were scared to drink it.

It is important to collect all the beer in glasses rather than buckets. Collect until just before it turns to water. You'll be left with twenty-three pints that the company is paying for. Drink up before lunch. Save in the fridge. Recarbonate later for end of shift drinks.

This I did.

It was a quiet music Thursday. We passed the time by racing the lines and riding bikes round a slalom of tables.

While I sent emojis to Molly, Allyn made strange plans for new homebrew equipment. He was staying to close and asked me, 'What're you going to do when you finish?' It was a Lahmacun Thursday. £1.50 from the Turkish restaurant next door and we ignored the delivery drivers and stupid too-soon customers knocking on the door as we ate. We returned the empty kegs, back-spinning new casks onto the crash mat in the cellar so they didn't bounce too much. In between deliveries, while the line cleaner was turning blue, we used our time to compare pump clips. Bad beer and band branding go together. 'It's a matter of pure imagination,' said Allyn. 'You can't make good beer if you can't draw a good picture.' He started laughing maniacal plans to himself, smiling at me with his mad beard and old fisherman's eyes, sketching label designs for his own homebrew bottles for the rest of the afternoon. 'Emphasis on minimal,' he said. 'Casual. The labels will be horizontal: Have you ever seen a horizontal label before?'

I said, 'No.'

He said, 'Why?'

I said, 'Because you're not meant to upturn the bottle.'

He said, 'Exactly. It releases the sediment. My sideways labels will say THIS BEER IS BOTTLE CONDITION. DO NOT TURN. Ha!'

Till One

04-02-14

SYSTEM – TEST PRINT

Make him live all his lives behind bars at once: when he pulls the pump he feels like every bartender he's ever been. When he opens the till. Hears the bell. Breaks chunks of ice in the bucket. Rotates the stock in the fridges. Once, a long time ago, he had to pour two hundred espresso martinis in twenty minutes with only one cocktail shaker. He was locked in a room by an older woman. He had been carrying a tray of drinks up to the third floor of a hotel. She asked him to run her a bath. After that all hotel staff carried a radio. In the pub with the drunken landlord whose wife had already divorced him, there was a box of pigs' ears for visiting dogs. A Jack Russell had a large grey scar on its back. It always sat by the fire, chewing a pig's ear. He worked in a theatre, was seeing a woman there. They came to a short-skirt-black-shirted understanding in the cellar. Locked the door. Fucked on top of a chest freezer while other bar staff couldn't get to new bottles of beer. The intervals went unstocked.

I lay on Ace's sofa bed but left it folded up. It was so uncomfortable, it used to get me up. Long mornings on Gumtree searching for a house. No, only teasing the idea, the fear of rent, the time spent on TFL's website. The overground from Hackney Central where a huge concrete hole had opened up. Preparations for potential Crossrail 2, or just another housing block which broke the foundations of the Turkish restaurant on the corner, opposite Marks & Spencer, until they had to close and move out.

I was staring at the ceiling, thinking about that afternoon when I'd gone to meet Max in Camden. This is a whole other fantasy story. London stock bricks weren't just dull with pollution. There was a young man on the overground with a mysterious puppy wrapped up. He said, 'It's not supposed to be in the country.' Some other guy had a Weimaraner.

I wanted the sofa to go on forever.

I thought about the previous Christmas when everyone left us to go mince around the tables and chair legs of parents in country houses. No one was from Stokey except the homeless man with the limp and the woman who took a shit in the alley behind the Thai restaurant. Only graduates stayed. And they were crying escape. And Jewish butchers, shopkeepers. I spent that Christmas with El Hell, dog sitting for his business partner near Finsbury Park. Allyn stayed to run the pub, as did Eloise the German Filmmaker, who hadn't yet begun working for the BBC. She was living with her parents, both doctors in Seven Sisters. We were the only members of staff still on for Christmas. Ace gave up his bedroom to visit our mother, but I still didn't want a bed.

We were pouring since ten or eleven for the Christmas hanger-ons, all buying us drinks, and even we could get drunk behind the bar back then, choke in great elongated smoking breaks, merry Christmas with every other customer and a lock-in to follow. No kitchen. Why bother? Not even a cockroach that day. Not even the crackheads with dirigible bellies and gaunt limps: 'I was coming here before you was born. You a professional posh kid, then?' The company wouldn't let any of the old regulars in when they reopened the place four years ago. They had a bouncer on the door. A bouncer all of their own. But none of them showed up on Christmas Day.

I'd been with Max. That's why I was drunk, lying on the sofa and staring at the ceiling, trying to stop the room spinning with my excess brain function. Keep going. Lie on back and breathe slowly. Low down and pool. Gargle, choke on vomit. Didn't want it. Couldn't soak Ace's carpet again. Not again. Fucking Camden.

I was drinking Stone Ruination, mostly, that Christmas day. Stone Ruination IPA is expensive to import. Order form only comes round every few months. Allyn got it in especially to coincide with Christmas day, smiling, drink, drunker, dunking my face in the dirty staff sink in the cellar. Refreshing. Drunk cycling after close on Nanna's borrowed Cooper, kick-back three-speed hub gears and a bent crossbar where she hit a curb and broke her leg, drunk, then, too. I went to find El Hell in his colleague's house in Finsbury Park. That was El Hell's Christmas dream. I was thinking about this while lying on the sofa because Christmas Day was my favourite shift. It was so quick. Molly was with her family. El Hell's colleague was married to an architect, so there was a bookshelf wall with a sliding ladder and wine and whisky and somehow cigars and, now that recall, The Shapes of Dogs' Eyes. Yes, a whole-roasted-clove-of-garlic wonderful Christmas night. There were two Basset Hounds and they were mourning Tulula. Tulula was a box of ashes, and probably still is, on the headboard of the double bed I would later fall asleep in.

Tulula was a Basset Hound.

Bernie the gay poodle, Noodles the Christmas angel, and Hedwig. That dog on the train to Camden was illegal. Barely born. Undesirable. I tried lighting a new cigarette but remembered I was inside without a match. Matches are cooler than lighters. Basset Hounds have droopy eyes, droopy lids like kids or kids' fingers: pink and sticky. Half the pupil cut in two, high, horizontal (like Allyn's revolutionary beer label). Can't see. Can't even tell if they're happy. El Hell kept having to stop them climbing onto the sofa with me, and that was a big slippery leather affair. A daunting prospect for such short legs, and one I regretted not sleeping on, when I went downstairs to the furry double bed in the cellar (it was where El Hell's colleague let the dogs sleep). I was watching National Lampoon's Christmas Vacation. That's an El Hell family tradition, apparently. I think he missed them. We shared some rained-on tobacco as we slid along the wooden terrace outside and thought about all the empty terraces of London. And that's how I felt, months later, lying on the unfolded fold-out sofa after a drunk afternoon with Max in Camden: a London dream. Max. Molly. Still lying on the morning cushion, wondering why estate agencies never update their windows.

'There's this client of mine,' said El Hell, at Christmas, with

Glenlivet outside on the wooden slip-slide of London terraces, perched on a flooded plant pot with specks and dots of cigarette butts underneath a layer of ice, 'this client,' and he was telling me a story, 'who wanted to go to Rome with me. She was married, but we'd been seeing each other in secret. I walked her dog. Still do, in fact.' He took a drag. 'I fucked her,' he said, with a cigar and a firework somewhere distant, 'in a hotel, but the next day I didn't meet her at the airport. So she went to Rome by herself, and I blocked her on Facebook.'

El Hell had a greyhound tattooed on his throat. When he coughed, it looked like the greyhound was barking. When he choked it put its tail between its legs.

I said, 'Last night I kicked out a homeless man. He came in begging. It was Christmas Eve and too much for me to deal with. I couldn't give him anything except a packet of crisps. He didn't want them. He said he wanted a roast.'

'You make me sick,' said El Hell, and patted me on the back.

I took Tulula's ashes off the head board and tried not to move for fear I'd stir up the fur, choke in my sleep and die. It was a good sleep. Months later, after Camden, I would think about sleeping there, on that bed of dog fur, only just able to lie on my side without the room spinning, while Max lay snoring on the opposite sofa. A twisted pile of jeans and t-shirt and leather.

'I think I've got a dick disease.'

'Yeah?'

'Yeah, it's really itchy.'

'Needs a wash, probably. Staying here all the time, in this studio, no toilet, sink, shower. It's bad for you.'

'I've been scrubbing it intensely. It's all red around the end.'

'Show me.'

'No. I'll draw you a picture.'

-

'Is this really what it looks like?'

'It's a caricature.'

'I had my balls scanned, once.'

'How are they, by the way?'

'Sore. I was lying there with this beautiful doctor and this beautiful nurse.'

'Man or woman?'

'Man and woman.'

'And they were looking at your balls?'

'And my dick. It was a cold room.'

'Ouch. And they didn't know what was causing the pain?'

'No. I think I'm going to ask for it again.'

'Yeah, I think I'm going to have to take the walk as well. But there's always a pretty girl or someone you know. Once, I saw my old tennis teacher in the waiting room.'

-

'I went to a brothel in Thailand.'

'Cool.'

'It wasn't cool, it was dark. We had just played the gig and our drummer tried asking some policemen for a light. He was holding a joint. Fucking idiot. Then some guys drove us to an abandoned hospital ward where some matriarch with a cane and a bar stool stood us in front of a load of girls and told us to choose. The girls were all lined up. I chose the little one. They were all little. We went into a room with a hospital bed, but in the end I didn't want to. It was scary. I still paid her, though.'

'So how could you have you got an STD?'

'I don't know. I can feel it.'

'I see.'

-

'There's a bar outside Liverpool Street called Dirty Dicks.'

'Really? But I think I got it off that girl in Camden yesterday. I went in bareback, and she does work at The Star. We did it in the toilet while you were at the bar.'

'Let's get some breakfast.'

Not long after that Christmas with El Hell began the great return of

Hackney humans and New Year parental visits. Our pub became a hub for lunchtime families. Meet New Year boyfriends, girlfriends, easy-to-read dads who wanted straight glasses because jugs were unfashionable when they were the same age as their sons. Straight glass and a pint of mild or best. Drab. Boaz ordered all the boring stuff because the boring breweries gave out free casks. Got to sell. The son would take the jug, the handle, the hoppy American/New Zealand pale. 'Made with, um, citra. Try it, dad.'

Dad said, 'Think I'll stick with my bitter.'

And there were dogs everywhere. Parents visiting children bringing dogs excited to see them. Excited in London chocolate Lab. Ace brought Gin, his tiny Maltese-Yorkshire mix, but she was scared of the tube. Someone drew a biro Labrador on an Evening Standard crossword. It was a prize draw: win a rally driving taste experience. Four down: amen. Five across: kiss. But unfortunately we weren't a summer pub. We had a pavement, but all London and London professionals gravitate towards the parks the grass the pubs with gardens when even the slightest hint of sun arrives. We were dark. Ruby. Brooding. Everyone was waiting for the winter to come back. Real drinkers still came in, but they were lonely. A guy outside stood by the door, scoping, stroking his beard in plastic backpack and boots. Empty chairs. He said, 'Ah, do you know how many bikes I've had stolen outside this pub? How many parts?'

I said, 'People carry their saddles inside.'

'Poncy twats,' he said, chewing his glasses. 'I used to love it here. It had the most beautiful round bar in the middle by the—'

'Pillars? Yes.'

'Hmm.' He paused, shook his head. He said, 'Ah, it's a barn, a barn.'

'I heard it was a little rough around the edges.'

'Ahhh,' shouting arms into the air showing shiny silver tooth inside the void. 'You don't know what rough is,' and he dug me in the ribs with his pipe. 'Oh, I love a bit of rough,' and he smiled at a New Year family having lunch beside the door: son, new girlfriend, mum with a wine, dad with a jug of mild.

THE SHAPES OF DOGS' EYES

For a while afterwards I kept seeing my mother's haircut cycling around London. Crossing the roads of London. Under the tunnels of London. Being hit by the taxis of black cab London. Canals. Towpaths. Just her haircut, from behind. My mother hasn't lived in London for twenty-six years. She lived in Kennington.

The bartenders' morning. Listening to Neutral Milk Hotel and cultivating a perverse affair with rainclouds which bred in me a compulsion to stop speaking. At school I was the child who said, 'I knew that,' after somebody else had already answered the question. Dogs' eyes. A Hackney studio. Max borrowed four grand from his mother and spent most of it on drugs. He said, 'I'm living a dream.' I'd become insane. This was thanks to hours alone in Ace's house, when the others had gone to work and the bar didn't open until four.

My mother had a bob when she was eighteen.

I wasn't sure if exposing The Shapes of Dogs' Eyes was a good idea. Life Behind Bars is a better title if you're feeling afraid, and I was. Canine customers keep bartenders entertained, like their owners. Stop them thinking about things that will convince them to get up and leave. Drop all the glasses. Stop listening to stories of endangered love triangles and drunk lovers dumped while lunch is trying to be served. Dee was managing on Boxing Day last year. That was before they made me supervisor. It was a quiet day. Nobody saying much in the way of words, mainly groaning. Dogs whining to go back outdoors, but the best cure for a hangover and sore wallet is to simply drink more booze. Hair of the dog. Insert like a drop. Three Irish guys kept buying pints for their table. And pints and pints and pints. Full. Losing carbonation because they were still drinking the same lager they'd bought when they first walked in. They were stocking up. When we finally called a tired last orders by flashing the hanging lights above the bar, they had four pints between them to drink up by half-past eleven. When two police women arrived at quarter past one they still didn't move, threatened me when I'd already told them to put out their cigarettes, called Dee a fucking Protestant and had grown three or four times their original number, women in Christmas dresses with eyebrows like hedges on one table and eye-bag men on another. One of them said he'd get all his mates to leave us if we gave him fifty quid. We were imprisoned babysitters waiting for police backup to chuck them out at around two o'clock. A few days later Bobby refused to serve an Irish guy who got so angry he pulled down one of the hanging lights and started punching it, threw a pint glass across the room and called everyone in the pub, 'A load of middle class cunts.' And they just sat there, looking anywhere but at him, listening, ignoring, fully aware that what he was saying was right. They were frightened, but it was fear of the truth. Boaz got him by the collar and landed several jabs to his stomach behind the door curtains. Guard beats up a prisoner. I watched through the taps, held onto them like bars, unsure whether I was looking into the cell or out of it.

A dog barked from under a table.

iMessage
Man, I was so drunk last
night. I called up this girl
I used to date. Big mistake.
She's crazy. But I needed
some place to crash and we
had sex and I felt so rough
the next morning I thought
I was dying. Def not on the
woops, drugs for a while.

Lol

Wanna hang?
Read

Max and I walked up the Kingsland Road from Shoreditch,

feeling bohemian, washed up, whitewashed in a world of shifty mannequin shop-front weddings, Turkish barbers and the memory of childhood seaside holidays which lived in the smell of the fishmonger on Stoke Newington High Street. I walked down this road with Nanna the day before, after breakfast on Church Street. Ace went home early, angered by all the children and the waiter who couldn't understand that the green tea Ace had ordered was actually lemon and honey. El Hell unhooked his dogs from the table and Nanna and I went to Beyond Retro for dungarees, had to cross the road by the fishmonger because she almost gagged. But that smell was my grip on an outside-London. A familiar. A memory of crabbing off rocks climbing out of the ocean, snorkelling, sneaking, parents bleating bedtime, can't bedtime mum, too busy watching Padstow across the water. A town lit up like a midnight dream of⌐—

Max. Raw haze of Halal butchers. English sheepdog hair except black, or very dark brown, which teased the poster-boys of barbershops pinned up in the early nineties and long since bleached with time. We stopped in The White Horse for a piss before my shift at five and there were pole dancers. Max said, 'I never knew,' and swore that he'd go back. But the place was caked in weird paint, opaque men and premium lager. We walked in line with the 149, road sodas opened for us by the grocer, whose keyring was a Dublin souvenir shop heirloom. A police officer came out of the Tesco in Dalston with a shopping bag, just finished his shift, and shot us a frown like he knew he should tell us, 'Don't drink on my street,' but thought FUCK IT and went on, uncomfortably, while we were offered weed outside a McDonalds. Up Kingsland Road, greatest road in London. Underneath the sun, the concrete. Everything was alright until I got to work and Carla the German Philanthropist asked our regular transvestite which pronoun she would prefer. Our regular transvestite said, 'Just give me your strongest beer.' Max sat at the bar, in the wooden gloom, and I fed him tasters from all twenty-three taps until they mixed in his stomach and he went back to the studio and slept.

Eloise the German Filmmaker came in, so we stayed after

with tequila and tales of BBC coffee patrols down in Central and slaughtering cockroaches in the ladies' toilet. We only had antibacterial spray, surface cleanser and degreaser with which to unattach them from their lives and that's a slow death, but at least we bothered. I saw a cockroach in Ace's kitchen and became fearful that I'd carried them in on my boots. Cut the head off, crush one, and a thousand eggs were let loose. Boaz left early, left me in charge to lock up, drink up, drink the wastage and by mistake not record the shots that would be missing from next Monday's stock count. Yet to be typed, already written. Smoking, on the Kingsland Road, inside. A joy. A complaint. Always a complaint about the music we play, from Arthur. Dee came in with her new boyfriend who was drunk. She said, 'Oh, he's always drunk to me.'

We finished at Lisa's. Last stop for the off-duty bartender, open until three or four with mutual bar staff lock-in to wind us down. Lisa's was a narrow Irish situation. Wray and Nephew head fucking rum in a 35ml shot and a dance around the jukebox to stop your head falling off. Craft beer inhibition prohibited when Guinness is all that's on draught. We smoked in a strange seated circle and Eloise told us about her boyfriend's new angle: stay at home. Wait for work to come in. He was in film as well. Independent. No company. But Eloise wanted always-money to afford a deposit and move out of her parents' Seven Sisters apartment. 'I miss you guys,' she said, though she'd rarely text. Coming to Lisa's was a new staff member's right of passage. And when you leave it's the place for goodbye drunk drinks and flailing dances and kisses you'll maybe regret. Biting nipples in the corners. Cycling to various homes at five in the morning, and once there had been an occasion for crying in the ladies', cramped, unrequited affection between bartenders from different stations: those available and those not. On my first night in here I thought I'd found real London. Later that night, I threw up on Ace's staircase and on the floor of his bathroom.

'When I was cleaning glasses today I had to try really hard not to drop each clean glass on the floor.' I was lying in Molly's bed. 'Allyn practically placed the back bar beneath my hand when I let go.' I was under Molly's duvet. It wasn't raining. Rest and recuperation. Soon jump back in because still I could not escape The Shapes of Dogs' Eyes, though I knew I wouldn't want to. I said, 'It's just the humans I despise,' which made trying to save them from domestic canine occupation all the more confusing. And only fuelled my self-loathing. 'People are buying more pugs,' I said.

'Pugs are fashionable,' said Molly.

'Their eyes are bulgy,' I said. 'Like a baby's. And that's probably why couples keep buying them.'

Molly sighed. 'Remember when I was on my last period?' she said.

I said, 'No.'

'Me neither,' she said.

'Was it when we went to see that house I didn't rent? We were on the overground from Camden Road to Homerton and you kept looking at that baby being held by that lady beside us. It was rush hour. You kept copying the noises it made.'

'Oh yeah,' she said, laughing. 'The look on your face. Remember when I told you I wouldn't have sex with you anymore if you didn't start calling me your girlfriend?'

'Yes. It was on the tube, after Warpaint in Brixton.'

'So you want a dog before a baby?' she said.

'Let's not do this.'

'Do you remember when we met?'

'Of course. We were on the District Line. I'd just come to London, but you had been here a while already. You said you liked my painting.'

'You said you painted it intentionally, just to impress me. I thought your chat-up sucked.'

'What was I meant to say? "My mother gave me this painting? She had it commissioned? It was her Christmas present to me?" Fucking hell.'

Molly smiled. It was her usual big smile. Her forehead smelled faintly of sweat. The painting was of my mother's dogs. The one with cataracts and the one without a brain.

'How was work?'
'We got a new drip tray for the glass washer.'
'Is that the most exciting thing that happened all day?'
'Molly, it's the newest piece of equipment we've been given in four years, apparently.'
'I see.'
'Now the dregs won't drip down behind the sink. The wood will dry out. There'll be fewer bar flies.'
'My agent phoned me.'
'Less stink of stale beer.'
'I've got an audition.'
'Less stickiness, too. Wood sticks to your fucking sleeves when you reach down for the bactericidal spray.'
'Something for TFL.'
'Bit late though, I think. Whole bar needs to be replaced. Wood's completely rotten.'
'A TV advert.'
'So is the floor. Vinyl keeps lifting up at the walls. Eloise almost broke her neck. I think it's one of the reasons she left. That, and the better job. Oh, you have a missed call from your agent by the way. She called this morning, while you were in the shower. She left a message.'

London rains, not the sky. London the cloud on by, the shadow. London rained the people. Two single girls who'd just broken up with their boyfriends, searching for drunk validation. A table of half-asleepers needing police to escort them when they wouldn't leave us just wanted a place to be for the night. Bathroom snorters turning the other cheek. And corner kissers emerging from each other with skin creases in immaculately styled imperfection. Sometimes the people were the torrent. They were torrential. They had the Hackney complexion: pasty cheeks, red eyelids and eye-bag shades and beards hide the men, whereas the women bear it all, pull off thick glasses that do not detract from the image but serve to enhance its confusing sexiness. A beautiful woman with dip-dyed hair and black jeans leant over the bar to me. She was alone and far from reach. She said, 'I've just split up with my girlfriend. She found out I had a boyfriend in Amsterdam. I wanted us to be a triangle, but she wanted me all to herself.' It was one of those days every day. Both tyres on her bike were flat. That didn't make for an economic recovery. It only enhanced the appeal of bus-route experiments. Fingers that smelled half of hand sanitiser, half sexual fluid. Sometimes the people were the torrent. Mostly they were the drizzle.

Evan came in looking jowly. He brought his short Scottish hair and black glasses with him, eyes you mistake for a frown but they're smiling in faint autistic consternation. '5am Saint and a¬—'

'Malbec?' I can still finish his one sentence for him. Pint of ale and a malbec for his wife. When I started there she had long blonde hair. By then she was bald. Chemotherapy, said Dee. Rumours of leukaemia, maybe, cap on, blue scarf. '5am Saint—'

'And a malbec?' Of course I was already pouring it. Evan smiled. Pleasurable state of late night hesitancy. Glancing over at his wife perpetually. Did his eyes frown? Lips in a constant state of pursing. He'd hold her gaze across the room and hold her hands across their table.

Remember to rotate the stock.

One night I saw a black cat pretending to be a panther. This happened in Hackney Downs, by Rectory Road. West Country myths were invading the disused chimney stack sprawl of Hackney, circumnavigating the city and crossing over the border that holds in the marshes.

I was walking home. Carrying myself home, rather, alone, towards another sofa in Lower Clapton – another terraced Victorian island where my friends Theo and Nemesia lived.

Ragged fox populations skulked warily, dragging nostalgia for bushy tails, pushing old tins of maybe baked beans or tuna through the street with ears pricked on Evering Road like narrow paintbrushes on an outside wall, longing for thinners, or neglected in a cupboard after decorating the bedroom of a child that would be stillborn.

The panther sat watching, unperturbed. I once had a girlfriend who liked cats. But I can't abide shitting in boxes. Someone had been sticking little flags in dog shit along the Regent's Canal. They'd climbed a mountain and conquered it. Blue flags that said, 'Thank you for sharing this.'

I Instagrammed it.

I'd been walking home with my keys clutched tightly between my fingers, wishing I could hear anything louder than the sound of my own footsteps. But memories of London news reports were fading. Jogger assaulted in Victoria Park one evening. Stabbings on Homerton high Street. And I was walking, never running. No bag for mugging. The only people I passed were lightless cyclists flashing, one girl with a limitless ponytail and midnight joggers on the lookout.

The night was warm.

A curiosity. The story. All dogs safely tucked away at the ends of their owners' beds. Dogs are a thing for the day, especially the little ones. Foxes rule the streets and eat the scraps of night. Molly's fox slept in the garden, curled up in a disused, rusted barbecue heap where a hole in the fence went through to the house next door.

Text Message
Sorry, can't iMessage. Think
you'd at least get 3G in the
middle of fucking London.

Have you called the doctor?

No I just went there and
the receptionist said the
results were normal but
the doctor wanted to see
me and told me to sit and
wait so I was sitting and
waiting and freaking out
because you don't get an
appointment that quickly
unless it's really important
but the doctor said all the
tests are fine and then he
stuck his finger up my arse
to make sure my prostate is
fine too. He said it is.

iMessage

Cool.

Boaz's dealings with what we presumed to be the Turkish mafia
kept us talking. Discussing all the different factions, from taxi
drivers, restaurant waiters in black with scimitar walls and finely
pruned beards. Whispering on corners while we stood at the bar
and watched. Strange men came into our pub every night asking
for money, even when he was not there. And none of us had the
balls to turn them down. We wanted to keep the rumours fuelled.
We wanted more free meals for silent men in the corner, and strange
handshakes by the door to the cellar. And who knew the contents of
the safe, anyway? It was not worth the time spent counting, asking,
wondering where Boaz and Arthur took the nightly takings, and
from whom they got it back in time to bank it.

Isi was gone. Our latest crazy protein shake chef, whose name
I have remembered to forget, brought in his photo album. It was
filled with photos of the French Foreign Legion and his time spent
in African brothels. 'Here's the bar,' he told me in schizophrenic

Hungarian English, half intonated with the flicks of knives that scared me into conversation. I couldn't understand him half the time. The staff complained about his short fuse: 'Customer says the ribs are not cooked through? Bastard.' Then went on smashing plates and syntax, swearing in Hungarian whispers for no particular ears. He was a self-made caricature.

'This is me in my combat uniform. Good boots. And, ah yes, the bar, like I was showing you before,' he went on, during some kitchen downtime when no tickets were coming through and Boaz was talking to a young guy in a beige fleece outside. I'd just come back from checking the floor, collecting glasses, when the guy approached me and asked for £180 in tens. I opened the till and he went back outside to speak to Boaz, who was just finishing a call.

'And Boaz won't give the homeless notes when they bring in handfuls of change,' said Timbo, resentfully shaking his head.

'What's the new chef's name, Timbo?' I said quietly.

Timbo said, 'I don't know. They come and go so quickly I don't bother.'

I went back to the kitchen.

'So,' leaning in with Latest Chef who was showing me a photo of a corrugated shack with a green roof. 'One girl for forty guys,' he said, and blew big air out of his cheeks. 'And she was cut, like, you know,' with his hands over his groin. 'You get me? Not so good,' shaking his head.

I went back to the bar where Timbo said, 'That's probably the most dangerous man you'll meet. He's an old friend of Boaz, apparently. He worked here ages ago, before you, and man, he was stacked back then. On steroids, like that Russian guy who always asks Boaz for a twenty.'

'Who?'

'The little dude. Scatty. Ratty. Stringy. Massive, no, not a crackhead. He's on heroin. And there's a funny story there, I tell you.'

A pause.

'Well no, not funny,' said Timbo. 'It's actually quite fucked up.

You know the Bourges? Who own the building?'

'No.'

'Yeah you do. They come in and Boaz makes us put everything they order on 99. Then he writes it off at the end of the night. There are echoes of the Krays about them.'

'Who?'

'Ah mate, pick up a fucking book.' He rubbed his forehead. 'They're two brothers who own the building.'

'The Krays?'

'Fucking hell. No! The Bourges. And the Russian guy, when he was normal, got one of their daughters pregnant, and they, like, forced him to bare knuckle box to make them money, in payment of the debt, or disrespect, or something.'

'Fuck.' I looked over at Latest Chef. He was standing in the corner, in the kitchen where the toilets once were, tripping over the hole in the floor where the wood was rotten, punching holes in the kitchen wall every time the grill stopped working, which was most days. It was blocked with ages of ash and grit. The little Turkish man they sent to fix it shook his head, 'Needs a service,' he said, 'cannot mend myself. Don't use because it's dangerous.'

'Course it is,' said Latest Chef, relighting it with the nub of his cigarette.

'And this guy?' I said to Timbo, who was yanking a hand pump aggressively to pull water through its line. Looked like pumping iron. A show. Looked like giant show-off wanking and Timbo said to me, 'Oh, the new chef? He's much calmer now. He got a dog. Got off the roids.'

'Psst,' said Latest Chef from the kitchen, 'come over here.' And I did. I stood, skulked, hunched, with Chef in the corner by the cockroach shelter, otherwise known as the condiment station. He had in his hand another photo, but this one was digital, on his phone. He was zooming in. 'That's my dog,' he said. 'A sausage dog, you know?' He laughed. 'He can't climb up stairs, and every night he takes up half the bed. He's small.'

In the corner of my eye the kitchen porter was cutting out naked women from a magazine to cover the holes in the plaster board.

We wanted to run the Bermondsey Mile. This plan was decided during the Monday deep clean up to our elbows in flies, fly eggs, stemware and glass matting of beer dreg stickiness, renovating the glass washer which had become full of orange slime. Allyn was very excitable. He ignored knocks on the front door, the big pain-in-the-arse windows for all the, 'Are you open yet?' fools of the Kingsland Road. Allyn, stretching his legs. Doing lunges. 'We're going to run the Bermondsey Mile,' he shouted. Allyn had been shouting since, apparently, he woke. 'I had an epiphany,' he told me, 'a dream. I woke up in a strange stress-sweat and knew immediately what it could mean.'

'The dream? You didn't tell me what it was.'

'Doesn't matter,' he said. 'All that matters is that I've figured out how to spend my Saturday.'

He hadn't had one off in over a month.

'Brewery tap rooms open in the afternoons. Not long. Got to be fast. Which, I suppose, is the point. It's a race,' he said, and I was grunting like the u-bend under the sink. Allyn was thumping his hand down on one of the two-seaters, which shook menacingly. The furniture was second hand, just like the plumbing and glass washer. Like the heel of my right boot, too, which was failing, and the leather, also, which was rotting under thick coatings of former beer. 'Would you rather not spend your day away from all of this?' I said.

Allyn said, 'Of course not.' He said, 'This is the only way to live.'

The Bermondsey Mile. A long line of railway arches that runs from South Bermondsey to Tower Bridge, with around six micro-breweries and their respective tap rooms underneath. 'I want to drink straight from the source,' said Allyn, and we cheered our coffee cups and we went on ignoring the knocking humans on our pub's front door, though we were eight minutes late to open.

Carla said, 'Why haven't I been shown how to change a cask?' We were in the cellar. I told her, 'Boaz doesn't see the point.'

She said, 'Because I'm a woman?'

I said, 'Yes. Sorry.'

She shook her head. She said, 'Whatever. I'll be leaving soon. I deserve to know how it's done.'

'Well you start like this,' I said, closing the tap in the empty cask and unscrewing the line (a transparent length of hosepipe). It was a pale ale. Citra hops. Very popular. 'Fill up that bucket with water, will you?' And she did. 'You put the line into the bucket, and if it's not busy someone upstairs will pull the water through for you, in order to clean the line. It's a rudimentary clean, not chemical or antibacterial. It just removes any blobs of sediment and yeast.'

A pause.

'There,' as the line started twitching like a long nerve dribbling on an electric chair, a vein. 'Bobby's upstairs pulling. And while he does that, we can drain the old cask.' Carla picked up the empty cask from its rack, removed the tap, took it out of the cold room and turned the whole thing upside down over the drain. 'It's not that heavy,' she said. I smiled. 'I know,' she said, 'it's the full ones that fuck up your back.'

'Ignore him,' I told her, meaning Boaz. 'It's a waste of energy to indulge. Besides, you'll be leaving soon, for the better.'

She laughed. 'Everyone's a beer celebrity even if they don't want to be. The problem with job applications is the odds. They get more imbalanced with every new graduation ceremony.'

'Still haven't heard from the company?' I said.

'Course not.'

'It's just an internship. Probably treat you like less valuable shit than here.'

'But at least I'd be the right kind of sewage. And anyway, I know a lady who works there. She's supposed to be hooking me up. She works for a charity, for fuck's sake. You'd think she'd be half nice.'

'Have you got a glass?' I asked. The line had stopped twitching. 'That means he's pulled through a bucket or so of water. What we do now is try every beer down here, until we find one suitable.'

Carla said, 'Couldn't we just check the rack board to find what beer is available?'

I said, 'But where's the fun in that? A professional gets drunk before going back upstairs, and is still able to function as though perfectly sober.'

Carla laughed. 'It's so fucking easy for you. Boaz loves people who aren't going anywhere. People with no ambition.'

'Um.'

'And Allyn. His whole life is beer. Career and hobby. It's just so fucking easy. Hey, maybe I'll go to Chile, if I don't get this internship.'

'Allyn will miss you terribly.'

She looked down and said, 'Whatever. I'll go back to Cologne first, I think, see my family.'

I smiled and said, 'I won't be sad to see you go.'

She said, 'Thanks.'

I rinsed a glass under the cellar tap, opened up the cask on rack seven. 'Keep in mind what's already on the bar. The selection has to stay balanced. When you think you've found something that'll go on nicely, always pour the first glass away. It'll be full of sediment. The casks are angled down, remember? This one is a rye IPA. 7%. See how it's clear?' holding the glass up to the light before taking a drink. 'Tastes fucking great,' said Carla as she screwed the line back onto the tap, opened it up and removed the spile from the shive to prevent a vacuum. 'So that's it?' she said.

I said, 'Yes. All that's left is to pull the beer through upstairs. But we better try a few more before that. How about this oyster stout?'

Today I was boiled alive. I was stuck inside a horror vision of beer kettle aluminium, titanium and chrome. Stainless steel that stained me. I was welly boot dry-hopped in a vat of pale ale, and that made me the secret ingredient.

It all began in Battersea Park, or, rather, on the way back to

THE SHAPES OF DOGS' EYES

Sloane Square. Allyn phoned me, said, 'What the hell are you doing in Chelsea?' I was with Theo. We met Nemesia, who'd been seeing a friend, on the King's Road for small Chelsea coffee, black metal fencing and the Victoria Line from Highbury & Islington. Everything clean. A bratty borough of nannies and absentee car wash parents having caffeinated affairs with Italian baristas. No corner shops or roti stops or speakers speaking out of windows. I said, 'Allyn, there's not even gum on the pavement.' I was scared. 'It's too much like where my parents live,' I said, meaning Hampshire.

'Did you cross the bridge over to Battersea Park?' he asked.

I said, 'Yes.'

'Horrible isn't it,' he said. The run down grand sherry-stained breath of Empire Britain. The white Albert Bridge painted so many times that the rivets have lost their shape.

I slid through temporary traffic lights, round parked-up Rolls Royce windows, trying to hear Allyn hint at my potential social promotion. 'So are you around tomorrow?'

I said, 'Yeah, why?'

'Pentangle need someone to help out with their brew day. I can't make it. I'm going to a Simpsons trivia night in Dalston and need all day to revise. Serious prizes. Bart Simpson skateboard Scalextric.'

My time had come. Allyn had friends beneath every railway arch. I'd been behind bars for so long, now I was going to be new. Be me. I could barely contain my excitement when I was almost crushed by a taxi. Renewed. I walked to the brewery in the morning and became the boiling sun. I arrived at ten to eight when they were opening the heavy metal gates to the yard, held them back with sand-filled traffic cones, yard full of rotting pallets, remains of spiles and labels. A former car park turned to meadows of barley malt wastage, crushed pellets of rettles, Irish moss in hops in bags and empty brown bottle populations waiting on cardboard plinths to be resettled in pub fridge campsites. I was introduced to the caustic soda, the branded boxes stacked by the bottling machine, the filler. The devil horn star of Pentangle. 'What do you use the mobile bar for?' I asked when I parked my bag in one of the lockers at the back of the warehouse. There was a bar on wheels with a little black cooler and taps and pipes for keg beer. 'We take it to events,' said Will, the owner. 'Sometimes we have our own events right here. Gigs. Sometimes we just hook up some kegs and get drunk at the end of a shift. Mostly drink straight from the tanks though, if I'm honest. Want a coffee? There's no drinking while on the clock,' as he lifted a mug to his lips and gave me a wink. There was a fridge full of labelling machine rejects – bottles too imperfect to box up and sell. And biscuits. And milk and coffee grounds. And microwave meals in plastic containers. And samples of another brewery's beers. Following Mick, one of the head brewers, I looked around the cold storage room, opened bags of hops in boxes to smell them, smelled all the malts stacked up like sandbag barricades on enormous shelves at the far end of the archway. The whole place smelled like a milkshake.

'Tea?'

'No thank you.'

This was my time to be the pub-brew celebrity. One of the faces in Dalston, Stokey, Clapton and Central Hackney, faces that stop a crowded bar to silence as they make their way through the curtained door. A saloon. Gangsters. Gun slingers except with recipes for beers on hips, not guns that stun crowds into whispers. Murmurs. Rumours of who put MDMA into last year's Christmas stout, or which bartender slept with which brewer the other night. Who grew a secret hop variety in the cellar, or which closeted ex-convict has been illegally selling alcohol. Different drug, different law. This was the edgy echo of a former East London. The sum of what legendary gangster business had been redeveloped and branded into. And I wanted it all. The intrigue. The cool. The hat that did not sit still, and that worn out pair of Doc Martens.

I stayed at Theo's house the night before, after we'd escaped from Chelsea. We sat up all night talking about it excitedly, boring Nemesia while she was trying to read. Theo's house: a third floor one-bed in Lower Clapton. A library. A mousetrap kitchen and a tiny study slash living room which had become my on-off dormitory.

This was more convenient than staying with Ace. Closer proximity to the brewery. Got up early. They gave me a little fridge space.

The brewery floor was blue and gritty. Mick said, 'We've got Thames Water snooping round in fifty minutes, can you clean these hops out of the drains?'

A sign on the wall said, "We pay London Living Wage."

I had a brush.

A large kettle of mash (that's barley malts and water) to clean out with a pressure washer that kept falling over and shoes that were not watertight.

I climbed inside. And that's when I was boiled alive. I think it was Allyn's decision. He saw me working at the pub, liked my movements with the pumps, my dedication to bullshitting when someone asked me something I didn't know about one of the beers, my economy of movement, never making too many trips down one end of the bar for tomato juice or crisps when the human I was serving was tapping his change a thousand miles in the other direction.

Allyn knew these guys. And I had to climb inside the mash tun with my legs dangling through the hatch at the bottom, arms deep in a pair of thick rubber gloves which stuck to my skin while heat seeped through them and scolded. The heating elements were still warm from the morning's boil, pipes out to the fermentation tanks, malts clinging like a tawdry perfume. I didn't wash my work clothes for days because the smell was heaven. The smell infects the nostrils and got me going. I was standing in near darkness between conspiracy blankness when someone grabbed my legs and shoved me in. They closed the kettle up. The heating elements, like great long whisks, or rulers, began glowing. They lit up the dark in a red streetlamp frenzy, and the dark became pierced by the screen on my phone. It was buzzing. And I began shouting. And kicking. I was shouting and kicking and hitting the darkness. And then the water soon filled and was boiling.

Now I'm base.

I came out in an afternoon bottling session. Capped, dried,

labelled. And at the end of the shift, leaning against the stacks of boxes waiting to be packed into the van in the courtyard, they all drank me. Allyn was there, on the way to his trivia night. He said, 'I just stopped in for a quick pint,' while America played Germany in the World Cup. I climbed out of the final bottle in confused anticipation of my taste and frustration. And so I sat, sodden, feeling blithe, on the rotten pallets by the gateway that went out to Hackney Downs Station, and I drank myself.

This all happened. I had a missed call from Max and a burn on my ankle to prove it.

I was ready.

On her day off Carla the German Philanthropist went to King's Cross Station and got on a train to Cambridge. She'd come to London after studying in Ireland – had only been in Hackney one day before getting work at the pub. She said she didn't know better and wanted to see the English elsewhere. Cambridge. Blind train to nowhere. She said, 'No one looks you in the eye here. It's infuriating.' She'd been pacing like a criminal, or perhaps like an animal. The bars were beer taps. Hand pumps. 'You can't look them in the eye anyway,' I said. 'The taps are just too high.' Forever. Carla. Her day off. But with nowhere to go, other than here, hence the train.

I finished early, had to wait outside the ladies' for some guys doing lines on the new clean toilet seats I'd spent forty minutes that morning trying to install, then went to Ace's and had a nap. And as I lay on his sofa, facing into the sun, feeling hot, unable to sleep in some kind of glass heat fever of blue eyelids, I dreamed the adventure. My mother had been in London for a business meeting with some businessman taking over her company. She was selling up. Moving on. They had lunch at a Thai restaurant in Green Park. She said, 'You'll have to meet him, he's so nice, but a little too charming.' She was suspicious. Didn't matter as long as the money was there. I met her on Great Marlborough Street for coffee. My mother said, 'Are you hungry?'

I said, 'Always.'

She said, 'Oh darling, aren't you eating? You really need a place of your own.'

I said, 'I'm more concerned with finding a toilet of my own.'

She shook her head.

I said, 'I'm fine in Ace's home. Don't worry.'

She said, 'Well, as long as his housemates are still ok with you staying. Do you want another coffee?'

The café was quiet. I went to the toilet in the cellar for five minutes of privacy. When I went back upstairs my mother had bought me a slice of cheesecake.

We left each other on the Northern Line. I took Central to Liverpool Street, the Enfield Train back to Stoke Newington, and sat and sighed and waited on the platform for fifteen minutes before it was ready to leave, contemplating Carla's decision to come to worn out England. I touched out in Stokey at the top of the stairs, stopped, ran back down to where my train had not yet left, quickly removed my shoes and threw my socks onto the floor of a carriage. Then I left.

I wondered if maybe El Hell would find my socks, if he decided to move to Enfield with his dogs. They'd be pinned to a notice board or pierced on metal railings by carbon monoxide birds of prey. Maybe they'd end up back in Liverpool Street to ricochet round dead end concrete and rivets?

My socks could be anywhere.

With Carla in Cambridge.

'So how was it?' I asked her, Carla, who sat at the end of the bar eating her five o' clock staff food: a plate of reheated rice and peas shrivelled by the microwave. Cockroaches were in the glasses, so she was drinking from a bottle. She said, 'I only stayed for two hours.' She had a white cardboard box.

I said, 'What's in that box, Carla?' I asked her.

There was cake in the box.

She said, 'It's fruit cake. And that's privileged information, by the way. Boaz and Allyn have been asking the same, but I wouldn't tell them.'

'I had a strawberry and mascarpone cheesecake this afternoon with my mum,' I told her. 'She thinks I don't eat.' I was standing there, polishing glasses in the doom of the empty pub, checking my phone surreptitiously while hiding behind the door to the bar and positioning my body so that the nearest hanging lamp – a large aluminium tube with a face cut into it – hung between me and the camera pointing my way from above the door. 'Don't let me forget,' I told her. 'Boaz asked me to change the fly strips hanging by the end sink later.'

'How's the cider trap working?'

'Pretty fine,' I said as I held up a half pint tumbler with an inch of cider inside and a squirt of Fairy Liquid. The glass was covered with a layer of clingfilm pierced here and there with a biro. 'Allyn said the washing up liquid makes the flies sink. The cider is what attracts them.' There was a centimetre of drowned corpses at the bottom of the glass.

'That thing's fucking grim,' said Carla, 'and I'm trying to eat.'

'Did you ever catch wasps in old jam jars filled with water?' I asked her. 'It was a summer ritual for me.'

She said, 'No.'

'I think they should give us cake,' I said, 'the pub, instead of sending out the rota each week. To compensate for how little socialising we get to do, how little we get to meet human beings without a bar between us, how little we get to see other places, and to smell clean. You came here and, what, got this job straight away? Where are you living?'

'With a woman and her baby, near Clissold Park.'

'Great, so you know Clissold Park and you've been to Cambridge.'

'What about the cake?' said Carla.

'Well, the nicer your cake, the worse your shifts will be.'

Carla laughed. I could see old bits of reheated rice and peas on her tongue. She checked her email for an internship and groaned, feeling little concern about the appearance of an albino cockroach behind the mirror at table 270. 'They haven't noticed anyway,' I said, nodding towards the couple who sat there quietly. They had a miniature schnauzer and a Labrador puppy. 'They must be letting their dogs do the talking,' said Carla.

'Maybe even the mating,' I said. The dogs were settled down. The humans were reading. They each had their own Kindle, each said, 'Bless you,' when the Schnauzer sneezed. The Labrador puppy started sniffing the schnauzer's arsehole.

The woman had dark red hair.

She matched the walls.

I went to Ace's to get an iPhone charger and found him besieged by the water pistol kids from next door who were giggling, climbing the front patio garden wall. I rang the doorbell and it kept ringing in an annoying relay until he answered. The water pistol kids stood in my peripherals, feeling ready and dripping from the nozzles. I shook my head, which must have provoked them – they squirted my back, assaulted my ears with their next-door-kid giggling. Something that usually permeates through the walls. At least I had my work clothes on: ripped shirt where the hem caught the buckle of my belt and some old navy blue chinos that had been carrying me around since my Southern English days of theatre bars and wedding receptions, ripped on the left knee, patched, ripped through again where I'd been kneeling to stock up the fridges. All the fridges. The right pocket wasn't there and the lining looked like dirty boxer shorts.

My phone rang. Clothes stained with beer.

'Is that you out there?' It was Ace, finally, from somewhere.

'Yes, of course it's me.' Then there was a pause. 'What's the matter?'

No answer. Just slowly the front window, the living room window, my bedroom window, began to open, and out crept, or slid, the shaved sides of his head, messy top tuft of hair like he'd just got out of bed. Turns out it was stress, like someone just touched him with lightning. The children whispered. 'Here,' Ace said, and he threw out the keys to the three front doors. I didn't see the keys until they'd hit the new patio floor. Ace said, 'Shit, didn't scratch it, did they?' The patio only went down the week before.

I said, 'Um, no,' down on all fours to be sure, the perfect water pistol target.

'Damn street rats,' said Ace, who retreated. 'Don't let them follow you in,' came his voice from somewhere within. The depths. The dog hair mess. The void with scraps of Weetos cereal packets and Turkish cigarettes, bought like playground drugs over counters on Stamford Hill.

Just then I turned around and found two kids wide with cheeky grins and water guns sneaking up the steps behind me. 'Not right now,' I said, with a look that they laughed at. Must have thought Ace was some curiosity, some Boo Radley of a bored Stamford Hill locality, only with less rumour. They laughed away and hid behind the front wall. 'Have you been inside all day again?' I asked Ace, who'd retreated to the small beige sofa and was standing on the arm silently watching the street, several feet away from the window. 'Man, they won't leave me alone. Is it the school holidays or something? They're just always around. It's a never-ending replay of my kitchen nightmare.'

'You mean the barbecue?'

'Let's not talk about it,' said Ace on the sofa. 'I've been checking the street every twenty minutes. They keep running up the steps and ringing the doorbell. Can you go down there and disconnect it?'

'We only installed it last week.'

He sighed. He looked like a sweaty mess. 'Have a shower, man,' I said.

Ace said, 'Okay,' and went off to the bathroom. When he came back he was holding the Nerf gun I bought El Hell for Christmas and shot me in the face, other hand wielding his iPhone. 'That's going straight onto Instagram,' he said. Then there was a knock. Some kind of plastic shock to the foggy household atmosphere. Ace straightened, rigid, knowingly. 'Did you lock the front door?' he asked me. I shook my head and closed my eyes.

Ace said, 'They're inside.'

The secret to eternal youth is in a whisky bottle. Because whisky only ages in the barrel. And anything will develop a personality, if it lives for long enough.

'I came to London for the pubs. I'd been up in Manchester, at uni. I studied economics. My friends did English. Pretty useless, really. Uni was only ever a way of getting free money, you know, money I spent in pubs. Time isn't an issue, is it, when you're a student. I had a girlfriend, a girl I was living with up there. Eight hours of lectures, most of them I missed anyway. Rest of the time I worked behind a bar, or drank in front of one. I was assistant manager at this place called The Dolphin. It had a big grill kitchen. One day the chef left. He quit because of some dispute over pay. I don't know. They said, "Allyn, can you run the kitchen for a few days until we've hired someone new?" I said yes. And that was a big mistake. Then the manager himself left. And they said, "Allyn, can you manage the place for a week or so, just until we get a new guy?" I said sure, saw it as an opportunity, of course. Fucking uni? Well, that was a ruse. A beard, covering a much bigger issue. I wanted all the beer, man. I wanted all of it. The PDQ systems. The ringing of the tills. All the lines. The drunks. I'd finished uni by this point, though. Got a 2:1 and split up with my girlfriend. One day – it was about four in the morning – I found myself peeling potatoes on an empty, upturned tub of Chef's Kitchen mayonnaise. Prep for Sunday lunch. And I was crying, hands all cut up, tears running down my face. But I wasn't sad, just exhausted. I broke my toe the night before by kicking the plate warmer. The new chef they got in was a cunt. Utterly useless and over-privileged. He made up a bowl of hand-cut chunky chips, forgot to put them on the counter and ring for service. I said, "How long have these chips been under the heat lamps?" He said, "About three minutes." I grabbed the bowl with my bare hand and it was so hot that I dropped it, shouted, kicked the plate warmer, broke my toe. Must have been sitting under those lamps for half an hour. And I really shouted at the guy, but he didn't care. He quit a week or so later. And they didn't even pay me the extra for those days in the kitchen, or the month I spent managing, because they still hadn't bothered to find a new guy. In the end, after that Sunday, when all the potatoes had run out and we closed the kitchen early, I said FUCK THIS and came to London. Started fresh. More pubs here, more progressive brewing scene, more beer. I wanted to own my own pub, or at least run it, and I mean properly run the place, by the time I was twenty-seven. It'd be a free house, mind, absolutely not tied. Fuck that. Tied pubs are dying because large breweries are greedy and lying. It'd be a brew pub, with a small, consistent set-up in the cellar. Fucking great. Want to do things all my own way. London Living Wage. No fucking kitchen. Kitchen is an unnecessary expense, a liability. I mean shit, just look at ours, and our insane, inane list of come-and-go chefs. Ha! Know what Latest Chef said to me? He said, "There are no English chefs anymore." He said, "No English chef would let themselves be treated like such shit by such shitty owners." He's Hungarian, isn't he? My own pub. Well, I haven't got there just yet, but at least it's my birthday. Hey, thanks for staying to have a drink with me, man.'

T heo's house was always steamed up. It was a sauna. The bathroom is at the top of the stairs. The front door at the bottom. The kitchen is to the right of the bathroom. The living room and sofa, futon and coffee table, to the left. At the opposite end is the bedroom. And you could not stand up in the shower. Theo told me to crouch. He'd rigged up some nylon string to hold a shower curtain because the ceiling is so slanted that it wouldn't support a standard railing. Steamed up. Extractor fan just barely working. The bathroom smelled of salt and vinegar crisps, raw onions and underarm musk. Needs a clean. We were all in need of a clean. Theo said I could do it – clean the bathroom, not him – in exchange for sleeping there free of charge, with cupboard space for stacks of ibuprofen and codeine. My left testicle was still hurting. He showed me a trick for extracting codeine from the paracetamol in co-codamol tablets. You needed boiling water and a coffee filter. NHS chucking me around, bumper car, get rid. Theo told me to drink the liquid. I did, and we stayed up playing GTA until four in the morning. Nemesia was on the phone to an old housemate, some dispute with an old landlord about the security deposit he wouldn't release. 'You tell him to send us the invoices,' said Nemesia, 'if he's going to take £64 off each of us for minor improvements. Fucking bastard has got to prove that we caused any damage.' She hung up. 'Fucking landlords.' Their one bed flat in Lower Clapton cost just over a grand a month. The agency told them, 'The landlord could ask for much more.' The agency, after Theo and Nemesia had paid off the admin fees, said, 'So be thankful. You're living in the coolest part of London.'

The toilet still leaks.

Theo had started working at a new bar near Old Street. I don't know much about it except that it had a roof terrace and attracted a lot of Peroni drinkers from the City. 'Sounds awful,' I told Theo.

Theo told me, 'The manager went wild when I told him I also work at Otterville. He actually said, "They're my favourite fucking brewery!" Exclamation and all. Shouting. It was a cool vibe.' Theo shook his head. I was rooting through his sock drawer, after my Wednesday managing shift, cycling home, feet so hot and sweaty in my vegan Docs that my skin was peeling off. Results in hidden wounds that sting. Weep. Stick to the polyester. Theo said, 'You should wear cotton.' And he had a whole menu on his feet back then. That day it was hotdogs. They were printed on his socks. I said, 'What was it yesterday?'

He said, 'Milkshakes.'

It was the pub's policy, apparently, to wear their products around. 'Day before it was pizza slices on a yellow cotton background.' They had a wood-fired pizza oven.

'Did they provide you with these socks, Theo?' I asked.

Theo said, 'Don't make me laugh.' He went to the kitchen, took a can of Otterville IPA from the fridge. I went into his bedroom and started fondling around in his sock drawer. I ticked a bag of weed off Max at the studio before going there. The band was pulling an all-nighter. Deadlines looming. Growing incentive to make more than £100 a week. On the way to Theo's I went via Carysfort Road where a tip off from Carla the German Philanthropist suggested an old standing lamp had been left outside number ten. When I got there the lamp was gone. Just the remains of a chipboard computer desk and a barbecue were left. The barbecue looked like Ace's. Small and pointless. And the wind was beginning to growl. I said, 'Sorry T, someone got there before me,' leaving tyre marks on the white walls of his corridor and stairwell, chaining my bike to the handrail just as an electrical storm broke over Shoreditch and Central. Thunder faintly grumbling above the Gherkin in the distance. No standing lamp to illuminate us and no desire to turn on the overhead bulb because it was clinical. Absurd. So we sat in the dark, facing the window. I said, 'Do you think lightning will strike the Shard?'

Theo said, 'I hope so. Wouldn't it be amazing to see it explode?'

'How much do you get paid at this new bar?'

'£7.00 an hour.'

'Time and a half on bank holidays?'

'No idea.'

Smoking cigarettes with incense and the window slightly open.

I said, 'I bet they don't.'

TV on. Muted news commentary. 'You hear about this Malaysian airliner shot down in Ukraine?' said Theo.

I said, 'No.'

'Why are you hiding weed in my sock drawer?' said Theo.

I said, 'It just seems like the right thing to do. Hey, turn this off will you? I'm trying to watch the lightning.'

In Gaza, a dog was sitting on rubble.

Ready salted salt and vinegar cheese and onion sweet chilli
Ready salted salt and vinegar cheese and onion sweet chilli
Ready salted salt and vinegar cheese and onion sweet chilli
Ready salted salt and vinegar cheese and onion sweet chilli

Max phoned me from the roof of Shoreditch House. He'd been drinking frozen margaritas with his manager and was drunk. I was moving 25kg sacks of barley malts. The malt varieties were Munich, Caramalt, Maris Otter, and I suppose there was some wheat in there. Caramelised sugars. Highly kilned. The Maris Otter smelled like a dusty protein milkshake. And Max was a telephone call. The brewery yard at Pentangle was forever blanketed with the splinters of broken pallets and former cask labels pressure-washed off and left to decompose. Max had just got back from a visit to his mother's and had a problem.

Max called me and said, 'I went to the doctor in Oxford. I was there for just about long enough to get an appointment. Got a cotton bud stuffed down my penis.'

I said, 'I hope your manager's gone to the toilet.'

He said, 'I'm stressing out man. He shoved his finger up my arse.'

'Your manager?'

'The doctor.'

'And?'

'I feel violated. Not the finger, though it was big. It's the fact that the results were inconclusive.'

'So you're fine.'

'Apparently.'

'Did you actually have a complaint in the first place?'

A pause.

'Listen. There's something in my body,' said Max. 'I can feel it. I know it.'

You've got to pour the malts into the hopper steadily. Don't overfill the auger. It only has a small capacity. A narrow tube and screw. The auger whirred loudly, filled the old railway arch happily with the sound of progress. Or the sound of a troubled car ignition, when it was channelling too much malt. Dust masks hung on the wall but no one wore them. Our clothes were covered in so much dust you could bake bread or thicken sauces with us. The water must fill the mash tank at the same rate as the barley. Max telephoned me from the roof of Shoreditch house, looking for a blood test.

'Have you seen the new pub yet?'

'The new pub in Wood Green? Is it open?'

'No. I've been making the menu for them. New bar, new kitchen, new everything. Man, I got them to get all new grill, fryers, ovens and cold storage.'

'Couldn't you get them to get new stuff for here?'

'I've been chef for fifteen years, right after the Hungarian army. Management? No getting them to replace what was once, a long time ago, new. If it works, even just a little, then to them it works a lot. My grill? It doesn't fucking work. But that's my opinion. Not theirs. Hey, you got any new tattoos?'

'No.'

'Want staff food yet?'

'Not yet. What is it, anyway?'

'Uh, chicken, fries.'

'No salad?'

'Uh, maybe.'

'Is the chicken leftover from Sunday?'

'Of course the chicken is leftover from Sunday. Don't look at me like that. It's Tuesday, yes, but it's fine. You know, the pub in Finsbury Park has the same kitchen as us too. I got them to make it exactly the same, when I first work for the company. It's a good layout. That pub was a dump. The first time I was chef here, before your time, they had only just bought that pub. It was shit hole, man – rats, no lights, fucking wasteland cellar. Husband and wife owned it, but the wife died, and they bought it cheap, the company, and say to me, "Can you stay the night please? Look after it?" because the locks were fucked and there was no alarm. That was the first day. They gave me £200 cash, so I slept by the bar with a carving knife, make sure no one broke in. That was when I lived in the flat upstairs. I was awake one night, in that flat, stoned. I had a machete, this big fucking knife I kept from the army, under my pillow – old habit, uh? – and I saw this figure, this black shadow, climbing up the side of the building, at the back of the roof where that flat bit is, and I rubbed my eyes because I couldn't believe what I was seeing, and they were dry because I'd been smoking so much weed. But the shadow didn't go away, and it started trying to open a window into one of the other flats. So I grabbed the machete and went out onto the fire escape, but it was gone. Maybe it heard me? Whatever, man. It was just my fucking neighbour all along, the girl who lived next door. She left her keys at home, went through the alleyway there, right? To the fire escape, break into her own house. Man, fuck, I almost chopped her fucking head off. Uh, here, before I forget, take my bank card. My friend is coming in. His name is Tamás, like the kitchen porter, yes, but different. T-A-M-A-S-H. Yes? Reserve him a table. Eight o' clock.'

'How will I recognise him?'

'He's a big motherfucker yeah? Ha, you'll see. We were in the Hungarian army together. He's a hired gun now.'

'A mercenary?'

'Yes. Take my card. He's got a date and he's nervous. Don't let him pay for anything.'

Molly said, 'Are you alive?' I'd been out of touch for a while, sending one word messages and seeing just a little bit less of her, offering excuses based on work commitments that were, in reality, vast shipments of beer flooding my guts, problems with my nuts which seemed to ache more the less I had sex, and ache more the more I got stressed. Two things which went hand in hand, never mind the impending doom of the canine conspiracy claiming me as its next victim.

I neglected an immediate answer, still somewhere deep in Limehouse, Cable Street, busy with wine glass meditation in a dank squat while actors performed an immersion piece based on the work of William Burroughs. I thought I was doing Molly a favour by not replying right away, saving her from some pit of young love despair: too young, too serious, just like so many generations of emotionally repressed parents before us. But my fingers were trying to be honest, my heart batting the bars of my rib cage saying, 'Let me at her, you idiot.' Fortunately, my brain was on pills, so I couldn't string two words together, anyway.

Max sat on a cushion beside me in the dark, eyes closed, couldn't see me secretly using my phone. 'I haven't read any of his books,' I whispered, embarrassed.

Max said, 'You don't really read him.'

'You sort of let him read you,' said Stefan on the floor by the mescal bar, which was a square hole punched through a tiled wall between what was once either a shop floor, now the meditation room, and a ground floor kitchenette. The room was very still. A woman ran her fingers round the edges of bowls in the corner, creating rumours in the air about Limehouse being the new Hackney, or Tottenham the new Dalston, which was almost as unsettling as the text I'd almost sent Molly, which said, 'Help me.'

When we arrived there was an old steel shutter half-closed with a sign that said TONIGHT: LECTURE ON SOCIAL EVOLUTION. The mangled Converse All Stars of a young woman were visible below, and she bent down under the shutter when she saw our Docs, Nikes and plimsolls, to let us in.

She said, 'Take a seat, the meditation has already begun.'

Uncross your legs.

Lie back.

Close your eyes.

Listen to the bowls.

Rub a finger round the rim.

About a dozen or so other humans slipped in and out of my

awareness, or tried to, lying against walls or draped on reclaimed oak chairs. I kept checking my phone was on do not disturb, background light dimmed right down, 'Help me,' to Molly, in some pathetic plea for attention.

When the bowls stopped singing we were invited to walk through a curtain where I asked an actor dressed as a doctor what to do about my testicle. He rubbed his nostril, turned his head to the side and prescribed three shots of mescal with a typewriter and an intentionally fading candle.

In the next room were the faces of writers and poets pixelated in poorly printed images dangling from fraying strings attached to the ceiling. A Christmas tree stood by another shutter covering another door, decorated with syringes dipped in unthreatening shit to give them the illusion of having been used. A sorry typewriter was being abused on a long central table by people too used to touchscreens. Max said, 'Are the drugs communal?' He wanted total immersion. Someone handed him a half-smoked joint as if to prove a mutual understanding of friendship and cohabitation. A tall man with long hair was slumped at the table. Someone said, 'Is that guy part of the act?' as he started throwing up in the corner. 'We should've brought another gram,' said Max. He was on it. In it. Under it. Applause. The tall man stood up, apparently fine. Thinking of Molly, heart thumping. Could be love. Could be k-holing. I didn't know.

'How was your walk?'
      'There were dogs and pigeons.'
      'What kind of dogs?'
'Two Chihuahuas.'
'Where did you go?'
'To St John at Hackney, by Clapton Square.'
'What were the Chihuahuas doing?'
'One was hiding behind its owner's leg, staring at me.'
'And the other?'

'The other was wearing a jacket.'

'The one staring at me had one pointy ear and one floppy ear.'
'Very unusual for a Chihuahua.'
'It was funny.'
'And the eyes?'
'Dilated. Bulgy.'
'Just as I suspected. Theo?'
'Yes?'
'What are your thoughts?'
'We're getting a puppy in two years.'
'Is that right Nemesia?'
'Yes.'
'Is that right Theo?'
'It's what Nem and I want.'

In the wake of this information I began collating The Shapes of Dogs' Eyes: writing ideas for creative medium on till receipt paper, strategies for publication and distribution. Strange weird drawings that lived in my pockets sprung to life – occasional doodles of letter-thoughts and the ramblings of drunken bartenders overheard. Max said write a song. Allyn said name a beer after my strange idea and get the world drunk on truth. It could be the taste of the story. Malts and hoppy. He was rethinking his grapefruit pale. Upped the ABV. Branding on the label, on a domestic-industrial level. Theo said write the manifesto, spread the word in bi-monthly leaflets and push them under the doors of those of us not already succumbed to a life of corner sofas and vet bills. I had to clear a headful of ideas first. It needed sweeping, the floor of that brain, which was different from the brain I have now. I had to get rid of the cockroach eggs, the cobwebs, the stains. The pub cellar was littered with half-hidden ancient stock lists. Bottles for the glass fridges. American. Belgian. Local British. Right to left. Littered with the discarded shadows of former staff members at midnight, long since re-employed and whose lives I might have saved had I discovered the plot sooner. A trickle of clues on a scavenger hunt to nowhere.

I hadn't heard from Molly in a week. I was convinced that she was how they'd get to me. The dogs. So I wrapped my life up in tinfoil, in a lunchbox ready to go, but the bread was squished, with a week old condom packet stuck to the fold and a replacement oyster card in need. I was hiding underneath a railway arch filling bottles. And I was shrouded by darkness afterwards. No dogs in the railway arches, where I found sanctuary from the front line of my conspiracy behind walls of branded boxes and cardboard ideas draped with ceilings of plastic dividers, wiping bottles with musky tea towels to remove condensation. Invited mould. Defeated glue. I spent hours labelling bottles, hands moving, autonomous, while behind the eyes I held meetings with the factions of my brain – the last refuge of a coward – deciding ways to expose the lie and save kids from becoming their parents.

Mick said, 'There was a problem with the porter last week. It wouldn't naturally carbonate. So we're a bit behind schedule and there's a lot of work to do.'

The only interruptions were occasional job alterations. Rinsing glass bottles in peracetic acid then hanging them on the bottling tree waiting to be filled.

Labelling bottles was more cathartic. I didn't have to maintain focus on not squirting diluted acid in my face. Brain dysfunctionally functioning. Molly texting and expecting a reasonable amount of effort from her boyfriend, which made me loathe myself and the prison I'd made.

Six hours of lunging until my knees hurt knocking gas canisters around in imitations of Anglo-Italian Skype conversations (the bottle machine had stopped working and tech support was in Tuscany). I was surrounded by gyle numbers, cylindrical pale ales and rye malts, a sweep of the warehouse floor. Citra and Amarillo hop dust. Bin men in green Hackney Council visibility rounding every corner. Something told me to wash off the caustic soda which had crept over the rim of my long protective gloves while I was cleaning some equipment.

It was my nervous system.

The acid formed a ring of seething bite around my forearm.

Mick said, 'Your girlfriend will find the scars sexy.'

His wife was pregnant.

T heo was angry because Molly rearranged his living room. He was going round his living room with a pencil and paper making notes and taking photographs of the crime scene. He had a refurbished Polaroid camera but only half of the pictures came out.

'Why don't you put the room back together?' I said.

He said, 'Because the room's evidence. Didn't you read the first paragraph in this section?'

'What?'

'You can't just let people fuck with your stuff and forget it.'

There was a pause.

'I thought you weren't sure about Molly, anyway,' he said. 'Why was she here?'

'I've developed a new strategy,' I said. 'I'm going to expose the conspiracy from the inside. Let them think they can get me. The dogs.'

'Then what?'

'Um.'

'Cool. Hey where's my record collection?'

I said, 'You only have three records.'

'Yes. And I can't find them.'

'They're there,' pointing to the corner of his messed up living room. 'T, your living room is ten feet square.'

He said, 'It doesn't matter. Aren't you sorry? You don't actually live here, remember. And she?' shaking his head. He went to a festival for three days with Nemesia. Molly and I slept in their bed.

Free house. Unoppressed sex. Theo said, 'You didn't, did you?'

Another pause.

He said, 'We're going to have a severe falling out if you fucked in my bed.'

I sighed. 'Did you always have that beard?' I asked.

'It's new.'

'Looks good.'

'Thanks. No, wait. I'm angry at you.' Theo sighed too. 'Someone stole my bike saddle. Right outside the front door.'

I put my hand on his shoulder.

Outside, an ice cream van. Theo started laughing, one hand resting the weight of his body on the recently misaligned futon and the chair I was using as a coffee table. 'Yankee fucking Doodle.'

I laughed too.

Yankee Doodle went to town, all the way through Hackney Downs.

'Maybe go stay with Max for a while,' Theo told me.

I said, 'In Lewisham? Theo, you can't do that to me.'

'Well, Ace then.'

'He's got some French girl from Tinder staying over.'

Theo paused. 'You're right,' he said, 'I wouldn't do that to you. South of the river gives me the shivers.'

'We didn't really have sex in your bed,' I said.

'Whatever,' said Theo. 'I'm surprised she's still with you.'

Molly. I'm still working this out. Molly. In my head. Molly. Asleep under red, under blanket, on the chair. She calls it comfort. That's the comfort of quilt. Molly. Red lips and black tights. Blinking, winking, lingering Molly. Howling in Hackney setting traps of clothes line wire to catch a neighbour's trespassing dog. Molly, for whom I got a slice of paper as a side to green tea in a Stoke Newington café. Bikes decorating the window and wooden floorboards, with pumps and inner-tube valves and oil. Closing hours awaiting Molly's imminent call, when she would give me the go-ahead. Thumbs up Molly on some deal.

I woke up with her, as a side order to a morning lot of hard-on back sweat and bad breath which only served to fuel me.

Molly, who I apologised to for being so useless the last few weeks then kissed profusely. Then, hours later, I was very slowly drinking my tea. 'I need your help,' she'd said earlier to me that morning, and kissed me in the white oven of her duvet. Damn it, that meant I couldn't refuse, and wouldn't have wanted to, anyway, feeling strong about my decision to try and beat the dogs with her, which I still thought was possible, then.

She walked, after breakfast, to the DLR at Bow Church, feeling turquoise. And I pushed Ace's black fixie – a borrowed luxury – beside her.

I said to Molly, 'Okay,' kissed her by the rails when her Birkenstock fell off, fell through the railings and became caught on pigeon spikes for clarity. This was sincere. This was spiky London. 'Okay,' kiss, then got on my phone and my way immediately, concerned about time and showing her how useful I was, or could be.

So I cycle-superhighwayed down to Bethnal Green, up Mare Street, Amhurst Road, Dalston lane and Dalston Junction back, then, to Kingsland Road, feeling pale in the early brick morning as I curved north in search of a music store. Yes, that is what I was looking for. But Hackney, like a nervous man who had bitten all his nails out so only the cuticles of an in-between land remained, was stuck behind a continual construction fence. Bright red. And the girders hoisted what was left above my reach.

As I was cycling my phone went off. It was Ace. He said, 'Where's my bike?'

I told him I had it.

'I have it.'

He said, 'I need it. I'm due at a race.'

'What race?'

'Got to be in Shoreditch on Paul Street for a meeting. Some advert about cough medicine. Could do it in my sleep but listen: they've got free hot drinks and Nicorette. I've got to be there. I want the job before I go on holiday.'

I was feeling a two-wheel imbalance.

El Hell, Ace and Nanna were flying to New York. They'd rented a Greenwich Village apartment. One bedroom, two sofas. The bedroom was for whoever successfully brought home an American. Ace said, 'I'll miss you on the sofa.'

I said, 'Why?'

He said, 'Because I'll have no one to annoy while I sit around doing nothing all day. It'll be boring. Reading unwritten novels. Trying to sell abandoned Airbnb belongings on Ebay.'

I was perched on the crossbar by Dalston Square.

'Where's my copy of Hans Fallada?' he said.

'I'm still reading it.'

'Slowly,' he said. 'Fucking hell, you've been staying with your mate so much. It's not fair.'

'You mean Theo?'

'I don't know. I don't care.'

'He has a bigger bookshelf.'

'Whatever. We've got a bigger collection of dogs.'

'Exactly,' I said.

A pause.

'Don't be lonely, Ace.'

'Don't worry about me,' said Ace. 'I don't get lonely, I get revenge.'

Click.

There was a dead lion on my tin of golden syrup. The tin of golden syrup was entirely for my benefit. Cats weren't really something I'd ever bothered to consider. I used to walk my mother's dogs for 50p a day. I was young, desperate, in the middle of the countryside and trying to save up for the guitar I'd later give Max. New musical horizons stretched from ploughed field to ploughed field, with no view to the studio wall where Max would one day watch it hang. And I was waiting, trying to do Molly a favour, slice of paper on behalf of Molly. Write this down. Try it out. All I was trying was golden syrup with the tip of my finger. My finger was too bitter. And the syrup was too sweet. Effects on brain arteries and vision unclear, but alarming. Fear of diabetes. Feet going numb. It was wet cycling through Dalston, pausing for Ace's inane telephone conversation. Fucking Shoreditch. He got the bus in the end, on the condition that I accompany him to Morrisons. It was a compromise I would pay for later, but since I was only down the road and still needed his bike to complete Molly's favour, I took it.

There were flies flying around the corpse of the lion on the syrup tin. Syrup flies. The only music shop I found open didn't have the right product and I waited on texts to know if she'd take an alternative version. Problems in acquisition. Molly. Table. Chair. Only Ace, whose meeting was over, was on the 149 back up here. He said he left early. He got the job but the coffee wasn't strong enough.

I got a call from Molly when my green tea had gone bitter and my smuggled Morrisons madeleine cake was eaten. Tea no longer green, even. More a tannin brown. Molly said, quite clearly, 'No no, they must be Vandoren, size 2.5.' Those weren't the type this music shop had in stock. No matter. I had an iMac list of clarinet reeds and stockists, as well as a whole day off. I texted Ace: 'I'm going to need your bike for longer.'

Ace said, 'Come swap it for Nanna's then. She'll be out for longer.'

So I did. But her bike had a bad seat-to-handle-bar-height ratio, a buckled rim and the memory of an Islington curb. Nanna, still limping each morning to work. Back at the flat, Ace said, 'How was your tea?'

'Alright. Thanks for the cake.'

We switched bikes through the door frame. Smell of cumin from the flat below. Nanna's bike a lot worse than I thought: riding it felt like cycling through syrup. I got as far as Newington Green before I realised Ace, who only gets revenge, had drastically reduced the tyre pressure.

I met Molly in Trinity Buoy Wharf after cycling up from Limehouse Basin, which should be filthy as a primary school post-painting session sink but was a CS3 housing development dream along Regent's Canal. 'Molly, I cycled to the Barbican for your reeds.'

'Thank you,' she said, then kissed me.

'Hi, by the way.'

'Hi.' She wore khaki trousers and combat boots.

'Molly, I rode all the way through London for you. There,' handing her the reeds. She'd been rehearsing a play all week. That night was the opening but she wouldn't let me go ('Best wait until it's been performed a few times, tightened up, you know?'). The car park outside the studio was awash with apathetic actors in a slumming pre-show luncheon. Sun bathing. Reading lines. A few of them, including Molly, practised instruments for musical interludes between scenes of fearsome Greek murder, rape, battle and laughter. Surplus camouflage was the chosen costume. Molly complained: 'The director decided to put a play within the play,' she said. 'I think that's overplayed.' She was fingering her clarinet in a tragicomic way. 'Come in two or three days,' she said, while I finished a malted shake.

The canal was a duckweed carpet, dense in underwater scrap forestry with me looking into the water, looking to the bed from goodbye-Molly. She had to get on rehearsing, lunch over, and Nanna wanted her bike back too. Looking into the canal, where all of London slept and retained its possibilities.

I went looking for a bike pump.

It was around this time I learned that people had been brewing craft canines. Like beers at home, they were brewing, breeding, selling, reaping dogs, who had infiltrated the population to a far greater extent than I'd realised. Human eyes began to rust in their sockets. When they moved, their imperfections caused friction like Labrador hip bones. And I knew that I'd have to act soon, play their game, defeat them.

A Belgian-shepherd-collie cross walked into the pub. I was in charge again, dressed in bow tie and tails, standing, wagging by the door curtain and greeting all the tailored dogs of London, their humans on leads, little humans in handbags for show. Lap humans, spreading out on old church pews and dribbling booze all over the floor. This dog, with eyes like charcoal and fur as dry as pavements, black underneath like dip-dyed roasted barley malts of a coffee stout that's 7% alcohol, 93% sorrow, had just arrived. Cream paws and legs and hips and a single pale spot on head, above right eye, or left. Creamy brown like creamy fobbing beer head. A porter. Latest Chef said, 'We should have a dog menu. I could be London's first dog chef.'

So, they'd got him too.

Patted head. Offered human a bowl of water. Severed pigs' ears would be a different book. Allyn was away in Manchester and Boaz was on holiday in Ireland.

I was dreaming. Leaning in solace with The Shapes of Dogs' Eyes against the bar. The Shapes of Dogs' Eyes leant with me. I stroked its head. A double agent. A Highland Terrier in a plaid jacket eyed me suspiciously, as though I were being tailed by the canine Gestapo. Behind me lurked an enormous Chow with the hair of a furry brown cloud, a lion, a burial mound and sink holes for eyes, ready to disappear me for good.

A customer said, 'Woof,' and that brought me back in. The pub. The wood. The BARK. Bar staff forgot to dim the Edison bulbs and one blew. They were only fitted a week before and replacements are expensive. We didn't have any. The office chair was a memory, the bag of old card receipts that kept overflowing downstairs behind the computer became a mystery. The mystery of the endless receipts. Fill a pool. Go for a swim. Someone yelped. A tail underfoot. Clumsy, barbaric humans. We should've used the old receipts to cover the floor and soak up all the people. Slopping. Sloshing. Scampering up and down stairs and dragging their backsides along the floor. Copulating senselessly in the corners and toilets. Endlessly consuming even when bellies were full or filling. So embarrassing for their canine owners, who sat patiently beneath tables holding jowly canine conversations, pricking ears, gnawing legs and whining with the passing of Kingsland Road sirens, the always soundtrack to a shift illuminated by the green neon Brooklyn Brewery light that hung above the crisps.

Allyn arrived to shatter the fun.

'What happened to Manchester?' I said.

'It's done,' he said. 'I slept in. Missed my train. Was up all night explaining lost love to Carla.'

'Love?'

'I mean beer,' he said, and got out a list of things he needed for his homebrew kit. 'It's too demanding. Keeps me up all night. It'd be easier to have a baby, but I'd have to have a girlfriend for that.'

'Or wife.'

He shivered.

'Or dog?'

He started showing me coils of copper pipe and wires and heating elements he was using to enhance his heated yeast reproduction, consumption, cultivation, production. Eat sugar, shit beer. 'Carla's not into it,' he said. 'She's leaving London. She's the smartest one of us all. I've been chatting to a girl from Camden, anyway. I want a more intense homebrewing sensation. She's coming round later, actually. Might stay until morning. These things – by which I mean beer – take time. Be up all night, I'm hoping.'

He winked.

'You slept with her then?'

'She wants to take it slow.'

'What about Carla? I thought you loved her.'

'That love is a past participle. And anyway, shh,' looking towards her, Carla, who was at the other end of the bar squinting through a whisky tumbler, making decisions or something, 'she doesn't know.'

'Um.'

'Does she?'

I changed the subject: 'So, what about Manchester? I thought you were going to visit your old uni friends? See the pub owner who fucked you over and tell him to go fuck himself?'

Allyn said, 'It's fine. I decided that I couldn't leave Hackney, anyway. I'm getting close, you see,' and he reached over the bar for

89

a glass.

I said, 'Allyn, take my bow tie and tails seriously. I'm running this place tonight and you're not meant to be here.'

Allyn said, 'Okay fine. Keep your draught piss and check this out,' reaching into his satchel and removing a bottle of his new grapefruit pale. 'That's right. Newest batch. A big improvement. Though, for some reason,' holding the bottle, which was brown, up to one of the working lights, 'it's come out dark.' I leant forward, looking into the shapes of his eyes. They were tiny. Deadly. Focused. They were eyes that knew what they wanted. And they were also eyes that were weary. Small, dark pools of car crash oil on a roadside. His beard was growing quickly, tangling with his shirt when he looked down, moustache creeping under his top lip and catching the ends of dregs with occasional rebellious strands that impersonated antennae. Sniffing beer, beard hairs conducting the first test. 'I've got a growler,' Allyn said, and grabbed a big bottle with one hole for a finger from his satchel. The impossible void of a narrow bag. 'They're selling them at Clapton Craft. Cheap re-fills from their taps.'

'Want to fill it up here?' I asked, walking behind the bar.

'No thanks. I need to get a big enough holder so I can carry it around on my bike. Hydration is key,' Allyn said to me, as liquid dripped from his beard onto his shoe. 'Now, are you coping alright?'

I told him I was doing fine.

He said, 'You're overdressed. Lot of dogs in tonight.'

'That's right. Lot of water requested. Had to raid the kitchen for more bowls. Latest Chef nearly exploded. As for beer, I'd say we've undersold.'

'Got to push up the GP, man.'

'What do you care?'

'More money, more beer, idiot. Hey, where's Timbo?'

'I sent him out for treats. We've had dogs panting and dribbling all over the place. All the excitement's been driving their humans insane. They've been so fucked they can barely maintain their composure. They keep wandering out onto the street for cigarettes and I keep having to usher them back inside, scratch them behind the ear, offer them more beer, burgers, nuts. The dogs are mad. Last thing we need is a lawsuit: "Oh, you didn't close the door and my human went outside and climbed into an unmarked taxi. Now he's missing.'"

Woof.

'You know what I was thinking?' I said. 'These dogs should get their humans cut.'

Allyn said, 'Excuse me?'

'Yeah, cut off their thumbs so they can open fewer doors.'

It was a bold statement. Too bold. I regretted it as soon as I'd said it. The beauty of the canine oppression was that no humans knew. When the words came out of my mouth every dog in the pub turned its head towards me. I coughed. They barked. One of their humans began gnawing my tails, drunk, trying to taste my fabric. I could see things were beginning to get out of control. I'd exposed myself. Allyn was looking around, mouth open, frowning. 'I don't know what kind of place you've got running here,' he said, necking a quick whisky chaser and paying his tab, 'but when I get back from Manchester, by which I mean my homebrewing session tonight with this girl from Camden, I'll be making some changes. You're letting power go to your head. You're barking mad, son. Tell me, how long have you spent sitting in the office, watching dog videos on YouTube?'

'Ten minutes here and there. It's research, though.'

'Be careful, he said. 'Don't abuse your position. Fuck man, you've got Timbo out buying dog biscuits.'

'We've got a table of six miniature schnauzers coming in at quarter to eleven.'

'Fuck me.' Shaking his head.

'Whatever, man,' I told him, gesturing to the door. 'You're not even here, you're in Manchester, right?' Then he left.

Carla walked over and said, 'I'm glad he's gone.' There were customers waiting, but they were only human. The dogs stopped barking because Timbo had just walked in, arms full of dental chews and dog-friendly chocolate. 'He's been going on at me on the phone lately,' she said. 'Really late at night. He talks on and on about the temperature of the cellar, how it's got to be less than thirteen degrees, and about bottle trees he's ordered, and kegging. I think he thinks it's a ritual, all this beer-talk, as though a prelude to handcrafted mating.'

'He thinks he's getting over you,' I said.

'Shh,' she said, 'I'm not supposed to know,' winking. 'Besides,' looking around at customers becoming impatient, 'he's been brewing with some girl from Camden.'

'Yeah, he said. Don't take it personally. You see, he's just drunk on yeasty rejection.'

'Have you seen them together? They're already on Instagram, dressed in black aprons with big bellies.'

'It's the beer, not babies.'

'They'll give birth any day now. Did you try his new grapefruit pale? He gave me some earlier, while you were cleaning up that puddle. It's black, man.'

'I know. They used the wrong malt.'

Carla was shaking her head. She said, 'She's not right for him, I can tell.'

That's when Ace walked in. He had Noodles with him. They were arm in arm. I hadn't seen him since he left for New York two weeks earlier. They sat at the bar and I offered Noodles a four-pawed bottle of water. Ace wanted a Hacker-Pschorr, which is, unfortunately, a lager. Noodles shook her head and began watching the adventures of a catacombing cockroach that Carla the German Philanthropist was trying to catch in order to save it from the eventual trap of Boaz's whenever-he-gets-back boot. She was on all fours, Carla, rather than the dog, who was on three – one paw raised and dangling in strange confusion: what was this human doing? Carla was on all fours, slowly stalking the bug as it navigated the filthy moonscape of the pub's beer-puddle floorboards, long covered with those little plastic tubes that once held cigarette filters and tiny springs of tobacco that somehow cropped up, and tinier pieces of glass which occasionally became stuck in her palms.

When this happened, Carla would give out a yelp.

'Will you lick this?' she said to Noodles, who was no less confused than before. 'Please? It's good luck when a dog licks your cut.'

Noodles refused.

'What's she doing?' said Ace, who was looking at Carla, who was missing her chance to catch the cockroach – it went through a crack in the bar and she was trying to crawl in after but the hole was too small. Point of sale beer pumps climbed to the ceiling like stalagmites. And Carla sat dejectedly at our feet, repeating the words, 'I'm in a cave. I'm in a cave,' looking defeated. She semi-shouted, 'FAG BREAK?' at me.

'You don't smoke, Carla,' I told her.

She said she just wanted some air.

Noodles wandered off to socialise. Sniff arseholes. Be polite and discuss grooming her human, El Hell. Usually starts by licking her private parts, then going right for his mouth and eyes. Noodles was standing on the table. 'She's talking to those dogs about mating you with their humans,' I said to Ace. 'They're bargaining. Sell a baby, make some money for that new chew toy. Dogs are enterprising, you know.'

'Cool,' said Ace. 'Just stick me in the back of a Subaru. Read the paper while I go at that bulldog's owner and hope that my aim is true.'

Nanna walked in. Nanna the Hackney fable. Leggings, bent bicycle, still limping even though her crash was months ago. She came here to discuss their tenancy agreement and the idea of living together – just them – should El Hell take his dogs up to Enfield. I had a haircut before opening the pub and there were little bits of hair stuck in my ears. Nanna started flattening down my fringe. It got rained on, came up greasy and long. Nanna said I looked like a wet dog. She said I smelled of burgers and chips and coleslaw, which I suppose is a fashionable way to smell around here. The rush of a birthday dinner – some terrier's seventeenth birthday, which I think is around eighty or ninety for humans, looking grey and blind and grumpy – made me sweat, panic-text the figures to Boaz who was too busy kissing the Blarney Stone to reply.

Somewhere someone was coughing. It was Carla, waging too close a war with the bug spray she was firing into the cavernous sink. I floated the word blitzkrieg, but she didn't like feeling British. She felt stuck in a hackneyed idea.

'Make sure you rinse the dog bowls out,' I told her, while Noodles was watching fleeing cockroach families disperse around human feet.

I told Molly I would drop her at Gatwick Airport. She was about to go to Italy with her theatre company. They stayed there a month to learn Commedia dell'Arte, ride bicycles, tan and eat gelato. I was watching Germany play Ghana in the World Cup with Ace and hadn't actually asked him yet if I could use his car. That's Ace on the opposite sofa. We were throwing occasional biscuits at each other. That's Ace going under, clingfilm wrapped around a new tattoo of Bart Simpson. Ace under a layer of Bepanthen. 'I'm too old to get free condoms from Boots,' he told me, intimating that I get some for him.

I said, 'I will if I can borrow your car tonight and tomorrow.'

The hood rats were yapping on Oldhill Street.

'Are you going to visit her in Italy?' he said.

I said 'Yes,' with paper on my knee.

'Just a minute,' said Ace, straining to get up, tracksuit bottoms, salad cream. He manoeuvred round the TV, the wonky Ikea coffee table which kept threatening to fall. He hobbled over my deposited blob of an army bag, spilling clothes and an old birthday card from Max beside the sofa. 'Careful of the dog shit back there,' I told him.

He said, 'I know. I'm going to let El Hell clean it up when he gets home.' He closed the window and stood watching, past the plane trees that kept scraping the glass, all the kids being mean to each other, now silent. 'Much better,' he said, then hopped back to his hole in the sofa, one foot up, the other on the floor.

I'd sunk into the beige two-seater. That's me on the sofa, again. The forever sentence. Going over in my mind all the things I had left to do that night: quick shower. Get petrol. Get to Molly's studio for the last night of her play. The women of Athens and Sparta had been denying sex all week to end a war. And I was trying to write a letter before I left to go see her perform, with a magazine placed under the paper, resting on my knee: a letter that held all the things I had been scheming to tell her, that I'd give her in secret so she could discover and read it when she got to wherever in Italy. She gave me a letter, too, and that was the pressure. One enveloped letter, or card I supposed, with who knew what lying dormant inside. A volcano. It could have said, 'I do not love you,' for all I knew, and that would have made sense.

'You cannot open it until the date I told you,' she said when she gave it to me a day earlier, and that was a week and a half away.

'Are things getting serious?' said Ace. 'I thought you were scared of being an adult?' He laughed. I kept writing.

'What do you want it for anyway?' said Ace.

I said, 'To drop Molly in Italy tomorrow morning.'

'That's quite a drive to do in twelve hours.'

'I'll take the M25.'

The game was over.

The score was 2-2.

I saw my death in the Blackwall Tunnel. This was an early morning affair. Part of a strange back-to-concrete ecstasy. An escape from the green of Sussex and Surrey. Auto-asphyxiation. Mouth against the exhaust pipe of narrow lane lorries beneath Thames London. It was death in slow motion. Death in rotation. Death in constipation. Death that kept on happening. Ace's car was a Citroen banger. The southern route was closed for roadworks. So we went west, on the way there. Took the A12 to the M25, crossed the river at Dartford and came off onto the M23 for the airport. The company was to meet in departures at seven, and Molly slept most of the way, having spent all her energy dying from a gunshot wound to the stomach the previous night. The northbound tunnel was open on the way back, and I went under alone, at quarter past eight, feeling thin with Max's band on the stereo plugged into my phone.

Soon after I went under, the roof cracked. The reinforced concrete snapped. The river rushed in and the painting was slowly filled. It demanded a drowning death. I felt all the weight of London crush me. Molly didn't know about the letter I wrote. I snuck it into her suitcase last minute, night before, after driving her back from the show in Ace's car.

Only thirty miles per hour.

I felt no fear when the water came in, only ragged in defeat, but at the hands of whom I did not know, and for what cause I could not say. I came out of the tunnel into a world of sweat-smacking thighs and Hackney Half Marathon sports bras, when I finally got round Victoria Park (Grove Road closed), and found the memory of Bobby telling me something about this a few weeks ago at work. His girlfriend was running it. I saw her on Lower Clapton Road while I waited for a wide enough space between runners to cross over and go to Theo's. And waited. And waited. She waved. I had to drive through Bethnal Green to Shoreditch in order to get the car back to Stokey. This proved difficult when my phone battery died and I had to navigate with personal geography. At least there was free parking at Ace's.

What are your negatives? Dark scans that show a different you? Something inside that does not yet officially exist? I met my old friend Sam at Stoke Newington Station. Another job interview had not gone well. He'd stayed in London afterwards, at Spitalfields Market. Got drunk, came up, at my insistence, to Stokey, to meet me when I'd finished work, after I'd run up to Ace's for a shower and a new shirt. Sam was slurring his way round the pavement outside the ticket office, balancing a bottle of iced tea on a black metal box full of high speed fibre optic broadband cables, chatting his monochrome blurb to some coke can loiterer outside the Roti Stop. He kept apologising to me. The following morning we were sitting in Dreyfus, the café by Theo's house on the corner of Clapton Square. He was drinking a coffee and waiting for an expensive full English. He kept talking about negatives at me. The night before we'd met Theo, who'd come down from Tottenham after another day in the tap room at Otterville and was carrying a case of their session IPA under his arm for later. For free. Theo was already tired from work. Negatives. And he didn't want to put up with Sam's shit after eight hours of bar service and less than two of knowing the guy. Foolishly, and before Theo arrived, I offered Sam Theo's sofa to crash on with me for the night. Theo, who wouldn't learn to give a shit until later, when Sam got really battered and called some guys cunts on the benches outside my pub, was fine about it. Why'd the interview not go well? What're you doing now? Didn't I tell you? I got a job back home. I'm going to be living with my parents for a while longer. Save up, you know?

'Christ, really?'

'What?'

'Man, that's a terrible idea.'

Sam looked at me. He said, 'Why?'

I said, 'You need to get the fuck out of there. Shit. I'm speaking to you as your oldest friend, so just listen to me. It's the truth.'

'But we never see each other,' he said.

I said, 'Yeah, well, stop living at home then. How's your mum, by the way?'

'You know about that?'

I shook my head. Negatives.

'That's right,' he said. 'Negatives. Remember when we were seventeen and my parents took us to Portugal for a week and we met those two really cool girls and then it got late and we didn't know what to do about it? Sleeping with them, I mean. And they'd left us and gone to bed anyway. Remember?'

'Yes.'

Our food arrived. I had a poached egg. 'How can you afford that, anyway?' I said to Sam, pointing at an obscene sausage.

'I told you,' he said. 'New job.'

'Then why were you interviewing yesterday?'

He said, 'Why not?'

'So what're you doing in this one?

He said, 'Selling.'

'Selling what? Stock keeping software? Insurance to insurance companies?'

'Actually,' he said, 'I have no idea. But my boss takes the whole office out on Mondays for lunch and we all get really drunk. He says everyone should treat Monday like Friday, and that seems to make everyone happy. £26,000 a year.'

'That's more than I make in two,' I said.

Sam shrugged. 'Pockets,' he said through a mouthful.

'What?'

'Your negatives. What are mine? Easy: getting fucked up and upsetting taxi drivers. Forgetting I told my friend that my mother has cancer because I was smoking so much weed.'

'I knew it.'

A pause.

'And yours?' he said, 'Yours are, well, you never check your pockets.'

'Are you referring to the holiday in Portugal?'

'We lost the room key and had that big stupid fight in the corridor while looking for those two girls we fancied. We almost killed each other because we couldn't get into our room.'

'And then you disappeared. Yeah, I remember. And I found you hours later by the pool. It was the middle of the night. The place was deserted and the key was in my back pocket.'

'What I'm saying,' said Sam, 'is that something really bad's going to happen one day, and it's going to have been in your pocket the whole time.'

'But Sam,' I said, standing up, 'look, I don't have any pockets.' I was wearing my work trousers and I was standing there with my hands poking straight through the holes where my pockets used to be.

Sam shrugged. Sam said, 'You'll have to buy new trousers eventually. I could lend you the money, if you like.'

The graffiti in the women's toilet was driven. It was handcrafted on a foundation of life advice and ideas for growing culture on cubicle walls. Things like, "It's the possibility of making dreams come true that makes life interesting <3," and "Those who are scared to climb mountains will forever sleep in ditches. Fact." The men simply drew penises above the urinal. Although, more recently, some poet had written, "I was born here + will be flushed away someday," behind the toilet seat, so there may have been hope after all.

I began to sense that something was beginning to end. But what it was I didn't know. When London and I first became acquainted it was autumn. We would soon go full circle. Superficial sunrises were breaking the morning mist that covered the tip of the Shard, the Gherkin, from Kingsland Road, Stoke Newington High Street and the attics of Lower Clapton. I hadn't seen Max in a week. 'It's been longer, no?'

'Yes.'

'Thanks for the Cuba libre.' On a bench.

When Max arrived I went behind the bar and poured us two glasses. 'Nice jacket,' I said. It was new, or new to him.

'Thanks. Got it from that vintage shop on Cambridge Heath Road.' Denim, big Mickey Mouse stitched onto the back, pale blue.

'So what's been happening?' he said. 'What's new?'

I'd just been accused of pushing an old man's bike over. He was now pointing and yelling and rambling in the street.

'This fucked up old guy keeps threatening to kill me, that's all,' I said.

'And I will, I will,' the old man said. 'All my, my mates,' he said, thumbing for a non-committal, or existing, ride back down the street, 'all my mates are coming to get you.' The old guy was perched, homeless maybe, on the edge of a child's purple mountain bike. His bike. Possibly his only possession. One flat tyre. The front.

I sighed. 'Mate, this is my pub. You've got to leave.'

He said, 'I've been coming here for fucking years.'

I said, 'You're not even drinking our beer man, you're holding a fucking can.'

Max laughed. Carla was there, still hanging on to the promise of a Skype interview and the pub's free wifi. She finished her shift three hours before the old man arrived, when the call from her prospective new employer was meant to arrive. She had her nose in her laptop and her eyes on the scene. Her eyes, so big and green, were wincing. They looked sorry. 'Just ignore him,' Max said, 'and he'll leave.' Max drank his free rum and coke. Jon, Carla's replacement, came out for a fag break and told me he would be issuing a formal complaint. 'I'm complaining,' he said, with tobacco teeth.

'About what?'

'About the tea,' he said. 'Our tea. You're the supervisor, right? The mediator?'

'You're the union boss, man,' said Max, winking at me, Carla sinking further into her tired 2003 computer. 'So what's happened?' I said.

'Arthur just came in and threw all our tea away. He looked me right in the fucking eye as he grabbed my cup and turned it upside down above the sink. And Timbo's cupcake too. Timbo had a cupcake he was saving for the end of his shift and he'd left it on the shelf by the coffee cups and Arthur picked it up and dropped it in the bin. He may as well have said it's not good for the customers to see that we're human.' Jon shook his head. Alex the Homeless Italian was doing the rounds. He had a big kit bag full of who knows what dangling from his back like the body of a dead conjoined twin. And he was limping. That was new. 'Where are your sandals, Alex?' I shouted. Boaz had bought him a pair of sandals from Sports Direct.

'Spare some change?' said Alex, because that's all he could say in English.

'Haven't got any. Sorry.'

The old man swore at me from across the road.

'I wish these old crackheads would fuck off,' said Max.

Carla the German Philanthropist closed her laptop and shoved it into her bag. She stood up and scowled at Max, who said, 'Where're you going?'

'To Chile,' said Carla.

I felt like cutting myself open. There is a lump underneath the skin of my forearm, just before the elbow. The lump moves freely. If you pinch the lump, you can lift it. Only the skin gets in the way. I was in a hotel room. In the dark. Shifting kegs and casks at the brewery. Pouring drinks and breaking blocks of ice from the ice machine into bits at the pub. Enhancing the size of my veins for wider blood flow. The new structure of my arms brought to the surface a fatty deposit. The lump. Reduced flab. All that appeared to be left of my waste product, not counting my mind. Storage. The lump was no bigger than a pea. A large pea. I kept thinking about Sam's mum. The doctor told me, 'It's fine.' She also told me, 'forget it.' It was a side note in the margin of a much more testicular problem. The problem was longevity. My testicle hurt when I was on my feet, and since I worked in a bar all hope seemed lost. The tests kept being inconclusive and the doctors kept scratching their heads.

So I got on a train out of London. But this time I was not alone. There were eight bartenders around me, including Allyn. The train was going to Retford. The company was sending us away to a hotel spa, a brewery, a bakery, a cheesemakery and wine tastery for two days. They sent a photographer to follow us, record us having a good time, so that they could show the London pub scene how well our low wage souls were keeping, thanks to them. I left Hackney with unease. I got off the bus early and walked down Pentonville Road to King's Cross where I met the others in a hotel bar that tried charging me £11.00 for a whisky. Drunker as the train wore on I became slumped, tired, and drifted vaguely through the day to lie wet, eventually, on my enormous hotel bed in Sherwood Forest. I was juggling memories of my old friend Sam's last visit to Stoke

Newington. I couldn't stop mulling him over as I walked, still wet from the shower, round my hotel room. The enormous bed. The tall window that stretched down to the floor, long curtains open a crack and a courtyard with a pathway through a garden to the pool. Molly and I had been texting between London and Italy. I kissed your vagina and we fucked against a tree. Just a dream. My somewhere love, which she didn't know about, unless she'd found that letter. I'm on a hotel bed. I'm on a train. I'm still with Sam, back in Stokey before he offended Theo so conspicuously drunk and embarrassed me. At first he was drinking iced tea, ticking rolling papers and tobacco as we walked back down Kingsland Road to my pub. 'How's Ace,' said Sam.

'Fine. Tore some ligaments while skateboarding.'

'Who's Theo?'

'He's a friend I met through the pubs and breweries. I've been staying on his sofa too.'

'Where's Max?'

'I don't know.' It was a good question. A prelude to the negatives of the next morning in Dreyfus Café. Where's Max: the endless question.

'I get a company car next year,' said Sam, drunk, fag dangling.

'But you haven't got a job,' I said.

'Yes I have,' he said indignantly. 'But we can talk about that at breakfast tomorrow.'

'Well I know you haven't got a licence.'

'I'm learning to drive,' he said. 'I'm learning. Hey, so where are we going?'

'We're meeting Theo at my pub.'

'Who's Theo?'

'Jesus Sam. He's that friend I met through the pubs and breweries. I've been staying on his sofa too.'

-

'So who's Sam?' said Allyn while we were still on the train. He was fitting free-pourers to our bottle of Johnnie Walker to compensate for the movement of the train. If we couldn't afford a single malt then we certainly couldn't afford to spill any, and he kept licking the drips from the side of the bottle as they tried to make their escape. 'He's an old friend of mine,' I said, 'who still lives with his parents.'

'They have a dog?' said Allyn.

I said, 'No. I keep telling him to get to London but he won't. I think they're giving him a car.'

'His parents?'

'His new company.'

Allyn made a face and sank another whisky. 'Drink?' he asked me. I yes pleased, drank one, drank another, drank three. 'Long train ride, my friend,' said Allyn, and it wasn't long before we'd opened the bottles of blueberry saison we brought along for that reason. 'Good notes,' said Allyn, with a bottle up to his nose. The other bartenders – supervisors and assistant managers from the company's other premises – were filling themselves with Schweppes and Beefeater. Cheaper. Someone said, 'Did we forget the lime?' There was a large, resounding sigh. Someone else went off to the buffet car for ice. 'Keep 'em steady,' said Allyn, refilling our shot glasses as I checked my phone for 3G.

NO SERVICE

The following night the eight of us sat around a table in the hotel restaurant with only our work in common. Every movement was a concerto of service industry criticism. We spent all day making artisan bread. Stone baking pizza. Cheating and reaping the benefits of three-day-old yeast cultures that had made the dough perfect long before we arrived. We ate what we cooked in the garden of a country estate, wondering if anything we were learning was transferable at all, or if we were just being used. I chose the latter. The photographer skipped around us like an anxious poodle. Smile. Toast. Glass stems. The only half decent beer on draught in the hotel bar was Guinness, but it was extra cold. The restaurant was an Ikea show room. There was a stag's head on the wall above a fake fireplace. It was wearing a bowtie. 'That waitress will have to reach across you to give me my dessert,' someone said to someone else, both of them shaking their heads. I chose brandy snaps and salted caramel ice cream. Allyn and I were judging the bottle selection. It was mainly mainstream premium lager, so we shook our heads too. It made my chair creak. No hope for reclaimed furniture. We were surrounded by one of the oldest forests in England, apparently. The waitress leaned. Someone raised their eyes. 'Shouldn't have pushed the table so close to the wall,' said someone else. On the train the previous day, before we'd arrived, Raj, human resources, said, 'If anyone mentions work, they have to drink.' We were all alcoholics as well as professionals, so we were quite drunk by the time the taxis dropped us at the hotel.

I was in the bath, sweaty from the heat of the water, trying not to throw up, trying harder to summon the courage to masturbate.
　　Bubbles.
　　I took a photo of myself and sent it to Molly. She said she'd been to a water park.
　　So hot in the water.
　　Molly Facetimed me. I was sitting at the desk reading tourist pamphlets. 'How's the course going?' I asked.
　　She said, 'It's amazing. We're learning so much. It's tiring, though.'
　　'Are there Italian students there too?'
　　'No, this is the summer school,' she told me. 'It's just us, the practitioner and his dog.' She was sitting on a balcony in the dark, pyjamas, wet hair. 'How was your shower?' I said.
　　'Grimy.'
　　'What breed is the dog?' I said.
　　'I don't know, some sort of terrier, I suppose. His name is Trolley.'
　　'Did you get a look at the shapes of his eyes?'
　　'I'll send you a picture tomorrow.'
　　'Ok.'
　　'Have you been wanking much?'
　　HA---Y-U-BE-N-WANK-NG---CH?

'Go find some better reception.'

'But this is the only place I can steal the neighbour's wifi.'

Data roaming was out of the question.

Everyone else was stoned, apparently. Someone had already been arrested for shoplifting laxatives. Eating disorders were rampant, as were young Italian men on scooters, feeling liberal.

'Did you open the letter I gave you?'

'Yes,' I said. 'Thank you.'

She said, 'I cried when I found mine in my suitcase, you fucker. How could you? How could you tell me you love me, for the first fucking time, while I'm in fucking Italy?'

I said, 'Same to you.'

—

I wanted to fall asleep on Theo's futon. Ace's sofa. The big sofa in Max's studio. The floor of Molly's bedroom in Mile End. Wooden. Slippery. Her bed frame was wooden, used. It still squeaked despite the inner tubes and brake pads we'd shoved in its cracks, so we had to be cautious, though caution only got us so far in those situations, before it went completely ignored.

Where was Max? No longer a question, but a statement. For a while I thought Max was everywhere: the memory of London, chewing Dalston mints and skint, rolling pinched fags and listening as songs were written around him. Max. In the hotel room I was having a crisis. But before it could morphose, someone knocked on my door. Allyn knocked on my door and I answered while partially naked. Towel. He had a notepad. He was excited. He said, 'I've been sketching designs for my bottle labels. Remember my sideways bottles? Bottle condition, do not turn over?' He started laughing maniacal plans to himself rather than me, while I stood dripping in the doorway. He was stuck in automaton mode, as though pouring five pints in his mind at once and twisting glasses and bottle openers through fingers like drummers spin drum sticks, or might. There was cash that did not exist. It was floating in his eyes. Great big dollar signs, for some reason. Dollars. I don't know. He was focusing on an imaginary customer behind me, just wait mate, this guy was first. I turned around. There was no one there. Just the window. Curtains slightly open because I enjoyed the thought of a stranger in the courtyard seeing me naked. Table. TV remote control and a tray of instant coffee and UHT sachets. Sockets for shaving. Allyn tapped me on the shoulder and shoved his notebook in my face. 'These are my designs for a real brewery,' he said.

'Allyn you're wasted,' I said. 'Go to bed.'

'But they're good, yes? Good? No, I can't sleep. I'm too excited. Germany won the World Cup. Carla will be pleased.'

'So?'

'Didn't you know? I love her.'

'What about the girl from Camden?'

'Her? She only wanted me for my beer. Besides, she's from Camden.' He sighed. 'It doesn't matter anyway, now that Carla's gone,' he said, and started sobbing. 'Can I come in?'

I shook my head.

I'd been spending more time at Theo's, using his coffee table as a desk upon which to gather my till receipt thoughts. I dropped a shoe on the floor and the table quivered, nearing orgasm at the thought of its own collapse. I'd been reading in the light of the window, reading into and out of the other side of midnight, on nights I was not working. And on nights I had been, I was reading until the sun came up. Theo and Nemesia would sit together one foot above me on the little blue two-seater sofa. The little blue two-seater sofa had a stab wound. The two of them would sit quietly, telling stories to each other with their eyes while I worked my way through their library and tried not to get in the way. They were stories of pyjama intimacy and vegetarianism. An old record player from the seventies sat on the rickety coffee table. A cardboard box of records sat next to the dog-eared contents of a bookshelf. There was even a typewriter and an old Dell laptop with an eleven inch screen and an exceptionally loud hard drive that sat between Theo and

Nemesia, whirring louder than a steam roller on a motorway. But it was only playing the highlights of Wimbledon. I was just sitting still, silent, with Molly's letter on my knee and a moat of conspiracy around me. Mutilation of truth. Thievery of people's mental possessions. Nemesia was looking at some photos her mother had sent her. 'Look guys, my mum's just got a new toller.' I looked, but I was suspicious. Toller. Canadian. An unpopular breed, though intelligent, energetic and useful. Hard to find a pedigree – most are the offspring of incestuous congress between cousins, or something.

'Apparently he's cross-eyed,' said Nemesia.

I was dreaming of her bedroom. Gasping with burger joints and greasy hands and sweat. Cold journeys between Hackney and awful places like Covent Garden and Oxford Street. London. Enjoy the joke. The lights reflected on the brown water of the river like innumerable muzzle flashes firing up into the atmosphere. But HMS Belfast was still. And when we got home we'd push Molly's duvet and bedclothes onto the floor to make a nest. Make a nest to wrap ourselves in and keep dreaming ways we could be caught having sex in communal spaces.

By now Max had dropped below the accurate detection level of my radar. X-ray Max would occasionally resurface in text message submarines with reams of, 'Shit, my phone is fucked again,' and threads that kept unravelling. 'Want to go for a swim this morning? Shit, I can't, but I'll come by the pub at some point.' There were rumours of new deadlines. Something was being set in yellow stone with further record labels. Knuckling down. 'Ah man, I'm even off the weed for a while.'

Delivered.

I shook up my life by knifing my way through Theo's front door, folding my arms and legs over the futon torso with a view of a London that was swinging in lonely forlorn early morning memory of pushing through crowds with Molly. Hackney was beginning to redevelop me. Burn me down. Nemesia got up early to open the café in Bethnal Green, get her name down quick for a take-home vegetarian burrito, free, so I missed her when she was leaving, while Theo would still be snoring, unconsciously preparing himself for another day's delivery of craft beer pump foolery down in Shoreditch, or up in Tottenham at the brewery. When he got home, I would have already left.

London kept me struggling to coincide with anyone back then. And I was left doomed in the knowledge that all of my immediate acquaintances were actually customers. Dee, my former supervisor, came in one night for her birthday. She'd been at the Auld Shillelagh with her family and what Max called the best pint of Guinness in London. Her boyfriend was coercing me into not serving her any more beer. I'd been filling her pint glass for free all night, with instruction: 'Now lad,' she'd said, 'I've been drinking since roughly noon. Work was a breeze but I'm starting to feel it in me now. Can you tell? And how's the job going, by the way? Do the other staff members hate you yet? Listen: keep me topped up will you? If my eyes look like they're quitting, prop them up with a shot of Patron.' Then a wink. A hug round the side of the bar. Boaz was already offering her tab the house bon. Freebies for two years of good service and dedication. Only the finest rituals for the human relics of a more joyful employee past. Ace had been printing t-shirts with some of Nanna's dreams on them. Not ambitions she hoped to achieve, like being able to walk without a leg brace or limp, but actual pictures of things that she dreamed. She drew them. A nude woman without pupils, breasts with no nipples but at least they had croissants on them. Customers had been mistaking the pastries for plasters. Taking the shirt as some kind of statement against cosmetic surgery. And mammary mutilations. Another woman had serpents for pubic hair. A sort of sexualised, inverted Medusa. She turned rock hard dicks away from stone, so they became more like new-born chicks who'd flown the nest and flopped down onto the ground below. I felt conspicuous. I needed more people to take notice. Not women, not for that purpose. Just acknowledgement that I was not alone. I looked up Carla the German Philanthropist on Facebook a few days later. There was something about group sex in the Andes, or farm labouring in some part of Chile. One like I left received a response: 'Are you still pacing like a caged animal?' she'd said.

Molly was watching the menu. The menu was dancing on a barrel that had been turned into an Italian table. We were outside an Italian bistro on the edge of an Italian square.

'Shall we get some wine?'

The answer was yes, of course. It'd be a refreshing break from the hop varieties of Hackney breweries and human sediments lounging at the bottom of dull brown bottles surrounded by thin tubes of plastic that once housed long colonies of filter tips, scrunched up receipts from contactless payments discarded at the whim of a wrist, and occasional splashes of dog piss.

The square was lined with the pale terracotta of a Mediterranean sun gone down, lights shone up and a two hour flight to Molly, who asked, when she met me at the train station, 'How was it?'

'The flight? It was fantastic. Almost missed the train to Stansted though.' This happened while walking back to her Italian flat. When I got off the train from Parma to this wherever Italian town I was so excited to see her that I kicked her in the foot and made her big toe bleed under the nail. I felt her hands tighten their grip on my back. She raised her arms up to my neck and pressed her lips against mine even harder. This was the result of the pain, though I think she'd been missing me, too.

There were trees all over the square. The trees were low and they were rigged with outdoor lighting. Every nighttime was a festival occasion. The lights were illuminating a natural canopy that hung over an empty stage set up for a band that wasn't there. 'Do you like the hotel room? I'm sorry we can't stay at my flat. My roommate's boyfriend is here for the weekend as well, but they won't be there on

Sunday night. We can push the single beds together. I think that's what they've done.'

A young Italian woman with thick glasses caught me grappling with the bus timetable outside the airport terminal, she going my way, which was to the train station, Parma Central, same train as well, apparently, though she went one stop further than me, to Bologna, where her mother and father and boyfriend were waiting to see her, debrief her and console her after an internship with some media company in Shoreditch. She told me she'd been living in Stratford while we waited. I said I was sorry and kept an ear out clearly for the name of my stop. This amused her. The carriages were empty. The train ran smoothly through a dried up Italian country.

Crisp.

Molly ordered a plate of salami with bread and olives. She said she'd been living off ice cream mostly. 'What's the beer like here?' I asked her.

'It's Peroni, mostly.' She shrugged, smiling at me. When we reached the hotel earlier, they'd upgraded us to a deluxe suite with a view of the town square. The reality of my London sofa thread quickly vanished, though the sofa was the first place we had sex. The window out onto the square was wide open and the curtains tickled us in the breeze.

Across the square young English actors paraded on faded pink bicycles they'd hired.

'You know Max and Stefan are flying to Pisa tomorrow?' I told her. 'They're staying in Florence for a week to write more songs for the album.'

She said, 'You didn't fly half-way round the world to hang out with your mates.'

I said, 'I didn't fly half-way round anything. It takes longer to get from one end of London to the other at half-past five.'

There was a pause.

I coughed. I asked her, 'How's your foot?'

She laughed.

I like you when your eyes go green. Your glasses look green in the sun. Your wide-mouth laughter which is silence. Your smack. Your slapping. When you come. My. Face. My laughing in the after. Ether. Your screaming. I like your dreaming which is wake-up rain first thing with you each morning. You're incoming. What was that? Your yoghurt yearning and yoga parking. Your canal running and crossbar cycling. So I'm giving you an endless tighten. I like your pirate voices, your choices to surprise me without surprises. And teasing. I like your canine keen and new love meltdown. I like your sofa cushions. I've lowered my life expectations – no future swimming pool, just a great big corner sofa will do. And sleep with you. With you. I like your. Tears. Your love and constant fears. And, most of all, your glasses when they're green in the sun.

No one exists in Florence during the daytime except tourists who slowly turn pink. Molly and I turned pink in the Boboli Gardens, eating watermelon by the big fountain in the centre of the big pond at the bottom of the long gravel path. We sat on the lawn at the top of the hill where we'd been deposited as if by a stream. We ate chocolate croissants and chocolate bars and drank orange juice and turned pink up there as well. Molly was wearing an orange dancing skirt and it was the colour of the rooftops. We turned pink on pink hire bikes. And ate pink gelato. And fell asleep on the sheets of some hostel campsite near Piazzale Michelangelo. An orchestra was performing in one of the squares and we sat on the ground and leant against a row of potted plants and she put her head in my lap or perhaps on my shoulder and we drank from a bottle of wine.

'So what else have you been doing?' said Max, who we'd met at a restaurant in Saint Spirito. 'You must be pretty relieved to finally see each other. What has it been, two weeks?'

Stefan laughed.

There was a pause. 'Feels great,' I said, looking at Molly, her bowl of gnocchi and glass of wine. She took my photo. She said, 'We've just been hanging around as though we were normal. We went to the Uffizi yesterday. We went round it twice, actually, trying to find The Birth of Venus. I don't know how we almost missed it. It's massive.'

She sighed.

She said, 'It's my favourite.'

I said, 'My favourite thing was the giant toe.'

'The giant toe?'

'There was a giant toe in one of the rooms,' I said. 'There was a sign next to it and the sign said, "Left big toe of a colossal statue." That was all.'

Molly's foot touched mine beneath the table. Her toe had stopped bleeding. I had mosquito bites all over the left side of my face from the previous night. We'd pushed the two camp beds together and made a queen camp bed and we lay on our queen camp bed with the door open – the tent was a canvas shed – and listened to crickets and humans rustling in Italian bushes. The next day we sat beneath a restaurant awning in Piazza Saint Spirito, the trees forming a city forest that time had lined with bars.

I drank my wine. Stefan rolled a cigarette. 'We've got a week to finish the album,' he said.

'What are the other guys doing?' Molly asked.

'They're working on drums in Dalston and lead guitars in Stoke Newington.'

Molly said, 'Max, where are your Italian friends?'

Max said, 'I don't know. They're both artists. They just sit around smoking cigarettes and drinking espresso.'

'Like you?' I said.

'I only drink negronis,' with a wink at Molly, the remains of her gnocchi, my beef, Stefan's risotto, which we pooled together in a terrible mess that the waiter topped with a snarl. Max sat back with a sigh in the Italian light and the promise of Italian night. He was escaping a woman, someone he'd been chasing for ages. He said, 'We've been endlessly texting, always flirting but ultimately failing to meet fleeting plans we kept drunkenly making. And texting quickly becomes a drag, doesn't it. No one exists as an entity except me,' still winking. 'Ah, I could chase her all my life round the hanging baskets of Hackney.'

We met Max's friends Dina and Francesco on the Ponte Santa Trinita, balancing on the edge, watching the shop rears of Ponte Vecchio, the Jewellers' Bridge, the window shutters of precariously perched first floor extensions closing in a sunset as gold as their contents. We were drinking wine out of the bottle and all the city came out to join us. 'Shame the Thames isn't like this,' said Max. 'We could drink tinnies out in the rain.'
    'Theo told me about a river in Hackney,' I said. 'Well, it's more like a brook, actually. Possibly a stream. He said it starts somewhere near Clissold Park, goes through Hackney Central, right by the entrance to Oslo then joins the Lea Navigation at Hackney Wick. Theo says it's all underground now, subterranean, like a forgotten vein.' The Arno River was flowing lazily. Shallow. Languid. Unthreatening as the wine and evening made us feel. Superb. Our train back north was later that night, the next day my plane back to London. 'We get a lot of Italians applying for jobs at my pub,' I told Dina and Francesco, bottle opener on keyring and Peroni, smoking copious cigarettes and staring at the water, the reeds sleeping in dreamy beds – but which way downstream was we couldn't tell. The water was moving so slowly it may even have been still completely. There was an artificial beach further down. It had a wooden shack and a bar inside the wooden shack and deck chairs and a net for volleyball. They were screening the World Cup before we got there. Now the screen was black and the sand was the surface of the moon. Undisturbed footprints and only occasional lounging tourists when Molly and I had walked back up to the campsite on Saturday night.
    Molly said, 'Look at all these tourists. It's disgusting.'
    'Just like London,' said Dina, open shirted, loose skirted. She'd been studying there the previous year. 'You know we got charged tourist tax at the campsite?' said Molly. 'Me. Tourist tax. Fucking hell.'
    'What did you say?' asked Max.

'I said I've been living in Italy for the last month.'

'It's only been two weeks.'

'Problem is,' I said, 'they don't really seem that keen about working for us. They hand in their CVs without enthusiasm (that's putting it lightly) and with only the experience of serving coffee. They're all studying something, I suppose, and want the extra money. But my boss prefers people who he knows aren't going to leave.'

'Who wants to work anyway?' said Francesco, stretching, only smoking and drinking espresso.

'And what did he say back?' said Max, illuminated.

'He said, "I don't care". He was bald and wore a white polo shirt. Italians can be so rude.'

'Yeah,' said Dina, finally, 'we can.'

R efer to addendum sheet for wiring instructions as product may fail to function if wired incorrectly.

El Hell came into the pub. I'd been cleaning tulips, occasionally dropping them on the floor and pretending it was an accident. When customers arrived and approached the bar I'd say to the other staff, 'Let's cover our eyes with our hands. If we can't see them they won't be here.'

It'd been a slow shift. A standard midnight close where every new customer added another five minutes to the last hour of service. Humid and sweating. Extractor for the kitchen not working again so the air was thick and greasy. A falafel burger sat expectantly beneath the heat lamps, waiting for its rightful owner who turned out to be some long-haired gaunt kid in double denim. The kid said, 'Hi.' He was timid and thin. 'I called up earlier and ordered a falafel burger?' The way he said it suggested he wasn't sure if it was true, that he needed us to prove it for him. I grabbed the burger from the kitchen and placed it in front of him but he said he'd asked for chips instead of fries. I said, 'I'm sorry man, the kitchen's closed.'

He said, 'Oh.'

I said, 'Um.'

He said, 'That's why I called. I couldn't get here in time to order in person.'

'Okay. Well is it a big problem?'

'Yeah, it kind of is. Is that the manager?' pointing at Boaz. It was Boaz who took the order. I grabbed Boaz from the kitchen. 'Boaz, he said he asked for chips.' It was bad timing. Boaz had been in the middle of some stress of waving arms and scraping feet on ends of legs with Latest Chef – GP, wastage, rota changes, I don't fucking care. He didn't want to hear it. The extractor fan not working. Ghulam over-ordering. The blocked gas pipes in the grill still flaring in spite of the botched job Arthur's man did overnight. Boaz said, 'Are you kidding? No he didn't. Kitchen's closed now, anyway. Tell him to eat it or leave it.'

I said, 'Did he pay?'

Boaz said, 'No.'

I went back to the bar. The kid looked at me expectantly. I said, 'Look man, I'm sorry. I can't change it.'

He said, 'Ok, well then I think I'll just leave it.'

'Leave it?' said Boaz, who'd followed me. 'What am I supposed to do with it?' Bobby caught my eye and smiled hungrily. The kid looked suddenly thinner, tried saying something like I'm sorry, but Boaz was shaking his head. He grabbed the plate, our hungry eyes following in dismay as he stormed back to the kitchen and smashed the hopes of our entire evening into a recycling bin, leaving the edges of the plate in shards all over the floor for all the customers to see. I turned back to the kid: 'Really sorry about that.'

He looked bewildered.

'It's been a pretty slow night. Stay for a drink?'

'Sorry, no.'

'Don't worry, it's on me. Well, it's on somebody anyway.'

He said, 'Thanks, but I'm okay,' then left.

A pause.

'Only an hour and a half left to go,' said Bobby.

El Hell, who came into our weird atmosphere twenty minutes earlier, drunk after an unsuccessful Tinder date, had seen the whole thing. 'What the hell was that?' he said, and I shook my head and went round to collect empty glasses, record wastage in preparation for tomorrow's beer battered fish. At ten past eleven seven new faces came poking their noses through our curtain. They were awake. They were gleaming. Why couldn't they have just come in after a curry on Church Street? At least then they'd be too bloated to outstay their welcome. Or, better yet, why couldn't they all just stay home? Use Just Eat, then fall asleep like the dogs of London wanted. The city was conspiring to make it harder for me to enjoy all the half-hour relationships I'd been crawling with since I began working at the pub. Some bartender from The Coach came in for CO2. El Hell was tapping the bar with his feet, description of housemate's loud sex pending, dogs down on the floor with paws covering eyes because they'd already heard it all in his van on the way over. 'Water bowl?' I asked

'No, this one needs to settle,' he said, stroking Hedwig's head. 'I don't think we'll stay long.' He treated them like children. 'But they're far more important than children,' he said. 'Understand?'

I did.

The dog winked.

El Hell said, 'It's too loud.'

I said, 'What's too loud?'

'The sex. I can hear everything.'

El Hell was becoming a dog. He kept looking at a cut on the top of his thumb and I was sure he was going to lick it.

'I just had a lift put into the van so I can pick up all the cages. Dogs are better in cages whilst driving. Otherwise they can't stand properly and that makes them worry, get shirty and argue on the backseat. Not good having a backseat with eight dogs arguing all the way to Hackney Marshes.'

He coughed. 'Can I have some water?'

I gave him a bowl.

'I'm the boss and they're the rabble,' he said, as I marvelled at how little he knew. 'I'm thinking of getting a pushchair for the little one,' he continued, 'the French bulldog. He gets tired legs. The others leave him behind.' He yawned. 'And I get tired too. So fucking tired.' He drank his beer. 'Have you got any Blu-Tack? What about Sellotape? I need to get some of these dog hairs off my hoody. Got a midnight date with bed and I've only just cleaned my room.'

El Hell hadn't slept all week. Ace was worrying. But he couldn't process affection properly so his caring resembled annoyance. Too many dogs all at once. It was too much for a single person to take. This is what relationships are for. And the dogs wouldn't even make use of themselves. Ace tried getting them to catch the mice that live in the skirting by the router but they wouldn't bother. They'd just shit behind the TV or piss in the corridor.

'Look at this,' said El Hell, showing me a photo of Ace's bed. There was a little, barely distinguishable puddle near where Ace would rest his head. The house that Ace, Nanna and El Hell built was crumbling. And I was getting more and more certain that Theo's sofa in Lower Clapton wouldn't endure. 'It's weird,' I said, 'that they can still get in despite the bedroom doors being closed.'

'Their agility training had been going very well,' said El Hell. 'I think they've learned to use handles. How was Italy?'

'Took the wrong bus to the airport and nearly missed my flight home.'

The night before, a fox had climbed onto the garden wall then onto the small roof outside El Hell's bedroom window. 'It must have smelled the animal parts I had in my combat jacket,' El Hell said, and began exploring the greyhound tattoo on his neck. 'It started licking my cheek and at first I thought it was Noodles, but she was staying with the Bassett Hounds in Finsbury Park. So I sat up and saw an orange tail shoot out the window. It was still dark so I shone the torch on my phone and it stuck its head back through, as if to check something. I don't know what it was checking.'

'Probably been fed before,' I said, putting the bar mats in the glass washer. 'Ace said he's going to sit at the top of the stairs all week with the Nerf gun and wait for the fox to come back.'

'Bobby, could you grab all the candles off the tables? I want to get out of here before Boaz has another meltdown.'

'I think he's losing it,' said El Hell, 'cooped up inside and stuck at his desk all day. Making TV adverts can't be easy on your brain.'

The kid who wanted chips instead of fries walked past the window with a pizza.

'You know,' said El Hell.

'Hold on. Bobby, do you want to write a stock list? I've got itchy feet.' I'd just wrapped some clingfilm round the tap nozzles to stop flies getting in. One tap was leaking. The clingfilm had swollen into a gassy bubble which resembled a dying testicle.

'When we first moved to London,' El Hell continued, 'Ace and I rented a flat in Whitechapel, in some disused Banglatown brothel. I slept in Ace's bed for the first week because I was scared. All curled up at the foot like a dog. We had weird men knocking on our door at midnight, old clients looking for women who were no longer available. Ace had a piece of wood with a nail through the end of it that he kept behind the door. I'm moving to Enfield anyway. Our tenancy agreement is ending soon.'

I said, 'Don't remind me.'

'Zone Four scares me more than the brothel, but,' he sighed, 'I've got to do what's best for the dogs.'

They were asleep at the foot of his stool. The smell of weed crept through the side door to the pub. I climbed on the church pew in the corner to switch off the heat lamps outside. One of the regulars ordered a couple more beers and we flashed our lights to call time as I bent down in attempt to crack my back.

'Sleeping on those cushions must be killing you,' said El Hell.

'It's fine. The frame's too loud when you unfold it and I don't want to wake you.'

He said, 'I've got a fox for that.'

Ace walked past the pub earlier that day. We exchanged middle fingers through the window and the weather which was sun. He was carrying a new, larger Nerf gun. And I wondered if it was the same fox I'd seen on Rectory Road the last few nights, dragging food and body weight and walking into me on the way to Theo's after work without so much as a sorry, just a grunt. The fox was staring, sharing its whatever garbage tin with some fox compadre.

'Are you drunk?' El Hell asked me.

'Can't drink at work,' I said, holding my mug, 'just instant coffee in here.' I winked at the dogs. 'It's the same fox. I'm sure of it. And the fox on Downs Park Road. And the fox that sleeps in Molly's garden.'

'What are you talking about?'

I leant in close and, to the dogs, who I'm sure were only pretending to sleep, whispered, 'The Shapes of Dogs' Eyes. That's all this is.' I looked around. I could see through walls. The local bars were humming in closing rituals. The bar staff of the borough were bending down to roll their vertebrae. Twelve hours of service gravity. Compression. 'They are the fox as well,' I said, expecting El Hell to at least raise an eyebrow, but nothing happened. A phone went off. Ace's voice in the air said the fox was still at large. The dogs of Hackney were having a party. El Hell shook his head then left me for bed. For dead. And I knew I couldn't hope to save him now. He was too far corrupted, a puppet controlled by dog leads as dogs lead him away from sanity and through an open window. Dreams of tongues. Of Whitechapel. Coffee cup booze until one. Drink up Bobby, Jon. Lisa's bar. Boaz chatting up two Danish women he didn't ask to leave, didn't flash his lights for. Drink up, on, out, fuck off. Still rolling my spine as El Hell grumbled out the door, something about being kept awake by a housemate's midnight liaison. It was a long shift, that first one after Italy, but soon the pub had sunk into a quiet only the squeak of the kitchen fridge and the click click CLICK of a cockroach roaming the work surface could pierce. Cigarettes lit and all the clean ashtrays soiled again. That building, its spark of life, kept my whole world moving. Ace's flour mite infestation, bleached cupboards in the house which stank, no food except in the fridge. Molly. Italy. Boaz squashing cockroach children quickly with his heel so this Danish lady didn't see the inhabitant descendents of centuries of public houses, true London locals, foxes, mice, chewing wires and ordering too-late falafel burgers, big-nosed rats shorting fuses, pumps, houses, as if all those creatures were conspiring in some futile kamikaze attempt to protect their long-established wall cavity communities from the blight of human development – something worth sacrificing, bug and rodent families, joined in a strange floorboard coalition, to preserve. The foxes were dancing between, but what shapes their eyes took I couldn't say. There were ropes tied around the bases of the pillars that held up the roof. They were all that stopped the sag of rain from caving in on everyone. A pub. A wild yeast strain growing in a stained woodwork cave of night, bloating humans like over-dead mice. But the people were more scared. Stomach hunger for lover's Italia, or wherever, her bed, pubic hair, scent. I'd been calling everyone mate, everything great, but something was rotting unseen. Boaz gave me a shot of Patron then told me, 'Go home to bed,' as he pulled on his a.m. jacket and offered the Danes a lift somewhere. Back to sofa and the cool calm light of early tomorrow. Confused birds singing too soon in plane trees, stuck on cycles of Molly, cycling down the Regent's Canal where it dives into an Islington tunnel, dark and incoherent. 'It's not even tomorrow,' I was shouting along Belfast Road. The cool gas light of the morning, more hopeful than the sad lovelorn sentiment of a lonely bartender's twelve hour ending.

Back in the flat I was afraid to turn on the light. The sofa was all folded up. The head I relied on to keep keeping on was whirling, drunk. Conjuring conjugal far away visits as I did my teeth and spat you out and washed my face and feet and looked at me and said, 'Who the fuck are you? You're not the same,' into the mirror. Here. Required food. Electricity. Not even paying rent. Ace was lying at the top of the stairs with an elastic band tied round his wrist and a GoPro strapped to his head. He was waiting for the fox. He'd have more luck catching the cockroach eggs as they fell off my shoes onto the carpet. Two pets were enough. The dogs were sleeping. They had agreed to keep keeping us contained. But the mice kept on crawling from under the sofa and into my peripheries. 'Morning Ace,' I said, half dead, 'I thought you'd be asleep.'

'Couldn't,' said Ace, 'there's dog piss all over my sheets.'

In an attempt to take my mind off Molly, Theo and Nemesia took me to a play in Chelsea. We took the overground to Highbury & Islington then the Victoria Line to Victoria Station then the District Line one stop to Sloane Square. Access to relics of London bohemia. Don't lose faith. The theatre was a galaxy. A submarine of steampunk rivets that seemed impossible to raise to a surface. And I was underneath it at the bar before the first act started. A bar in a cellar with a jet black counter. Good for housekeeping, easy to wipe clean, does not just absorb the remains of a half-sunk pint of Meantime lager sneeringly ousted by some pink-trousered man from the plastic cup the bartender gave him. We were on a strange tangential current. Dark pushchair tributaries of day-tripping families were flowing into us. Silver taps. Points of sale. Espresso. It is customary to loathe anybody who asks for a coffee, but this is just what I did. I wanted to watch the black shirts squirm in this strange cataclysm of drama students trying to earn some food, deluded into thinking that serving drinks in a theatre may actually help their acting career. Took fifteen minutes to get served. Theo and I split up. That's the standard co-op tactic. Gently shunt other customers towards the end with the dirty glasses where no bartender will pay them attention. And never wave, whistle, click or tap. Eye contact, yes, but only once. The person serving will decide which human is next. Fifteen minutes. I hate being human.

Nemesia found a table while we were waiting. Theo and I sat down, yawning, and drank our coffee on the fringes of the restaurant area. Bowls of spaghetti. Sourdough. Avocado and chilli. Our spindly cigarettes lay between an archipelago of spillages from previous sitters. We weren't used to the exquisite quiet of that kind of bar. Theo said the staff were good actors.

I said, 'Yeah, they really look like they enjoy working here.'

Nemesia was less than convinced.

'Not a bad selection of whisky, either,' I said. 'Mostly bourbon, I'll admit, but there are at least three alright Scotches.'

Nemesia said, 'I think I'll quit the café and try getting work as a nanny.' She'd been spying on Chelsea prams all evening, weighing the eyeballs of mothers with the depth of their strain, the goggle-eyed brows of their toddlers who were confused because instead of juice they'd been given babyccino, and when they turned to complain their fathers were nowhere around.

Woody showed me the shapes of his eyes. They are spaniel eyes. Molly had fallen in love with him. He'd been resting his head on her knee. He knew how to press her. So do I. She'd been resting her head on my chest. And I was wearing a soft jumper. On a yellow sofa – a three-seater – in a cottage in the countryside darkness: a strange position. We were at my father's house. And I kept stealing Ace's Citroen to drive with Molly. She said she liked it. Being driven. She falls asleep with the vehicle's motion. My father said, 'It's so good to see you.' That was for me. 'And so good to finally meet you,' which was for Molly. 'How long has it been? Almost a year? Hey, want to take all your old stuff back with you?'

'I don't have a house, dad.'

'It's just so good to see you. Whose car is that anyway?'

'Ace's.'

I borrowed it to pick up Molly from Gatwick. She kicked my toe emotionally and we hugged for what felt like lives.

Pause. Yellow sofa. Three-seater. Red chair in the corner near the remains of an old Parkray heater he'd recently torn from the living room wall. My father, always tearing down his houses, renewing, rebuilding, reauthenticating to original pastoral specification and then moving. 'There are beams up there, I'm telling you. Old oak beams underneath that plasterboard ceiling. I'm going to uncover them. I'm going to discover their secrets. Hey.'

THE SHAPES OF DOGS' EYES

'Yeah?'

'Want to see something cool?'

My father went into the under stairs cupboard by the back door. That's where he kept his tools and guns and cartridges and cans of long-life food. 'Here,' handing me a strange piece of gear. 'It's a probe,' he said, and, back in the living room, shoved it into the old chimney. 'Look at the screen,' he said, which we did, squinting through the dusty darkness of the cavity, though somewhat reluctant to remove ourselves from the sofa, tired from the drive and what remained of Molly's Italian hangover. 'You can see all the histories of this chimney. All the homes this house used to be. The smoke of people. It's listed, you know.'

'It looks like the bowels of an abandoned ship,' said Molly.

'Or a robot's impacted colon,' I said, 'if robots could shit.'

'Cool, don't you think? I'm waiting for the flue to arrive. Had to hire a crane. Think you'll be around to help out? There's a new wood burning stove to install. It's in that box your coffee is sitting on.'

'We're only staying one night.'

'How's your own house hunt going?' he said.

'House hunt?'

'It's six hundred a month for this cottage and garden,' he said.

'Get a double room in London for that.'

He kept shaking his head. 'Why do it to yourself?'

I said, 'I don't.'

'It's the only place to be,' said Molly, but I'm not sure if she was talking about Woody's eyes, or Hackney.

We arrived out of the blue. The blue was the haze that had risen off the M11, the A14, the A11 and the north, the east, the promise of some Norfolk sea. The flat country. The blue was the sky. It was hot. My father and stepmother were hosting a paella party in their enormous back garden. It's so big my father bought a ride-on mower. We left Ace's car parked on the driveway next to my old Skoda. I patted the driver's side door and shook my head at the rust in the wheel arches before they shunted us into a world of flint and brick friendships. Shook hands. I'm an actress. I'm a bartender. False condolences. Don't worry, a more substantial career awaits. Correcting the airline pilot on his knowledge of Belgian beer. There were some bottles of beer going around, but I drank the wine instead. 'Will you fill everyone's glasses?' my father said, and handed me a bottle. My stepmother said, 'Don't make him, he gets enough of that in London,' laughing. Somewhere, a wiry brown puppy was in her first season. She was spinning around and flying up and down the pathways my father had mown through the long wild grass of the garden, bothering Woody who is still brandishing his testicles, or plums, as my father calls them.

'Just a warning, Molly, but Woody is a bit jumpy.'
'Oh?'
Molly, trying to sleep in the passenger seat beside me.
'Well, he's just a bit happy.'
She said, 'I don't like jumpy dogs.'
'He's very friendly. Wouldn't hurt you.'
'Is he big?'
'He's a spaniel.'
'What kind of spaniel?'
'A springer spaniel.'
'Hmm.'
'Just wait until he shows you his eyes.'

Woody ran in the North Sea shallows. Tennis ball in the current, Woody too frightened to recapture it so my father ended up going in. Quite uncharacteristic, since his heart operation. The tide was in and loving it, so we jumped off the concrete sea wall and fell into the ocean. The tide was slapping like skin on skin, unsure why the concrete wouldn't slap back. 'Should be five feet deep,' said dad, and it was. Molly, holding conversations with her teeth, swam over. She said, 'The concrete reminds me of home.' It was still hot from the afternoon sun. My father was still glad to see us, would tell us some more later, when we got back to the three-seater sofa.

After the beach we sat in the dust sheet living room where Woody showed me the shapes of his eyes and dragged his feet across the floor. 'You know, I'm so happy to see you. And Molly, It's so good to finally meet you. You'll both have to come up for longer next time.'

Molly smiled. 'The stars are so good here,' she said.

'Maybe we could help with the work,' I said. 'Molly's good at pointing bricks.'

She said, 'I did it once when my parents replaced their chimney.'

The house had been there for hundreds of years. It was brutalised by the nineteen fifties. Like London, blitzed and rebuilt badly. My father enjoyed uncovering the past. He wanted to fix it but didn't really know how.

'Where do you live, Molly?' asked my stepmother, just out of the bath and wrapped up in towels.

'Mile End, but I want to move to Clapton,' said Molly, hand on my leg, Woody pawing for nonexistent scraps of langoustine shells. 'I was going to move to Dalston, but it's become so expensive.'

Woody kept his chin on my hand on her knee. A fleshy, sea salt tower.

'Why don't you find somewhere together?' said my father. 'Get him off his brother's sofa.'

Molly smiled. I coughed. Woody blinked and I had a feeling he knew something I didn't. My father said, 'You must take some food home with you. Do you at least have a fridge?'

'I have become acquainted with several,' I said. 'Half an onion on Shacklewell Lane, though I don't think I'll see that again. But there's some milk in Lower Clapton and a bag of frozen peas in Stoke Newington.'

'Wonderful.'

Molly told them about Italy. The heat, the training, the gelato. On the second-to-last day the company put on a show in someone's villa. Before the show Molly sat under a tree in an orchard, listening to David Gray and eating plums. She sent me a photo. Woody lay on the floor. My father, with drooping red wine eyelids, looked down at the dog and said, 'Look at that guy,' pointing an accusatory finger, a joke, the dog lying there on his back, ears splayed out like great creeping glaciers that had been hearing things for centuries but never said anything back, greasy fur of sea salt, salt water, still damp and further dampening the air around him, creating a musky canine atmosphere populated with revolving dreams of an East Anglian sunset all orange and pink and a concrete barrier being swallowed by the leech of a sandy pier creeping into the sea. His ears. Listening. His fur. Which was bad to smell. Gums which poked through his drooping dog lips, stranger shades of brown and pink and teeth all upside down. He was found by the RSPCA in a shed. I tried stroking him with my foot but feet scare him. He doesn't like the feet of humans because his last owners used to kick him. He reached down around his armchair and stroked one of Woody's ears. Woody smiled at Molly and it was a tear-inducing smile. It was a smile of the eyes. Big dark pupils with invisible whites. She kept it together. And I loved her. And Woody lay back down, his tongue squeezing through the gaps between his teeth as he lay there, sniffing, sneezing, wheezing wisps of hair on his fleshy belly, not caring about The Shapes of Dogs' Eyes but just happy.

Theo phoned. 'Come back to mine if you want to,' he said. He was angry that Molly and I had sex on his sofa. 'Nemesia and I are going to my parents' for my brother's birthday . You can use our bed.'
   'Thanks Theo,' I said.
   'Just don't have sex in it.'
   'We never did.'
   'Liar,' said Molly, too far from the phone for him to hear.

I n The Shapes of Dogs' Eyes London was a midnight bus ride. A trip through an immersive performance. Clapton Pond needs a clean. A dredging. Dredge it like a soul. Preen it like pubic hair. Maybe it was from hanging out with Theo, but I was starting to see poetry there. In every bus driver's tired glare. In every thanks that went ignored and every romance peaking with each blown up high. Panic smells of urine. Plastic prams squeaking let me off, let me alone. Bus 488. Bus 276. Through Hackney, east. The Wick. Homerton Hospital. Each rise of the driver's hydraulics was a nuptial therapy. A melding of flesh and commodity, a glimpse into foul stinking existence between privileged observers and his or her love affair with a stranger's telephone tears or the dialogues of cruel, jealous school children in garish blazers. Aches of muscular proportion in all the ankles. Bromley-by-Bow. In The Shapes of Dogs' Eyes London was a bus ride liaison with hospital and bed in a dream of asbestos in warehouse shares and syringes that didn't exist but which could still suck language from the air. The walls were peppered with buckshot and phantom pregnancies and STDs and synthetic shops for breeding duckweed on Clapton Pond and diabetes. I rode with Molly. I rode with Theo. I rode with Max and noticed something. Not a threat from dogs controlling humans but a suggestion that everything could be ok. A door opened. Someone said my name. It was a urologist.

'Now, this may be a little cold, but just try to relax.'
    'Shouldn't we close the curtain?'
    'Oh no, it's fine. No one will walk in.'
    'Who's that guy?'
    'He's the chaperone.'
    'Oh, I don't think I need one of those.'
    'It's hospital policy.'
    'So how do they look? Can you see anything?'
    'Could you just hold your penis against your stomach for me?'
    -
    'Hmm. I can't see anything.'
    'That's embarrassing.'
    'Lumps, I mean. They look fine. Is that uncomfortable?'
    'It's a little cold.'
    -
    'I think we're all done. Here, dry yourself up.'
    'That was quick. Are you sure you checked both of them?'

'Could you turn on the lights please? Yes, they both look healthy. There's nothing to suggest that swelling is causing the pain you described to your GP. But I can't be one hundred percent certain at this stage. If you come back in a few weeks we'll have the complete test results.'

'Um.'

'Have a nice day.'

I found Max on a wall outside the pub. The wall was by the door of the Jewish butcher. The Jewish butcher had no sign, just a sun-bleached hole where a man in rolled-up sleeves appeared and took delivery of plastic-bagged animal bodies. That was all. I found Max on a wall near the road where the man in the black Mercedes was robbed at gunpoint for his Rolex. He had four thousand pounds wrapped around his wrist like an adolescent pipefish. The men who did it must have known. Tailed him. Waited. I wonder if I served him? I gave Max a vodka soda. He gave his last money to a crackhead who wanted tea. It was a fifty pence piece. Max said, 'That's the thing about your place,' passing me a joint, 'it's just far enough for the crackheads to bother, but if you sit outside the pubs a bit further down the road you don't get nearly as many people asking for money.'

'Just a load of couples pushing prams and buggies.'

'How's work, anyway?' said Max.

'Fine thanks. Six more hours to go.'

'Let me know when you're finished. I'm staying at the studio tonight. You should come round.'

'Thanks. What're you doing now?'

'I'm going to Dalston.'

'Wish I could join you,' I said, yawning. 'Our regular transvestite came in earlier and started cutting herself in the middle of the floor.'

It was a warm evening.

There was Irish whiskey in my mug. Back inside we were celebrating a belated IPA Day with an experimental Pentangle prototype. I had tried it at the brewery a week before. We had the new batch on tap. Limited release. Allyn worked three days a week for them so it was no coincidence that we had it. He wouldn't sleep. He'd sweat and dream beer. Allyn, listening in on the narration, said, 'They're installing some bright tanks for more carbonation. They're having a complete brew floor clear out. Less collaboration with tight spaces and pain for knocked elbows and knees. The office, so I've been told, is going to move outside into a large transportable unit, so the space where the current office is will hold the yeast fridge, and there'll be no walls in the way.'

'Seems a shame,' I said.

'It was a good location. Kept everyone together. Labour and administration. But they've got to upgrade to a twenty barrel kettle in order to double their output, if they want to stay in the game.'

'Theo says one of the brewers at Otterville quit.'

'Yeah?'

'Apparently. He said the brewery has got too big.'

'The bald guy with a beard and tortoiseshell glasses?'

'Exactly.'

A pause. I was standing still in a forest of dirty glasses. It resembled a wrecking yard or Hackney Wick in the rain. I let the new staff get up to their wrists in wastage sheets and customer information. Stem polishing. Replying to the kitchen's claim that we didn't have chicken wings on the menu because Arthur had the last plate earlier. I was arriving later for each shift. There were cameras in all corners and problems convincing new bartenders to drink. They seemed afraid to try. Afraid they might be fired for stealing.

'Not so promising,' said Allyn. 'How are they getting on?' tilting his head at the new guys while they were scratching theirs.

Bobby was draining tea bags and Timbo was telling a story. He said he fell asleep on the Metropolitan Line, which was about when the kettle clicked and I ignored the tick-tick-tick of some impatient customer waiting for a drink. Timbo had arrived in Ruislip.

'Drunk?'

'Drunk, yes,' said Timbo. 'It was two o'clock and I stumbled out of the station, confused, thought I may as well find the nearest pub.'

Bobby laughed. 'You didn't think to find a way home?'

Timbo said, 'I just thought to myself why not?' Lucy was grappling with a fobbing red ale. Timbo stopped his story to watch her. 'Use a wider straight glass,' he said. 'Remember the surface area,' then turned back to us. 'Jesus, this job is scripted. We're acting in reruns.'

He added a sugar.

'Anyway, I found some random pub, can't remember its name, and in the aftermath of some party I got talking, drunker still, to some people and before long I was rolling around with some girl on the floor of a marquee in the garden,' which was when my tea became drinkable. 'And then we were rolling around in the car park waiting for a taxi when some hands suddenly appeared on my shoulders, pulling me away, and on her shoulders too, doing the same. It was her friends. They were screaming at me, telling me to get off her.'

'Was she drunk?'

Timbo yawned. 'Of course she was drunk. But she was also underage.'

'Under which age?' said Bobby.

Timbo shrugged.

'New staff are good,' said Bobby, nodding at the faces at the end of the bar then sipping his tea and turning back to face Timbo and I. Timbo had a curved moustache back then. It was curved at the ends. We'd all agreed it looked pretty cool. Even Latest Chef. 'So why do you look so tired?' I said. 'It was only two a.m.'

Timbo said, 'Mate, it was this afternoon.'

'And Zone Six, too' said Bobby

Molly was freaking out about Ebola on the sofa. She said, 'I read this article in The Daily Mail about, like, what if someone with Ebola didn't know they had it and somehow poured infected water from a glass they'd been using into the water supply.' She said this while rolling a fag. I was heating up a gram of coke on the hob, trying to break it down. Nem laughed. Nem said, 'Think about where you read this.'

Molly said, 'Yes, but how would they know?'

I went to the shop with Molly's umbrella. It'd been raining again. End of summer.

'But water gets cleaned and filtered after it goes down the drain,' said Nemesia. 'Otherwise you'd have already drunk enough bad stuff to kill you a million times, way before you even knew what Ebola was.'

Molly said, 'And I'm not even sure about that.'

I got back from the shop with less change in my pocket, but at least I had a packet of Hobnobs. Nemesia was sitting on the window sill smoking. I was leaning by the door to the kitchen, racking up lines and drinking wine. I said, 'There was a scare in Lewisham recently. Some guy claimed he had Ebola and when he went to a hospital all the staff went nuts. They totally panicked. They only had some rubber gloves, aprons and masks to deal with a potential virus outbreak. There was an uproar all over the internet. I can't believe you didn't see it. The comment section was fantastic. People getting so fucking frustrated because the hospital staff were so unprepared. They let him use a public waiting room toilet, apparently, and a pay phone in the foyer.'

'Shit,' said Molly, 'really?'

We'd given up taking it in turn to perch by the window, just closed the door to the hallway instead, lit more incense and began smoking on the sofa and futon, dropping ash into empty wine glasses.

'Yeah, I'm not kidding. It's in The Guardian. And it turns out he didn't even have Ebola.'

Molly shook her head. 'I want to live in Islington,' she said.

The next day Nemesia got mugged on Dalston Lane. She'd been walking to the Job Centre, following Citymapper while I was in her kitchen making coffee. She appeared like some apparition in the doorway, tiptoed into her own home and, shaking, explained how a man on a bike swiped her phone and when she tried to grab it threatened her with a knife. The map would still be recalculating. Shaking, Nem rolled a cigarette and told me not to tell Theo, who was working and would have dropped everything to come home.

We sat in Hackney Downs Park airing out Theo's pop-up tent while London, hoping for an Indian summer, was beginning to get colder. After weeks behind the sofa Theo's tent had begun to smell like a ferret. It had cigarette burn marks like stars on a fly sheet sky. Ace wanted to borrow it and take it on a fishing trip with El Hell and the dogs. He'd been feeling pastoral, had been searching for good camping spots in the Lake District and stocking up on knives. I slung the tent over my shoulder like a Saxon shield and Nemesia and I marched through the park, up Rectory Road to the police station where we waited so long to be seen by anyone, or to even see anyone behind the glass, that I was beginning to think bringing the tent was a good idea. 'Pitch up, camp out. Occupy the London Met.' Nemesia laughed in fragments and shards, battling with shock and tears. 'Fucking thing had a crack in it anyway. What was that idiot thinking?'

Very slowly, like an hourglass in reverse gravity, a man appeared in front of us and sat behind a computer. He said, 'Is there anything that might distinguish the assailant? Skin colour, clothes?' Nemesia said that the bike was blue but we spent most of the time on the phone to EE trying to block the SIM card. EE were only interested upgrading her contract. So we went back to Hackney Downs and sat in the park next to Theo's pop-up tent, airing our bodies out, leaving the Job Centre to hang on while Nem read Crack and a woman in a wheelchair pushed herself backwards along the path by Queensdown Road, one leg stuck out like a rudder. Nemesia sighed and I wasn't sure if I should have felt bad for not giving her a hug when she appeared in the door to the kitchen. At least I spilled my coffee. It burned. It made the shape of Hackney on the floor. Everything the man in the police station wrote became a strange inky dribble that squabbled with DO NOT LEAN OVER THIS LINE signs on the counter. His words looked like a dark winter tree branch clawing its way out from the black bubbles of incident bullet points. The man yawned. He wore a blue shirt. Wasn't actually a police officer but I did see one with an Alsatian only a few moments before. Suspicious. Direct infiltration. I felt trapped and immediately tried to pick Nemesia up and leave, but she teared up. I think she did it on purpose. She wanted to get a rise. I put my hand on her shoulder and my left eye, the one with astigmatism, on the German Shepherd.

Something cold had come. The only warm light of London was that part of the sun still unhidden by trees. Playground. Basketball courts. Monkey bars by the path. Football pitches and kids playing five-a-side with tracksuited community coaches. Nemesia and I kept picking up the pop-up tent and moving it away from the advancing shade. It was staging its winter offensive. Nemesia was more annoyed about missing her appointment at the Job Centre. Hackney Council required their approval for housing benefit. Needed proof that interviews are attended. Bank statements. No cash giveaway ever intended. All about to go online but the website was rubbish. She'd quit the café, anyway, so wasn't entitled to an allowance, but at least she had a new iPhone in the post already.

The last heat of the sun was licking our hair. It was the death rattle of Gelert the dog, and we were Llewelyn the Great. We felt strange. The sun shrugged in reflection off the wheelchair lady's direction, now poised, paused, backwards. Her rudder-leg was kicking the air by the benches and tennis courts where tennis balls flew with the same energy I spied in the eyes of an uncastrated Alsatian who walked over while his owner called after and took a long piss on the tent.

A morning off in nude murk, musk, sex and Molly on the desk. At the desk. On the cold leather chair. Shivered. Warmed it with her cheeks. Sitting beside The Shapes of Dogs' Eyes. With me. And the ragged scraps of Theo's life, the speakers he rigged to his wall playing

Beach House, reminded me of you. Jeff Mangum too. Theo was at his parents' house for his brother's eighteenth birthday. They were having a teenage barbecue.

We were naked. Loving together. Inhabiting each other and not getting rained on or wading through puddles of floor plans. She, looking for a new flat and I, simply looking. Sex on the counter in Theo and Nemesia's kitchen. Anywhere but the bed, he said, or implied. I left a condom, unused and removed from the packet, beneath their duvet as a joke.

In the morning we awoke with relentless Hackney sirens and the whine of the Yankee Doodle ice cream van pervading our half-sleeping senses. The carpet in the flat was scattered with crumbs. My t-shirt hung from the handlebars of Theo's bike, which was leaning against a wall of old paperbacks from the bookshop on Lower Clapton Road. Molly's knickers snoozed on the small Persian rug, having tired themselves out giggling all night. She'd been selling her clothes on eBay to raise money for a security deposit, stressed out and trying everything in her power to avoid being deleted by London. New property, tenancy, meant re-applying for housing benefit, and that's not as easy in Hackney as it is in Tower Hamlets. Nostalgia for Mile End dying hard, here. And I wished that I could help her, but I knew nothing. We woke in heaps of Hackney and our own flesh. Rain spattering our toes at the end of the bed through the crack in the window. Condom packets on the floor and everything moving outside. With a sigh I pulled her closer, feeling at home as I held her. Molly said, 'What's that noise?'

It was a thunderstorm.

Engines sounded through a hoarse outdoor throat. The wind was in the oesophagus street which was struck by a midnight lightning bolt, setting car alarms off all along it. But we hadn't even tried to sleep. Our electricity was lingering. Rain dampening the coarse wild grass of each other, spooning. Nude morning. I'd not thought about The Shapes of Dogs' Eyes all night. And I didn't know it yet, but my brain had decided that being there, with her, was enough.

'How was the barbecue?'

'It was fine. Nem and I went for a walk.'

'Did you take your dog with you?'

'No we didn't take him. He went missing the other day. My mum and dad were walking him in the woods and he ran off. They found him three hours later under a tree, with a gluttonous look about him and a broad black canine grin. Turns out he'd snuck into a Co-op and stolen a loaf of bread. He wouldn't shit for days. That gave it all away. Now he's banned from all future excursions.'

'That's a shame. Where'll he escape to?'

'Don't worry, they're getting a puppy to keep him company.'

'What kind?'

'How should I know?'

I'd been thinking about the first dog in space. Laika. Part husky, Samoyed and terrier. She was a stray, a descendent of the hunting dogs of Siberia. She was also a type of beer, a canine namesake made with wheat. She had a herby taste. Eyes that had seen more than mine, providing windows were built into her spaceship.

It was late. A cheeky white terrier scuttled round the floor and condiment area. It looked remarkably like an Old English terrier but they're extinct. Molly texted me and said, 'Did you get a chance to see the blood moon tonight?' but it was too low to see.

Laika.

Couldn't see the stars either. Light reflections on glasses polluting pavements with shards that punctured soles, tyres locked up in the gutter, arses that clattered back-pocket keys when there were no more chairs left to fill. People stood, lethargic. I was getting angry at a customer for not paying enough attention to me. It was a passive anger. It started with bland repetition. Repeat the order back to him at a significantly reduced pace. He turned around to ask his friend which topping he wanted on his medium-well burger.

Cheese. No bacon.

I was about to commence shouting but then saw his hearing aid. I think the dog was part Jack Russell. Its tail was long and curved. Docking is not necessary in the city. Purely aesthetic. No risks taken. Dogs were disposable tools for fixing relationships, not for rooting out foxes and thorn bush pheasant corpses. They were for wallowing in the glory of artistic poverty. But reality was rich. It was a better kept secret. And the dogs were fools for keeping it. There was nothing tamer than a fox strolling through temporary hunger. Now Laika was running the bar, taming every customer. Two guys walked in and said, 'We want some lager.'

'Cheap lager. Cooking lager. Tinny lager.'

'And what's a good cider?'

Drunk and drunker.

Molly texted me. She was dealing with estate agencies and the prospect of an expiring railcard: 'Well?'

I typed, 'No,' then looked up at whoever was asking for beer.

'Twenty-two-years-old this one, and can't handle his beer,' said my newest customer.

I said, 'This is a good cider. And this is a good cider. Do you want it still or sparkling?'

'Um,' said the younger man.

'We're builders,' said the older man.

'We're professionals in construction,' said the younger man, bowing.

'How about this one?' I said, pouring them two tasters.

'What do you think?' looking at each other. 'Okay. One of them and a Camden.'

Money crossed over the cracks in every finger. Cracks filled with ash and the dust of Polyfilla. Shirt stains could be food, could be tar. 'We came straight from our site down in Angel, via a few places on the way.'

The younger man said, 'I always thought bartending and building were a very similar type of trade. They are humble. Practical. Honest. Got any snacks?'

'We've got ready salted salt and vinegar cheese and onion sweet chilli.'

'Not crisps. Nuts.'

The curly tail of the terrier sailed on the surface of floor-dwelling handbags. A great white shark that sniffed the blood of discarded dishes. The dog followed the trail thirty feet across the room, through the nasal din of cacophony footprints and spillages to where a group of drunken men had spread their food across the floor. The rot. The invisible cockroach eggs we'd never truly got rid of. The dog's nose was very impressive. My senses were completely shattered by even the sound of human din, my brain function reduced to automaton standards. When I approached the cellar door after changing a keg or cask I started to tremble. The noise from upstairs rushed towards me the closer I'd get to turning the handle. Back up. I'd begun to hope that the broken step would break when I pressed my feet on it and that I'd fall into peaceful darkness.

Molly said, 'Shame. It was beautiful.'

The moon.

One of the builders, the older, amused, least drunk of the two, said, 'Did you know this place before it was taken over? Before the bar was at the side, and it was part of the middle interior? Nice bit of work, there. I know a carpenter who worked on it. He doesn't live round here anymore. Enfield's much cheaper.'

'I heard it was a dive bar,' I said. 'Rough, like a broken record.'

Timbo, fitting a new bottle of gin to the optics, laughed.

'My dad,' said the younger man, with knots of blonde hair and a bent nose, 'my dad, hey how old are you?'

'Twenty-four.'

'Pleased to meet you,' holding out his hand which was chalky and yellow as bricks. Gritty. A good hand. 'My dad used to come here too. There was karaoke until four in the morning.'

'But you were too young,' said the older man.

'I was too young,' said the younger man, blinking wildly. In a swift fist-to-mouth manoeuvre he sipped and swallowed some beer. He asked me if I was local.

I said, 'I don't have a postcode.'

'Better here than Angel. That's where our site is. It's a piece of shit. Too expensive and close to the bullshit.' They both smiled. In the corner a bowl-cut man with a goatee was playing the flute. 'You live here?'

I said, 'Stoke Newington and Clapton, mostly.'

'You do get around. Got a degree?'

'No.'

'Thank fuck someone round here hasn't. Everything is so up-and-coming. Fuck, even Walthamstow's on the way. Which means it's a dump right now. But soon, mark my words. People don't need the fucking City. Better further out, except then everyone realises and everywhere gets filled with poncy cafés and fancy beer. No offence.'

The younger man said, 'You know these Romanian people?' then paused, smiling at me, but more like through me to the broken tiles on the back wall behind me. 'They call them immigrants. They're all coming here and they're immigrants. But I think everyone's an immigrant because everyone's moving. I'm moving right now.'

He was swaying.

He started tapping his chest. The older man was shaking his head.

'You know what I say?' said the younger man. 'I say follow your feet.'

'That right?'

'That's right. I've got a tattoo on mine. It says, "Keep smiling." And that's me. And you've got to.' By now he was on his second pint. 'You've got to be honest with yourself. So if I don't, sorry, mmm, don't keep smiling, then I'm not being myself. So I've got to trust my feet and always follow them. Your feet carry you, mate. You should always remember to listen.'

'But what if you're so busy watching your feet that you don't see where you're going?'

'Ah ha!'

Another customer approached the bar, empty glass in hand. 'Looks like that man needs another,' said the older man.

'What's your name again?' the younger man asked. I told him. He said, 'Pleased to meet you. I'm in construction. I'm a noble architect. Can't you tell? My father? Why, he used to come here all the time. He designed the building and built the bar. He's dead now but I'll find a picture for you, you'll know him.'

The older man said, 'Come on you idiot,' still shaking his head. 'I want a cigarette. Have you seen the moon tonight?'

I don't feel healthy I don't -feel-healthy- I can feel my body swell up.

I went for coffee with Max. His friend Lauren was waiting for us cross-legged on an old leather sofa slippery with ankles and soda water. The two of them were having a discussion. Lauren said she was thinking of becoming a writer. But there was a problem: she gets too distracted. She had these two second-hand paperbacks in front of her. She got them from a guy selling second-hand paperbacks on the pavement outside the Church Street entrance to Abney Park. That was three hundred yards away. Lauren said, 'Modelling is fine but I used to write loads when I was a child. When I was a child I could focus on things,' she said. 'But that's hard when you have to make money, isn't it?' I didn't really know.

'Are you still in that band?' I asked her. I'd forgotten the name, or I didn't know it in the first place. She said, 'No, and I'm not modelling much either. I got a cat recently. Here,' and she showed me a picture.

I said, 'Why didn't you get a dog?'

She said, 'Because I don't want a boyfriend.'

'But you could write about The Shapes of Dogs' Eyes for me.'

Max said, 'How's that going, by the way?' It was a corner-of-the-mouth kind of question.

'I'm stuck in a rut of uncaring,' I told him, 'but I don't want to give up. Maybe commissioning a writer to document my findings is a good idea?'

'What shapes?' said Lauren.

'Like hexagons. Dogs' eyes have edges. Cats' eyes don't, as far as I know.'

'What about people?' said Lauren.

'People? Yes, some people resemble The Shapes of Dogs' Eyes.

Hexagonal. Distraught. Like when a dog is looking at you, begging for food, or it's tied to a lamp in the rain. I see it at work all the time. A couple sitting at a table, begging for a reason to leave each other. Begging for food. Eyes wet. Nose wet. Got a cold. Great big Spaniel ears of hair, pursed Maltese lips, tails docked at birth. People misshapen, interwoven. Sometimes they're interweaving. Mostly they're unravelling. They just want something to keep them sane and a dog, it seems, provides that.'

Lauren said, 'It's the people distraction.' I nodded. 'That's why I didn't get a dog. Dogs are for sharing. They know too much for one person to handle. If I'm ever going to start writing again I need a clean empty bedroom.'

Max said, 'Impossible. Your room is a tip.'

I told her, 'Try it. I need to see this on paper.'

She said she'd think about it.

We went to Lisa's after work. It was Jon's birthday. When we'd finished stacking chairs and removing the lingerers and updating the whiteboard with newly racked, vented and tapped beers, we necked a few shots of Jägermeister. Written off the stock count. No matter. At Lisa's Jon said, 'Last time I was here, that guy Joe, the one with Tourettes, was leaning against the bar and that dealer on roller skates who roller skates round the area came back from the toilet and Joe called him a cunt. The dealer, feeling ignorant, started a fight. Even the bartender jumped in. She was trying to, excuse me, she was pulling them apart. It was funny.'

Timbo handed Jon a shot of Wray & Nephew.

'Thanks lad,' said Jon. 'Anyway, I was leaning against the bar with my mate and this guy with crutches dropped his crutches and started bashing the dealer's head. Meanwhile my mate necked Joe's glass of wine while no one was looking. Fuck, I was twenty-nine then.'

I said, 'How old are you now?'

Timbo was trying to bite Lucy's nipple. Bobby was fiddling with an old set of decks that never seemed to get used. I don't think the turntables had needles. The jukebox was maxed out. It swallowed my two pound coin before This Charming Man could start then told us all to fuck off.

Jon said, 'I'm thirty but I feel younger. I'm definitely not an adult yet. The last time I lived in Hackney we thought there was a gas leak in our flat. That was five years ago. It was a big block of flats but I can't remember where.'

I said, 'Why?'

He shrugged. 'I'm bad with roads. Somewhere between Victoria Park and Dalston, I think. Near a pub called The Gun. We called the gas man and he checked the boiler which was fine. He said it was more likely we had a slow burning fire smouldering somewhere cavernous, like the attic, but that seemed like an unfathomable space considering the size of the place. He suggested we call the fire brigade immediately and then promptly fucked off. I think he was scared he'd be one of about a thousand people about to go up in flames. But we'd been smelling it for at least a day and a half.'

'Shit.'

'I know. About thirteen fire engines arrived and I was the guy, the sort of spokesperson for the entire block, because none of the other tenants knew what was going on. Turns out it was the flower pot on our balcony we'd been using as an ashtray. An old aloe vera plant had caught fire. And we were high up, so the breeze had taken it through the whole flat. The fireman who found it called me a twat.'

'No he didn't.'

'You're right he didn't. But he may as well have. After that I moved to the warehouse on Green Lanes.'

I tried going for a piss but someone was throwing up in the toilet. Lucy was berating Timbo, who'd grown bored of offering lap dances to unwitting chair-bound customers. Rage Against The Machine between Blondi. Jumping up and swiftly swooning. A strange stage in the corner, empty except for a stiletto-shaped chair. Almost no other customers there thanks to Timbo's harassing. Doors locked and cigarettes lit. Boaz didn't come with us. He never did. Besides, there was a crack opening up, a divide. Heavy concern for fake fifty pound notes and announcements that staff would be paying for any loss of stock or money with the abolition of their 25% discount and the confiscation of their tips. We broke a Saturday night record the previous weekend: almost eight grand in one day. Then someone took a bad fifty without checking the hologram in the UV light by the fan, so the contract of trust between customer and staff was going to be used to reimburse the company. Excuses for use of passive protest: quiet lips, annoying enough, but busy fingers pouring after-hours pints go unpaid with talk of revolution. Timbo, still finishing his shifts earlier than us, hung around and waited for Lisa's, racking up a tab the size of his earnings and calling in an air strike. Some things never change. But it was one hundred for a gram, so at least it was the good stuff. Allyn was schmoozing at a brewery in Kentish Town. Another railway arch booze function or launch of some new highly-hopped lager. He said, 'It's always good to network. Nothing wrong with an increase in the number of hops.' The rest of us went to Lisa's. Sunday, closed half an hour early and Lisa, the manager, wouldn't kick us out for a few more hours. That bar was perfectly placed. Ace's not-long-for-this-world sofa was just around the corner. Perfect. Only a short walk past The Birdcage, by then closed, banners indicating over forty years of Stamford Hill service, when it was the only cool pub in Stoke Newington and ours was still a dive. Forty years became nothing. It was to become another Turkish restaurant. The last time I went there was with Max and Stefan. The place had just had a refurb. Pool table, new paint on the walls gave you headaches, big shiny open island bar fully-staffed with Italian women who had almost no experience. 'We got a CV from one of them the other day,' said Lucy. 'It made me sad.'

'Like a column of refugees seeking asylum,' said Timbo, who was holding a pint of Guinness. 'Guys, shall we get out of here?' They were already selling fireworks in preparation for November 5th and Timbo wanted to buy some. But the vote was unanimous: too cold out there. Yet it was too warm inside. Eyes were dry. Temples throbbing in anticipation of a comedown. We smoked a joint on the way up the hill. It didn't go far being passed around six people. Timbo shrugged and rolled out the door and we didn't see him again that night. He probably went off to convalesce and gestate plans for an explosive finale. Bobby trailed off, slurring. And Lucy wanted to get chips. But all the shutters outside were down. I stayed for another drink, a tonic I told Jon contained gin, but that's only because I found another tenner in my back pocket and thought it best to use it quickly before anyone noticed. Jon said, 'What's the time?' pushing his arms against the wall where old sepia photographs of Kingsland Road were hanging, trying to recalibrate his spine. I told him it was half four. He yawned and said, 'It takes me ages to cycle home and I need new brake pads. Is it raining? Good. It's mostly uphill on the way back and I don't want to get too hot. I've been using my ankles to stop.' He showed me a hole in the sole of his shoe. 'That's right. I put so much money into my latest film project that I'm broke. No staff tips? Guess I won't get new brakes.' When we went outside Jon unlocked his bike from a streetlamp and put his backpack in the basket. The basket was broken but somehow still clung to the handlebars. He checked the chain was secure by turning the cranks, one of which he'd nicked from a derelict frame in his warehouse. Then he looked up at me. He said, 'If I don't show up tomorrow, it's because I'm dead. Make sure Arthur and Boaz know that.' He stomped out his cigarette. 'And all for a dud fifty quid.'

We didn't see Timbo again until the following week. Strange posts had been sighted on Facebook. Posts from a man no one was even sure came from this planet. They were crying for revolution. It was Bonfire Night and Timbo arrived at the pub at nine o'clock, drunk. He brought his housemate, a ukulele and a trilby hat. The trilby hat was green. The table was drenched in the languid cackle of conspirators. Jon was there. So were Lucy and Allyn and Heather. Those two Irish girls from the pub across the road were rolling fags. The guest of honour was a black bin bag filled with fireworks. The cash-up was easy. The chairs stacked completely and the cellar shut down. Done by quarter past twelve. Time for a cigarette round 250 and a couple of outdoor tinnies while Timbo got started, letting off a rocket outside. Bang. Through the curtains. Bang. Doors locked, lights, ashtrays swept for smouldering aloe vera plants. Bang. One rocket almost separated Jon's face from his head when we were walking to the Common. This was at one in the morning. Jon and I pushing our bikes next to Lucy and Heather, no Allyn after he'd said an Irish goodbye and disappeared without us realising. Timbo and the Irish girls were ahead and Timbo lit a rocket and turned round to fire it and the rocket flew past Jon's head then exploded next to a parked taxi. The driver went mad and sped off towards Seven Sisters. For some reason Timbo wouldn't hold the rockets vertical. For some reason Timbo held the rockets. The orange plastic launcher stayed in the bin bag. Most of them exploded by the railway tunnel and in the trees on the other side of the Common or near the playground or, once, when Timbo ran forward and turned around and pointed a rocket towards us, we scattering, the thing flashed up into the plane trees around us then tumbled down onto the road, blowing up in green and pink smoke just as an OUT OF SERVICE 73 went past. The crowd were poised to run, fearing police. Heather said, 'I've already been arrested twice. It can't happen again.' But fireworks go off all the time. Ten minutes after we began some rivals of the night started answering from the direction of Clissold Park. We used our fireworks up in conversation. Exhausted our ability to communicate on a social level. Timbo lit a rocket while we shouted, 'Let it go, let it go!' by which point all of the rocket's thrust had depleted so when he did finally release it the rocket just plopped two feet in front of him and exploded in the grass with our laughter. The Irish girls went home and Timbo went to the bus stop, leaving Jon, Lucy, Heather and I on the corner of Rectory Road while in the distance Timbo waved the orange launcher like a sword.

At one o'clock I went to the pub watch meeting. It was in the cellar of The Full Stop on Stoke Newington High Street. There were supposed to be free sandwiches and coffee. Allyn was meant to be a regular attendee. But Allyn sent me in some compulsory favour because he, hungover, couldn't be bothered. The cellar of The Full Stop had its own bar and stage lighting and the shaved off ends of books used to decorate the wall by an espresso machine. I was the first one there so I grabbed a coffee. There were no sandwiches. I sat in a leather corner underneath a light pointing everywhere but onto my head. No silhouette to give me away. That's good. Stay hidden. 'Avoid questions,' said Allyn. 'Don't speak to council members (our unavoidable enemies).' I told Allyn I could pass on his concerns. The time of our bin bag collection had been changed from whenever to one hour between eighty forty-five and nine forty-five. Very impractical.

Allyn said, 'I know. But don't bother. Boaz will deal with it himself.'

Slowly more landlords and managers arrived. No lowly supervisors. Lisa was there. She smiled at me. Another lady sat next to her and a man with crutches plus two or three council members, their notes, their numbers.

The debate came down to four points:

1: changes to the conditions for issuing temporary event licenses for pop-up bars and kitchens in the areas of Shoreditch and Dalston. 'How many applications did we receive last year, Karen? Almost two thousand? Yes, unfortunately we can't stop people from wanting to put events on, we can simply slow down the application process, make it more difficult to avoid the regulations we've been redefining with the police, who've been very supportive.'

Drinking my coffee.

2: altering the conditions to existing premises licences. 'This is linked in part to point number one. Our current number of licensed premises in the Stoke Newington area alone mostly have standard closing hours. Those are between eleven and twelve at night. That's fine. And for those who possess existing late service licences, like you Lisa, this condition will remain as such.'

Someone said, 'Good. Lisa's bar is about as far up Stamford Hill as you can go. It has to stay open late, otherwise the place has nothing.'

The council member said, 'Understood. However, all new applications for late service licences will be granted only under stricter adherence to a new set of rules currently being devised, with the police, in order to co-operate with point three.'

3: containing the abuse of illegal substances in bars, clubs and pubs, with the complete reduction of their use in mind. 'The main area of concern is, in particular, Shoreditch. From a recent study undertaken by our agents and in conjunction with local police, we can see that, rather disturbingly, more women than men are abusing illegal substances in public areas. The study found evidence of substances and, um, residue, in a number of women's toilets, and the number of reports certain establishments have been filing are increasing dramatically. Any thoughts, everyone, on the reasons why our young women may be taking more drugs than men?'

Disregarding the words of Allyn, I said, 'You've got it all wrong.'

'Oh?' said the lead council member, a man with stubble, a suit and fake leather shoes. I crossed my legs. High-top Doc Martens. Gutted mate. He continued: 'Who are you?'

'I'm the supervisor at –'

'Oh, you're from the place that sells the craft beer. That stuff is very popular right now. Business must be good.'

'It's not doing so well, actually, since the council made us remove our benches and tables from the pavement.'

There was a pause.

'Right. Well, anyway, you were saying?'

I said, 'There are no more women than men taking drugs in pub toilets. The men go into the ladies' to do it. It's obvious. That way they don't get caught. Bartending is predominantly a male occupation, and people aren't followed into women's toilets.'

Someone laughed.

'And you've seen this?' the council member said.

I said, 'Yes. It happens in our place all the time.' Lisa was sitting there wide-eyed, as though I'd just inadvertently divulged a precious secret kept by a league of rebellious publicans. The man from the council sat up in his chair. He raised his left eyebrow to show he was serious. 'And you allow it?' he said.

I coughed. 'Um, no, no of course not. We kick them out if we catch them.'

'And confiscate their drugs? And hand them in to the police as part of your incident report?'

I said, 'Yes, yes of course.'

Lisa sniffed.

The council member paused. He shuffled some notes that no one else had been taking. 'Good,' he said. 'You had me concerned there, for a moment.'

But something kept me from stopping: 'What about our bins?'

'Hmm?'

'Our bins. Recently we've been denied the ability to leave full bin bags outside on the pavement where we used to. Now they have to stay overnight in our cellar because we've been given just one hour to get rid of them. Eight forty-five to nine forty-five in the evening. Which is right when we don't need to empty them. They make the cellar stink and that attracts pests which I think are a bigger concern than whether or not some people do a line in a toilet to celebrate not being at work.'

'Well –'

'Have you ever actually worked behind a bar?'

Another pause. I sat there, looking around for support and feeling very pleased with myself. Most faces, and there weren't many, just looked at their phones or their coffee. Poor attendance. Should've provided sandwiches. The man from the council said, eventually, 'I'll look into the bin situation for you,' but he didn't write anything down. 'Shall we move on to number four?'

4: preventing the use of illegal substances in outdoor public places, after having successfully completed objective 3.

On the way back to work I walked through Abney Park Cemetery after shuffling my way down Church Street. Allyn allowed me an hour for the Pub Watch meeting. It lasted twenty-five minutes. I spent the extra thirty-five looking in shoe shops and card shops and considering cafés and rummaging through bushes to read the obscure names on the gravestones of Hackney's ancestors. The paths through the cemetery are a labyrinth littered with joint stubs. I kicked empty canisters of laughing gas as I circumnavigated the remains of the chapel, contemplating another eleven hours of pouring beer and ignoring drug takers in the toilets.

Till One
16-11-14
SYSTEM – TEST PRINT

REMEMBER: record as many hand dryer brand names as possible, as well as their ability to dry hands after A) superficial hand splash (number 1), & B) thorough hand scrub (number 2).

Also, soap dispensers.

I'd hoped to offload my till receipt notes on someone who could make them legible. Who could consolidate and compress them and email them to me in a .zip file that I could infect every household computer with. When Timbo introduced me to Alice Unknown I had a piece of paper with a large question mark drawn in pencil. Alice the Writer. Alice the Spook. Fabricated on layers of heat-sensitive till paper and Theo's insistence: he said I had to DO SOMETHING if I was going to expose The Shapes of Dogs' Eyes to the public. At this point I wasn't even sure it was possible.

But I was bored of everything and had nothing else to do. I was going to help them break up, make changes, stop sitting around repairing broken pieces of human furniture with Tinder and beer cooled down in a cellar. But my hands were sticking like glue. I was beginning to lose sight and, crucially, I hadn't yet realised that, according to The Shapes of Dogs' Eyes, I was supposed to. Back then, I still thought I could fight.

Theo suggested I find a writer, but Timbo introduced me to Alice. Max's friend Lauren was too distracted. I needed help.

Sunday, Stoke Newington: Timbo and I were on split shifts. We didn't need to be because the pub was overstaffed and empty, but, well, that's just how it was. I asked Boaz for an extra two hours. Twenty minutes free every six hours was an employee myth. Also the law. But never seen. And Sunday was always a long day. Timbo was my co-conspirator. It was against company policy to drink while temporarily off-duty, so we left the premises. Walked one hundred metres down the High Street to The Coach. A few days earlier, Timbo had said, 'Do you know Alice the Historian?'

She went by many titles.

I said, 'No.'

Timbo said, 'I should probably introduce you. She may be able to help with your investigation.' But there was no answering the wrong question, and that, I now know, is what I was chasing. What was Alice making? In another life she was an agent, an investigative journalist like Tintin in a dreamy midnight Berlin. There she crossed the border and fell in love with a man in an East End bar, who'd tried to turn her in.

'I've seen you in our pub before,' I told her, outside The Coach on my two hour break. 'You always complain about the state of the cellar.'

Timbo said, 'Shh, you'll scare her off.' He said it quietly.

Alice, sat across the bench from me, was smoking Hamlets and only drinking from straight half pint glasses. She said, 'I wasn't complaining, merely stating my concern that the beer was hazy.'

'But haze comes naturally,' I said. 'All that keeps it away is a fining agent. Do you know where fining agent comes from? It comes from a sturgeon's liver.'

There was silence. After a while, Alice undid the zip on her green puffer jacket. She did this very slowly and only part of the way. It was a slow-to-undo-the-zip kind of manoeuvre. At no point did she take her eyes off me. 'I can see you know your stuff,' she said, 'but how do you think I can help you?'

I said, 'I'm onto something. A situation that has been developing in London over the summer. Specifically, at least to me, in Hackney. The Shapes of Dogs' Eyes is taking over. Forcing people into drinking craft beer, swelling bellies and bank accounts with just-in-case savings and Ikea decorations. Then, and this may shock you, babies. Yes, babies. But it starts with puppies.'

A pause.

'Were you really an investigative journalist in West Berlin?' I asked her.

Alice said, 'Yes, but I wasn't in love. I told a man I met that if I went with him back to his house – it was in some grey Soviet block of flats – I'd leave immediately at even the slightest hint of trouble.'

'And?' said Timbo, skinning up.

'There was a man behind the door. A spook, I'm sure. East German Police. Stasi. Or some other Soviet lackey. So I left. Didn't get what I needed for my story.'

'What was that?' said Timbo.

Alice sighed. 'I was reporting on East German apartment doors. Brutalist flat block staircases that lead to love affairs and dares and, well, that sort of thing. Something, anything, good. Feeling, I suppose you'd call it, and how it's represented in aesthetics.'

'Did he have a dog?' I said. 'It's important to know if he had a dog.'

Alice shook her head. She said, 'I don't know. I was young and ambitious and scared. What have dogs got to do with anything?'

I said, 'Twenty-somethings are retiring. They're buying dogs with their partners because they're frightened.'

'Of what?'

'Living. They're quieting, settling, drinking and barely speaking. They're unhappy, I know it. And they're under the dogs' control. The dogs have been redeveloping. Have you ever looked into their eyes? They're not entirely round. Their eyes have edges. The pupils. This is why I wanted to meet you. Something strange is happening to the lovelorn, scared young people of London. I guess in East Berlin there were bigger things to deal with.'

'You mean bigger than relationships?' she said. 'Bigger than love and sex? Not at all. But this is not a contemporary phenomenon. Dogs having been controlling humans since humans began. There's no escaping it. Hackney isn't Neverland but everyone, young man, is at least a little scared of growing up.'

For a moment I said nothing. I nodded, breathed a lot, put my hands on my chin and scratched the stubble. I looked at Alice Unknown and then it dawned on me: I was a movie. A caricature of everyone's anxiety that wasn't, as I'd thought, chosen by me to resolve. It'd been projected upon me, dumped on my shoulders and then ignored. While I thought I was running round Hackney, saving the world, the world was carrying on as normal without me. I thought of Molly. I felt a fool. I looked at Alice Unknown and, after a while, said, 'When did you move back to London?'

Alice said, 'I moved to Camden in '92. Married my husband in Highbury then moved to Hackney a few years later.' Timbo was on his third beer. He had to be back at work in less than half an hour. I said, 'How come I've never seen your husband in the pub?' but that was none of my business. Alice said that they'd always had cats. She said, 'Listen, I'm busy at the moment. Did you want me to write something for you? Is that what this is about? I'm writing a book on a particular event during World War Two. I won't say which. And I've not much time for The Shapes of Dogs' Eyes. The truth, more often than not, will be right in front of your own.'

'Cats?'

She shook her head and sighed.

Timbo stood up, said, 'Fuck this, guys.' He looked at Alice, nodded and said, 'As always,' then at me: 'I'll see you back at the bar.' Alice was right. Something had changed. Some new arrangement with The Shapes of Dogs' Eyes had been made without my knowledge. A kind of choke-chain device or humane shock collar. 'Cats?' I repeated, shaking my head. Despite the big question mark I knew what she meant.

Molly.

I was groaning for midnight lahmacun, stalking in walkways to make way for curbs, protesting, tripping out of the Earl of Essex with Theo and Nemesia, while Hackney was a bitter peripheral sigh, a memory, another dried-up name-brand identity. I was in denial, having accidentally had The Shapes of Dogs' Eyes deciphered for me on a personal level, but then found myself unable, and, looking back, unwilling, to stab the pub, the people, and Molly, in the back. I knew what I had to do, but instead of going to Molly, instead of saying goodbye to The Shapes of Dogs' Eyes, fuck you, I went searching for orphaned answers in the belching contents of Islington bars. The answer had been texting me all night, but my phone was on airplane mode.

Molly.

There were deer heads on the walls. Monolithic statues of fashionable people that moved by with waxy candour. Three pints down me and we sat, bloated, by the dumbwaiter, considering the expense of chips. No conversation. Nem looking angry. That was Saturday, and though I knew what Alice Unknown had meant, was sure I felt it lying in Theo's bed with Molly during that thunderstorm – that there's no fighting the canine trend – I still had to make sure. There was a large chrome fermentation vessel behind the bar. The bar was a dark island in the middle of a human sea. Swamped.

The bartender surveyed the busy room as the curator of some grotesque exhibition. His pub an interactive museum. His shirt had bulldogs on it, so I knew I was close to something. I rarely saw what walk-in life felt like on that side of the bar. Curious school kids prodding lethargic, bloated animals behind a cage clogged up with gakky ephemera, struggling to lift their gouty feet when they needed to get up and take a piss. Why not just do it there? It's been known.

Nemesia was scowling. I tried talking to her but she couldn't hear me. So I looked at my half-empty glass and considered throwing the rest of it over a human rather than fill my stomach with more sugar. It seemed like none of us could abide being inside a crowd anymore. I was bloated with belly-full drinks and hunched over, concerned I could have an internal yeast infection, getting drunk so often and too easily. My stomach lining felt like a cellar floor grown mossy. Trying to shit was a persistent two a.m. hassle. I'd been waking half sunk, bent in the middle like the spine of a torpedoed ship which had buckled and been scuttled on a cushion reef. I didn't want the enemy to board and seize me, whoever the enemy was. When Theo said, 'Let's get out of here,' Nemesia was on her feet faster than the head rush that sucker punched me. The bartender smiled a child's smile.

We walked, a sort of disillusioned tripod, parallel to Essex Road beneath the brick chins of Islington townhouses, brown and grey with white window panes and age and money.

My sleeves rolled themselves up. Cold air sobering.

'Time for one in The Cock?' said Theo.

'It'll be closing soon.'

The North Pole was all but empty. The staff looked happy to see us which aroused our immediate suspicion. We knew better. We were hardly even happy to be there and I quickly became captivated by an enormous remote controlled plane hanging above the door to the toilets. Theo and Nemesia ordered two halves and I pulled out another flurry of tenners.

Theo said, 'They give you a pay rise or something?'

We sat smoking in a pot plant courtyard of plastic chairs and memories of old acquaintances from lives we'd outgrown.

I was an anthropologist.

My phone vibrated.

Theo said, 'I could write The Shapes of Dogs' Eyes for you,' but I wasn't paying attention.

Nemesia didn't think it was a good idea.

'Is it a memoir?' Theo asked me.

'It's an investigation. My father said I should write a story called Life Behind Bars.'

Theo said, 'Yeah, you told me.'

'I think he was sad I didn't go to uni.'

'Don't worry,' said Theo, 'he needn't be,' as he rubbed the bruise of a degree.

Nemesia sighed impatiently, waiting for something to come along and take us somewhere new.

My phone vibrated again. It was Molly. She'd been with her sister somewhere and there was a chance to coincide. I wanted to drop everything and go. Fuck the dogs, the beer. The place was slick with emptiness. It made me think of The Albion on Lauriston Road, its boarded up windows and broken sign. That time I saw the fruit machine through the accidentally unclosed door. Where have all fruit machines gone? Hidden, desperately, by council members in attempt to attract foreign investors. This information kept me feeling like the holder of some secret, some voyeuristic taboo. A fruit machine. An obscene artefact from the days when Fuller's was a much smaller brewery and pints with handles were too old-fashioned and ceilings were yellow with generations of smoke before smoking became so bad for you. 'I think we're done here,' said Nemesia, poised on a reclaimed church pew. My body was struggling to process. Liquid kept filling my stomach but I never needed to piss. I could feel my bile rising. Throat intermittently stinging. Body hating. Theo said, 'Are you around tomorrow? There's a big event going on at Otterville. Brewery collaboration.'

I said, 'I don't care anymore,' and my phone lit up on the table. A pause. Contemplations of whisky. The candour of bartenders was becoming a myth, and I was considering temp agencies and internships.

Indoors, a woman sat with a poodle on her shoulders like a curly haired mountain goat with legs too close together, back arched awkwardly in fear of falling and a head it couldn't hold up. The mountain was drinking a glass of white wine and kept the goat there the whole time she was in the bar.

In the corner by the window three people got up to leave. They made a lazy wobble for scarves and fluffy pockets for wallets and keys. Check. Bartender ticking off his closing down list, wrapping clingfilm round the pump and tap nozzles, turning chrome things upside down on the bar surface. Everything upside down.

Nemesia began to panic. She said, 'We can't become those people.'

She meant lingerers.

Theo got up to leave. We left our glasses on the bar, stepped out and breathed a sigh of relief, of confirmation – that what Alice Unknown had told me outside The Coach on Stokey High Street was real. My phone vibrated.

I found a poisonous spider in the courtyard outside Pentangle. It was enjoying the warmth of a bin lid. Hops and malted barley were scooped, still steaming, out of the mash tank. They were so hot they could scorch your skin. I was reorganising the courtyard in preparation for the new conditioning tanks. All the pallets needed moving, stacking, throwing away if they were rotting. And a lot of them were. Yard sweeping. The poisonous spider was thinking about moving to the empty boxes of kebab lunch relics. Strange rusting car parts were half stuck in the new layer of tarmac laid down by the taxi company in the railway arch next door. A layer which crept under the fence like lava and created a miniature mechanic's Pompeii out of discarded sweet wrappers and metal. Allyn had the day off from the pub as well. He spent eight minutes Instagramming the poisonous spider who was having a good time being introduced to the sun. Captions of near paralysis. Death tagged as a flirty friend, who, with its own handle, also liked it. A strange hand reaching out to [almost] touch it. The rest of the crew were having lunch. Lunch was microwaved lasagne in night-before plastic containers, apples and cigarettes fat with over-tobacco. Discussing tap-takeovers at various Hackney bars and meet the brewer days and live brewing events. Sam, from marketing, was filling envelopes with handfuls of bottle caps, unused, for a craft beer enthusiast who wanted them for his collection. John, the drayman, was smoking on a stack of bottles he'd been filling the van with. He was running his steel toe caps along the cracks in the surface of London which had been steadily filling with pub names washed off old casks. More columns of maggots and sugary deposits to flush out and inspect with torches. The cleaning machine used steam to blast dirt out and sanitise. Place casks face down on chrome spikes. Hit the pink button, feel the vibration punch the ceiling and ejaculate. But bar fly larvae is tough to break. After selecting the appropriate filter for the poisonous spider Allyn asked Mick if he could use the old fermenting tank they kept in the back. He needed to move house first, acquire more brewing space. I caught the poisonous spider underneath a London Living Wage mug, rehomed it in a derelict flower pot by the gate to the courtyard then ate my lunch on a pallet by the fence, watching them. The crew. The beer. All kids at a sports day relay running round in recycled conversation of crepe paper and sequins stuck together with PVA glue, types of bottles used and label adhesives. An alcoholic vigil, drunk on industry ritual but like the tail end of a comet trailing off and burning up harmlessly in the atmosphere.

A lot of money had gone missing from the pub. We'd broken another record. Freakish displays of beer consumption in an otherwise haze of dry business. Must be the coming of cold weather. Eight and a half grand in thirteen hours. Most of that was between eight in the evening and midnight. I was managing. They paid me fifty pence more per hour to do the same job. Arrive at three. No need to key in the alarm code, it would have already been done by the cleaner, who never turned it back on. Get the lights on, count the floats for each till. There should be two hundred in each. We made a record taking. A tenner was always missing but it wasn't a problem until Boaz or Arthur got round to adding it up. Print off the manager's checklists, email food special costings, tweet updates for new beers, clear bookings in the diary and display reserved signs on tables. Do this by four o'clock. Get it done by twenty past three and have a cup of tea, a Virgin Mary, some crisps. Tabasco helps to shit when all you really drink is beer, keeps you clear and weightless to designate jobs for otherwise co-workers. Someone else would set up the bar but I'd always clean up the shit from the leaks in the toilets because I was conscientious and staff tips had been abolished, or rather, requisitioned to fill the void of missing money that hadn't actually been missing when I cashed the till. Swiped the supervisor card through the PDQ machines and pressed the big Z. Downstairs in the big office chair the CCTV kept me knowing, phone call up and how's it going? Want to leave. I counted the takings three times. All fine. Boaz said the stock count was low. Money missing but the bosses were always dipping into the safe, so why couldn't we take a tenner as well? If you stood behind the hanging lights the cameras couldn't see you operate the tills. The whole situation had me counting pennies on the bar, having finished another shift early with staff not happy. They'd been trudging through checklists since emails were released indicating disciplinary measures and big concern. Wrong input. No offence. A young man playing harmonica on 140 set the tone of their discontent. A service industry soundtrack. I had a pint of porter. Didn't know where to place my feet over the fence. Allyn, finishing up that night, said live music was too faux old-school. I'd suggested we get a piano for the corner to play us out as we all quit together, ceremoniously, signing our names on some sheets of music to display a big fuck you on the toilet wall with the other eternal graffiti. But the company would never condone unnecessary expenditure. In the wake of the missing money, and apparently a lot more that had gone unaccounted for previously, I was sure that Allyn was right. 'I'm doing some tinkering for Pentangle,' he told me, leaning on the kettle. I was stacking coins in tiny towers and trying to ignore him. 'You know the Christmas village that the council's building in the park? Pentangle were asked to organise the bar. But there's a problem: they're worried that the temperature will fuck up the beer.'

'Too cold?'

One two three four one. One two three four two. One two three four three.

Twenties.

Allyn said, 'That's right. If it's below nine degrees chill haze can occur. They want to figure out a way to keep the beer warm.'

'Never heard someone say that before.'

The harmonica kept things low. Heart rates subdued. People wanted to hear what he was saying. Only talking in borderline whispers. The harmonica man's friends, a couple who sat across the table from him, looked warm, stroking their dog.

I envied them.

Allyn laughed. 'Which is why there's no specific way to do so. But you know those water-cooled jackets you put on casks in the summer? I've decided the function can be reversed if you replace the cooling element with a heater. Then circulate warm water over the casks. Make the Christmas village a boozy mess. Just how Christmas should be.'

One two three four six. One two three four. 'Six eighty in twenty pence pieces.'

'It works in theory,' said Allyn.

'Your heater?'

'Yeah,' said Allyn, sniffing his fingers. He'd just oiled his beard.

'Can you do it in time for Christmas?' I said. 'It's only a month away.'

I changed the coins into notes from the till, slipped them into an envelope, wrote the date and amount. Only forty-five quid. Lucy and Jon were whispering together in the corner by the crisps. They'd both inadvertently turned up wearing grey t-shirts and black jeans: an accidental anti-management uniform.

The Shapes of Dogs' Eyes

Walking up Clarence Road from Mare Street.

NARRATOR (INTERNAL) We flirted with cinema ideas, as though going on a real date, while sitting, drinking in The Cock Tavern, then decided not to watch anything, left and went towards the plastic crap of kitchen goods and feeble bin bags that line Narrow Way. Molly wants to check out the junk shop to see if they've got a picture frame she can put her poster of Venus in. She's been carrying it everywhere, ever since we went to Florence, just in case she needs the measurements. She misses Italy, and London is a grey job misery. A place to feel trapped in, now that bartending is about to delete me.

Shop Proprietor sleeps on an old deck chair, wakes up with a start.

NARRATOR (INTERNAL) I guess that's the shock of customers. There's never anyone here.

Shop proprietor stands up, peers outside, fingers lingering on the pavement sign, checking for anyone else.

NARRATOR (INTERNAL) It all makes me sad: windows of Buffy the Vampire Slayer box sets on VHS, the pawned porcelain of dead grandparents and prints of pastoral thunderstorms that never truly had the chance to break. And still no frame for Botticelli.

Outside, a bored construction worker pokes the belly of a garden spider as it clings to the centre of its web.

> **NARRATOR (INTERNAL)** If I wasn't amused I'd tell him to stop. Poor thing's waiting for a fly, not the end of a twig. What's the guy waiting for, anyway? A supply of oriental rugs to be unloaded from that lorry outside Pembury Circus, by the looks of things. Decorate the show homes of yet another addition to Hackney.

Molly leaves the shop.

> **MOLLY** Still no frame for Botticelli.

> **NARRATOR** You'll find one eventually.

The pair walk up Clarence Road.

> **MOLLY** We were cast in some Chekhov play today. It's called Three Sisters. I'm playing the youngest sister. What a surprise. The practitioner was like, "I want you to reach out and take whatever you want most in the world." And I was like, "What? I'm so over this." All I could think about were cashew nuts. And you. That's not acting.

A woman with a lurcher walks past. The lurcher, wearing a muzzle, starts to growl at a man smoking outside an electrical motor repair shop. The woman, ventriloquised, casts him a wary look.

> Text Message
> On the train. Why didn't we have
> sex this morning? I keep getting
> erections ;)

Since the money went missing they'd been giving me fewer shifts. When Boaz was on holiday I was managing Saturdays from eleven to six. It was a good two weeks. All the staff were relaxed, except for when Arthur came in. He'd ask for £300 from the safe and expect me to give him a grand, check X readings then throw our tea away and tell us to keep moving, keep moving. I was told that a manager needs to stand still. Boaz said, 'Dee used to stand still at the end of the bar and look around, check out the tables, see if food was waiting and who was coming in and going out.' This was the service scan: knowing who was where and what was working. The key points of service were reduced to two: hello and goodbye. It was in the training pack they gave you, the same one I'd been failing to take new staff through. When I started working there I arrived for my first shift at two in the afternoon. Dee was sitting on 250 with a Macbook. 'She was more of a dictator than you,' said Boaz. 'Do you know what I mean?'

I did, sort of.

When Boaz went on holiday we were all on the same side, stayed for drinks after closing every night, helped ourselves to the taps and crumbled hash into fags on the bar. When he returned he began to act strangely. Putting prices up. Not giving us free drinks on a Saturday night. Pressure from Arthur. Then the money went missing and things began to get worse. Morale was low. Boaz told me to be less friendly with the staff. But they were pissed off. He called me into his office. I knew it was about the email I'd sent. Boaz wasn't happy with me. He hadn't been for a week. Theft could not be proved, but neither could negligibility.

Boaz said, 'I'm a fair boss, aren't I? I help you out, and this is how you repay me?'

I said, 'No one is stealing.'

He said, 'Tills don't make mistakes.'

Boaz had the email up on the computer. It was an email I'd sent to Arthur. It was about the staff. How they all felt undervalued, mistreated, the victims of theft and that he was the perpetrator. The money didn't matter to us. There were talks of a bartenders' strike. I didn't read Arthur's reply. Boaz said, 'You shouldn't have gone behind my back.'

I said, 'We've been breaking sales records and this is a small loss. A loss on takings, not on stock. The cost would be a lot lower, less than half. The staff are pissed off.'

He said, 'Listen, a grand went missing after one of your shifts. You'll have to pay it yourself if it can't come out of their tips.'

I said, 'Then I quit.'

–

When I went back upstairs Ace was sitting on a chair by the window with Noodles. He said, 'I saw that guy you work with today, down in Hackney Central.'

'You mean Allyn?' I said, as I stroked Noodles' head.

He said, 'That's right. He was at the bus stop at the end of Clarence Road.'

'What did his eyes look like?'

'Tired.'

I gave Ace a free ginger beer and took a shot of Patron. Ace asked for more lime but I said, 'We should probably get out of here.'

–

As we walked along Church Street towards Clissold Park Ace said, 'He had a big plastic container on a sack truck.'

'Allyn?'

'Yeah.'

'I think Pentangle gave him their old fermentor,' I said. 'He makes his own beer, remember?'

Ace said, 'He asked me the time.'

–

'Sorry I couldn't help you,' I said. 'Did you get everything packed up?'

'Mostly,' said Ace, swinging his empty bottle of ginger beer and pulling Noodles who'd stopped to drink from a puddle. 'We found an old dog shit under the sofa. It was grey.'

I said, 'That explains the smell whenever I went to bed.'

Ace shook his head and said, 'I can't wait to get into the new place. How's your search going?'

I said, 'I'm on Gumtree every day. If you've got a real gun to kill that fox yet you could always use it on me.'

'I don't want to kill that fox. And you'll be fine, anyway. You don't need that place.'

'But I can't even get Jobseekers',' I said. 'London's going to delete me.'

'Have you thought about moving in with Molly?'

I shrugged. Somewhere far below me a dog barked. It was Noodles. I knelt down to stroke her. Ace said, 'She wants you to throw this for her.' He was holding a tennis ball.

I'd tried talking to The Shapes of Dogs' Eyes but The Shapes of Dogs' Eyes wanted to sit quietly in the corner, licking its paws and communicating on Tinder with emojis. I wanted to say that I understood it. That I'd do what I could to forget it. After Molly made me see that The Shapes of Dogs' Eyes didn't hear me things began moving in different directions.

The receptionist at the walk-in clinic gave me a form. I asked her, 'What's this?'

She said, 'It's an information sheet for another clinic, one in Shoreditch. It's for people without, um, addresses.'

I said, 'You mean homeless?'

She smiled. I sat down and texted Ace, who laughed.

I texted Theo and he sent sad face.

:(

I'd locked Nanna's bike up outside but I'd forgotten to lock it to something. It'd still be there when I left, but Max had got me worrying. All his cautionary diseases and Thai brothel stories had caused me to rove endlessly in the shower. Hands. Nuts. Body lipoma. Testes still in pain, a downer on a rare sunny day with nothing better to do than convince myself I had cancer, thanks to

London. Why else would my testicles hurt? Breathing the air is like smoking sixty cigarettes a day, apparently, and I almost did that already.

I had my last walk back to Stokey that morning. Ace and Nanna were at their new two-bed, El Hell was on Walthamstow Marsh, Instagramming Noodles and Hedwig. The house on Kyverdale Road was empty and I was alone. I went there to drop off my key and see if there was anything left behind worth taking. There were some stains on the carpet that wanted to stay, a partially-broken bike light on the stairs and some batteries. AAA. I left them, yawning. I'd been with Molly that morning. The first alarm went off at six thirty. That's pre-emptive. A warning. It got our brains working. A kind of work which wasn't dreaming. Her narrow curtains withheld us from outdoor-nothing so the cold London white of drizzle clouds or pre-sun mist made getting back to sleep too hard. Pooling blood in province limbs surreptitiously wrapped around our torsos. Molly sleeps close to the wall, even now. She'd catch cold from the patch of mould by the skirting. I'd take the side by the cupboard door, her arse pressed up against me, my back and elbows knocking the bedside table, wobbling pint-half-empty, or full, when she moved. Responsibilities when lying here included turning off the lamp at night and disengaging the morning alarm. Twisted, easily done. Movement woke us up enough to rub ourselves together, dream-eyed, groping sleepily, coming tight but quietly before words like good morning were freed. Sex only wants more sleep. The second alarm would deal with this. It went off at six forty-five and we ignored it and left it to fight for our attention until sometime around seven, while we were waking up, getting more energetic with our genitals and spending energy trying not to wake up the sleeping young professionals that surrounded us. That's when Molly, blinking, rolled over in nude good morning to reprimand me for continuously pressing snooze, as though it was a year ago and I'd just moved to London and had yet to find somewhere else to go during the daytime, which, then, was true.

So I'd stay underneath, vaguely conscious of her slipping into a new pair of knickers after showering, little feet stepping round condom landmines in search of black leggings, she disappearing for twenty minutes then returning, bag dangling, on the very edge of a world built for leaving. I'd wake up two hours later in an empty house with a note she'd left me. Something about looking too happy to be woken up. Today I made breakfast while she showered. That's tea and buttered toast. Crumbs from late-night housemates returning drunk and burning pizza. Then I left the house with her, walked to Mile End tube and said goodbye. Another day of acting. Another walk back into Hackney, and I was the only person walking towards Roman Road and its chicken bones cleaned up by bin bag foxes and boxes of rotting oranges and tomatoes left over from weekend markets.

Max met me at Homerton Hospital. He said, 'I heard it was more like eighty.'

I said, 'Hmm?'

He said, 'Eighty cigarettes a day, not sixty. But that's a respiratory thing, right? So it'd be lung cancer, not a tiny little lump on the side of your ball. Anyway, I thought the ultrasound technician said they were fine?'

'She said wait for the results. Anyway it's small. You can barely feel it.'

'That's what she – '

'Don't say it.'

There was a pause.

'Want me to check it again?' Max said.

I had wanted a third opinion, and Theo had already looked. A few days before he was on one knee in his living room, as if proposing to me with my own scrotum, when Max came in from the kitchen after hot plating a gram of cocaine to offer his opinion.

The 276 to Stoke Newington always stinks of piss and salt and vinegar crisp packets and all the sticky hands of school children in bright red blazers and stubby, disproportionate ties that remind me of not knowing what to do with my life. I'd only take the bus during rain. Smears on the window obscured refound, rusting goal posts and outdoor gym sets on Mabley Green that feared the salt of neglect. Smears made by the last great greasy head to lean against the glass, tired, sweating under the shadow memory of red intestinal towers watching over the Olympic Park, bobbing to the surface of a scum enveloped pond like a faded rubber fender tossed indifferently from a narrowboat. Or bus ride heads on necks that can't support them. Too sick to look out the window. Too sick inhaling moisture growing cultures on the seal. The armpits of a man behind me always smelled like a dusty library and almost made me jump off in Hackney Wick and impale my neck on sticks of steel rods stacked up in its rusting ex-industrial yards.

Max said, 'It's a good thing I came with you. Trust me, you'll feel better with someone here.' He was holding a plastic pot which I'd just pissed in. He was throwing the pot and he was catching the pot. He held the pot up to his mouth as though he was drinking a pot of beer. He said, 'Do you and Molly use protection? Have you pissed since this morning? You need at least an hour's worth of piss to make these people happy.'

I said, 'Yes.'

'Have you cheated?'

I said, 'No.'

Max looked at me.

I said, 'Fuck off.'

I'd walked through Victoria Park via Gun Maker's Wharf. When I reached the fountain I looked up and remembered The Shapes of Dogs' Eyes and how I was walking home to it for the last time and how I liked that feeling. Found it relaxing. Losing weight. Like I've only always been here a month and am still navigating. I crossed the wet grass away from Tower Hamlets and ran aground on the confused sand bar of Victoria Park Village. It was peppered heavily with buck shot dog shit litterers running round in all four canine jackets catching balls thrown by plastic arm extensions, tugging leads from the hands of their owners in a growl Theo had convinced me was poetry. I walked up Lauriston Road passing closed-up cafés and bars and queues of communal travelling humans hesitant to get on nightmare buses for dull appraisals in office buildings. I walked through the traffic lights onto Well Street, past the broken sign of The Albion where the terraced seclusion of Victoria Park Village transforms into brown brick stairwells and giant retail outlets for Burberry, Pringle and Aquascutum, whatever the hell that means, opposite the railway and the Tesco on Morning Lane, lollipop lady, bike path and primary school up the hill to St John at Hackney cemetery, where I first realised, walking home to Ace's sofa over a year ago, that London already knew it all and that I shouldn't bother.

But I did anyway.

By the time I reached Stoke Newington Common I was sweating. Am sweating. Will always be drenched in prickly London perspiration. And that was only at the bottom of Ace's road.

When we met at Homerton Hospital a few hours later Max said, 'You should've given them Molly's address. Haven't you moved in with her?'

I said, 'We're looking for a new place together.'

'You'll get a dog next,' said Max, laughing.

I looked at all the waiting humans. The baby crying. The ankles compressing. The lives spent undeciding in the heat. Max said, 'Check out that guy,' and pointed at a man standing at reception. It was Alex the Homeless Italian, blood all down his head, neck, grey shirt.

'Where're his sandals?' I said.

'What?'

He was only wearing socks.

I said, 'Boaz bought him a pair of sandals during the summer.'

'Ah.'

A pause.

'What does The Shapes of Dogs' Eyes think of that?'

'Think of what?' I said.

'Of you and Molly moving in together.'

'I wouldn't know,' I said. 'We haven't spoken in a while. As far as I know it was last seen in Clissold Park, rolling in its own shit.'

Max said, 'You think?'

I shrugged.

When I think about The Shapes of Dogs' Eyes and that time last Autumn when I first came to London, I think about Ace's road. At night, when it's illuminated by street lamps that speak through plane trees and colonies of confused four a.m. birds. When I stood in the Bermuda Triangle I saw my mother and her bob riding bicycles around London with her dogs. Except she was older and the dogs were blind. Their eyes were dull like shards of glass left in an ocean. They had no edges, just smooth circles around them. The ghosts of old possessions, lingering, waiting to be spread over the dry luminescence of Hackney and make midnight dogs prick their ears and stare nervously into the corners of rooms while the sticky feet of post-shift bartenders put dog bowls through glasswashers, even though they'd been told not to.

The receptionist looked flustered. She was trying to hand Alex the Homeless Italian the same form for the Shoreditch Clinic she'd given me, but he couldn't understand her. 'You need to go to A&E,' she kept repeating, pointing round the corner from her desk. She couldn't understand him either. He kept saying, 'Please,' and touching his forehead and checking the ragged flight case he'd brought in with him and wouldn't let go. She asked him, 'What's your address?' but he must have been drunk on blood loss because he kept shaking his head. I said, 'He doesn't have an address. And he doesn't really speak English. He can only ask for change.'

The receptionist looked at me, embarrassed. She said, 'Do you know him?'

I said, 'Um.'

She said, 'Are you a friend?'

I said, 'No, I kicked him out of the pub I used to work in.'

She nodded, slowly. It was a suspiciously slow kind of nod. Alex stood looking at me for a moment, swaying, then wandered off in another direction.

Max was scrutinising my urine sample. 'There are little bits floating around in your piss,' he said. 'That could be trouble.'

PUBLISHING THE UNDERGROUND

This book was published as part of Dead Ink's Publishing the Underground project and supported by Arts Council England. Publishing the Underground aims to bring readers closer to authors and enables them to support their work and bring them to publication.

Dead Ink and Harry Gallon would like to thank everybody who supported this project. Without your help the publication of this book would not have been possible. To thank you all for your dedication we have included your names in order to acknowedge the contribution that you made.

If you would like to support future Dead Ink titles and keep up to date with our authors then please stay in touch via our website.

WWW.DEADINKBOOKS.COM

Aaron Kneen
Akiho Schilz
Alan Clarkson
Alex Hoyes
Alison Layland
Amelia Collingwood
Andrew Wilkinson
Angelika Harris
Anna White
Anthony Finucane
Antony Scoulding
Becky Radcliffe
Ben Spiers
Bobby Gant
Calum McConnell
Charlie Handy
Christopher O'Brien
Claire Fuller
Daniel Coxon
Daniel Grant
Ella Beedham
Eric Waring
Frank Burton
Gerard McKeown
Helena Blakemore
Ian McMillan
Jack Flanagan
Jaimie Batchan
James Allen
Janet Gallon

Jayna Makwana
Jeanette Duncan
Jessica Badger
Jim Williams
Jonny Keyworth
Jordan Philips
Joshua Beever
Judith Heneghan
Katy Woodward
Kumar Kolar
Lidia De Petris
Lilli Bowers
Lorna Riley
Lydia Unsworth
Lynn Earnshaw
Malcolm Ramsay
Margaret McCormack
Michelle Ryles
Miss Leeming
Natalie Marshall
Neale Long
Nicholas Dwyer
Nick Bell
Nyle Connolly
Paul Banks
Peter Gallon
Poppy Steveni
Rebecca Reid
Rupert Evans Harding
Rupert van den Broek

Samuel Mildner
Simon Lohrenz
Simon Middleton
Sophie De Val
Stephanie Baird
Steve Dearden
Tom Gallon
Tom Preston
Tracey Connolly
Val Harvey
Valeria De Petris
Vicky Pointing

New Voices
2015

New Voices is Dead Ink's annual publication of new books from new authors. New Voices 2016 is...

The Shapes of Dogs' Eyes
by Harry Gallon
9780957698598

The Wave
by Lochlan Bloom
9780957698567

When Lights Are Bright
by Wes Brown
9780957698550

Available from deadinkbooks.com

LEARNING BY HEART

Family secrets never die...

Just when success seems set fair for Zeph's writer husband Nick, she discovers that he has been having an affair. Wounded and angry, she turns to her mother for support, only to discover that the past has also come back to haunt Cora, a person who always seemed utterly flawless. For now comes evidence of Cora's own long-ago relationship with a famous man, a man who so adored Zeph's mother that he never forgot her. Zeph is forced to see her own childhood in an entirely new light. Was her parents' happiness a sham, as hers and Nick's threatens to be?

LEARNING BY HEART

LEARNING BY HEART

by

Elizabeth McGregor

Magna Large Print Books
Long Preston, North Yorkshire,
BD23 4ND, England.

British Library Cataloguing in Publication Data.

McGregor, Elizabeth
    Learning by heart.

    A catalogue record of this book is
    available from the British Library

    ISBN   978-0-7505-2796-5

First published in Great Britain by Bantam 2006

Published in Large Print 2007 by arrangement with
Transworld Publishers Ltd.

Magna Large Print is an imprint of Library Magna Books Ltd.

Printed and bound in Great Britain by
T.J. (International) Ltd., Cornwall, PL28 8RW

All the characters in this book
are fictitious, and any resemblance
to actual persons, living or dead,
is purely coincidental.

non vo' che da tal nodo Amor mi scioglia

I do not wish Love to loose this knot
                    Petrarch: the Canzoniere

I warmed my hands before the fire of life
                    Walter Savage Landor

Sicily: Easter 1973

It was after midnight when they came out into the Via Roma. They could hear music in the street towards the cathedral, locked behind its roofs and steps, now cloudy in the darkness, only the vaguest shapes of buildings showing. She let the others go ahead, and waited on the corner of the piazza by the hotel, to see if the band would come towards her.

Her husband's friends were walking across the square, threading between the wooden trailers and the sports cars, over discarded flowers and candle stubs. She looked again up the dark street and saw that, while they had been in the restaurant, all the torches that had been burning high on the walls along the route of the procession had been extinguished. Where the crowds had stood, silent on each side of the road as the guilds of the churches went past, carrying lanterns or wreaths, there was no one now.

Cora stood in the closed doorway opposite the smaller church of the piazza and tipped back her head to gaze at the sky.

It was then that he stepped into the doorway next to her, put his hands on her waist

11

and kissed her.

Then she heard the band coming down the hill, playing loudly and fast. Pietro stepped back and she stood with her hands on his shoulders.

'They are celebrating,' he said.

And she thought, The beginning of the vigil until Easter Sunday. She looked at him, at his shadowy profile, as he lifted her hand, and turned it so that the palm faced upwards. He kissed it, then her wrist, and overwhelming desire, which felt like desperate thirst, suddenly astonished her. She hadn't felt it in years; perhaps she had never felt it like this – the racing, inarticulate need to have his mouth and hands on her. And somewhere in the back of her mind, the objective part, the part standing to one side and watching them in this darkened doorway – perhaps the part that Richard had made in her, of unemotional scrutiny – she heard the wife criticize the lover, the abandonment, the selfish carelessness of it all. Yet she still put her arms round his neck, this virtual stranger, and pressed her body to him.

At last, they stood back from each other. As guilty and dazed as greedy children, they began to smile.

'It's the end,' she murmured, meaning that it was the end of the Good Friday mourning, the end of the candles, flowers and torches, and the end of the crowds that had pressed hard down the narrow hill, and filled the balconies and rooftops, the steps of shops, public buildings and galleries, and pressed close to the doors of the convent. The crowds that had pressed all the way to the end of the town on its rocky outcrop, to the gates of the cemetery, where the wreaths and garlands multiplied; and the smell of the almond trees in bloom, ashy canopies in the shadows, was almost too sweet.

'It's the end,' she repeated, and tried to remember the look he had given her an hour ago.

'No,' he replied. 'It's not the end. It's the beginning.'

Sicily: Easter 2004

It was the warmest April that anyone could remember, so warm that the hills were green by the time the month began, and fruit was on the trees.

Some people in the hilltop town said that it was summer for Caviezel, so that he might enjoy the last weeks of his life as he had lived them.

But that was only the women: the men indulged no such fantasies. It was only Caviezel dying in that red-shuttered place, with its overgrown garden, its fading, iron-fenced balcony, and the upper rooms where he lay with the windows open, the air rushing through, even the evening chill. By all accounts, he was still himself: foolish, talkative, barefoot and grinning, joking with the nurse from Syracusa. Still turning his face to the light as if he were thinking of writing about it – as if he had not written enough – listening to the cathedral bells and comparing them with the lesser voices of the other churches, talking about a woman, even on the day he died.

Caviezel had seen the priest in the last few hours of his life. There had been no raised voices – impossible, now, for Caviezel's voice to be heard above a whisper, he who had sung so often and who could dazzle any company with his talk. Caviezel, who had become thin and stooped, who had been so upright and dark, no longer fired with the electricity that had made his hands move, his voice run breathlessly. Caviezel had become a grey-haired ghost in his dawn forays, whispering his poems to himself, sitting on the Casina Bianca, looking at the fountain, or at the coffee-shop bar, eating the almond kisses, refusing the syrupy chocolate he had once enjoyed.

They buried him as he had wished, according to the instructions he had written for them: a plain coffin, the cheapest they

14

could find, few prayers.

There was a shower of rain, unexpected, as the coffin came out of the cathedral. The mourners held back, for a moment, at the great copper doors and watched the clouds race over the rooftops. Caviezel had asked for something absurd, two white roses on top of the coffin, and as the bier halted, they fell to the ground. A murmur ran through the church, an intake of breath. A woman pressed her hand to her throat, and the words and breaths vanished, driven upward to the roof as the rainy breeze bore inwards. The roses fell down the steps, and the sparse congregation stared at this moment of Caviezel's, this line of his verse come to life: the falling of the flowers.

Afterwards, when she was clearing his rooms, his housekeeper Grazia found the book. It was held together with a plain rubber band. Once a fine leather, it had been rubbed pale red over the years. Grazia had held it on her hand, with the desk drawer wide in front of her. She was tempted to open it – very tempted.

She could see that there was more than just journal pages inside: the little book was stuffed with other papers, newsprint, from what she could guess, and thicker sheets, like the kind of cartridge paper he had used for drawing. She weighed it speculatively in her hand, and wondered if it was full of secrets,

15

like the man himself. And she thought suddenly that she might open it and find the names of people she knew, women, on the pages, that it might be thrilling for a moment, and devastating for ever afterwards.

So, ten days after he had died, and two days after the flowers had fallen onto the cathedral steps, Grazia sat down, took a large brown envelope from the desk and put the journal inside, with all the receipts and bills and magazines that were in the couple of drawers she emptied. She sealed it and addressed it to the lawyer, as Caviezel had asked her.

One

Nick thought, as he came through the door and heard her voice, that the flowers were too much. They were too showy, three dozen blue iris. They looked like an apology. He stopped inside the door to shrug off his coat, awkwardly holding the flowers in one hand. They had been almost giving them away – the flower stall by the station in Charing Cross Road had been closing. But all the same…

His wife Zeph came out of the kitchen, and stood in the light from the room half-

16

way down the hall. Joshua, their two-year-old son, trailed her like a shadow, one end of the comfort blanket stuffed into his mouth, the rest following him, a grey bridal train. 'You're late,' she said.

'I had to call in somewhere,' he told her. He walked forward, gave her the flowers and kissed her. He looked down at Joshua, then back at her. 'What is it?' he asked.

She didn't answer. She lowered her face to the flowers, then went back into the kitchen and opened a cupboard for a jug to put them in. He was puzzled by the set of her shoulders, her half-averted face. She said no more but, then, there had been so much silence in the past year. He turned his attention to his son and picked him up. 'Hey,' he said to the boy. 'You stink.'

Joshua crowed with delight and waved his arms. Nick realized he still had his keys, the script and the tickets in his hand, and put them carefully on the nearest work surface. Zeph glanced at them, at Joshua, then stood, a hand on her hip, leaning against the door to the garden.

'What time are you going tomorrow?' she asked.

'Early,' he said. 'Five, half past.'

'Is someone coming to collect you?'

He paused. 'Why would they?'

She raised an eyebrow.

'No one collects me,' he said, smiling. 'I'm

17

just the writer.'

'I thought someone might call and share their car,' she said.

He heard the edge in her voice, the chill. 'What car?' he asked. 'Who would share with me?'

She said nothing, just turned to the stove. He watched her back as she stirred the contents of a pan. 'It's just three days,' he said. 'Maybe four. Only Paris.'

He stood there for another few seconds, waiting for her to respond, and when she didn't he went upstairs, hoisting Joshua over his shoulder so that his son dangled down his back. It produced the usual fit of delighted screams.

Nick set the child down in his room, then went to run the bath. He came back and found Joshua struggling with his laces, then placing his shoes by the bed.

He looked at the line of figures that formed part of the complicated design on Joshua's floor, and at Joshua's bent head, the thick blond thatch. Joshua was like him: the broad forehead, the unusual combination of brown eyes, fair skin and hair. Sometimes Nick even saw his own past in his child, or his current preoccupations. Joshua's insistence on orderliness, in the way his books were stacked on the shelves, his clothes folded in a drawer, the almost obsessive precision were his. And only the other day he had seen

18

Joshua screwing a piece of paper into a ball and trying to bounce it on his knee. Now the memory brought a lump to his throat. He turned back to the bathroom, looked down at the swirling water. 'Hey, little guy,' he called. 'Get yourself in here.'

Joshua came to the door. 'Going to the pictures,' he said.

'Yes,' he told him. 'I'm going to help make a film. Only a few days. Be back soon.'

'See Harry's party.'

One of Joshua's playschool friends was having a birthday party at the weekend, the event so shrouded in mystery and excitement that Joshua had had sleepless nights over it.

'I'll take you there,' Nick promised. 'Don't you worry.'

'Saturday.'

'Saturday.' His heart turned over with regret. He would make it up to Joshua, he thought. Joshua, who didn't even know that he had been betrayed.

After supper, he packed his case upstairs, then went down. It was ten o'clock.

Zeph was watching television, a glass of wine balanced on her knee.

'So,' he said, sitting opposite her, 'suppose you tell me what's the matter?'

'Is anything?' she asked, her eyes on the screen.

'Come on,' he said.

'What?' Now she looked at him.

'That face,' he told her. 'That expression. Have I forgotten something?'

'No,' she said.

'At least give me a clue.'

She held his gaze. He got up, went over to her and put his hand on her arm. She recoiled, and he half-crouched to her level. He had been going to kiss her. He wanted more than that, too – he wanted to make love to her. Josh was asleep. He remembered the days when they took each other anywhere, even here, on the floor in front of the fire. Not so long ago.

She had tucked her arm into the depths of the chair, and sipped some wine.

'Zeph?'

'Why don't you go to bed?' she said. 'You've got an early start.'

'Come with me.'

'I'm watching this,' she said, and nodded at the television.

Puzzled, he considered her, then straightened up. 'Are you sulking?' he asked.

'What do you think I've got to sulk about?'

'My going to Paris.'

'No.'

'Or going anywhere, probably.'

She flashed him a look, took another sip, and stood up. 'I don't begrudge you going anywhere,' she murmured, and turned off the television. 'That was a story you concocted.'

'Excuse *me!* You made a big deal out of my going to Hay-on-Wye, and I was a fucking speaker, for Christ's sake.'

'Don't swear at me,' she said. She walked out to the kitchen.

He followed her. 'Well, you did,' he insisted.

He heard her sigh. 'I don't care where you go,' she said.

'Oh, is that so?' he retorted. 'You don't care – and that's why you create such a bloody atmosphere every time.'

His wife was washing the wine glass; slowly and methodically, she dried it with a tea-cloth, and placed it on the shelf, aligning it precisely with the others.

'All right,' he said. 'Come with me.'

'I'm going to my mother's,' she replied. She folded the tea-cloth and faced him, leaning against the draining-board.

Her answer took the wind out of his sails. He thought she had been angling for an invitation to the set, to Paris.

'Somerset?' he asked.

'Yes.'

'But you haven't been in months.'

'I rang Mum this afternoon. I'm going in the morning.'

'Well, ring her again and say you've changed your mind,' he said.

'Why?' she asked. 'To please you?'

He laughed in exasperation. 'No, to please

you, you silly bitch.'

She eyed him levelly. There was a long pause. 'Why do you do that?' she asked.

'Do what?'

'Use that kind of language to me.'

'Use that kind of language?' he repeated, astonished. 'What's this? The Campaign for Clean Speech? Who the hell have you come as tonight? Did I miss a scene change?'

'You ridicule me,' she said quietly.

'Well,' he replied, 'don't be ridiculous and I won't have to.' He spread his hands and grinned at her. 'Problem solved.'

'You think you're very funny.' It was a kind of weary admission to herself.

'But I *am* funny,' he objected, still grinning. 'It's one of the things they pay me for. Didn't you know?'

'But you're not funny,' she said tonelessly. 'You're facetious.'

He took a breath. 'OK,' he said. 'So I'm a not very funny bastard. OK. Slap me, huh? Slap me hard. Come to bed.'

She didn't reply.

'Or to Paris,' he said. 'Or both.' Still there was nothing.

'Look, Zeph,' he told her. 'It's fucking late.'

'Stop saying that. Josh copies you.'

'He does?'

'Yes.'

'He said that?'

'Yes.'

22

'When?'

'A couple of days ago.'

'He did?' Nick laughed. 'Cute guy.' The idea creased him up. 'What a cute guy.'

Zeph put a hand to her forehead. Once, she would have laughed too – in horror perhaps, but certainly at the absurdity of it. She wasn't laughing now. She wasn't even smiling. She was pressing her fingers to her eyes, then her mouth.

'Look,' he said, 'come to Paris – please. Or don't. Whatever you want. Come to bed or don't. But, Zeph, don't give me this routine. If I've done something, for God's sake spit it out, and if I haven't, well, goodnight. I'm sorry you're pissed off about whatever it is.' And he turned to go.

'I won't come to bed with you,' she said, very softly, at his back. 'I won't do that again.'

He thought he'd misheard her. He looked back. 'What?' he said.

'I'm not sleeping with you again,' she said.

He started to smile, thinking it was some kind of wind-up. She used to tease him quite a lot. They had shared an understanding about it, that she could wrong-foot him and make him almost lose his temper before he realized it was a joke. It had been quite a turn-on. She could do it superbly. But it hadn't happened for a long time now – like everything else that had come easily to them. They had lost it somewhere, the ease

23

of being together. Some time in the past year, or maybe some time since Josh was born – anyway, so recently that he could still believe it was how they really were and that, one day, he would wake up and find that they had rediscovered the old ease and humour, and that the awkwardness between them had been a dream.

'I'm not joking,' she said.

He walked back into the room and stared at her.

She held his gaze, then went to the bookcase and took out a sheet of newspaper that had been slipped between two paperbacks. She glanced at it, then gave it to him.

It was the gossip column from that morning's tabloid. There was a photograph of Nick and the actress in the film he was working on. They had been caught, mid-stumble, coming out of a club. His arm was round her waist. She was gazing up at him, her hand on his midriff.

He read the short article beneath it, 'Bella James Steadies New Scriptwriter's Nerves,' then something – his heart thumped grudgingly – about this being his first script, and how the lovely second daughter of dashing theatre impresario, now a star in her own right ... seen dining together...

When he looked up, Zeph's expression hadn't changed. It was as inscrutable, emotionless, as it had been all evening.

He felt short of breath, nauseous. He held out the page, angled towards her. 'It's just a picture,' he said.

She waited, gauging his reaction. 'When?'

'When what?'

'When was it taken?'

'I don't know,' he said. 'Maybe last month.'

'It was one of the nights you were late,' she said.

'It might have been,' he said. 'It doesn't matter.'

'An occasion that doesn't matter?'

'It was Patrick's birthday,' he said, remembering. 'I just got roped in.'

It didn't feel as he had thought it would. He had dreaded being found out. He had tried to imagine Zeph's reaction, and pushed the thought from his mind a hundred times. He would never be found out, he had reasoned. Bella would never say anything. He certainly wouldn't. It had been short-lived, and it was over.

Zeph went to the window and drew the curtain tighter, rearranging its folds, her back to him. Then she pulled the chair straight.

'Zeph,' he said, 'it's just a picture.'

'Oh, yes?' she murmured. She turned back to him.

'You know what the papers are like.'

'Actually,' she said, 'I don't. You didn't, either, until this film.'

'Well, what am I expected to do?' he

25

asked. 'I can't say no, can I?'

'You could invite me,' she said.

'It was just a drink, and it turned into a party on the spur of the moment,' he told her. 'It was nothing.'

She began to laugh. 'And you a writer!' she said. 'I'd have thought you could come up with better dialogue than that.' She shook her head.

A strange sense of injustice choked him. She should be crying. Wasn't that what wives did, when they suspected their husbands of infidelity? Why didn't she cry?

'I can't believe you could get so worked up about a photograph,' he said.

'So you're not having an affair with the...' Zeph glanced at the newspaper article, which he was still holding '...the lovely second daughter?'

'An affair?' he echoed. 'You'd believe this bloody journalist?'

She fixed him with a stare. 'No,' she said. 'I wouldn't.'

Relief washed through him. 'Good,' he said. 'It's just ... you know what they're like...'

She held out her hand in a gesture designed to stop him coming any closer to her. 'I wouldn't believe it,' she said, 'unless someone else had told me it was true.'

Such was the shock that he actually stopped breathing. 'What?'

'Unless someone else had told me,' she repeated.

He opened his arms helplessly. 'Who would tell you a thing like that?'

'Jess Turner.'

Nick's stomach dropped. They had known Jess Turner for several years. He was an actor, and had dated one of Zeph's girl-friends. They had made up foursomes for more than a year. 'I haven't seen Jess in months,' he said.

'Neither have I,' she replied. 'Until today.'

He watched her sit down again. She brought her legs underneath her and crossed her arms composedly over her chest. He thought that he saw a flicker of the pain she was holding in.

'Look,' he said, 'Jess...'

'He's in *Equatorial* at the Duke of York's,' she said.

'I know that.'

'And so is the *first* daughter of the dashing theatre impresario.'

There was a beat. Two.

'Of course she is,' Nick said dully.

Zeph looked at him as he sat down opposite her. He felt the drag of defeat, the exhaustion of the secret carried and revealed.

'I was going down St Martin's Lane,' she said, 'to the National. He came out of the theatre.'

Nick put his head into his hands.

'He came up to me and said he was sorry.' Nick said nothing. 'I asked him what he meant,' Zeph went on. 'I hadn't seen the article. He walked me across the road and bought me the paper.'

That fuckhead, Nick thought savagely, his hands obscuring his face from his wife.

'Everybody knew,' Zeph said. 'Everyone but me, apparently.'

A terrible prolonged silence descended. He dared not look up. He feared her implacability, the face he had seen when he first came through the door, more than anything else.

'Don't go to Somerset,' he said, into his hands.

'Why?' she asked.

'I won't go to Paris.'

'But you're needed there,' she said bitterly. 'And she'll be there.'

He dropped his hands. Zeph was getting out of her chair. He scrambled to his feet as she made to walk past him. He caught her arm. 'No, no,' he said. 'Zeph, please. Listen to me.'

'Let go,' she said.

He heard the tears, although she did not shed them. 'Zeph,' he said, 'I've been tried here, judge and jury. Don't pass sentence on me. Please.'

'You don't deny it's true.'

'No,' he responded finally. 'But Zeph ... it

wasn't like that.'

'Like what, exactly?'

'It wasn't ... it was just...' He dropped her arm. She made no move to leave.

'How long?' she asked.

'Not long.'

'A month? Two months?'

'I saw her half a dozen times.'

'Since just before Christmas?' she asked.

'Yes.'

'When you started work on this film.'

'Yes. Zeph–'

'You started an affair the first day you met her?' Zeph asked. 'Did you sleep with her the first day?'

'It doesn't matter,' he said.

'Where did you sleep with her?' she insisted, her voice rising.

He stared miserably at his feet. Suddenly she snatched the article from him and tore it in two. 'You bastard,' she said. 'She must be ten years younger than you. How the hell did you get her to want you?' She threw the pieces down in revulsion. 'What did you say?' she demanded. 'That your wife didn't understand you? Some cliché like that? That we really hadn't been getting on, maybe had never got on. Perhaps you told her I didn't love you.' She stared at him. 'Let me think,' she said. 'That we never had sex – that's a good one. It would have made her determined to give you what your wife wouldn't.'

She was staring at him intently. 'You did,' she murmured. 'That's what you told her.' She let out a gasp. 'Oh, Nick – you liar.'

'I didn't say exactly that,' he protested.

'Oh?' she said. 'Not *exactly* that? Well, what the hell, *exactly*, did you tell her?'

'Zeph–'

'Tell me!' she shouted. And she hit him. She bunched her fist and hit him in the chest. It was so unexpected that he fell backwards a couple of paces. 'Tell me,' she repeated. Her voice dropped low. 'Tell me, or I swear I'll kill you, Nick. Tell me.'

'All right,' he said. 'That's what I told her.'

'Oh, Jesus,' she whispered. She turned away from him and put her hands over her face. 'Oh,' she said, 'I can't believe this.'

'I know I'm to blame as much as you–'

She wheeled round, aghast. '*I*'m to blame?' she cried.

'No, no... I meant... Christ,' he muttered. 'I don't know what I mean. Just that we haven't been close for months – a year even, not since Josh, really...'

'And that justifies it, does it?' She was staring at him open-mouthed.

'No,' he said. 'It doesn't. I'm just trying to tell you. I've missed you, I–'

'So your answer was to take up with a stranger,' she said. And her façade crumbled. She started to cry.

'I didn't think it through like that. Darling, please don't cry. Don't cry.'

She doubled up as if he had struck her, hands folded over her stomach. He tried to put his arms round her in that awkward position, but she stumbled backwards, pushing him away. When she stood up he saw something of Joshua in her: the fragile, helpless look of terror that he wore sometimes when the world seemed too huge to handle.

'You did it,' she whispered, as if confirming it to herself. 'You really did. All day I've been hoping... I've been thinking it can't be right, it can't be true...'

He cursed himself. He should have denied it, he thought. Blamed Jess, the newspaper, anybody, rather than admit what he had done. 'I didn't think,' he mumbled. He sounded crass, shallow, stupid.

'You're damned right you didn't,' Zeph replied. She wiped her face with the back of her hand. When she spoke again her voice had hardened. 'But you'll have plenty of time to think now. In fact, you and your girlfriend can think it through together. You'll have all the time in the world.' She tried to push past him, but he stepped back to bar the doorway.

'What are you talking about?' he asked.

'I'm going down to my mother's, and I'm going to stay there,' she told him.

'But for how long?'

31

'You're quick to catch on, aren't you?' she said. 'For good, Nick.'

'You can't do that.'

'Oh?' she said. 'Well, hey, I'm doing it.'

'But Josh...'

'We'll work something out,' she said. 'You can squeeze in your visits between paying for hotel rooms. Although, actually, come to think of it, you won't need them now, will you? You can bring the deliciously pouting Miss James here and screw her in our bed.'

He grabbed her shoulders. 'Don't take Josh.'

'What do you expect me to do? Leave him with you and that bitch?'

'Don't take Josh,' he repeated, and meant it. 'I've seen other fathers at weekends, trying to find their wives who've gone off to God knows where with their kids.'

'You should have thought of that before,' she said furiously. 'But, oh, I forgot. No man thinks with his head when his dick's engaged.'

'Don't punish me with Joshua,' he said.

'Or what?' she demanded. 'What are you going to do about it? I'll take Joshua and I'll do as I like. That's the price you're paying, Nick.'

'I need him here,' he protested.

'Oh, really?' she said. 'Going to teach him that that's what daddies do, like you've taught him to swear?'

32

'You're not taking him away,' he said.

'Yes, I am,' she said. 'That's exactly what I'm doing.'

'Then I won't go to Paris.'

'Don't,' she said. 'It'll still happen.'

'I'll stay here,' he said. 'We'll talk this through.'

'Stay or go,' she said. 'Talk until you're blue in the face. Look what you've done to us! You bastard.'

Some fuse, some thread of caution, broke in his head. 'And you're a saint?' he said.

'What?'

'You're so wonderful, so caring, you never think of yourself,' he told her. 'You won't sleep with me, and when you do, it's under sufferance. You don't talk to me. You're always in a bad mood. I feel like I'm treading on eggshells. You belittle what I do. You haven't any patience. You talk down to me in front of Joshua.'

'I do not!'

'Yes, you do, Zeph. You always have. You've done it so much lately, it's like routine. Let's make fun of Daddy. What a bloody liability Daddy is. You know you do. You make me feel like a shit.'

Zeph hesitated. 'You *are* a shit,' she said.

'And now you can prove it,' he said. 'Now you can tell Cora and anyone else who'll listen to your catalogue of woe what a complete waste of space I am, and they'll all

33

agree with you, and I'll be Public Enemy Number One.'

'That's right,' she said grimly.

There was a second or two of complete silence.

'And you can believe it?' he asked.

A fraction of a second's pause. 'Of course I can. It's true.'

'But I take Josh to school, don't I? I pick him up most days, too, if I'm here.'

'Oh,' she said, 'congratu-fucking-lations. Once in a blue moon.'

'All right,' he said. 'Not as often as I should.'

'You sit up there in your ivory tower and act like you're the important one.'

'All right,' he said. 'All of that. I sit up there working when I could help you out maybe.'

'There's no "maybe" about it!' she exploded. 'I work part-time and I run this place full-time. And then you expect me to be a rampant nymphomaniac for your pleasure.'

'For our pleasure,' he said. 'Remember that? For *our* pleasure.'

She was silent. Gradually, her face softened. He saw something else in it: regret, sadness. His heart felt as if it had taken a single great beat of relief.

'Zeph,' he murmured.

'Yes, I remember,' she told him quietly. 'But once it's gone you can't get it back.'

34

'You can,' he protested, and tried to take her in his arms.

She pushed him away. 'No,' she told him, with finality. 'You can't, Nick.'

Two

Cora glanced at the sky as she came out of the house. The forecast had been for rain, but there was nothing yet, merely iron-dark clouds, sweeping in from the Quantock Hills. She stood in the yard of the farm-house, shrugging on her rain-jacket, so old that even the waxy finish was threadbare in places.

'Denny!' she called, narrowing her eyes to focus on the fields, where the dog might have strayed. 'Denny!'

The Labrador was elderly; he had gone out first thing that morning, and not come back, as he usually did, fifteen minutes later. Cora had opened the window and called him to no effect. Worried now, she had come out to find him.

The farmyard was in almost permanent shadow from the three sides of the house that surrounded it, but in a few paces the route through to the fields brought her to a slight slope thick with hawthorn. There was a gate in the hedge, and beyond that, two large horse-chestnut trees at either side of the path. In late spring, Cora would wake to see their vast banks of white candles; last year, they had been particularly abundant, and she had lain in bed for some time on May mornings, looking at them. She always woke at first light, and never drew the curtains. She had seen the trees as thick with snow as with leaves; seen them, too, bent against the westerly gales.

She gazed at them now, as she came through the gate, then lifted it to secure the latch. The timber had cracked and the gate had dropped; it was another job that needed doing. She hunched her shoulders automatically, and looked back at the house from her vantage-point.

Two things characterized her day more than any other. First, there was the view of the house below the chestnuts, a sanctuary whose roof was sunken in the centre, a peculiar warping of age above eighteenth-century walls. The overgrown lane and the road to Sherborne beyond it, invisible unless a car was passing down it. Beyond that, she could see field after field, tree after tree, and the distant grey-green rise of the Blackmoor Vale.

She turned away, and leaned against the gate.

Second, there was this view to the west of

the farm, now laid out before her; this was the passion that had kept her going in the last few years.

Nine thousand trees were planted beyond the gate. Dabinetts and Michelin, Yarlington Mill and Ellis Bitter. The Dabinetts were her favourite, prettier than the Michelins, by her reckoning. The cider-apple orchards occupied a slight rise in the ground, not high enough to be called a hill yet raised to avoid frost pockets and waterlogging. The field closest to her was almost one prolonged, round-headed mound, so soft was the contour and so gentle the falling-away of the land into the woods.

She walked forward, still calling Denny's name.

The trees were planted in rows far enough apart for several people to walk abreast between them. She set off now along the first, stopping every now and then to run her hands along the branches and feel the end of each with her fingers. She looked carefully at the tips for signs of winter infestation: for aphids' eggs, or spider. Sometimes, in the spring, she would overturn nest after nest of minute caterpillars, curled in a wad of sticky white wool. Their intent, slow-burning attack fascinated her: their fuses were primed to blow in slow motion and take the autumn crop from her.

After two hundred yards or so, she

stopped and called again. 'Denny!' She would be surprised if he had gone as far as the woods. Ten years ago, perhaps, but not now. Not when he knew that she would soon be putting the kettle on the stove.

They were a deserving couple, she thought, as she stood against the wind, a solitary figure in a great sweep of planting. A wry smile came to her face. A woman coming up to her sixty-fifth birthday, and a dog to his fourteenth. That made him almost a hundred in human terms. They were two old basket cases together.

She felt in the pocket of her coat for a headscarf. Inside her wellington boots, her feet were bare, and she had tucked her cord trousers into the tops. Like a child, she wriggled her toes inside the boots. Still functioning. No arthritis. Cora balanced on her heels, rocking backwards and forwards as if to reassure herself. She dreaded the onset of a telltale ache in her wrists and knees.

She lifted her face to the wind and closed her eyes. She could taste rain. She had become good at detecting it, or the slightest change in the weather, just by standing here. But perhaps there would be no storm, just this sweeping, dancing, grey-on-white sky.

She looked at her watch. Nine fifteen. She had to be in town, at the solicitor's, by eleven, and it was a good half-hour's drive.

Denny usually came with her, trundling through the crowds at his snail's pace, submitting to being tied up – and petted – outside while she did her errands. He would stand by the car if he realized she was going out, and refuse to leave the spot until she had ushered him on to the back seat. She frowned, and glanced back at the house.

As she was walking back, and came within sight briefly of the lane, she saw the post van. A few moments later, Jim Blake came to the fence, holding the mail in one hand. 'Blustery,' he called, as she got closer to him.

'Yes,' she said. 'Is there much for me?'

'A few bits and pieces,' he said.

She got to the gate and opened it. 'I can't find Denny,' she told him.

'Want me to go and look for him?'

'Goodness, no,' she said. 'He'll probably turn up any minute. Come inside and have some tea.'

They went into the hallway. Flagstoned and dark, it was full of boots and coats. Tied bundles of newspaper ready for recycling lay under the stairs. On the black dresser there was a tide of circulars, bills, receipts and magazines; notes, too, that she had made for herself and, just as quickly, forgotten. There was a bowl of clementines, almost desiccated with age, their skins shrunk to the texture of coloured, crinkled cardboard.

'Put it on there,' Cora said, indicating the dresser with a wave.

Jim looked at the mail in his hand. 'There's a little parcel,' he said.

'People are hounding me with all sorts of things,' she told him. 'I'm sick to death of the lot of them. Estate agents. The bank. I have to see the solicitor this morning. I've had to find the deeds...'

'This is from Italy,' he said.

She was half-way to the stove. Blake put the parcel on the long oak table, and sat down, rubbing his hands and glancing out of the window. 'Coming into leaf, are we,' he asked, 'down there?'

'Not yet,' she murmured. 'Soon.' She looked at the parcel.

'Did you know that the Sampsons are selling up?'

'No,' she said. 'You mean the house?'

'The whole place. There was an auction sign on the fence when I came by this morning.'

She shook her head. 'I haven't seen them in weeks.'

'Somebody told me they were going to their daughter's in Spain.'

She brought the teapot and cups to the table.

Blake watched as she poured the tea, and handed him a mug. She smiled at him. She had known him for years; known him as a round-faced boy of twelve coming up to help with harvest. Seen him married; seen him divorced. She worried about him from time to time; she wanted very much, with what she supposed was sheer nosiness, to ask if there was another woman at home for him now. He was the sort of man who needed a wife, someone waiting for him, filling his empty house, making it a home, giving him children. But Cora wasn't used to asking such questions and he was not the kind of man to volunteer information about himself. So she watched him as he drank her tea every other day, and went on wondering.

'You're not worrying too much, I hope,' he said, 'about all this. About the money.'

She raised her eyebrows.

'You'll not sell, like them?'

Her eyes strayed again to the parcel, but she made no move to open it, or even to bring it closer to her. 'I don't think I have a choice,' she told him.

'But you've had this place a long time.'

'Yes,' she said. 'Thirty years.'

And she looked long and hard now at the brown-paper package. There was a white label on the front, covered with a printed, flowing sepia script, a company name, bearing a large postage seal in one corner, and a line of stamps.

Blake followed her gaze and turned the parcel towards him with a fingertip. 'Syracusa, Sicily,' he said idly. 'Who do you know in Sicily?'

Thirty years.

She had been born in Sherborne. She was a local girl, who couldn't wait to get out of the county. It was the end of the fifties when a schoolfriend at Leweston had told her that her father was letting his house in Camden. She was asked to go, with another girl, and she had leaped at the chance. She remembered getting on to the train – the little railway station within sight of the abbey – one Saturday morning, her mother and father standing anxiously on the platform.

'You'll be careful?' her mother had said. 'You'll phone us tonight?'

'Yes,' she had replied, already far away in her head, too excited to care what they were thinking or whether they were worried.

'Listen to your mother,' her father had admonished, rather half-heartedly. He often feigned disapproval, and was terribly bad at it. She saw his kindliness. She had noticed, as she slammed the train door, that her mother had taken her father's hand surreptitiously, and tried to hide the gesture behind the folds of her skirt.

Cora had leaned out of the window. 'I will ring,' she had promised, 'and write.'

She had sat down, after a brief wave, to watch impatiently as the countryside went past: Temple Combe, where she had spent most of her teenage years helping in a riding stables; Buckhorn Weston, where her mother's friend had the rectory and an idyllic garden full of old English roses, and almost too full of scent. She watched as all the beautiful names blurred away – Abbas Combe, Fifehead Magdalen, Coppleridge – and the train gathered speed, great clouds of steam rushing by the windows, and they left behind Cranborne Chase and Salisbury, and wound on into ever more populated suburbs, until finally they were clanking and grinding into Waterloo.

Cora had let down the strap of the window, to the disapproval of two other women in the carriage, and had breathed in the dusty, oily smell of the capital. Nothing had ever seemed more sensual or exciting. She had put on the coat that her mother had given her the previous Christmas, then pulled down her leather suitcase from the rack, with a canvas bag that she suspected had survived the war and still smelt heavily of camphor.

Her friends had been waiting for her on the platform and, as soon as she descended the step, she saw them. They bundled her up, all talking at once. Now, when Cora looked at this picture in her mind, she thought they had been like a group of birds squabbling in a hedge, a flurry of wings and sound, a tight little knot of animation.

The next day, Jenny had introduced her to a friend of her father's.

'What does he do, Jenny?'

A toss of the head. Jenny was interested in City men – stockbrokers, bankers – the kind of man who could buy her a house like the one she had been brought up in – not art. 'He's something to do with books.'

'A publisher? A writer?'

'I've not the remotest idea.'

He was a literary agent. His name was Brian Bisley. He looked old, but Jenny told her he was in his early forties. He gave Cora her first job. He had a house by Camden Lock, filthy, five-storeys. The Lock was twenty-five years away from being fashionable, and when she opened the front door, already slightly ajar, to go in on the first morning she worked for him, a waft of stale cooking and staler manuscripts, with an even stronger stench of alcohol, greeted her.

At the party where they had been introduced the previous Friday, he had seemed fun, if a little drunk, full of scandalous stories about writers and actors. He was selling the film rights that week, he told her, in a well-known novel. The following month he was going to New York. He was a rich man – that, and a dozen other lies.

On that Monday morning, she heard him calling her name as she went through the

44

door. 'Cora?' he shouted. 'Is that Cora?'

'Yes.'

'Come on up,' he yelled.

She did so. The house felt cold, even though it was a beautiful morning. Not only cold, but damp. The door to the bathroom was open, half-way up the stairs: she glimpsed its mildewy interior, and clothes slung on the floor in a heap.

'I'm in here,' he shouted. She made her way to the front upper room of the house.

It had once been magnificent. In forty years, when she came to London again, she would return to it, stand in the square and look up at it in all its restored splendour; but now it was slowly decaying. She glanced up at a magnificent Edwardian plaster ceiling, and down again at the mess in the rest of the room. Brian Bisley was sitting in a chair by the window. He was dressed, as all gentlemen dressed then, in a three-piece suit. It must have started out very correct – he wore all the right accessories: the watch-chain across the waistcoat, the laced brogues, the pinstripe shirt with its separate starched collar, the cufflinks at the wrist – but, as if the effort of dressing had been too much, it looked all wrong on Bisley. The suit was shiny and flecked with cigarette ash, the shirt collar a little frayed, and the shoes were unpolished.

Next to him on a small table stood a pile

of papers, a black Bakelite telephone and an overflowing ashtray. That was the only small area of order in the place.

There was a row of government-stock filing cabinets on one wall. There was an open fireplace. There was a red carpet, stained brown in parts and faded almost to pink in others. And that was about the extent of what could be identified as something other than paper. Great drifts of letters, manuscripts, magazines and crumpled notes flooded every surface, and fell on to the floor.

Bisley was wiping his nose on a crumpled handkerchief; his eyes were reddened. 'Are you all right?' she asked.

'Did you see the kitchen?' he asked, by way of reply. 'Pass it on your travels?'

'No,' she told him. 'I came straight up.'

'It's on your right as you come in at the door,' he said. 'Be a love, and get me a couple of aspirins, will you?'

'All right,' she said.

'And a large Scotch.'

'Should you?' she asked. 'It's only half past nine.'

'Look, darling,' he said, 'do you want a job, or don't you?'

'Yes,' she replied. She had enough money to pay two months' rent, but no more. And, besides, fifties girls of good county stock were brought up to be grateful, not independent. Particularly if a man offered you something. A drink, a chair, a job, a lifetime of stultifying marriage.

'Well, that's the first thing you do every morning,' Bisley informed her. 'Stick the kettle on. That's for you. Open the Scotch. That's for me.' He winked. 'One of us has to be sober at teatime.'

He wasn't an unpleasant man; he wasn't aggressive. He was simply a drunk. How he remembered anything was a permanent source of astonishment to her; but he did. He didn't need the overflowing filing cabinets because every book he had ever sold was logged in his head, and his memory was miraculously accurate.

He would tell her the most intimate details about writers.

'He has a friend in Harlow whom his wife doesn't know about,' he explained one morning, when she had taken a phone call from someone who had been critical of an author's contract. The secret man in Harlow, as it turned out. 'He does my client's accounts, poor bloody sod,' Bisley had continued. 'Little thanks he gets for it. Our genius will go over to Harlow when he and Glenda have had a falling-out. Which they do every six weeks or so.'

'What do he and his wife fall out about?' she had asked.

'Bichon frisées,' he told her.

'What?'

'They're dogs. Snappy little beasts. They have four. Surrogate children. How he ever writes a line with them yapping round his heels I'll never know.'

She had thought, on that first morning, that she would try to last the week. Bisley had turned out to be rather more rackety than she had hoped. He was not the kind of man her parents would have liked her to know. She would get a week's wages, she had reasoned, then look for something else. In those days, it was easy to walk out of a job on Friday and be at work somewhere else on Monday morning. London was flooded with girls from the provinces, an inexhaustible supply, from Brighton, Esher or Woking. Nice girls flooding in from Saffron Walden, Chertsey and Bracknell, filling the trains to capacity. And London needed them to replace all of the typists and telephonists, clerks and shopgirls it consumed. She was one of those girls, leaving the little house in Camden at nine, taking the tube two stops, getting out near the corner shop, where she bought the daily pint of milk and a loaf of bread. Besides Scotch, toast kept Brian Bisley nourished.

But by that Friday, something had happened. For one thing, he had made her laugh twice with his outrageous gossip. And then there was Thursday. At four o'clock Bisley had rolled in from lunch and demanded to

48

know what she was doing.

'I'm tidying up,' she told him.

'What's that?' he demanded, pointing at the windowsill.

'It's a plant,' she said.

'Where'd you get it?'

'I bought it.'

'What the hell for?'

She blushed in confusion. 'It's pretty.'

'Jesus Christ!' he had exploded. 'What do you think this is, a fucking florist's?'

'It's just a plant,' she objected, colouring deeply now.

'I don't like flowers,' he said.

'But everybody likes flowers!'

He had slumped into his chair and eyed her for some time, shaking his head. Eventually, unable to bear his gaze, she had picked up her coat.

'What are you doing?'

'If you'd rather I wasn't here...'

He slapped his hands on to his knees. 'Put that down!' he bellowed. 'I pay you to stay until five thirty! It's now...' he made a great effort to look at his watch '...eleven minutes past four.'

'But there isn't anything for me to do.'

'Sit down,' he insisted.

Reluctantly, she did so, with the coat across her knees, and stared at the carpet.

'What are you doing here?' he demanded.

'Helping you,' she said. 'Typing. Answering the phone while you're out.'

He laughed to himself. 'You are not,' he said. 'You are here to further the cause of literature.'

She couldn't help smiling.

'Ah, I see I have caused you amusement,' he said. 'I'm so very pleased.'

Now she raised her eyes.

'Nevertheless,' he added, 'I am perfectly serious, though it may seem a great joke to you.' There was a pause. Bisley gave a great sigh, and pulled a wry face. 'Actually, I'll tell you a secret, dear girl,' he said. 'It *is* a joke. The vast majority of this,' he waved his hand over the sea of manuscripts, 'is complete rubbish. We all hope that we're going to get the next Rattigan, but the truth is, we bloody don't.' He gave another laboured sigh. 'When I was a teenager, I fell in love. Not with a woman. Not with a man. But with books.' He rubbed his eyes wearily. 'Real books. Do you ever read books?'

'Yes,' she lied.

'I mean literature.'

'Yes,' she repeated, flustered.

'Name one,' he said.

She said the first thing that came into her head. *'War and Peace.'*

Bisley laughed. 'You haven't read *War and Peace,'* he said. 'Nobody has. All right. Forget the ancestral greats for a moment. Name one book published in the last ten years that you have read.'

She stared at him.

'A book in the last year, then. One title.'

Her mind was a blank. Abruptly, he got up. He walked to the door, saying, 'Follow me,' without looking back.

They went upstairs. For a horrible moment she thought they were heading for Bisley's bedroom, but he opened a door on the landing and began to climb a smaller flight of stairs. There was another door at the top. He took a key from his pocket, and, fumbling, unlocked it. He looked back at her. 'Well, come on,' he said. And, as if reading her mind, 'I won't bloody molest you. I haven't the strength. Or the inclination.'

The attic, unlike the rest of the house, was clean and ordered. This was long before the age of loft conversions; even so, a series of skylights illuminated the space, which ran the entire length of the house. Bookshelves were arranged on one side, and a long table on the other beneath the windows. There were several small reading lights.

Bisley walked to a shelf, and took down a volume at random. 'How long have books been printed, rather than written by hand?' he asked.

'I don't know,' she said.

'Caxton?' he prompted.

'I'm sorry,' she said.

'What did they teach you at school, apart

from how to embroider a cushion cover?' he muttered. He took the book to the table and laid it down carefully. 'Come here,' he said. 'Look at this.' He smiled. 'This is my secret passion.'

The book he had opened was small and leatherbound. The cover looked soft: worn calfskin as pliable as silk. The flyleaves were patterned with a dull pink; the edges of the pages were gold leaf.

'Do you know who John Keats was?' Bisley asked.

'A poet?' she guessed, having trawled the dim recesses of her memory.

'A poet,' he confirmed. 'One whose name is writ in water.'

She gazed at him blankly.

'Never mind,' he said. 'This is his last volume. 1820.'

'It's very old,' she observed politely.

'I'm not showing you because it's old,' he said. He turned round, stumbling, and stared at the shelves, then went to another and selected a larger book. 'William Langland,' he said.

Cora felt the hot-behind-the-eyes embarrassment that had sometimes crippled her at school. She had thought she'd left it far behind; now it swamped her, filling her eyes with tears that Bisley didn't notice.

'What did William Langland write?' he demanded.'

'I don't know,' she murmured.

'*Piers the Plowman*,' he said. 'Don't you know your own heritage? Don't you care? This man tells you everything you need to know about the society he lived in. It's a satire. Surely you know what satire is.'

'Yes,' she said. 'Like sarcasm.'

He put the book down on the table. 'This is a volume of English poetry,' he said. He enunciated the words clearly and deliberately, pausing between each one. 'It starts at Langland and it ends with Auden.'

She looked down, afraid to let him see her face.

'You sit downstairs and imagine I've brought you here to tidy up and put bloody flowers in my face,' he said. 'I suppose you think about some Brylcreemed bloke who's going to shove his hand up your skirt – or the price of bloody shoes!'

'I certainly don't,' she retorted, stung.

'Well, if not, I don't know what you do think about, because you haven't a clue about writers.' He turned and looked at the room and gestured at the desk. 'They make these,' he said slowly, 'all those posturing gits that you've seen this week. All those queers on the phone. All the frigid, screwed-up little women you pass in the street who come up my stairs with their packages wrapped in brown paper, and all the loud-mouths, and the silent ones who can't speak for nerves. They're all writers. It doesn't matter what they sound like, what they look like. They look different and sound different, and you couldn't be paid to sit next to some of them on a bus. Some are so psychologically bereft that they'll nurture a grudge for decades. A few – just a few, mind you – are reasonably decent.'

He turned back and examined her face closely. She had never heard anyone talk like that. Certainly never heard anyone swear like that. She wasn't at all sure that she should listen. But she was listening.

'They all have one thing in common,' Bisley told her. 'They've sat down and produced something. They've scoured what passes for their soul. And some of what they write is mediocre. Some are convinced they're a literary genius when they couldn't write a coherent laundry list. And some of what they produce is so bad that the best thing to do with it is light a bloody big fire.' He scratched his neck. 'Of which the vast proportion is sent to plague *me*, God help me,' he muttered. 'But some of it...'

He looked for some point of contact, of understanding, in her expression. 'Sit,' he said. He went to another shelf, took down a thin volume and put it in front of her. 'Wordsworth,' he said.

'Oh,' she said. 'The Lakes.'

'Ah,' he answered, smiling. 'The great

Lakes poet. Correct. Thank God. You've read something.'

'I...' She paused, then opted for honesty. 'We had a holiday in Grasmere,' she said.

He slapped a hand theatrically to his forehead. 'And bought the tea-cloth with the daffodil rhyme on it?' he asked. 'Oh, Jesus.' A grin escaped him. He went to the first anthology, leafed through it and slammed it down in front of her. 'Walter Savage Landor,' he said. 'An author. A poet. Read it to me.'

She looked at the poem on the page, a four-line verse. 'I'm not very good at reading poetry,' she told him.

'I'm astonished,' he retorted drily. 'Read it.'

'"I strove with none, for none was worth my strife,"' she began.

'Speak up.'

'I strove with none, for none was worth my
  strife;
Nature I loved, and, next to Nature, Art;
I warmed my hands before the fire of life;
It sinks, and I am ready to depart.'

There was silence in the room. Distantly, very distantly, as if London had moved away a little, Cora heard the trains and the traffic, the passing of feet in the street below.

Bisley gazed at her for some seconds, as if registering her for the first time. 'You are rather a sweet girl,' he observed, without passion. 'Yes, rather a sweet girl. One rarely sees true innocence. And do you know? I believe that you are that. An innocent.'

Cora didn't know whether to take this as an insult or a compliment. 'I'm not a child,' she told him.

He nodded. 'No,' he agreed. 'But you are one of Nature's nice ones, I think.' He smiled. 'Poor little sheep,' he added. 'Why don't you go back to deepest Dorset before you're eaten up by all these bastards?'

She bridled a little at the implication that she was too weak to stand up to London. 'I'm perfectly fine,' she said. 'I want to stay here.'

He gazed at her for another second, then held out his arm. It was a gesture that told her to go through the door and back down-stairs. As she got up and walked over to him, he said, 'You'll come up here every day for an hour. You'll read these books.'

'All right,' she murmured. 'If you say so.' Privately, she wondered if he was slightly mad.

He let her walk down the flight of narrow stairs. When she paused at the bottom, he was looking down at her, stuffing the key into his waistcoat pocket and searching in the other for his cigarettes.

'We're going to warm your hands, Cora,' he muttered. 'If you insist upon being part

56

of this roaring bloody beast called society, we're going to expand that shrivelled brain of yours, if it kills us both in the process.'

On the tube home, she decided that Bisley was eccentric. She rather disapproved of his talk of warming her hands at the fire of life. All his talk of writing. Certainly she agreed with him that writers were a mixed and uncertain lot. She had seen the people who came to the house: scruffy or strange, or both. One this week had looked like a bank clerk, very proper, quiet and neat; and yet the first two chapters of his novel, which she had been obliged to retype, were absolutely obscene.

And look at Bisley.

When had he warmed his hands at the fire of life? He didn't have a family that she knew of. No one he ever mentioned, anyway. He didn't seem to have any close friends. He didn't write: he simply repackaged what other people wrote, and talked about it as if he'd breathed a spark into it. And that was his life. That was what she was supposed to warm her hands in front of, a life like that.

Bisley wouldn't know life if it jumped up and bit him, she thought, with all the vast experience of her nineteen years. She got up and waited for the tube doors to open.

After three months, she went home to Sherborne for the weekend. It was June, the first time she had been back, and some friends of her parents were having a party to celebrate their silver wedding. There was a blessing in the abbey, and tea afterwards in a marquee.

As she sat in the abbey, Cora realized how soothing it was, listening to the choir and the service, looking at the well-known faces. These people were polite and well meaning; they were kind. No one boasted; in fact, in the kind of society that Cora's parents moved in, boasting was considered one of the deadliest sins. Even if one was accomplished, it was terribly bad form to mention it.

She looked sideways at the profiles across the aisle. She wondered what they would make of Bisley, what they would say if they read some of what she typed for him. She could imagine her father frowning at the things she read in the attic room. She blushed beneath her fashionable hat, and clasped her hands in her lap.

Wilt thou go with me, sweet maid, say, maiden, wilt thou go with me? whispered John Clare, in Cora's mind. She had been reading him yesterday, while below Bisley cursed on the phone. *Through the valley depths of shade and night...*

The hymn began to play. She stood up

next to her parents and lowered her gaze to the book.

The lips that kissed whispering I knew not what of wild and sweet: Tennyson.

Come to the window, sweet is the night air! That week Bisley had made her read Matthew Arnold for a whole day. She felt she was being invaded by the lines, by their insistence. Sometimes she loathed their intensity. Sometimes – especially lately – she found them murmuring to her when she did not want to hear them. Matthew Arnold – oh, God, she hated that name! Bisley went on about him, like a dog growling over a toy.

'Do you know what he was, Cora?' he had asked. 'An educationalist. He wanted the spread of culture. Of culture, Cora!' He had lowered his face almost to hers, grinning. 'People like you, Cora. Ignoramuses like you.'

It was a joke. She knew that. But she couldn't get the wretched voice out of her mind. *Come to the window, sweet is the night air...*

'Do you know what he wanted most of all, Cora? "Something to snatch from dull oblivion". That's what he wanted.' And Bisley had prodded the open page. '"From dull oblivion". You know what he called men? Do you know how he described their lives? "Striving blindly, achieving nothing ... no one asks who or what they have been."' And he smiled at her, as if she were part of the human race that would vanish into nothing, having run about blindly all her life.

She glanced at her father. Was he one of Arnold and Bisley's blind men, she wondered. Was that how they would describe him? Her father saw her look and winked at her. Well, she thought, suddenly passionate, they were wrong. This flood of self-conscious feeling was wrong. The world turned on small, quiet loyalties and understandings. No one ever cured anything by standing on a mountaintop declaring their misery. She smiled back at her father, deliberately pushing away the thought of Bisley's poets; the hymn, of which she hadn't sung a word, came to an end.

After the service, out in the sun, the Abbey Green was packed. The colours of the summer clothes were almost too bright after the gloom inside.

As they stood in the sunlight, her mother touched her arm. 'That's the man I told you about,' she whispered, and pointed to a figure coming across the green.

When Cora had got home the night before, her parents had been recounting a story of how a stranger had come to their door and said he was buying the derelict buildings in the fields at the top of March-bank Row, a lane that ran parallel with the back of their long garden, and the fringe of trees at the bottom.

Marchbank Row was the narrowest of lanes, unsurfaced, and was rapidly deteriorating; hundreds of years ago it had formed a packhorse track that ran for miles above the valley, all the way from Petherton to Shaftesbury; now, other farms and properties had encroached on it and obliterated it in places, and it was only for a few hundred yards here and there that it remained, a narrow, muddy echo of its past.

'We told him we were glad someone was taking them on,' her mother had continued, referring to the broken-down buildings on the other side of Marchbank Row, behind the vastly overgrown hawthorn hedges. Since the previous owner had died, an old man in his nineties, the fields had run almost to ruin, thick with nettles and ragwort. 'But you'll never believe the most peculiar thing,' her mother said. 'He's going to live in them.'

'Live where?' Cora had asked, confused.

'In the sheds!'

Cora laughed. 'But there's no water,' she said, 'no heating or light, no electricity. The roofs are coming down.'

'Nevertheless,' her mother had replied, 'that's what he's going to do.'

'I give him two months,' her father said, over the top of his newspaper.

And now the same man was walking

towards them. Cora inspected him closely. He was tall and thin, with sandy hair. He was wearing work-clothes – painter's dungarees, a frayed shirt. He walked up to Cora's father and held out his hand; she saw her father hesitate for a second before he took it.

The man saw it too. 'I'm afraid I'm very dusty,' he said. 'I've been loading stone into the lorry.' He nodded down the hill, to where an open pick-up was parked. He glanced at Cora, but did not smile or introduce himself. 'I was wondering if you would object to my opening a gap in the hedge to take the deliveries through.'

'Deliveries?' Cora's mother asked.

'Well, the stone,' the man said, 'and timber. And there would be some machinery next week to dig drainage.'

'You're digging a drain?' Cora's father asked.

'Across the field to join the mains on New Drove.'

'I see,' her father observed.

'I hope not to cause too much disruption,' the man added. 'I don't want to disturb you.'

Cora was listening to his voice, which had a northern accent: Yorkshire, perhaps. 'Where are you from?' she asked.

Her father laughed. 'You must excuse my daughter,' he said. 'Since she's been working in London she's become very forthright.'

'I have not,' she objected.

'Oh, goodness,' her mother murmured. 'I never saw one person change so much.'

'But I've not changed at all!'

The man held out his hand to her. 'Richard Ward,' he said. 'I come from a place called Rannerdale, in Cumberland.'

'Army fellow, I hear,' said Cora's father.

'Not for some years now.'

'No, of course,' Cora's father said. Ward's tone had been almost curt. But, then, the war had been over for fourteen years, and plenty of men wanted to forget it.

Cora took his hand, and felt the smooth silicate of the stone on his skin. She guessed his age at forty. He had, she noticed, a scar – if that was what it was, a fine line – that ran round one side of his neck like a red thread.

His fingers closed round hers. He had lowered his head, and was looking at her, frowning a little.

'My name is Cora,' she told him.

Three

She spent that spring, the last spring of the 1950s, in London; March was unseasonably warm, warmer still in Bisley's attic at the top of the house, where the air barely circulated even though she opened all the skylights.

Day after day she carried on reading as a dogged duty, resisting everything she read, and particularly the siren calls to indulge her heart and get – as she put it to herself in what was probably her mother's whispered voice – *carried away*. Whenever Bisley asked her, she would tell him the facts about a poet; she used a biographical dictionary, and found that she could easily remember all kinds of things about the writers.

In one of his fits of pique, Bisley came close to banning the dictionary. 'You're like a bloody parrot,' he told her, after she had been reading Blake. He had sighed deeply. It had been a bad week for him. He had lost one of his authors to a rival – one of what he called the wide boys coming into London: younger men. Younger men who had some idea of business that didn't rely on an old boys' network. Younger men who refused to follow rules and poached clients. 'London's changing,' he had muttered, all week. He was used to doing business in the Wig and Pen, a gentleman's club, not in the pubs or on the streets.

But the usual mild insults no longer bothered Cora. She had begun to feel affection for him. One day she had unearthed a few photographs of Bisley from a box of dusty manuscripts, and she had seen a handsome version of his present self: a smiling, relaxed man, arm in arm with a woman whom, when she asked, he would not name.

Sometimes – very occasionally – he would be reading poetry himself when she got there in the morning, and he would recite to her, remembering whole passages by heart. It was at these rare moments that she saw someone other than the sarcastic, bombastic man he showed to the world.

She adjusted to his comments. He was spiky, he was rude, but, she realized, he was passionate about what he did and knew. And even if she couldn't share his enthusiasm, she respected it. Now she bore his brief, wordy rages with a kind of humour. They had ceased to embarrass her.

She had been standing in the downstairs room when he made the comment about her parroting Blake's biographical details. It had been a slow day. There was nothing much for her to do. The warmth made the place smell fustier than ever. Smoke almost choked her as the day wore on. She had brought the volume of Blake down and had been reading it at her tiny desk.

'He was an engraver by trade,' she had been saying.

'Tell me his dates.'

'1757 to 1827.'

He shaded his eyes. 'You said that without looking at the book.'

'I just remember things.'

'Remember one of his poems,' he said. 'And not "Tyger, Tyger".'

'I can't,' she admitted. 'Not right off.'

'Is it doing you any good at all, do you think?' he asked. 'All this?'

'I know more than I did,' she said.

He laughed. 'You're so very composed,' he said. In the silence that followed, she saw that he did not look well. He seemed exhausted.

'You're different,' he remarked suddenly. Automatically she put her hand to her hair. The night before, she had sat in front of the kitchen mirror while Jenny wound her thick blond hair round little bone-like spin curlers, winding them close to her head until her scalp ached all over. Cora had held the striped packet, doling them out. The stench of the perming lotion had filled the room, strong enough to strip paint. She had emerged looking exactly like Jenny: her natural wave had been replaced with rigid, tight curls, set in place with a thick lotion.

'I've done my hair,' she said.

'Hmm,' he said. 'I suppose you want to be like the rest of them, more's the pity.' He studied her. She had dressed carefully that day; like every girl in London, she wanted to look like Bridget Bardot, a tiny waist cinched with a broad white belt, and frilly petticoats under a gingham skirt. The starch in the skirt made her flesh itch, but it was worth it.

Bisley made his usual God-help-us sigh. Then, crossing his arms over his chest, he said, 'Tell me about the place you come from.'

'Sherborne?' she asked. 'It's just a town. A little town.'

'In Dorset?'

'Yes,' she said. 'There's a boarding-school ... an abbey.'

'Tell me about your parents.'

'They're very ordinary.'

'What does your father do?'

'He's a solicitor.'

'Of course he is,' Bisley murmured. He did not ask what her mother did. In those days, mothers of a certain class did nothing but worry whether they could afford to keep the cook and gardener. 'Tell me about your house.'

'It's in the country...'

'A big garden,' he said. 'Hybrid tea roses, fruit cages and a lawn.'

'Yes,' she said. She resented that he spoke as if in criticism.

'And you lived there until you came up to London, nowhere else.'

'Well ... yes.'

'And I bet nobody in Sherborne wears a skirt like that.'

She blushed. Her mother, when Cora had last seen her, had been wearing a smart day dress with a white collar. Somewhere back in the dim recesses of time Cora remembered wriggling into liberty bodices and Chilprufe knickers. At home, she still had a wardrobe of frilly party frocks, white gloves for church and Clark's sandals, all with a little flower pattern in the leather upper. She glanced down at the winklepicker shoes that pinched her toes, then gave Bisley a little smile.

'Oh, Cora,' he said resignedly. 'Go back and get married. Bring up a batch of similarly self-satisfied children.'

'I'm not self-satisfied,' she objected, without rancour. 'And I don't want to get married,' she added.

'What, never?'

'Not yet.'

'Why?'

She shrugged.

'You've never met a man,' he said.

'I don't particularly want to,' she replied. She didn't like the City boys that Jenny and the others seemed in awe of: she thought them boring and stuffy. And she was programmed, despite what she felt to be fair and liberal-minded, not to consider a working-class man.

Bisley gazed at her for some time. 'You don't want to be sullied with all the mess of it, do you, Cora?'

'It won't be a mess,' she said.

'Oh, God.' He half smiled to himself. 'The fire of life. The wild, abandoned passion of it.' He took a deep breath, which rattled in his throat, and coughed protractedly. Concerned for him, she waited until the bout was over.

'Anyway,' she said, 'I don't know why you're always telling me that I don't understand life, or people, or all these poets. I mean, it isn't as if you've ever married.'

He remained absolutely still, frowning. 'You think me a cold fish, do you?' he asked.

She tilted her chin defensively. 'You seem to dislike everybody,' she replied.

'And you think that, if I were married,' he said, 'that would be proof that I'd had some kind of real life?'

'You told me yourself that you fell in love with books, not men or women.'

Bisley went to the window and stood very still, looking out at the street. 'I was married when I was twenty-two to a very lovely woman,' he told her. 'She died four years later, and so did our daughter.' A note of venom came into his voice. 'Childbirth in the enlightened technological age.'

A great rush of shame flooded colour into Cora's face. 'Oh, I'm so sorry,' she whispered. She didn't know what to do. She stood up. Her natural urge was to put an arm round him to comfort him, yet she remained where she was. 'Can I get you anything?' she asked eventually.

'Yes,' he said. He seemed to shake off his ill-humour as he turned back to her. 'Fall in love and get your heart broken,' he told her. 'It's the only way you're ever going to understand what you've been reading.' He waved her away, telling her to go home. 'Do me that favour, Cora,' he said, as she went to the door. 'Get your heart torn to pieces. Just for me.'

She did as he had asked, although she hadn't planned it.

She met David Menzies at one of Jenny's parties. Her housemate organized them at every opportunity, especially at weekends. In fact, there had rarely been a free weekend all summer, and Cora had begun to tire of the endless fraught Saturdays preparing the house, usually in the company of Jenny's gaggle of girlfriends from the shop where she worked in Regent Street. It was an interior-design place, full of overpriced curtains and cushions in what Cora thought secretly were awful designs of black, white and scarlet, but it was very fashionable.

This, it seemed, required a staff of ten, all girls below twenty-five, who pandered to the fifty-something male owner, Terry Ray, placating and admiring him as if he were a performing poodle. Cora hated him. He tried hard to look younger than he was – much younger – and, in her eyes, succeeded only in making himself ridiculous. But that wasn't the reason for her dislike: he was cruel in his attitudes, nasty with the girls.

'Oh, he's a love,' Jenny would tell her. 'Such a giggle. Such a gossip.'

'I don't think so,' Cora had told her.

Jenny had turned wide eyes on her. 'How would you know?' she demanded. 'You're not exactly a social butterfly, are you?'

Cora looked at her friend speculatively: Jenny had changed lately, become less optimistic, more cynical. Once, she would never have made a sarcastic remark. Now, it was all she could do with any feeling. 'Just something about him,' she replied. 'Something strange.'

'But he's like another girlfriend,' Jenny said. 'Really, Cora, you are dim.'

Cora hadn't pursued the subject. But she had seen how Ray looked at Jenny and another of his staff, his narrow, possessive glances, his mean little face peering out from behind the primped façade. She had heard him criticize the girls to customers, then watch their bodies, their mannerisms, his eyes on their breasts and shoulders.

It was Terry Ray's birthday on the night that Cora met David Menzies. He came with other guests, on the periphery of Ray's group. They arrived at half past ten, two hours late, eight of them, mostly the worse for wear, straight from a restaurant. The house was already full, but Jenny was humiliated by Ray's late arrival. After all, the party was in his honour, and he came through the door in a tetchy, picky mood, making fun of the house, the road and the neighbours. Cora saw Jenny blush; afterwards, Ray cornered her, and Cora noticed his hand pinch Jenny's leg, hard, through the wide skirt and petticoats.

She had turned away, and found Menzies next to her, with an empty tumbler. 'Shall we save her?' he asked.

'Do you know him?' Cora asked.

'He's a customer,' Menzies replied.

'What do you sell to him?'

'Glass.'

'What kind?' she asked.

He didn't answer. He held out the tumbler. 'Could I have some water?'

'Not Scotch? We have plenty. Someone gave it to us. There's gin, too.'

'I don't drink much at these things,' he

told her.

'You must be the only person in London who doesn't.'

'Ah,' he mused. 'I'm a bit dull, then.'

'No,' she said. She took him into the kitchen, and ran the tap. 'Are you a friend of Terry's?' she asked, over her shoulder. Menzies was standing in the doorway.

'Not really,' he said.

'Do you know much about him?'

'No. Other than that he has another shop in Sussex somewhere. And an ex-wife.'

'He's divorced?'

'He has two children,' he said.

'And you,' she said. 'Are you married?'

'No,' he answered, smiling. 'Are you?'

Menzies was a sociable person. It sounded dreary, *sociable*, but it was this that she liked in him straight away, his lack of arrogance, his good humour. He had a friendly way with women: he put his arm round them a lot.

'He's not quite real, is he?' one of her housemates asked her one evening, after he had dropped her at home.

'What do you mean?'

'He's always the same. A bit unreal, if you ask me.'

'Yes,' said Cora, secretly pleased. She didn't want to waste her time crying in her bedroom over being treated badly, like this girl did.

73

'He's a bore,' Jenny opined.

David worked alone in a warehouse in east London. Cora went to it early one Saturday, following the directions he had given her. She passed a pub on the corner, a row of terraced houses, and the street ended abruptly in a high wall, with a few lock-up sheds lined up against it. The old dock warehouses were mostly boarded-up, some derelict, only the ground floor used by a strange variety of trades. Just up from David's workshop there was an Indian garment store; rack upon rack of saris were being wheeled into vans as she passed. She glanced in and saw the clothes on endless rails, bright bands of scarlet, purple and yellow in the gloom. The Indian men pushing them stopped to let her pass; they stopped talking, too, regarding her politely, watching her every move. Once she had passed them they began to speak again, in a rising and falling pitch, a soft catcall.

Other doors revealed anonymous brown cartons almost from floor to ceiling; a photographer's studio; a furniture-removals office; a shoe wholesaler. Then came several empty units. David's workshop was at the far end. As she knocked on his door she saw that the warehouses were six or seven storeys high, red-brick, weathered. Pulleys that had once hauled bales or packets to the upper floors hung from the second or third floors of some. They were rusted now, and

74

the big doors behind them decayed.

'Come in,' he called.

She stepped into the ashy darkness.

'You can leave the door open,' he said. 'Let some air through.'

She propped it with an empty iron crate; the breeze came in slow draughts from the river.

As her eyes grew accustomed to the light, she saw open racks down both walls; on one side there were small tumblers, perhaps twenty or thirty dozen. She saw that they seemed ordinary until you noticed the speck of colour, a drop of blue or red, in the base of each. The glass was thick, and speckled with air bubbles. She reached out a fingertip and touched the cool, smooth surface of one.

David walked forward.

'I've seen these somewhere,' she told him.

'Liberty's,' he said.

'In the window.'

'Yes, they have a display this week.'

She nodded at him.

He smiled. 'Look at the other things,' he said, 'while I close up the office.'

She crossed to the racks on the other side. These pieces were quite different: larger pieces, all unique. Red bowls with bright pink circles; glass sculptures, abstract, with frosted threads running the length of them. She recognized one as an outstretched hand with what looked like capillaries in the palm and fingertips. It made her shudder. Others were quite pretty: globes with flowers inside. But too big for her taste.

'Those are commissions,' he said. He had come back and was standing behind her.

'They're unusual,' she commented.

'You don't like them.'

'They...'

'Neither do I,' he said. 'The flowers are wanted by a bank. They have six in the foyer of their building in Cheapside. Six continents, a different flower for each one. Hibiscus ... rose...'

'Oh,' she said. 'I see.'

'A corporate motif,' he said, raising his eyes to heaven. 'It pays my rent.'

She laughed.

'The hand is my own design,' he said. 'I'll take it to the next exhibition.'

She said nothing. It was the one thing she really hadn't liked.

Menzies grinned. 'You can't hide what you're feeling, can you?' he said. He took her arm, easily and companionably. She didn't like to retract it, even though it was the wrong way round; her arm surely should have linked his.

'Where would you like to go?' he asked.

'For a walk,' she said.

'You're a cheap date,' he told her. 'We'll walk to Soho.'

She had never been there before. Some-body at a party had once referred to it as a 'den of vice', laughing, then gone on to talk about clubs elsewhere, more discreet and more daring: Soho had lost the titillating glamour of the thirties. 'Nobody runs between theatres in body-stockings any more,' he'd said. He was an older man, who sounded weary. 'Feathers and opaques and body-stockings,' he'd said. 'Those were the days.'

Neither had Cora ever been to an Italian restaurant, which was where David now took her. It was all green and purple paint. David ordered a jug of water, and a Cinzano for her. When the food came, she was mes-merized by it; she had never had spaghetti before, except the kind that came in tins.

'Do you eat here often?' she asked him.

'Someone told me it was just like the pasta in Venice,' he said. 'They were right.'

'You've been to Venice?' she asked.

'For six months,' he said. 'To learn the trade. In Murano.' And he talked for a while about Venice and its islands, about boarding the waterbuses for Murano, Torcello and Burano; about the colours of Burano, strung between a bright blue sky and the bright blue lagoon; about the fishing-boats with the great ferries passing between them as the evening light faded, and the mist came down over the water, and the isolation of the marsh-strewn approach to Torcello, and the cypresses forming green avenues on its neighbour, San Francesco del Deserto.

He talked and she listened. After twenty minutes or so he asked her where she had visited.

'I've never been out of England,' she admitted.

He reached across the table and took her hand. 'You've got to go to Italy and Greece,' he said. 'And Spain. Go to Spain. I'll take you there.' And he went on to explain how the trains were unbearable down into the heart of Andalucía, but the journey was worth it; and all the time she left his hand on hers, that brief, warm pressure; and she knew that she could never tell her parents she was going to Spain alone with a man and, because she could not lie to them, this meant that she would never get off the train in Andalucía, at some little station that David was intent on describing to her.

She had an overwhelming sense of life passing her by.

She thought of the family visits to Cornwall, and of pier concert parties, and of sitting on the windswept beach outside Padstow, shivering in her woollen swimsuit, and of her mother and father carrying tea-trays across the sands, the complicated orchestration of deck-chairs and parasols, sandwich tins and Thermoses. That was all she knew:

the road down to Cornwall's north coast in August. They hadn't even crossed the Channel to France. They had been nowhere at all. She felt again the irritated shame she had experienced with Bisley, and a hunger to sit facing the sea on Murano, in Bordeaux, or Tuscany.

'Where is Fréjus?' she asked abruptly.

'On the Côte d'Azur,' David said. 'Why?'

'Oh, someone I know went there on holiday,' she murmured. 'Someone at school. She said it was wonderful.'

'All of the Mediterranean is wonderful,' he said.

At last she looked through the plate-glass windows at the street.

There was a narrow frontage opposite, with navy blue curtains across the windows. A man stood in the doorway and spoke to people as they walked past. It was some minutes before she grasped that the photographs stuck haphazardly among the curtains were of naked women, and that the foyer where the man stood was the entrance to a strip show.

Her face must have dropped.

'I'm sorry,' David said, 'but the food here is good. And cheap. Best not to gaze at the scenery.' He smiled at her.

David didn't look across the road at all. He didn't seem interested. It was only she who stole curious glances. The bill came, and David counted his money. Cora saw a woman come out into that dingy foyer opposite, lean against the door and cadge a cigarette from the man, talking to him and laughing at what passers-by said to her. The woman – she seemed very young, maybe not even twenty, Cora's age – wore a sweater and a pencil skirt, not so very different from Cora's. When David got up to go to the lavatory, Cora saw a man come up to the woman; he stepped forward and she stepped back. Cora saw him put his hand almost casually between her legs. She saw his fingers move. The woman tipped back her head and held his gaze until, just as casually, she removed his hand and placed it on her hip. Cora caught her breath.

Then, there was an unspoken law for any girl: you could kiss a man, but never let him touch you below the waist. She had endured all the usual teenage fumblings, but the idea of taking any pleasure in it was terrifying. Nice girls didn't. Nice girls wouldn't let themselves be touched in the street either. The look on the woman's face, of calculated interest, had also astonished her. Cora felt like a voyeur, an embarrassed witness.

David came back, and Cora gathered up her bag and gloves. He helped her into her coat, and as they walked out, she looked in the opposite direction from the doorway and the photographs. But in her mind's eye all she saw was the moving fingers, and the way that the woman's legs had parted to accommodate them. Every image felt shameful.

'Shall we go to a club?' David asked, as they turned into Shaftesbury Avenue. 'A jazz club? Do you like jazz?'

'Oh, I...' She put her hand to her head.

'What's the matter?' he asked.

'Nothing, really.'

'Are you feeling all right?'

'Yes,' she said, 'but I think I'll make my way home.' She smiled at him. 'Thank you for the meal.'

'It's very early,' he told her. He seemed intrigued, puzzled.

'Yes. I have to be at work early,' she said.

'On a Sunday?'

'Yes,' she said. But she couldn't lie well. He took her hand. 'What is it?' he asked. 'Something I've said?'

'No,' she replied. The sensation of his hand against hers was electric.

'Come here,' he told her.

He walked her back towards the strip club and stood in another doorway, a closed shop, and she leaned against the door. When he kissed her, she trembled. She couldn't help it. All evening she had been battling a feeling of excitement, of schoolgirlish anticipation; and now, with her back pressed to the door and his hands on her shoulders, she wanted to drop through the ground, and

81

sink. The image of the man's fingers, and the more distant, slowly increasing voices of the books, the poets with their intimacies, swept her out of the street into a kind of sweet, rushing darkness.

He parted from her. 'Oh, Cora,' he murmured, amused.

'I must go home,' she said. 'I must catch the bus.'

She couldn't let him kiss her again. The thought went through her mind that if she kissed him again she would lose herself. She would lose her grip on everything she knew, everything that was comfortable. She felt she was in great danger, and she hated it yet wanted it at the same time.

'Come home with me,' David said.

'Oh, no,' she replied, and stepped out of his grasp, horrified.

He took her hand again, then walked her down Charing Cross Road to her bus stop, with the evening crowds going past them in laughing, noisy groups.

She felt old as they waited at the stop, as if she had lived a dry, uneventful life, and possessed a body that was featherlight, desiccated, mummified, wasted.

'May I see you next Saturday afternoon?' he asked.

It was the politeness of it.

She would never have said yes if he hadn't been so polite.

Four

In the end, it was easy for Zeph to get away. It took just one lie. Nick had followed her upstairs and watched as she got into bed. 'You're acting cold,' he had said. 'But that's all it is. An act.'

Zeph didn't want to waste words telling him that he had never been more wrong. She wanted to say that he would soon find out, and the bitter triumph of knowing that she meant what she said was on the tip of her tongue.

Nick stood at the end of the bed. 'I won't let you out of the door,' he had said.

Despite herself, she had almost smiled at his bravado.

'There you are, you see,' he went on. 'Just acting.'

'You look exactly like your father,' she had said. A deliberate jibe.

It had struck home. His widowed father had brought Nick to England when he came in pursuit of a job. Selfish and critical, smug to a fault, he had hardly been mourned when he had died five years before. Nick's face dropped. He walked to the window, to the closed curtains, then to the wooden box at the foot of the bed and sat down.

'I'm going in the morning, Nick,' she said.

'I won't let you,' he had murmured. 'You're not leaving.' Stubborn, sulky.

Contempt for him nudged the deadness she had felt all day. She had seen the fear cross his face when she had held out the newspaper cutting to him, and it was hard to say, but perhaps if she had seen shame in his face, she might have relented. Just might.

And now he wanted to fight his corner. She wondered at the man she had married, where he had gone. This wasn't him at all, this person sitting at the end of the bed.

'Please, Zeph,' he said quietly, 'Please.'

He irritated her, and that was why she could lie. 'All right,' she had said, in a sad voice. 'I won't go.'

He had glanced up, then got to his feet. 'You won't?'

'If you don't want me to.'

'Oh, Zeph,' he said. He almost ran to her, clasped his arms round her, tried to get her to sit up so that she could put her own round his waist. He had kissed her in desperate gratitude, and not noticed that she didn't kiss him back. 'I'll make it up to you,' he said. 'I promise – that's a real promise, Zeph. Cross my heart and hope to die.' And he demonstrated by running an index finger across his chest. 'Do you forgive me?' he asked.

'I didn't say that.'

'No,' he said. 'No. It'll take time, right? I know.' He looked earnestly into her face. 'I know I've done it all wrong, Zeph,' he continued. 'I look back on it and think, Was that me? Why did I do it?'

'You were very stupid,' she said.

'That's right,' he said. 'Stupid.'

She disengaged his arms. 'We'll talk about it when you come back,' she said. She pulled the sheet over herself.

'I love you,' he said, suitably contrite.

She didn't reply. She saw him glance at the other side of the bed, obviously wondering if he would be welcome. 'Do something for me,' she said.

'Anything.' She heard the relief in his voice.

'Sleep next door. Don't wake me when you go.'

He paused, unsure.

'Go,' she insisted. 'We'll sort this out when you get back.'

He held her gaze for a second longer. She could see that he believed her. 'I'm so sorry, Zeph,' he said. 'Do you believe me when I say I'll always be sorry?'

'Yes,' she said, and her heart lurched. *You will be sorry*, she thought.

He left at five. She heard him open the door and look in at her. She lay on her side and

85

willed him to go away.

As he went down the stairs, and out of the street door, she heard him whistling softly. His keys jangled as he spun them round his finger. He always did that in anticipation of travelling. He was happy – she could tell by the sound of the keys and the jaunty whistling. She stiffened as she turned on to her back and stared at the ceiling, arms crossed tightly over herself. She listened to the taxi draw away from the kerb.

An hour later she got up and packed two cases for herself and two for Joshua. Her son regarded her with interest from the breakfast table as she went in and out, picking up toys, taking washing from the tumble-dryer, folding everything neatly and compactly so that she had room for more. 'My toy,' Joshua observed, just once.

'We're going to see Grammy,' Zeph told him. 'See the horses at the end of the lane.' She glanced at him. 'Ride one, if you like. You want to learn to ride a horse, Joshua?'

He gazed back at her, slightly unfocused, thinking of something else. 'Harry party,' he murmured.

'Hey,' she said, smiling, 'how about your own horse, Joshua?'

He frowned at her. She picked him up and sat him down in front of the television. 'I'll just be a few more minutes,' she told him.

When she had cleared her clothes from the

wardrobe upstairs, she found that there was nothing else she wanted. She paused for a moment over the photographs on the bed-side tables: one of her and Nick at a formal dinner, one of their wedding day, one of her, Nick and Joshua on a beach. She stood by the last one and bit her lip. Then, methodically, she took the photo out of the frame and tore it carefully so that she had the picture of herself and Joshua, and left the image of Nick. She put it back into the frame and looked at it. She felt nothing. But she hoped to God that it would hurt him.

She didn't glance back at the house as she turned out of the street, the home they had scrimped and saved to buy, that they had renovated themselves. On the day that they had bought it, it was crumbling, neglected. They had put in the new kitchen and bath-room themselves. She had even learned to plaster walls. They had dug out the garden together, and made the patio. A memory nudged into her mind as she pulled out of the street: a mattress on the newly laid stones, in the pocket of ground where they were not overlooked by neighbours, and the sweet-chestnut tree in next door's garden hung over them. Sweet dark shade in the day. They had lain there naked, far too drunk for Nick to achieve anything, but he had set about loving her with determined fervour, the two of them laughing. Sweet,

sweet darkness. His tongue and hands on her. It seemed like another world, long ago.

She put her foot on the accelerator, trying to obliterate the memory.

It was almost one o'clock when she reached her mother's house. Coming down the lane, she felt nervous. She slowed the car, trying to avoid the potholes in the track. Everything looked the same: the trees still overhanging the lane, the roof of the house showing through, a red patch in the green. The blackthorn was just starting to blossom.

She had not been down since the end of last summer, and felt a little frisson of guilt that she had left it so long. At Christmas, she, Nick and Joshua had gone with friends to Scotland, guests at a house party. At the time it had seemed like too good an opportunity to miss, and it had been the first time that Zeph hadn't seen Cora over the festive season; but the sound of her voice on Christmas Day, far away, but purposefully bright and cheerful, had made Zeph feel low all holiday.

Whenever she rang her mother, Cora always said that she and the farm were fine, but Zeph knew she was lonely. Or, at least, that she felt alone. She knew it not because her mother complained of it but because Cora would talk at some length about going into town, or about someone she had met in a shop, or a conversation she had had with the factory about spraying the crop. These things seemed to preoccupy her to an exaggerated degree. It was aloneness, or loneliness, one of the two. Now, as she turned the last bend and saw the house and the yard, a greater pang of guilt touched her.

The yard was in as bad repair as the lane, she noticed. She stopped the car and leaned on the steering-wheel, frowning. Why did her mother never get anything repaired? If Zeph lived here, she would have had the lane and the yard resurfaced. There were plenty of farmers about with the right machinery, she reasoned. But her mother wouldn't ask for help, wouldn't trade something in return for the favour of the road repair. Cora liked to keep herself apart. Insanity, Zeph thought. Something she would have to talk to her mother about if she was going to live here.

She turned off the engine and rested her head briefly on the steering-wheel. She had worked herself into irritation because she was nervous of telling Cora what she had done.

'I never left your father's side,' she imagined she would be told.

And there would be an argument.

But her mother came from a different world. Her mother had never had to put up with the things she did, a husband who disappeared with his work for days, sometimes weeks, at a time.

She wished her father were here now. Richard would understand. He would take her side. He would say that she had done the right thing, and that Nick's behaviour was intolerable. She could imagine his voice, with its Cumbrian burr as he turned to his wife: 'Cora,' he would have said, 'this is unforgivable.'

Cora would gaze at her with that flat, unreadable expression; she would shake her head, and look down at her hands. She had reacted in this way since Zeph was a child, and Zeph had never been able to fathom what it meant. Her father would have strode across the room to hug her. He would have threatened to go up to London to find Nick. He would have clasped his daughter's hand until it ached and she was forced to withdraw it gently.

But she couldn't imagine that Cora would do any of those things.

Zeph sat in the car trembling, wishing her father back more intensely than she had done for years.

When at last she got out, she realized that the house was empty. She tried the front door. It was locked. She walked round to the barn and saw that Cora's car was gone. She took out her mobile phone and dialled her mother's number. To her frustration, she heard the mobile ringing somewhere inside the farmhouse.

She stood on the doorstep and tried to imagine what would make her mother forget a phone call she had made only twenty-four hours ago. She tapped her hand against her thigh in confusion. What time had she said she would be here? Lunchtime? Early afternoon? Suddenly, she couldn't remember. Perhaps she had said early afternoon. Two, or half past.

She went back to the car and released Joshua from his safety seat. He wriggled out and ran for the door.

'Grammy isn't in,' she called after him.

He swerved, arms held out in imitation of an aircraft. Two fat pigeons on the path that led to the side of the house launched themselves upward in protest. Joshua roared after them, yelling at the top of his voice.

'Don't go into the fields,' she called.

He glanced back at her.

'Don't,' she repeated.

His pace slowed. He tripped a couple of times over his feet, and began to kick at the dust.

Resignedly, she trotted after him and took his hand. 'Come on, then,' she said. 'We'll just go to the top of the hill.'

She walked through the orchard trees. She had been recruited every year, from the moment she could walk, to harvest the seemingly endless tons of apples. It had been her job in particular to crawl under the low-sweeping branches and attach the thick canvas bands to each trunk, so that the crop could be shaken down. No need to take care with cider apples: bruising was immaterial. Just hours later they would be crushed in the factory forty miles away.

The smell of the trees, almost sickly sweet, the pungency of the ripe and overripe fruit, the sticky residue of juice on her hands and clothes had characterized those weeks at the end of each summer. Sometimes, in bed at night, she could not get the smell out of her mouth and nose; it had permeated the bedclothes and her own skin, no matter how hard she scrubbed her fingers and arms before she went to bed. Today, as she took the left-hand path and climbed the incline towards the woods, she looked appraisingly at the bare rows below her.

Joshua stood uncertainly by the stile at the entrance to the woods. Reaching him, Zeph helped him over. The ground under the trees was damp, the first blades of bluebells and wild garlic showing through. The trees looked spindly, almost cold: between them, Zeph could see the other side of the low valley. If they climbed to the top, they would see the Sherborne road, the way they had come, the route back to Nick.

It's the past, she told herself severely.

But he was in her mind anyway.

She watched Joshua run down the path. All morning she had avoided looking at her son because he reminded her of his father; she stopped now, out of breath, and watched him ahead of her. It was a terrible admission, that she could not look at Josh because of what Nick had done. She put her hand to her face. No, that wasn't right. The truth was that she couldn't bear to look at Nick because she was angry and vengeful. Because she would prefer not to imagine him on the planet, prefer not to have met him, not to have any memories.

Yesterday she had wanted to hit him. If Nick had walked through the door during the afternoon she would have done so, whether Joshua was in the room or not. She had wanted to draw blood. It wasn't until later, as she made something for Joshua to eat, that it had occurred to her that this might be wrong.

What am I doing? she had thought, while she was laying Joshua's place at the table. *What am I thinking?* The realization that she had spent three or four hours waiting for Nick to come back so that she could attack him was like being hit herself or, worse, violated.

Suddenly she felt so sick that she had to sit down. She was all churned up inside. There was a knot in her stomach, constantly tightening and releasing, tightening and releasing. And violation wasn't too strong a word. The person she had been before had been degraded; everything they had together was degraded.

Joshua had come in and stood at her side. He had been in the hallway, watching her through the open door, and, although she had known he was there, she hadn't spoken to him.

'Mummy,' he said, coming to the side of her chair.

'I've got a poorly head,' she told him, the best explanation she could come up with that he might accept.

Gently, her son had put his hands on her temples.

Now he turned back and looked at her.

He was so like Nick.

Please don't let me hate my son, she thought.

This is Joshua, not Nick.

It's not Nick.

And that was when the first acute sensation of pain caught her. In a rush, she remembered the first weeks in the house, and the time before that, a holiday in Greece, making love behind closed shutters in the vast, blanketing heat of the afternoon; Nick's soft American voice, which had attracted her the first time he had talked to her, that same voice whispering. She remembered how astonished she had been the first time they had slept together: he was so unlike other men she had known. He talked – about them, about the future, about what he felt. And he said wonderful things. Things so romantic that she might have been tempted to think he was joking, but a glimpse of his face confirmed that he was not.

One morning, as she had come back into the bedroom from the bathroom – they had been living together for maybe a month – he had opened his eyes and said, 'You are so stunningly beautiful.'

She knew that she wasn't beautiful, or anywhere near it, but she could see that he believed what he had said, and it wasn't a line, or an attempt to get her back into bed. He loved her, and found her beautiful. That memory made her gasp, as if she had sustained a physical blow.

Her little boy was pointing at something between the trees. She put her hand to her mouth, fisted it against her lips, as if to hold the sound inside her. She mustn't cry. It would upset Joshua. She would not cry. All those things were past, gone.

She began to walk faster, and, as she got closer, she saw that Joshua was bewildered.

'What is it?' she asked.

He looked over his shoulder.

She wondered if he had seen a dead bird. The first time he had seen one, killed by a neighbour's cat, he had been fascinated, prodding it and turning it over, watching intently while it was buried. But then he had become fixated by death, watching herself and Nick. The next time they had crossed the park on the way to play-school, there had been feathers on the path and he had cried so hysterically that she had had to take him home.

'What is it?' she repeated, dreading another bird and the scenes that would follow.

She looked to where Joshua was pointing.

The dog – Cora's dog – was lying on his side in the undergrowth. He looked as if he was asleep, the black flank showing between the bushes, the curve of his shoulder.

'Denny,' she said. 'Denny?'

La Rosa

You remember there is a road that runs south from Syracusa, along the side of the sea? My father has bought a second house there on the coast. It is a little way from where we stayed, a little way from the first house, but it looks east. My father is building it bigger; it is for tourists to stay.

The local people think that no one will want to come to where there is no beach, that they will only want to stay at Taormina or Cefalu, and that south of Syracusa there is nothing for them. But he says that people will want the quiet; they will want the view of the sea. And he says all this without knowing what the place gave to us.

I have been to the second house and it is not the same as the first. For one thing, it is much bigger, and he is making it bigger still. I have spent the last month there with the builders, with the carpenter my father brought from Enna, and the men who have made the new foundations and the new walling to the land. You told me that Richard had made a new house on land that no one wanted, and I think of him as I do the same job. And what else I think I dare not say to you, dare not repeat. I have told you too often.

There is a room in the new house that runs almost the entire length of the ground floor, and the workmen are making large windows there, almost all windows, so that you may sit in the sun for hours at a time and watch the water.

I am waiting for you, Cora, as you asked me to. Six weeks have passed. It is like six centuries.

I am waiting, and I think of that terrible day when Richard came here to reclaim you, and I think of the expression on your face as you told me that you would return with him to England. But I believe your promise to me. I believe that you will come back to me soon, very soon. Before this year is over you will be here, in the cottage near Syracusa, and all the waiting will be over.

Remember our place, darling. Keep it in your mind. Think of me there. I shall try to be patient, though every day is long. It is our house, that cottage, our place, with its single room and the broken-tiled floor. I have thought of you so many times sitting beside me there, lying in the bed, and I cannot put down on the page what my heart carries. I feel it too much, you would say.

You will be surprised to know that I have planted the rose. It is so funny to see an English rose in this garden. It will flourish in the spring but I am afraid that it will be burned to ashes in the summer. I have planted it, nevertheless, in the shadiest part. I have asked the woman on the farm if, when her sons are passing, they might water it. She nodded, but she thinks I am crazy. I can almost hear her sons laughing. 'To water a rose? A rose? He thinks we have time to water a rose?'

'Roses that sicken...' I have been reading as you taught me. It is not easy to find English poetry here. But I have the books, and I have been reading them all. I have read John Gray. Why is he not more known? I have found 'the roses, every one, were red...'

It is a poem just like us. It is a poem about this country. Did he ever see this country? 'The sky too blue, too delicate: too soft the air, too green the sea...' The sea is sometimes green when a storm is coming, or in the morning, occasionally, where it touches the land, green under the bridge to Ortigia. I stand on the bridge and think, She put her hand on this rail. I put my hand over her hand. Do you ever think such things, Cora? Will you ever think of the rose trying to grow by our house on the road that runs south from Syracusa?

The roses are not like Gray's. They are white. There were no red roses, though I asked for them. Will you think of them, perhaps think of me planting them? They say I am possessed by madness.

I walked six miles with the rose to plant it.

So perhaps they are right, after all.

Five

Cora stood in the doorway of the abbey, waiting to catch her breath. For the past five minutes, no one had passed her in the shadowy entrance, although she had made a great show, when she had first stepped inside, of reading the announcements of services, flower rotas and lectures that were pinned to the notice-board, in case anyone should come. She didn't want people to think that she was there with no purpose. She didn't want people to see her as an old woman who needed a seat, an arm, any kind of help.

So she stood by the great door and gazed at the times and places of events that she had no intention of attending, waiting for her heartbeat to slow, and the narrowing, choking sensation in her throat to subside.

She had been married in this ancient place, where the first kings of Wessex were buried; so lovely with its subtle, honey-coloured walls and arches, and great soaring roof. She had stepped over this threshold forty-five years ago on Richard's arm, at midday on a beautiful September morning, over this very stone where she was standing now. She had been a girl of nineteen with a husband of forty.

Suddenly a man strode in from the abbey green, tutting to himself, complaining at the cold. 'Oh,' he said, brought up short when he saw her. 'Hello.'

He was in his sixties, she guessed. 'Good morning,' she replied.

'It's a blowy one,' he remarked.

'Yes, it is,' she agreed. 'Quite cool.'

He turned down his collar, and she saw that he was the priest. 'Anything I can help you with?' he asked.

'Oh ... no.'

'Just sheltering?'

'Yes. Just for a minute.'

He looked into her face. 'Would you like a cup of tea?' he asked.

She heard the concern in his voice. 'No, thank you,' she replied. 'I must get on.' She gathered up her bag and gloves from the floor. When she had come in, she had been blinded for a while; she had thought she might faint. It had been sheer panic, but it had passed. 'I must get on,' she repeated.

She thought that perhaps he was watching her progress as she stepped out and started across the green, but she didn't look back. She walked down towards the car park behind Long Street, purposely looking into the shop windows, taking more time than usual. It wasn't until she reached the car that she realized she had forgotten to buy the food she wanted, and the flowers for the table in the hallway. She had been going to get a few daffodils for there and for Zeph's room to brighten the place up. She looked back across the car park, and it seemed a marathon, all the way back along the street and up the hill to the grocer and the florist, negotiating the cobbled lane and the uneven kerbstones.

For the second time that morning, she wanted to cry.

The first had been with her solicitor. The tears had sprung quickly as she had gazed down at the papers on the desk in front of her.

The solicitor had got to her feet immediately. 'Oh, Mrs Ward,' she had said, 'there's a solution, I'm sure.' She had given Cora a tissue.

She was a nice girl, although Cora had never quite got used to Alan Rendall retiring and this pretty, black-suited professional taking his place.

'Won't you reconsider selling the land alone?' Miss Miles asked now. 'It would keep the wolf from the door.'

'They would need to have access through the lane for their machinery,' Cora said. She wiped her eyes.

'You might build a separate access.'

'I'd have strangers coming up and down the lane at all hours. There would be no privacy.'

'But you would keep the farmhouse,' Elizabeth Miles said. 'Or you could reconsider selling the barn, perhaps, and keep the business.'

Cora put her hand to her head. She felt an overwhelmingly loyalty to Richard. She must keep together the farm and the land, everything for which he had striven so hard. But all she heard everywhere was 'diversification'. Divide and rule. Or, more accurately, divide and survive.

All around her, farmers were selling off or letting their buildings and taking up sidelines: craft workshops, bed-and-breakfast, holiday cottages. But she couldn't bear the thought of a continual stream of outsiders coming through the house.

'Did you get a valuation for the barn?'

'Yes,' Cora said.

'And that would be ... how much?'

'Fifty thousand,' Cora said. 'It's the oldest part, older than the house.'

'Fifty thousand is a great deal of money. It would solve your current problems.'

Cora had looked out of the window. Fifty thousand pounds would restock the orchards, replant the trees: the majority were coming to the end of their thirty-year life. It would pay for transport for the foreseeable future. It would renew the irrigation lines and pumps, and she could repair the roof of the house, which was long overdue. But it wouldn't pay for anything to be done inside – the boiler, the bathroom, the kitchen. It wouldn't pay for the lane to be resurfaced or for a new generator. She would be living in a house that was falling down around her, and forced to witness the barn's conversion into some ghastly executive home.

And there would be people. Builders, contractors, then the family who moved into the barn. People under her nose, peering into the yard.

And she didn't want people.

'I don't know what to do,' she murmured. And then, 'I must replant the trees.'

'Or there is the other option we discussed,' Miss Miles said. 'To sell everything, land, farmhouse, barn.'

'I can't,' Cora said, recovering a little. 'The terms of the will.'

Richard's will lay among the documents in front of them. She could look at it more calmly now: the first time, it had been terrible – she hadn't seen it since the funeral.

Richard had made it clear that the land and the house passed to her as an indivisible unit. When she died, it was to go to Zeph – *to Persephone, my darling daughter and only child* – and to her children. It wasn't to be parcelled out, cut into pieces.

'I'm sure that Mr Ward would have understood,' Miss Miles said. 'There would certainly be a legal way out.'

'From the terms of the will?'

'Yes. Would you like me to put it in writing to you?'

'I'm not sure...'

'Just to set out the various options, and how they might be achieved.'

'All right,' Cora agreed.

Miss Miles had given her a patient smile. 'I'm afraid that simply doing nothing is no longer among the options,' she had said quietly.

Richard had bought the farm in the spring of 1975. London retreated, with everything she had known and done there. For that, at least, she was glad.

It was the reason she had come home: to obscure London. To obliterate it. To erase it from her life.

She had met David Menzies the following Saturday, as she had promised.

It had been an unusually frantic week at work: Bisley had secured a new writer and a book that excited him and, on Thursday morning, the book had been accepted by a literary publishing house. There had been all sorts of talk about it being nominated for an award. Such was the luminosity of this young author, a man of twenty-one who had recently come down from Oxford with a first. It was a curious and clever little book about the history of common objects, and she had never seen Bisley so animated. She had been taken to lunch on Thursday and Friday, first with the author and then with his newly acquired editor. Bisley had introduced Cora as his 'right hand' and she had felt that her world had moved on a little. She could keep up with the conversations and the gossip; they laughed at her jokes; she understood some of the literary allusions.

So, when Menzies rang her on the Friday afternoon, she answered with a new sense of worth, of having some of the past week's glamour. That day Bisley had remarked, as she brushed her hair before lunch, 'Cora, you look quite reasonable today.' He had winked at her as she smiled at him.

'May I cook for you?' David Menzies asked her, over the phone.

She was gazing out on to the street and the patch of green square they could just glimpse from the window. It was hot, and a faint trace of autumn hung in the air; the leaves of the trees were turning dry and brittle under summer's assault.

She didn't think twice about it: she was still euphoric from the week's events. 'Yes,' she said.

He gave her his address, somewhere different from the workshop.

'Is that where you live?' she asked, puzzled.

'It's a friend's flat,' he said. 'He's gone away until Christmas. It doesn't smell so much as the other place.' He laughed.

'Shall I bring anything?'

'Just yourself,' he said.

It was a smart part of town, just behind Cheyne Walk. Unfortunately, the block of flats where David's friend lived wasn't as attractive as those that faced the river and the Embankment; but, nevertheless, it was Chelsea.

He answered the door with an apron tied round his waist, and a glass in his hand. 'Champagne,' he said, and gave it to her.

She took the glass on the doorstep. 'You might have let me get over the threshold.'

He opened the door wide, and waved her in.

She was charmed. She had never seen her father make a cup of tea, let alone cook – or more extreme yet, wear an apron. No man cooked unless he was a chef. Men sat in chairs and waited to be served; they smoked cigars, as her father did; they cut lawns, as her father did; they went to work, as her father did. Nothing else. To do more, or to do different, was not being a man.

She watched David as he walked back across the room, and felt liberated and happy. David was different, and successful, and charming. Different enough, but not so very different that her father wouldn't recognize the gentleman in him, his background of public school and European travel. She found herself wondering when she might take David to Sherborne and show him off.

'Make yourself comfortable,' he said.

The flat was painted white, bright and modern, instead of being furnished, as the mews house was, with dark period pieces – she always felt a bit stifled there, in the house she rented with her friends; threading her way between vast mahogany tables and cupboards that the owner had evidently brought up from a bigger place in the country. Cora looked round the sitting room: there was nothing that would have been in

107

her parents' house. No fireplace, no piano, no panelled doors, no sideboard. Instead, one sofa, like a box with a straight back, in a red and blue pattern, a spindly-legged coffee-table, a starburst clock on the wall, two bright orange lamp-shades on two Chianti-bottle bases.

'I hope you like fish,' David said, from the kitchen.

She went in to him. He was cooking trout in almonds: she had only ever seen a photograph of it in a cookery book. 'I'm impressed,' she said admiringly.

'You should be,' he told her, and raised his glass as if to toast her.

'Where on earth did you get trout?' Such things were like gold dust; she and the rest of the girls in her house subsisted on toast with sardines, and corned-beef sandwiches.

'Someone I know sent it down from Scotland.'

'Sent it down?'

'Packed in ice.'

'They caught it themselves?'

'Yes,' he said. 'She caught it herself... Wild,' he murmured. 'She should have been a backwoodswoman. Follows hounds, shoots...'

'Who is she?' Cora asked.

'A friend of a friend. Nobody important.' There was another bottle of wine on the Formica table. He began to open it.

'Let me help you,' she said.

'No, I'm rather good at this,' he told her. 'I'm rather good at everything.'

She didn't know that the champagne, the wine, the dinner, the remark, meant anything in particular. She had not been brought up to know.

He was attentive through dinner, insisting that she sit while he served her. The dessert was crème caramel – 'I cheated – I bought it,' he had said. There was coffee, and liqueurs. He gave her a crème de menthe, which she didn't say she disliked, both the colour and the taste. They sat on the hard sofa.

'Anyone would think you were trying to get me drunk,' she joked.

'I am,' he replied. And kissed her. She knew what kissing him would be like, and hoped that this time it would be more gentle, measured, romantic. But it wasn't. He put an arm round her, held her chin with the other hand, and forced his mouth on hers so hard that he pushed her lips against her teeth. It was not a dry kiss. His mouth was wet. He smelt strongly of the brandy he had drunk.

She drew back, taken unawares.

'Cora,' he said, and pulled her towards him again, still with the arm round her shoulders. She straightened her back and tried to slide sideways a little. She didn't like to ask him to stop: she felt obliged to let him kiss her. She had a feeling that women weren't supposed to be awkward, or object.

'Don't tease me,' he said.

She didn't know what he meant. 'I must go home,' she told him.

He laughed. 'Oh, darling.'

'No, I must.' She tried to push him away from her.

'Didn't you like the dinner?' he asked.

'Yes, of course.'

'Don't you like me?'

His face was very close. She tried not to look at the wet mouth. 'Of course I do,' she said.

'Well, then.'

She submitted to another kiss. She wanted to feel affection for him; she wanted a romance. She liked him; she would have been pleased to let him put his arms round her waist and ask her out again. That was what she had expected. She tried not to mind his insistence. She waited for the end of the kiss, trying to keep upright, folding her hands in her lap. In her mind she could hear a schoolfriend saying that when men began to breathe heavily, they lost control. That was how naïve she was, how much of a child. She was listening to the pace and depth of his breathing, and it seemed normal.

It's all right, she thought. I'm quite all right.

He moved his hand down her body; first,

fleetingly, to her breast, then to her thigh.

'I have to go,' she repeated. She tried to get up.

'Don't be silly,' he told her.

'David,' she said, 'please let me go.'

His hand ran down her leg and quickly under her voluminous skirt. She felt it snag on her stocking. She closed her legs tightly and made a determined effort to stand up. 'David,' she said. 'Please.'

He took away his hand, but only for a second. He pushed her backwards on the couch.

'No,' she said. 'No.'

He put his left arm across her, holding her down. He pulled up the skirt. She was wearing the usual net petticoats underneath: three starched layers that took so much trouble to wash and keep straight. Underneath them, she wore a silk slip to stop them scratching her legs. David Menzies' hand found this now. He made a noise in his throat and forced his fingers higher.

'Oh, don't,' she said.

His arm was almost on her throat. Her own right arm was pinned beneath her, but with her left hand she tried to pull his arm away. 'I can't breathe,' she told him.

'Will you lie still, for God's sake?' he said.

She trembled in panic. 'Please let me go,' she said. 'I promise not to tell anyone.'

He looked shocked, then laughed. He

stopped what he was doing. 'Not tell any-one?' he said. 'What are you talking about?'

'Just let me get up,' she said.

She had never let anyone touch her before. She had never made love to anyone. Over his shoulder, she could see the starburst clock on the wall. It was eleven thirty. She saw the minute hand move. She watched its progress, thinking that she would be home in an hour. She would be behind her own door. She could lock it and get undressed. She could wash at the basin in her bedroom. She would wash him away.

'God,' he said. 'You are a tight little girl.'

When he had finished, he stood up and went out of the room. She heard water running.

That's what I want to do, she thought. I want to wash.

He came back in. She was still lying where he had left her. He took a drink from the glass on the table, and regarded her for a moment or two. Then, he came over and pulled down her skirt. 'Don't lie there like that,' he told her. 'You look like a whore on her day off.'

She stood up. Her skirt was creased. She had spent ages ironing it that day, to look nice. I will have it do it all over again, she thought randomly.

'Did you get a taxi here?' he asked.

'No,' she said. 'A bus.'

'I'll walk you to the stop,' he said.

'No,' she told him. 'It doesn't matter.'

He yawned. He glanced at the kitchen, then smiled at her. 'Don't bother about the washing-up,' he said. 'I'll do it.'

She stared at him, and he continued to smile at her.

She picked up her handbag and went out into the hallway to where he had hung her coat. She put it on, thinking of nothing except that she must get out as quickly as possible.

'You're a nice kid,' he said.

She went down the steps into the street and walked quickly to the embankment. At the river she stopped, put her hands briefly on the wall and looked down at the water. She could feel something soaking her underwear: she wondered if she was bleeding. She pressed herself against the wall, feeling sick, and closed her eyes.

Behind her, two buses came and went.

They passed, rattling along the road, their destinations backlit in black-and-white, their interiors yellow oblongs. Faces looked out at her. Eventually, she turned back towards the street and watched the tail-lights passing towards Chelsea Wharf and Battersea Bridge. She watched the taxis come and go. She watched the lights being turned off in the flats opposite her.

And when next she looked at her watch, it

was twenty past midnight.

She turned east, and began to walk.

When she got home from Sherborne, it was past two o'clock and she saw her daughter's car in the driveway. Zeph was sitting on the doorstep with Joshua.

Cora got out quickly. 'I'm sorry, darling,' she called.

Zeph stood up. 'I was beginning to worry about you.'

She walked forward and kissed her mother's cheek. Cora bent down to hug Joshua. He hung back behind his mother's legs. 'What's the matter, baby?' Cora asked.

'Where have you been?' Zeph said.

'I had to go to the solicitor's, and then I forgot the food. I had to walk back. How long have you been here?'

'An hour.'

'Oh dear,' Cora murmured. 'There's a key here – look – under the stone pot by the door.'

'You didn't tell me,' Zeph said, 'and you didn't take your phone. How can I get in touch with you if you don't keep it with you? And how am I supposed to know where the key is?'

'I know,' Cora said. 'I was in a rush this morning...'

'It's what it's for,' Zeph said, 'the phone. For keeping in touch. You should always

114

have it. You should make it a habit.'

'Yes,' Cora said, hearing the note in her daughter's voice. She looked from Joshua to his mother, and back.

'You're bloody hopeless.' Zeph sighed heavily. 'Let me help you with the shopping.'

They took it into the house, and as they crossed the doorstep Cora saw disorientation in Zeph's expression. Joshua went straight to Denny's bed in the hallway under the stairs, and lay down in it. He curled himself into a ball, and stuck his thumb into his mouth. She hadn't seen him do that since he had started to walk and made a beeline for the Labrador slumped lazily in the big wicker bed.

'He's all right,' Zeph said. 'Leave him. He's tired out.'

Cora followed her daughter into the kitchen. 'What is it?' she asked. 'What's the matter?'

Zeph had sat down at the table and put her head into her hands, surrounded by the laden carrier-bags. Cora hesitated by her side. When Zeph took away her hands, she looked defeated. 'Mum, sit down,' she said.

Cora obeyed.

Zeph glanced briefly at the hallway. She got up and pushed the door almost closed on Joshua. She came back to the table. 'I've left Nick.'

'What?' Cora wondered if she had heard her correctly.

'I've left him. This morning.'

'But why?'

'He had an affair.'

There was a beat of silence. 'Oh, no,' Cora said. 'Oh, no.'

'He admitted it.'

'When?'

'Yesterday.'

They stared at each other. 'Please don't think of defending him,' Zeph warned. 'Not over this.'

'I wasn't going to,' Cora said.

Zeph closed her eyes briefly. 'You always seem to take his side.'

Cora was astounded. 'You think I'd support him in this?'

'I'm not going back.'

Cora reached across the table, but Zeph didn't take her hand. 'Don't try to persuade me,' she said.

'I'm not going to,' Cora said, 'and I'm not going to defend him.'

At this, Zeph began to cry softly, her shoulders shaking. Cora got quickly to her feet, went to the other side of the table and put her arms round her. Zeph sat rigidly, closed in on herself. 'Where is he now?' Cora asked.

'In Paris. Working.' Zeph took a crumpled tissue from her pocket.

'He's gone to Paris – after this?'

'He went because I promised not to leave. I waited until he'd gone.'

Cora dropped her arms. 'But he'll come after you,' she said.

'It doesn't matter. I can't go back. I can't bear it.'

'What about Joshua?' Cora went back to her chair and looked at her daughter, distressed.

Zeph sighed, as if she might be trying to find words. Eventually, all she asked was, 'Can we stay here or not?'

'Of course you can,' Cora said.

Zeph glanced back, once, towards the almost-closed door to the hall. 'I know what you're thinking,' she said, 'but you don't know what it's like. You and Dad were always working together. You never had to worry. So please...' She frowned, shut her eyes, and held the palm of one hand outwards as if to ward off further comment or criticism.

Cora hesitated, torn between taking the hand, and frightened that the gesture might drive her daughter out of reach. 'All right,' she said.

Zeph stood up and went out to the hall, where Cora could hear her whispering to Joshua. She picked up the nearest shopping bag, and took it to the cupboard. There, she stopped. The brown-paper package that had come in the post was still sitting there, unopened. She put her hand on it, on the Italian postmark.

'Mother,' Zeph said, from the doorway.

Cora looked around. 'Is Joshua all right? Does he want a drink?'

'In a minute.'

'You'd better lift him out of Denny's bed. It's not very clean for him.'

Zeph walked a pace or two forward. 'Do you know where Denny is?' she asked.

'I couldn't find him,' Cora told her. 'I looked everywhere this morning.'

'If I can get Josh to sleep in a little while,' Zeph said quietly, 'we'd better go up to Border Wood. Just you and I.'

La Lettura

My letter is returned to me. The letter I sent you has been returned to me. There is my handwriting, across the envelope. I wrote it down exactly as you told it to me, so it cannot be wrong. It cannot be.

Yet it has come back unopened again. This is the second time that it has come back inside another envelope, a larger one with the note attached that I sent when I returned it – the note, the little letter. Did you see it, darling? I write, I write. Did you not see the little letter, Cora? and I do not recognize the handwriting because it is simply printing in capitals. I have looked and looked at it, wondering if you printed the capitals across the envelope, sealed it over my own letter to you, and returned it. Nothing else in the envelope, no letter, no note. Nothing. Just my own letter and note, opened and resealed.

It is two months since you were here, Cora.

I wonder if you know what you have done to me with this. Not only with your absence, but with my letter. It is an insult. It is not right for a woman to insult a man. A man should be respected: he should not be ignored. I am not one of the village boys who hangs around the street. Never did I insult you. You told me you knew that many Sicilian men wanted to marry a rich girl from abroad, an English or American girl, and you smiled when you told me that some had already proposed to you, without asking if you were married. Proposing within an hour of meeting you, in the days before I saw you. How funny you found this, too: you found my country funny, I suppose. Perhaps you found me funny. Perhaps when you got home you laughed at me, and I have been insulted without knowing it.

But I know this is not true. Even as I write it, even as I am angry, I know it is not true. You were not lying when you told me all your heart.

Something must have happened to you to make you return my letters and not write to me. I am in despair that it is something bad. This is

119

why I shall do exactly as you have done. I shall put the first letter – it is myself, Cora, at least look at me, at least open the letter – and I shall put a third letter inside a larger envelope, and I shall return it to you. You will have three letters. And if there is anything bad, if you are ill, if you have changed houses, gone away, if you have a new address, you must tell me it all, Cora. For I have a right to know. You are mine in every way that truly matters.

I shall be more careful about the third. I will prove to you that I am patient and that I can wait, even if this would be shameful to any Sicilian man, to be made to feel like a child waiting for his mother's approval.

What is wrong? Is there trouble with Richard? I can't write that name. I can't write it again. I wonder if he touches you. That is what I wonder all the time, if he is touching you as I am sitting here alone in the house, writing these lines. He is touching you, and you allow it. That is what I think. Right now, as the ink drains from my pen and stains the page, he is drawing you out like thread through fabric, a needle sewing up the divisions between you.

That is his work, to make the seam tight, to bind the two of you together. That is his right, and your duty. I would not deny a man his duty or right, and what I ask for myself is sinful. I know that I have sinned and that I continue to sin. I go to church but it is all for nothing. It has no more meaning. It is terrible to lose the centre of your life like that. The pity of Christ I feel will pass over me: even He will exclude me because He knows that I think of what is denied me; He will know that I thought of the needle and the thread. And that needle passes through me, too, tying my heart to my spine. That is what it feels like. I have shrunk inside until my heart touches my backbone and ribs. I am so full of shame.

But I will still write the letter.

I cannot bear this separation any longer. And something keeps you from me and from the promises you made to me, I must understand what it is.

Write to me. Write to me.

For you made me promises, and I gave an oath to you.

Six

Cora was in Border Wood when she saw Nick. She had gone back to Denny's grave – they had buried him where he lay, at almost midnight, after Joshua had gone to sleep for the day, walking up through the trees and finding the dog with the aid of torchlight. It had been eerie, in the darkness, digging among the knotted undergrowth, branches brushing their shoulders, the wind pulling at the tops of the birches and sycamores.

121

Cora had been worried that it was worse for her daughter, almost, than it was for her. She had brought Denny home as a puppy when Zeph was sixteen.

It had been one of those teenage years when Zeph had felt nothing was going right. She had no boyfriend, she had fallen out with her closest girlfriend, and she had spent long hours in her room. Cora had hoped that Denny would bring Zeph out of herself, and it had worked. Denny had been Zeph's slave until she had gone to university in Kent two years later. For weeks afterwards, Denny would go to the bottom of the lane and stand by the gate, where Zeph had got off the school bus. Once or twice Cora had noticed the vehicle slow as it rounded the corner. Denny's tail would give a tentative half-wag as it went past.

The dog had represented Cora's own lost feeling: an empty house, with no one coming home at night. They had rattled around together, Denny following her as she moved from the kitchen to the sitting room, with her supper tray, to watch television. She had turned on the radio and TV constantly, so that she could hear voices, and it seemed like company. After a week or two, she allowed Denny to come upstairs and lie by her bed at night. He never had before, but she couldn't bear the sound of him walking up and down the flagstone hall, stopping by the front door. She couldn't look at his almost comically mournful face: she saw too much of her own self-pity in it.

But last night Zeph had borne the task with resignation. When Cora couldn't roll the dog's inert body into the ground, it was Zeph who, with a grimace of unhappiness, did the job. Cora had reached down and felt him.

'What are you doing?' Zeph had asked.

'I'm trying to make him comfortable,' Cora had replied, out of breath.

'Oh, Mum,' Zeph had said, with sympathy. 'It doesn't matter which way he's lying, you know.'

'It does,' Cora had whispered, as Zeph scooped earth into the grave. 'It does.'

They had come back very cold, and saying little. In the relative warmth of the kitchen, Cora had switched on the kettle and held up a cup to Zeph. Zeph had merely shaken her head, and Cora's heart had gone out to her child, who looked ghost-like.

'Not a particularly good day, all round,' she commented, hoping to see a smile of black humour.

'I've had quite a few better ones,' Zeph replied. She paused. 'Are you all right?' she asked.'

'Yes,' Cora had replied. 'I'll be fine.'

Zeph had gone slowly out of the room and upstairs to bed.

Now Cora saw movement on the path out of the corner of her eye. She looked up and Nick was standing there.

The two gazed at each other. There was no greeting. 'Where is she?' he said.

'She's out,' Cora said. 'She's taken Joshua to the doctor.'

Nick glanced briefly at the ground behind her. 'We had to bury Denny last night,' Cora told him. 'He died out here during the day.'

'I've been looking for you for a while. What's the matter with Josh?'

'It's just a sore throat. A cough. And she wanted to register him.' As soon as she had said it, she realized how tactless she had been. She walked away from the grave and on to the path.

'I couldn't stay in Paris,' he said. 'It seemed all wrong.' He gave a wry, painful smile. 'I wanted to surprise her,' he said. 'But it was me who got the surprise.'

'Nick,' she said, 'she's very angry. Perhaps you'd better leave her alone just now.'

'I can't do that,' he told her.

They walked back down the hill, across the first orchard.

'How did you get here?' Cora asked, because Zeph had brought their car.

'I hired a car,' he said, sounding irritated. He took a deep breath as they came into the second orchard. 'Everything's looking real

124

nice,' he said.

She smiled inwardly at the compliment. Nick had always been charming with her, as he was with all women. When Zeph had first brought him home, Cora had liked him at once. Oh, of course it meant little, she could see that, to be able to say pretty things at the right times. It was a facility rather than a strength. But it was pleasant all the same to be noticed and complimented. And Nick was good at telling Zeph how wonderful she was, and how beautiful. Cora had watched her practical, pragmatic daughter melt, and felt pleased. She had only ever looked as happy as that with her father – although Nick was nothing like Richard.

Nick was laid-back where Richard had been hard-working, artistic where Richard had been practical. Richard would probably have criticized his wit and apparent carelessness, his philosophy of letting tomorrow take care of itself. Richard would have said that Zeph needed security and money, not the hand-to-mouth existence that Nick offered.

Looking at him through Richard's eyes, Cora could see that a struggling writer was hardly reliable, hardly a provider, and she worried that it was Zeph, not Nick, who got the part-time jobs, a whole variety to make ends meet. When Nick and Zeph had first set up home together in a tiny flat, it was

Zeph, not Nick, who worked in a bar and, at nights, as an usher in a theatre. She even went temping, doing days here and there in City offices, filing and running errands. Anything to bring in the money while Nick worked on his first novel.

It would pay off when the book was published, Nick would tell them, with a wink, a smile and that fantastic American drawl. That was how Nick got along, Cora saw. And the first book came and went, and couldn't find a publisher; and the second found an agent and a publisher, but no money. Then the third. And by this time Zeph was pregnant, and the mortgage lender was about to foreclose, and Cora had even thought they would have to come to Somerset to live with her. But Nick had sold his screenplay, then got a job writing TV commercials, in the same ten days, and they were off, heads above water, not rich when Joshua was born, but no longer desperate.

They had come through all that, Cora thought, as they reached the gate to the farmyard and the house. Only last year Zeph had hinted at them buying a second home, somewhere near Cora, on the back of Nick's success with his fourth book. Her heart had leapt in hope. Only last year. And yet, Cora considered, there had been a weariness in Zeph after Joshua was born, an uncharacteristic depression. When she asked Zeph how she felt, Zeph had brushed aside her concern. Yet it was almost visible: a barrier between her and Nick.

As he held the gate for her, Cora looked at him. He was very handsome. Not just attractive, but handsome. You almost never saw that now: a man who was glamorous, like a forties movie star. A dangerous man, the archetypal image of a womanizer, a seducer. *And that's what he is*, she thought suddenly. *That's exactly what he is.*

'Why?' she asked him, made abruptly furious by this, and by her own easy acceptance of his appearance. Richard would have thrown him off the land, she knew. He would probably have hit him. 'What was it for, with this actress?' she asked. 'How could you have been so stupid?'

'I don't know,' he said.

'I thought you were better than that,' she told him. 'I'm ashamed of you.'

He looked wounded. 'Are you?'

'Of course! What do you expect me to feel? Proud?'

'I never had it in my head to hurt Zeph, Cora.'

'Well, you did. You have. You let a stranger tell her.'

'I won't see the girl again. It's over – it's been over for weeks.'

'What rubbish,' Cora retorted. 'Zeph told

127

me this morning that you're working with her.'

'No,' he said. 'I didn't stay to do any rewrites in Paris. I asked to work from home. I just saw who I had to, and came home by the first train this morning. I don't want to see Bella. I don't want her.'

'Well, now nobody wants you,' Cora said sharply. 'Congratulations.'

She had begun to walk across the yard, but Nick stepped in front of her. 'Cora,' he said, 'please help me.'

'I can't. What can I possibly do?'

'I can't lose Zeph,' he said. 'Or Josh.'

'What do you expect of me?' she said. 'I can't do anything.'

'You can talk to her.'

Cora smiled grimly. 'I can't talk to Zeph, Nick. You know that. She wouldn't take any notice of me at the best of times.' She paused. 'And I don't think I should,' she said. 'I shouldn't get involved. I should help my daughter do whatever she wants to do.'

'She doesn't want this,' he said. 'You know in your heart she doesn't.'

'I'm sorry,' she said, 'but I don't know that at all.'

There was a noise along the lane: the sound of a car.

As Zeph turned into the lane, she was thinking of her father. The thought had been

128

triggered as she had come past the lower field, the one turned to pasture. The grass was full of thistles now, and seemed beaten by the winter cold; she saw the dark areas of scrub and moss in the far corner.

Richard had always been careful to keep that field properly; he had put the two horses in there and built them a stable. When she was only eight she had helped him with it, gone down on the tractor, towing the trailer loaded with corrugated-asbestos roof sheets; stood by while two other men helped him put up the girders. He had told her long, complicated stories about building the other farm, of how it had been a ruin, and how he had learned at night school to lay brickwork and to plaster walls. How the thatcher had come and he had passed up the reeds, and how they had set traps so that squirrels wouldn't run over the ridgeline. And how the rain had rushed down the new thatch and washed away the loose stone path that he had put by the windows, and how he had got down on his knees and relaid them, mixing cement with a spade, angry that nature had tried to defeat him.

Her father could build anything. He told her how no one had wanted the land where the first house had been; how only one person had bid against him in the auction. He told her, laughing to himself, about her grandparents: they had been aghast at his plans to dig through the whole site for the drains; but her grandmother had relented, and come to see him one afternoon when he had been working all day, bringing him a tray covered with a cloth, and tea laid out beneath it, with a little white napkin and a silver knife, a pat of butter for the scones. 'She was a very correct woman,' he had told Zeph, smiling broadly.

She had no clear picture in her mind of her grandmother, who had died suddenly just before her fifty-second birthday, collapsing in the garden. Richard, from his vantage-point above the lane, working on the top-storey windows of the new house, had seen her fall.

He had gone down immediately, and found her by the flower-beds she had carefully tended. She had had a stroke, and was barely breathing. He had held her hand, felt the tension pass from it and realized that she was no longer focusing on him.

Cora had come home soon afterwards. She had not been back long from London, and that day had been trying to get work in Salisbury. She had driven a long way, he said, and had come into the driveway at speed, then got out of the car in a rush, slamming the door, and had seen him standing on the doorstep. 'What are you doing here?' she had asked.

Zeph had often wondered at the rest of the conversation, if her mother had wept and her father had had to support her. If he had played out his role as the knight in shining armour all day, all week, all month. All the weeks until they married. She had looked at their wedding album, and seen them standing in the stiff, formal group that did not include Cora's mother. She had studied how Cora leaned almost too heavily on Richard's arm. And she had decided that Richard had done everything you might dream of in a husband, or a man: he had rescued Cora; he had stood by her; he had given her his arm to hold on to.

He could do anything. That was Zeph's unwavering impression of him. He had fought in the war and been a hero; he had come home wounded from Sicily and not let the injury deter him; he had built up what he owned from nothing. He had planted all the orchards himself. He had made toys, her bed and all the cupboards in her room, and carved little animals as door handles on each one. She opened them all daily, for the fun of pushing down the elephant's trunk to lift the latch, or the tiger's paw, or the donkey's tail. He was clever like that, clever, resourceful and funny.

And he would sit with her at night, and not with her mother. Cora was always somewhere else.

131

Zeph had glanced again at the state of the field as she slowed the car. He would have hated to see how Cora had let things rot where they stood. He would have hated the state of the stable, with the roof panel cracked and letting in rain, the doors standing open. He would have hated the state of the lane.

She looked back to the road and the yard, and saw Nick and her mother waiting for her.

'Oh, no,' she murmured.

She pulled up and got out.

'Shall I take Josh?' her mother asked, worried.

'He's asleep,' Zeph replied. She glanced at Nick.

Cora spoke again: 'What did the doctor say?'

'He thinks it's asthma,' Zeph told her.

'Asthma?' Cora repeated. 'But he's never had asthma, has he?'

'Living in the city,' Zeph said. This time she stared at Nick.

'He hasn't got asthma,' Nick said. And there was something about the way he said it, with the American *z* instead of the *s* that seemed, unfairly, to set him apart from the two women, to mark or define him as separate.

There was an icy silence. Cora went to the car.

'Don't touch him, Mum,' Zeph said. 'It's the first time he's slept since five o'clock this morning.'

'I thought I'd take him into the house,' Cora said. 'You and Nick can talk.'

'No.'

Another silence. Nick hadn't moved. He kept looking at the car.

'I'll go inside,' Cora said. 'Shall I?'

'It doesn't matter,' Zeph said.

'Yes,' Nick countered. He looked almost pleadingly at his mother-in-law; she turned and left them, once glancing back anxiously at the car.

In the copse beside the chestnuts at the back of the house, rooks began to caw. Zeph frowned at the noise.

'You lied to me,' Nick said. 'Why?'

'Because I knew I'd never get out of the house otherwise.'

'You think I'd have stopped you leaving, if you'd talked to me?'

'Yes.'

'What – physically?'

'No,' Zeph said. 'You'd just have talked and talked until I couldn't think any more.' She looked at her feet.

'And that's a bad thing, right? Talking?'

'It is, the way you do it,' she said. 'What you call talking.'

'I don't know what you mean.'

'Never listening properly,' she told him.

'Just nagging and nagging about what you want.'

'I don't nag you.'

'You browbeat me,' she said. 'You're doing it now just by being here.'

Nick laughed shortly. 'What did you expect me to do?' he demanded. 'Sit at home on my hands?'

'Respect my wishes,' she said.

'Oh,' he said, 'I'm meant to respect you when you lie to me and leave the house with our son?'

'Yes,' she said. 'You're meant to try to work out what's happened to us and think about how you caused it, not run down here making demands.'

'I haven't made a single demand,' he told her. 'What have I said?'

'You're about to tell me to come home. No,' she corrected herself, holding out one hand, palm upwards, 'you're about to say that I *must* come home.'

'You must. You've got to.'

'There you are.'

Nick put a hand to his forehead. 'Jesus,' he muttered.

'I don't care if you accept it or not. I don't care what you feel,' Zeph countered hotly. 'Do you understand? I don't care what you feel or what you want.'

'I don't believe you,' he said. 'I don't believe you don't care.'

'I want to be away from you,' she retorted, her voice quivering. 'I want to think. I *have* to think.'

'Zeph,' he said, 'I can't allow this.'

'Allow?' she echoed. Her expression darkened. 'But you've got no power, Nick. You've got nothing. Don't you get it? Do you want me to be understanding? Do you want me to forgive you? What – you want me to try to forget that you've had another woman, that you've slept with her?'

'To forgive me, not forget. I made a mistake.'

'And that excuses everything?'

'Of course not. I'm just trying to tell you I'm sorry.'

'I always thought it would be different – I thought you'd be different when Josh was born,' she whispered.

'What do you mean?'

'Not go around with your tongue hanging on the floor, for one thing.'

'What?'

'The way you are around everyone.'

'What do you mean?' he asked, confused.

'You've always got to...' She took a deep breath. 'It doesn't matter.'

'No,' he said. 'Go ahead. You may as well tell me.'

'Just always pawing people. Always got to kiss the women. Always got to be at the front. Always the one pouring the drinks and telling jokes – like – like–' She was floundering.

Nick stared at her. 'You're criticizing me for being friendly?' he said. 'For *talking* to other people?'

'You don't just talk,' Zeph replied, angry. 'You ... you're false.'

'What?'

'You heard me,' she said. 'You're not real. You're fiction.'

He was staring at her, appalled.

'Even Josh swearing at me is a joke to you,' she muttered. 'It's a game. It's a laugh.'

'I'm sorry,' he said. 'How many other ways can I say it?'

'You're not sorry,' she told him. 'You're just terrified because I won't play.'

'Zeph,' he said. 'Look. I'll do what you want, OK? I'll go home. Is that what you want? You want me to be away from you. OK. I'll go. I'll wait. But in a week or two you'll feel different, won't you?'

'No,' she said.

'You'll change your mind.'

'Oh, my God,' she murmured, 'you think I'll come round. You really think that.'

'You have to.'

'Why?' she demanded. 'Why do I have to? Because it's what you want – it's what'll make you feel better?' Unconsciously she screwed her fist into her chest, her thumb pressing hard against her breastbone. 'You know what I'm doing now, what my busi-

136

ness is now?' she said. 'I'm going to make you feel as bad as I do.'

'Holy Christ!' he said. 'It's not as if I'm a murderer.'

She lifted her chin. 'Listen to me,' she said. 'I'm not some forgiving wife. If you've painted me like that in your head, you can erase it.'

He spread his hands in a gesture of helplessness. 'I don't think of you like a character in a story,' he said.

'You don't know what's real and what isn't,' she said.

Nick looked at the car, then back at her. Then he walked rapidly towards it and put his hand on the door. The child lock was on.

'What are you doing?' she said.

'I want my son,' he told her.

'Get your hands off the car, Nick.'

'Open the door. I want to talk to him,' he said, and pushed Zeph away from him.

'No!'

'Give me the keys.'

'No.'

'The keys,' he said, caught hold of her wrist and twisted it. She gasped, and sank a little lower to relax the pressure of the grip. Inside the car she heard Joshua murmur.

Nick held her gaze. Suddenly he pulled her to one side and against the bonnet of the car. She struggled to free herself. Then Cora's voice came to them across the yard:

'Nick!' she was calling. 'Nick!'

Joshua began to cry, and then to scream.

Nick dropped his hand. He stood still for a second, staring at his wife.

Cora ran to them.

Zeph lifted her wrist to her mouth.

'I'm sorry, but this isn't what I want,' Nick said. 'I want you.'

He looked at Zeph a moment longer, then took a step back and put his hand on the car window, beside Joshua's face. He held it there for a second, then walked away.

Seven

Cora had come home after the nightmare of the night with David Menzies. Her mother knew that something was wrong, but Cora denied it. 'I'm perfectly all right,' she told her parents.

She could visualize them now, sitting in the dining room, her father at one end of the table, her mother at the other, and she between them. It was as if she had regressed several years.

'What's the matter with her?' she had heard her father ask, the day after she got home. She was on the landing; they were standing below her in the hallway and had

138

not heard her footsteps.

'Perhaps she had an argument with Jenny,' her mother wondered.

It was the opposite: Jenny had begged her to stay. She was about to get engaged to Terry Ray, and she wanted Cora to help her with the party.

'I'm going home,' she had told her friend.

'But you can't leave me,' Jenny had said. 'There's too much to do.'

'I have to go.'

'Why? Is somebody ill?'

'No.'

'Are you ill?'

'No.' This was a lie. She had felt sick since the night she had left Menzies' flat. She was terrified as to what the reason might be.

'What about David?' Jenny asked. And a light dawned on her face. 'What's he done?' she demanded.

'Nothing. It's not him.'

Jenny frowned deeply, trying to read Cora's expression. 'Bisley, then,' she decided. 'That miserable bastard's done something to you.'

Cora bit her lip. Bisley was the one person she didn't want to leave behind.

'I knew it,' Jenny said, seeing her hesitation.

'It isn't Bisley at all,' Cora told her, 'and I'm sorry not to be here for the party.'

'It's on Saturday,' Jenny said, 'five days away. Surely you could stay five more days.'

'I'm sorry,' Cora repeated.

But in fact she wasn't sorry to miss seeing Jenny with Terry. She suspected that he was the same as Menzies. She had seen the bruises on Jenny's arms, the marks on her face. She knew that Jenny was attracted by his money, but she didn't dare to speculate whether she was slave to some other need or desire. She didn't want to think about what men did to women, or what pleasure women might expect, or what humiliations they might be prepared to endure – or even enjoy. She could see that because she was so naïve, with childish notions of romance, she had been a liability to herself; and because she had trusted Menzies, the thought that she might be in danger had not occurred to her. She had no doubt that whatever he had done to her, and however he had behaved, it was her responsibility.

She was supposed to give Bisley two weeks' notice, but in the end she gave him only two days. She had put off speaking to him until Wednesday evening, by which time she had bought her train ticket for Saturday morning.

She had expected a scene. She had dreaded it.

But he simply looked at her levelly for a few seconds, then asked her to sit down. She obeyed, and gazed past him at the edge of the desk and the spines of the books stacked there. 'London hasn't suited me,' she said. 'You were right. I ought to have stayed at home.'

'I was only teasing you,' he told her. 'You know, really, Cora, you would be very good in this business. You have the right sort of objectivity. Better than me, actually.' He smiled. 'Probably because you don't drink.'

She said nothing.

'Can't I persuade you otherwise?' he asked.

'I'm sorry.'

'I shall miss you very much,' he said.

She found herself in tears. Bisley got up immediately, came to her side and put his hand on her shoulder. 'What is it?' he asked.

She shook her head.

'It isn't me, this job?'

'No.' She put her hands to her face.

'Can you tell me?' he asked.

'No,' she said. 'I can't tell anyone.'

He pulled another chair alongside her. He waited until she took a handkerchief from her bag. 'Is it so bad?' he asked.

'Yes.'

'You're afraid of something?'

'I must go home.'

'Will you be safe from it there?'

She would never be safe anywhere, she thought. She felt vulnerable, naked. She felt as if she were still on the couch in Menzies' flat; she would always be there. 'No,' she whispered.

'Is someone trying to harm you?'

She put her elbows on her knees, her hands again over her eyes. 'Dear child,' Bisley said, 'has it already happened?'

'Yes,' she said, still whispering, through her fingers.

'A man?'

'Yes.'

He was silent. She sat in abject grief.

'When was this?' he asked eventually.

'On Saturday.'

'You were attacked?'

'It was my fault,' she said, still into her hands. 'I went to his flat. I went on my own. It was my fault.'

Bisley got up. She heard him pacing about the room. When she wiped her eyes, he was standing at the window.

'Who is he?' he asked.

She lowered her hands. 'It doesn't matter,' she said.

'I would very much like to know who he is.'

She shook her head.

'Have you told the police?'

'No,' she replied, horrified.

'But this man assaulted you.'

'I can't tell them,' she said, panicked. 'How could I?'

'Why do you think? He's committed a crime.'

'But I couldn't tell anyone,' she said. 'I

couldn't possibly. And I went there. He didn't drag me. I went of my own accord. I just didn't understand.'

'Cora,' Bisley said, 'this man raped you.'

'Oh, no,' she said. 'It wasn't like that.'

'He didn't rape you? He didn't touch you?'

'I should have known.'

'Cora,' Bisley said. 'My dear girl.'

'I made him think it was all right.'

'How?' he said. 'What do you mean?'

'I ate his meal, I accepted a drink...'

'For God's sake, Cora,' Bisley said, 'cooking you a meal doesn't give him *carte blanche*.'

He was standing in front of her, frowning. It occurred to her suddenly that this man, with all his experience of London and men like David Menzies, was probably better qualified to be her parent than her own father, who would be paralysed by fury and mystified by the circumstances in which she had found herself. In her father's world men did not attack women: they behaved with utter formality.

Bisley returned to his chair, pulled it closer to her, and took her hand in his.

'You see,' Cora said, tears running down her face, 'I couldn't tell the police because they would say I encouraged him, wouldn't they? They would say that I had made him think it would happen. It would be my word

143

against his. I haven't any evidence, have I? And he's such ... he's so plausible... He seemed such a decent, interesting man... I thought he was romantic.'

'Oh Cora...'

'I didn't know,' she continued. 'I'm too stupid to know.'

'You're not stupid.'

'I must be,' she said. 'You used to say that I was like a sheep. Naïve, brainless. You were right. I don't know how to behave with men.'

'Cora,' Bisley shook his head. 'You are not brainless. And not naïve. Innocence is something quite different.'

'Is it?' she said. 'I don't think so. I expected him to behave like the men who write these poems. To think like them. For it to be like that. Poetic. Romantic. And it's not, is it?'

Pain crossed Bisley's face, which she did not see. After a moment, he said emphatically, 'You are a very sweet person. That's worth far more than being like some other girls.'

'No,' she said. 'You're wrong. I tried to stop him. But only at first. That's the terrible thing, you see?' she muttered. 'I thought if it was over quickly... I thought there would be a terrible fuss if I struggled – I thought it would only make things worse, so...'

'Did he threaten you?' Bisley asked gently.

144

'Did he hurt you?'

'No,' Cora replied, in misery. 'That's why it's my fault. It's all my fault. Because I just let him.'

Everything was the same at home. It was comforting: the pattern on the curtains, the window-seat in her bedroom, the quilt on her bed. It was like being a child again.

'Are you staying long?' her mother asked.

'I've given up my job,' Cora told her. 'I've given notice at the house.'

'You're not going back?'

'I don't know,' she said, although she did.

Seeing her mother's doubtful expression, Cora had hugged her. 'It's all right,' she said. 'I was homesick.'

'Oh, darling.' Her mother laughed. 'You are a funny old thing.' She held her daughter at arm's length. 'That's all there is to it?'

'Yes,' she said.

'Well, perhaps you'll find a job in town,' her mother suggested.

The first evening, Cora found it hard to sleep. She got up and sat in the window to look out on the long garden. There was still a faint residue of daylight: it was high summer. She opened the latch, and put her hand on the thick green leaves of the magnolia that pressed close to the house. In the spring, the pale flowers framed the window and almost invaded the room. She reached out, took a waxy leaf in her palm and stroked it. Spider mites ran across her fingertips. Under the roof thatch, the scent was dank and green; webs infested the underside of the reed. Off to one side of the garden, she could see the rising ground and the edge of the lane, and through the trees she thought she could see a light. It flickered once or twice, then disappeared.

She looked back into the room, and saw herself suspended between one life and another, whispering against the walls of the house like the magnolia, pressing against the window without inhabiting the room, drifting like the light beyond the trees in the lane.

'Nothing is over,' Bisley had told her. 'Don't think that it is.'

He had given her a book of poetry: Shelley and Byron.

'For love and beauty and delight/There is no death or change,' he quoted. 'Remember.'

'Shelley eloped with two sixteen-year-olds and drove his wife to commit suicide,' Cora said, 'and Byron's wife left him after a year. They are not good examples.'

'Make me thy lyre, even as the forest is,' Bisley said.

She had shaken her head, but was touched by the gift. 'I'm not a lyre,' she told him, 'and it's words, just words.'

'Don't lose faith,' he said, tapping his finger on the slim leather volume. 'That's an order, you know.'

She didn't want to believe in poems any more: she had listened to too many. She closed her hands tightly over the book. 'Thank you anyway,' she said.

'What will you do at home?' he had asked her.

'Oh, I'll get a job,' she had told him. 'It won't be difficult.'

'Doing what?'

'Typing.' There wasn't much else for a single woman to do in a county town. 'Or I'll work in a shop.'

'Selling what?'

'Clothes-pegs,' she told him. 'Sheep drench. Wellington boots. Cattle feed.'

'Ah, the delights of the country.'

They had smiled at each other. 'Come back,' he had said, 'when you're ready. Please.'

It was mid-April. She had an interview at an office in Salisbury; her mother had loaned Cora her car. She had been home a fortnight. She left early, before ten, glad to get out of the house, which was in a flurry because her mother was helping at the village fête in four days' time. The hallway was stacked with books for the second-hand stall, which gave off the stalest odour

147

imaginable. Cora had pulled a face as she stood by the mirror, pulling at the jacket of the two-piece costume her parents had bought for her when she first went up to London.

It was scratchy brown tweed, an almost exact replica of one of her mother's. Round her neck she wore a string of pearls; on the hall table stood the large leather handbag that had been a Christmas present. She was gazing at her reflection, wondering who the person was who stared back at her. At that moment her mother emerged from the kitchen. 'Don't forget your hat,' she said.

'Nobody wears hats now,' Cora said witheringly.

'They might not in the city, but they do here,' her mother said. 'You want to make a good impression.' She smoothed Cora's hair behind her ear and surveyed her.

'I shall do very well without a hat,' Cora snapped.

'I wish you wouldn't drive all that way by yourself.'

'It's not that far.'

'Perhaps I'll come with you.'

'You're busy.' Cora had snatched up her bag and the car keys. 'And I'm not a child,' she said.

'I can see that,' her mother had murmured. 'Be careful.'

Cora drove the Wolseley out of the drive,

the street, the town. The road through the valley and rising up towards Shaftesbury was almost empty. She felt neither excited nor apprehensive: she felt nothing. The inside of the car smelt of her mother's perfume, Evening in Paris, and of cleaned leather.

On the dashboard there was an invitation to the Ladies Circle Dress Ball. Cora had been invited last year: she had danced the valeta and the dashing white sergeant, watching her parents go down the line of dancers, her partner a boy from her father's firm. It had been another life. A secure, familiar life. She recalled the heat of the Methodist hall, and the doors open to the night, the bowl of fruit punch, the politeness and ordinariness of it all. The local band playing slightly off-key; the reddened faces of the dancers; the women in their old-fashioned wartime crêpe-de-Chine; the food lined up as if for an army – tins of Carnation milk standing next to glass bowls of blancmange, the sandwiches curling, tinned fruit salad, slabs of home-made cake. Red, white and blue bunting strung above the fiddle players, a relic from the Festival of Britain and the Coronation, brought out on every occasion afterwards.

She had a sudden mental picture of herself in a replica of her mother's life, going down some other neat garden outside some other neat house, with a basket over her arm and scissors in her hand to cut the roses; sitting by the coal fire in winter, darning; arranging photographs in albums, fiddling with the little white corner stickers to hold them on the black pages. Setting her hair before a mirror, waiting to go down to dinner, asking the housekeeper to turn and sew sheets, and to keep camphor and lavender bags in the linen, because to be a good wife was to be solid and economical. Counting the weeks to a holiday by the sea, or to Christmas.

Half an hour later, Cora was driving along the Tollard Royal road, having gone south of Shaftesbury to pick up the faster route into the city and to get to the company where she had the interview, which was on the south side. Suddenly she couldn't look at the road any longer. She turned down a lane she didn't know, and found herself in a village she had never seen before. 'Ashmore', read the sign, and she found herself in a ring of old stone houses. A woman was walking along with a spaniel; behind her was an enormous millpond.

Cora got out, trembling.

'Good morning,' the woman said. 'Can I help?'

'I took a wrong turning,' Cora said.

'You're in the Cranborne Chase,' the woman told her.

It was a bright, warm morning. The reflection off the sandy path round the pond made her eyes ache. 'If I go along here...' she said, shading her eyes.

'You'll come to Fontmell Magna, and Sturminster.'

'Thank you,' Cora said.

The woman watched her get back into the car.

She drove for another half-hour. The Wolseley began to overheat. She pulled into a lay-by, looked at the temperature gauge, then turned the engine off and on again, lost as to what she should do. Eventually, she turned it off altogether, and stared at the landscape, the crops in the fields, the gently rolling hills. Nausea swept over her and she got out and took deep breaths.

What would she do if she was pregnant? she wondered. Did women feel like this when they were? The world looked as if it had been overpainted, the green of the trees too acid, the grey of the road too dull. The hedgerows were picked out in extraordinary detail, the hawthorn, the ivy and nettles. She would have to bring up David Menzies' child. This was the fear that had been in the forefront of her mind for days. She closed her eyes, overcome with dread. The shame would kill her parents. They would never get over it. And she had brought it on them with her carelessness.

She got back into the car and, after twenty

minutes or so, found herself far out of the way either for Salisbury or Sherborne. She had gone in the wrong direction: she was almost at Cerne Abbas, beside the giant figure etched in chalk on the hill. She put a hand to her head and felt her clammy, cold skin.

I'm going out of my mind, she thought. *I must go home.*

Safe at home.

It was one in the afternoon when she got back to the house. By then, her hands and arms were trembling as she gripped the wheel. All that she could think of was to get inside, get to her room. The sight of the roads had begun to terrify her. Disoriented, panicked, she couldn't depress the brake properly, and came into the driveway too fast.

She gasped when she saw a man standing at the door. He was familiar, but she couldn't place him.

The car stalled; she sat staring at her fingers on the steering-wheel. When at last she got out, she noticed that the man seemed apprehensive. He was holding the phone in his hand, the black Bakelite receiver. The heavy cord curled back to the hallway table. Stopped in the act of dialling a number, he looked almost frightened.

Cora faltered as she walked towards him. He put out a hand, as if he might be able to catch her, although he was ten or twelve feet away.

She thought she heard him say that he was sorry.

'What do you want?' she demanded. 'What are you doing here?'

Eight

As soon as he walked back into the street, Nick saw her.

Bella James was standing on the doorstep, the mobile phone still in her hand. She glanced at it, then put it into her handbag. All the way along the street, she watched him.

She was very tall and slim, almost as tall as he was. Her long dark hair was caught up in a complicated arrangement at the back of her head, fastened with combs.

As he got to the three steps in front of the house, he stopped.

'You look wrecked,' she commented.

His hand lay on the guard rail. 'You shouldn't have come here,' he told her.

'I don't see why not,' she said. 'I want to see Zeph.'

'Zeph?' he echoed, aghast.

'Where is she?'

153

'She's not here,' he said. 'She's gone away.'

'Because of this?' she asked. And she held out the newspaper article, taken from her handbag where it had been folded into a small square.

'Yes.'

'I thought it would help if I came and told her it wasn't true,' she said.

He realized how insensitive she was to anyone's feelings but her own. For a beautiful girl from a fabulous family, she was also, it transpired, very stupid. 'Jesus, Bella,' he said. 'It's complicated.'

'No, it isn't,' she told him. 'Not at all.'

He pulled the door key out of his pocket.

'She knows everything,' he muttered. 'I told her.'

Bella raised an eyebrow, then stowed the paper back in her bag. 'I don't see why you couldn't brazen it out,' she said. 'I would. I will, if you like.'

'Why?' he asked, confused.

'Because I like you, Nick,' she said. 'Helping out a friend and all that.'

'By lying to his wife?'

'Make her feel better,' she said. 'Patch it up between you.' She grinned at him. 'Good girl, aren't I?' she asked. 'Make it all right. Be a good fairy for you.'

'Christ,' he muttered. 'You don't understand what's going on here. It's not something that can be patched up just like that.'

'I'm good at lying,' she said. 'I do it for a living. I can act outraged. Like, it's so not true that we ever had an affair. *So* not true.'

'That's not funny.'

He stepped up to the door and put his key into the lock. The first thing he saw as he stepped over the threshold was a pair of Joshua's boots under the coat-stand. He slumped down on the staircase, and put his hands over his face.

'So what happened?' Bella asked, coming in after him and closing the door.

'It was terrible,' he said.

'What did you expect?'

'Do you know what I've been through today?'

'She doesn't deserve you.'

'I can't talk to you now,' he said. He went into the sitting room, and she followed him.

'Why did you come back from Paris?' she asked. 'I thought we'd have dinner, you know.' She grinned at him. 'Or whatever.'

She was standing coquettishly, hands on hips, swinging her body from side to side in a gentle, rhythmic motion.

He shook his head, and laughed at her expression. Half laughed, anyway. 'You have the biggest fucking ego in the western world.'

'No dinner? No whatever?' She was still smiling broadly.

'No,' he told her.

Bella looked at him speculatively. 'She'll calm down.'

'She's keeping Joshua from me.'

'It won't last.'

He glared at her. 'You have no inkling of what's involved here. You haven't got children.'

'Thankfully.'

He returned his head to his hands. He didn't want to look at her; he couldn't think straight when he did. She had never been married and claimed she never wanted to be. She'd never even been in a long-term relationship. She had a reputation for being footloose, a free spirit, which had aroused his interest. He had had a kind of fascination for people like that, who seemed not to operate on the same rules as everyone else.

She was so pretty it almost hurt him to watch her, even now. She wore a permanent expression of elfin sweetness. She had been in one or two good films now, and her name was known; not so long ago she had been the girl-most-likely-to-succeed at RADA; she had done all the publicity stuff – morning telly, radio slots, and wearing next to nothing at premières.

'I'm stopping at all the bases,' she had joked, the first time they were together. 'I'm putting together my portfolio.'

'Sleeping with the writer isn't a base,' he

had told her, laughing. 'It's not even in the bloody ballpark. In fact, you're doing the fucking-around equivalent of sleeping with a parking attendant.'

'I have to start somewhere,' she had replied, rolling on top of him and letting her hair fall round his face.

But she had started before him, he knew that. He had seen a picture of her on the arm of a producer who was not known for his fidelity to his wife of thirty years. It was said that he had got her the part in the first film.

He had pulled her hair back from her face. 'You don't need to start anywhere,' he had said. 'You don't need to sleep with anyone. You're beautiful.'

'Beauty doesn't matter,' she had replied. 'There are thousands of beautiful girls. Talent counts.'

'Well, you've got that.'

'Yes.' She had nodded. 'I have. So have you.'

He liked the flattery. She had read the character of her part well; she had understood it. It was good to talk to someone who had enthused so wildly about the woman he had created on the page. It had been amazing to watch her bring his creation to life.

And he wanted her. No surprise in that. Every man on the set wanted her. She had something indefinable, an air of sensuality. She didn't try hard at it; in fact, she didn't try at all. She wore ordinary clothes: sometimes skirts down to the ground, sweaters that swamped her – she still looked fantastic. He found himself following the lines of her body under her clothes. She was catlike in more than one sense: lithe, lazy, and greedy.

She put her hand on his shoulder. He jumped.

'Bella,' he said, 'I've got to think.'

She got down on her knees, took his hands from his face.

'No,' he told her.

Slowly, she ran her hand along the inside of his thigh, almost experimentally.

He took hold of her wrist. 'No,' he repeated.

She leaned forward and kissed him.

It was a strange thing to admit to, but when she had kissed him on that first afternoon, he had been taken aback by distaste. Her mouth, which looked so sensuous, which framed his words and repeated them to him, had been too insistent. He had wanted to make the move; she had made it for him. He had wanted to persuade her. She had needed no persuading, and she had fallen back on the bed, laughing, trying to take off his clothes, while he, in turn, had been going for the slow seduction.

He had thought that that was what women liked. In truth, he had had only the vaguest idea of what a woman such as Bella would like, because at heart he was old-fashioned, and he had had a picture in his mind of taking her out to dinner and bowling her over with his stories and jokes, the things that had made Zeph laugh, and had made Zeph look at him in that surprised, appraising way.

But Bella was not Zeph. She was nothing like her. She didn't hold anything back; she appeared not to have moods; she didn't seem to care what the world thought of her or what was the appropriate thing to do. She had no conscience. She pleased herself.

'Come here,' she had said to him, as she had lain there, and he had looked down at her in confusion and anxiety, wondering if he should turn for the hotel-room door before it was too late.

She was a bolt of lightning that knocked him off his feet, drowned the world and the rest of his life, and any sense of right or wrong.

She didn't make a sound when he screwed her. He thought he had done something wrong, disappointed her until, when he was finished, she smiled broadly, her body stretched sideways across the bed so that her head hung over the edge.

'You're a demon,' he said, meaning it as a

compliment but feeling that it was the truth.

'That's right,' she said. 'A regular imp. The kind that's supposed to prod the damned, you know.'

'Prod?' he repeated.

'The damned,' she confirmed.

He had lain on his side and gazed at her. 'I don't know anything about you,' he had said.

'Yes, you do. Check the CV.'

'Tell me more.'

She had turned to face him. 'That's what you writers like,' she said, 'isn't it? To know the details.'

'The key to all things.'

'Suck out people's souls.'

'What?' he said, leaning up on one elbow.

'Suck us in and churn us out. For research.'

'You have very warped ideas.'

She had run her hand down his body and caught hold of him. 'Oh, you don't know the half of it,' she had whispered. 'I'm going to show you how–'

'Oh, Christ,' he said.

'You'll see,' she had replied, laughing. 'No stopping now.'

She had slithered down his body and taken him into her mouth. He couldn't remember the last time that that had happened to him. When had it gone away?

'Oh, God,' he had murmured, and he had tried, just for a second, to hold on to a picture of Zeph stepping out of his reach, walking away down an empty road. He saw her quite clearly for a second, dropping his hand and striding away without once turning back. And then she vanished, and he rushed headlong down the same empty pathway, the landscape fragmenting behind him, caught up in a torrent, a whirlwind. Shreds flickered past him, parts of conversations, flashes of places, scraps of the look and feel of things he knew. And then he was standing nowhere.

Bella was getting off the bed, smiling.

'You blast me away,' he said. And he meant it: he had been thrown out of his secure places.

'Good,' she had said.

He didn't question what had happened. It sounded bad to say so, but he didn't think of it much, and he didn't feel guilty. He woke up the next day at six o'clock in the morning and, full of anticipation, had run five miles through crystalline streets. They had looked like pale, clean versions of kaleidoscopes, a slowly rotating jumble of cool colours with hard edges: kerbstones, the chrome on cars, the reflections in windows, the closed doors of shops, their lettering. It all seemed wonderfully highlighted and precise, every few yards another tableau to be wondered at. He had stopped half-way round, out of breath, leaned on a wall and watched the lime trees

161

moving gently in the wind. He felt as if he had taken mescaline. Once he had used it for a few weeks; given it up years ago. Now he remembered its heightened perceptions, the curious taste in his mouth. He wanted to run off the edge of the world and keep running.

He had thought of Bella that morning as he worked, and eventually gave up and rang her. She did not answer her phone, and he left a message. There was no reply that day, or the next, and by the time she answered on the third he was disoriented by the need to see her.

He had gone to her flat. As she opened the door, he pushed it away from her hands, slammed it behind him and almost forced her in the hallway.

'What's this?' she asked, entertained by his need.

'I want you,' he told her, pushing her backwards. 'Where have you been?'

'What's it to do with you?' she said.

He went on for perhaps two weeks in this numb need, giving Zeph barely a thought. His wife and child moved through him like shadows; he couldn't recall anything she asked him to do, and there were arguments when he forgot.

'What on earth is the matter with you?' Zeph had asked, one day. 'Do you feel ill? Is something wrong?'

He put his phone on redial for Bella's number. He drove past her flat time and time again at night, waiting to see the lights come on. He once drove past early in the morning, at about six, and saw that the curtains had not been drawn the night before. He had stopped his car at the end of the street and crouched over the wheel, crippled by the thought that she had been with someone else.

When he worked, when he looked at the keyboard, he couldn't conjure up the images he was supposed to be concentrating on. All he could think of was her, the things she did. Once, at a read-through, he had followed her out on to the grimy terrace where other actors went to smoke. The concrete floor was littered with cigarette ends.

She had rested her back against the door, pulled up her skirt. He knew they might be seen from the street; there might be a knock on the door at any moment.

'You shouldn't do any of this,' he said, turned on by the casualness of the action and the sight of her.

'I shouldn't,' she said. 'You're right.'

He would lie awake at night. It was a puzzle to him how wanting Bella made him want Zeph all the more. For moments at a time, the two women became indistinguishable. He would think of one while making love to the other. It was during one of these times when, for a second, he was so lost in the act, so driven by a kind of raging, blinding emasculating thirst, a lust so out of hand, that the desire broke, and he realized he didn't know the woman beneath him, and looked up to see Zeph's eyes closed, her hand flung behind her head. It was the first time in a long time that they had made love, and he was struck with terrible guilt.

He had stopped suddenly, and buried his head in the pillow next to her face.

'What is it?' she had asked.

He couldn't look at her.

'What have I done?' she had asked, trying to turn his face to her. 'Tell me, Nick, please.'

'Nothing,' he told her. 'I'm sorry.'

It had been two weeks, almost three, until he had felt the guilt.

There had been not a moment of it beforehand.

The next time he saw Bella, he told her that it was over. 'I never wanted to hurt you,' he said.

'You call this not hurting me?'

'It wasn't for always,' he told her, trying to be truthful, and seeing at once how dismally he was handling it.

'Well, it didn't last long,' she said.

He felt staggered, mortified. He had thought she would be more upset. 'I've got a wife,' he said, trying to justify himself. 'A son.'

'You had them six weeks ago.'

'I know.'

'So, what's changed?'

'I can't do this,' he told her. 'It's like cutting myself in two.'

Bella had put her arms round his neck. 'Then don't cut yourself in two,' she said.

'It's not as simple as that,' he said.

'You make it difficult,' she said, 'when it isn't. You hardly ever speak to each other. You told me that yourself.' She dropped her arms from him and walked to the window. They were in another hotel; the view was of a corner of Hyde Park. 'You can give me up, just like that?' she asked, with her back to him. 'Well, I'm sorry,' she said. 'It's a waste.'

'Don't be angry with me.'

She pulled an ironic face.

'I should never have started this,' he said.

'You're right.'

He couldn't understand her reaction. 'Are you angry?'

'I don't know what I am,' she said. 'I thought it would last longer than this,' she murmured, 'but why should it? You got what you wanted.'

'Don't say that.' He was hurt.

She glanced up at him, shrugged. 'It's true,' she said. She walked to the chair and picked up her coat.

'Don't go,' he said abruptly. She smiled as she put it on.

'I mean it,' he said.

'I'm late already.'

'For what?'

'I'm meeting Peter Maynard.'

The actor who played opposite her. 'Why?' he asked.

'Why not?'

The answer shocked him. She picked up her bag. He jumped to his feet. 'Is it work?' he asked.

'Look,' she said, 'it really doesn't matter one way or the other, does it? Not now.'

'Are you seeing him?' he asked. 'Are you sleeping with him?'

'What difference would it make?'

'Every difference!' he said, and a surge of jealousy went through him.

'I don't see why,' she told him. 'You sleep with someone else, don't you?'

'Bella,' he murmured, 'please don't go.'

'I'm doing what you want,' she said.

'No,' he told her. 'It's not what I want.'

She regarded him for a second or two, then leaned forward and rested her head on his shoulder. 'Why can't you leave her?' she whispered. 'I could make you very happy. I want you more than she does.'

He didn't think so, but he didn't care. He would have sold his soul at that moment to put his hands on her, to have her in bed with him, to possess her, keep her with him. 'I will leave her,' he lied. He stroked her neck, then wound her hair round his fingers and pulled her head back so that she was looking up into his face. 'For God's sake,' he said. And he tried to draw a deep breath. The thought of her with some other man was crushing, asphyxiating. He felt as if someone had put a match to his throat, his chest.

'Please,' he had said, and pulled her close, opened his fingers, felt the weight of her hair, its texture. 'Please, Bella,' he repeated, 'tell me you're not sleeping with him.'

He opened his eyes to the sight of her on her knees in front of him. Two months had passed since that day; and he knew now that she had lied to him. She had been with Peter Maynard all along. He had found that out after they had parted. And he had felt, when he was told the truth, that Bella had been right when she told him so carelessly that he was damned.

He saw that he had been standing at the gates of the underworld, and condemned himself freely to hell.

'Get up,' he told her.

She sat back on her heels, smiling. 'There's no reason why we can't take up where we left off,' she said, 'if you like.'

His eyes ranged over her. 'You are unbelievable,' he said.

'That's what you always told me.' She put her head on one side and accepted what she thought was his appraising gaze.

'I don't know what I was thinking of,' he said softly.

'I do,' she retorted.

He stood up, grabbed her wrist, pulled her to her feet.

There was a moment as he gazed into her lovely face, felt the flesh under his fingers, when he could willingly have gone back down the road. He took a breath, closed his eyes for a second. 'Just go,' he said. 'This is real life, now. Please. Just go.'

Nine

In those days, there was no accurate, accepted description for what Cora had, and there was no discussion of it. Of course people knew that she had not been at the funeral, and that she was not at home.

At the nursing-home she was allowed to sit out, and the gardens were pretty. From a seat by the main house, she could see the driveway and the Somerset levels beyond. The flat plain of fields was mesmerizing: a haze hung over it in the morning and late in the evening; during the day, in the heat, ripples ran over it, currents of air drugged with a sweet green scent.

All she did in the first ten days was sleep, sent into oblivion by sedatives. It was like being in a boat, far away from the shore, on a whispering ocean.

Her father came to see her every day.

'What have you told everyone?' she asked.

'That you've gone back to London,' he said.

'Why don't you tell them the truth?' she asked.

'Because I don't know what the truth is,' he said. 'I don't know what's happened.'

She saw the shock in his face. He had aged since her mother's death. 'I feel a fraud,' she told him softly. 'You should be here, being looked after. Not me.'

'Cora,' he replied, 'you've had a breakdown. It's not your fault.'

A nervous breakdown. People would say that about her for a long time afterwards. *You know that she had a nervous breakdown when her mother died?* They would say it at the wedding; she would overhear them. And Richard would be spoken of in admiring terms, as the man who had brought her back to life; the kind man who was not afraid of being with a woman whose personality could not withstand a death in the family.

'Richard Ward has asked about you,' her father said.

She looked down at the teacups, neatly arranged on the tray in front of them.

'Would you like to see him?'

'Not here,' she said.

'When you come back?'

'Perhaps.'

'He was very good that afternoon.'

'Yes,' she murmured. 'He was.' She glanced up again to see her father's worried expression. 'Cora,' he said, 'I've been speaking to Jenny.'

'When?'

'She phoned me. She'd heard about your mother.'

'I see.'

'She tells me she's getting married.'

'Yes, she is.'

He hesitated. 'She mentioned a man,' he said. 'David Menzies.'

Cora closed her eyes. In the room behind them – the windows were open – someone had put a record on the gramophone. The scratchy, tinny tones came drifting out into the garden. It was an old Frank Sinatra song from seven or eight years before: 'Three Coins In The Fountain'. They had the same record at home, all the ballads: 'Cara Mia', 'Oh Mein Papa' and 'Outside Of Heaven'. When she had been a teenager, those were the tunes that were played after dinner. Sometimes, if it was a party, her mother had put on comic songs, like 'She Wears Red

Feathers'. She could remember her dancing about, a glass held high. One Christmas. One new year.

'Who is he?' her father asked.

'No one significant,' she told him.

'Did he cause this?'

'It doesn't matter.' She could see that her answer disappointed him. 'I'm coming home,' she told him. 'I'm not going to stay here and cost you a fortune.'

He had put a hand to his eyes. 'I only want you to get better, darling.'

'I am better,' she said. 'I am.'

When she got home Richard came to see her. He walked into the house in the middle of a morning about a fortnight later, in the first week of May, through the open kitchen door, calling her name. 'Cora?'

She was standing at the big kitchen table, with the crockery laid out in front of her and all the cupboard and pantry doors open.

'You're busy,' he said.

'Everything's dusty,' she told him. 'I'm washing it all.'

She had been up since six. She didn't sleep well. After she had seen her father off to work, she had emptied the linen closet, bringing down all the sheets and towels, napkins and pillowcases. She had inspected them minutely, opening them out. Some bore yellow lines, starched and unused for years. Some smelt of lavender, sprinkled by her mother. These she held to her face before she plunged them into the washtub. She worked relentlessly, as she had seen her mother do sometimes with the cleaner who came on Mondays and Thursdays. It was hard, manual work, taking the linen through the mangle and carrying it all, dripping, to the vegetable patch where the clothes-lines were. Now, at lunchtime, the rows of washing slapped in the wind.

She noticed that he was carrying flowers: nothing from a shop, all from the hedgerow, dog roses, grasses and strands of ivy. 'Not very glamorous,' he said, holding them out to her.

'Thank you,' she said, 'all the same.'

'They're growing everywhere,' he said. 'All down the lanes.'

'Are you nearly finished at your house?'

'Yes,' he said. 'Finished.'

'What, everything? All the rooms?'

'I've whitewashed them,' he told her. 'I don't know what colour would be best to paint them.'

'And furnished?'

'Ah,' he admitted. 'Not quite.'

She walked up to the lane with him.

At the gate, she looked over the thistle-strewn patch to the low buildings.

Richard Ward stood beside her, saying nothing. He leaned on the gate, and she glanced at his profile, at the scar above his collar. His arms were muscular, but thin; she wondered how he cared for himself, living alone.

'It's taken a year,' he said.

'Yes,' she murmured. And she thought of that year: of Bisley, the books and the poetry. Of champagne. Of a clock stuck for ever at eleven thirty.

He turned to her, and straightened. She realized, with surprise, that he was nervous. 'Would you like to go to the cinema one evening?' he asked.

'You and I?' she said, and blushed at the stupidity of the question.

'Only if you would like to.'

'All right.'

'Shall I see what's on?' he asked. 'In town?'

'All right,' she repeated.

He smiled broadly. 'Fine,' he said. 'That's good.'

But as she walked back through the garden, shutting the gate to the lane, passing the budding roses, and then the lines of white sheets, she felt horribly panicked. She had to stop, resting one hand on the wall of the house, and glanced back along the path, the way she had come, and thought about telling him she had made a mistake.

They saw the Ernest Borgnine film *Marty*.

'I'm sorry it wasn't very cheerful,' Richard

said, as they came out of the cinema.

People brushed past them. They stood awkwardly, several feet apart. 'I thought it was very good,' she said. 'It was unusual.'

'It won an Oscar. Best Film,' he said.

It was still light: it was only nine o'clock.

'Would you like to go for a drink somewhere?' he asked.

They were in the centre of Yeovil, a twenty-minute drive from Sherborne. 'I would like to go home,' she said.

He nodded. They walked alongside each other. Richard had parked the pick-up van in a side-street; when he had come to collect her, he had apologized for it, saying he didn't own a car.

'I don't mind,' she had told him. She was staring at him now, seeing that he had taken trouble to look smart. She was wearing the same blouse and skirt she had worn all day, although she had brushed her hair and put on lipstick. It was only the pictures, not a date. They were only going together to see a film; she would pay for her own ticket; they would come straight back afterwards. That was how she had thought of the evening, yet now, looking at Richard, she realized it meant something more to him.

He had on a jacket, tie and flannel trousers, a little out of date, but all clean and pressed. He had obviously tried to comb his curly hair flat, and Brylcreemed it with a severe parting that showed a scalp reddened by the sun. She felt an enormous surge of regret and pity. She was not going to be anyone's girlfriend.

They drove in silence. Only when they got to her house did Richard speak again. 'Would you like to see *Gigi* next week?' he asked. 'It's a bit livelier.'

She turned sideways in her seat to face him.

'I don't think they ever get new films here,' he said, smiling.

'Richard...' she began.

'Do you like Hitchcock?'

'I haven't seen any,' she said. 'My parents never went to the cinema.'

'We had a film club in Italy,' Richard said. 'Not even *Rebecca?* Not *The Lady Vanishes?*'

'When were you in Italy?' she asked.

'I was in hospital for two months,' he told her. 'One of the officers got us a projector. All they sent us were Hitchcocks and horror. And when we objected, we got all kinds of things. *"G" Men*, and Busby Berkeley musicals, Bing Crosby. Godzilla. *How Green Was My Valley.*'

'You were wounded? In the war?'

'In Sicily.'

'Did you stay in Italy after you left hospital?'

'I was posted back to a desk,' he said, 'in London.'

'Did you live there until you bought the land?'

'No,' he said. 'I left the army. I travelled.'

It was getting dark now: she could barely see the borders of the garden, the trees at the edge of the drive.

'Richard,' she said, 'you're very kind to take me out. I enjoyed the film. But I don't want to impose on you.'

There was a silence. Then, 'I see,' he said.

The worst of it was, she felt nothing, not even guilt. She was not even sensible to his disappointment. She had gone tonight because she had been taken off guard, but all she wanted was to be left alone. She felt truly anaesthetized. She wanted to get the world around her straight and in order; that was all she cared about, or concentrated on. She didn't stop all day. Any day. Her father had already objected that she was unbearably restless, but it had troubled her to sit quietly with him, helping him with the crossword as her mother used to do. She knew what he was saying, but she couldn't help it. The world was flattened somehow, all the interest taken out of it. She forced herself to move because she felt lost, sunk in the grey, if she was still.

Richard opened the door, got out and came round to her side to hand her down from the pick-up. He walked her to the front door. She could feel the imprint of his

176

fingers and she wanted to get inside.

'Cora...' she heard him murmur, as she turned her back on him.

She banged loudly on the door, the heavy iron knocker making a sound that reverberated down the passageway inside. Her father didn't come. 'Daddy,' she called. 'Daddy.'

She knocked quickly and repeatedly with the flat of her hand, and then, through the single glass panel at the top of the door, saw the shadow of her father walking out of the dining room.

She turned to Richard to thank him for the evening. He was standing back from her, a distressed frown on his face. 'Good night, Cora,' he said. And, under his breath, 'I'm very sorry.'

It was another fortnight before she summoned the courage to go and see him.

He was working outside his house, digging out soil behind it to make a flat area. When he saw her climbing the slope, he stopped and wiped his hands on the seams of his trousers.

As she drew near, he smiled.

It was a close day, the sky overcast; warm and oppressive. Sweat marked the cotton of his shirt, the back and shoulders.

'Are you making a garden?' she asked.

'I thought I'd lay some flagstones,' he said, 'so there would be somewhere to sit out and look at the view.'

He indicated the hill behind her; she turned, and saw her own garden, the street beyond, the edge of the little town and the hills in the distance.

'This was how you saw what had happened to Mother,' she murmured.

'Yes,' he said. He dug the spade into the ground.

'What will you do when you finish it all?' she asked. 'Will you stay here or sell it?'

'I don't know,' he said. 'I may sell... Would you like to see inside?'

He took her in through the front door, which faced the lane. A rough driveway of broken chalk and flint had been laid. She glanced up at the building, thinking that it was very plain and serviceable, a man's house, perfectly square, with a large window at either side of the door.

They went into a short, straight hallway and from there into the kitchen. There was a sink, an electric stove and a large, floor-standing boiler. In the centre stood a red Formica-topped table, and four chairs, all very new. In the food cupboard opposite her, with its drop-leaf door and two glass-fronted shelves above, she saw the bare essentials: salt, bread, gravy browning, and cans of soup.

The room was white. Everywhere was white – the sitting room, the two bedrooms, the bathroom. Except the two rows of bright green tiles around the bath.

'I'm not very good with colours,' he admitted. 'The tiles were cheap, though. What do you think?'

'I think...'

'Be honest.'

'I think I know why they were cheap.'

They smiled at each other.

'Would you like some tea?' he asked.

'Yes,' she said. 'Please.'

He brought the cups to where she had gone to stand outside, looking in the opposite direction this time, to the brow of the hill behind. The grass and thistles were yellowed, sprayed with weed-killer to keep them down. To the left-hand side, in the sheds, she could see piles of bricks, railway sleepers, ironwork and roof tiles.

He handed her a cup of tea. 'If I built it again, I'd do it differently,' he said.

'In what way?'

He shrugged. 'I think it lacks something,' he said. 'It's rather boring and square.'

'I think it's amazing that you built it yourself.'

'Do you?' he said, turning to her. 'But it needs a woman's touch.' To her surprise, he blushed, and turned his profile to her again. 'What would you do with it?' he asked, nodding at the land.

'I don't know,' she said. 'The soil isn't very

good. It would take a lot of improving.'

'Perhaps I chose badly all round,' he said.

'Oh, no,' she replied. 'You would surely make a profit if you sold the house. But you could dig out a lawn, and plant trees on the rest. It might be very nice in time.'

He was standing with his arms crossed, frowning at the land.

'You're very critical of yourself,' she observed.

He said nothing.

'Richard,' she added hesitantly, 'I came to apologize. I was very rude the other night.'

'It doesn't matter,' he said.

'My father was annoyed that I didn't bring you in.'

'I asked you too soon,' he said.

'It's not that,' she said. 'It's not you.' She finished her tea, and handed him the cup. 'Would you come to dinner tonight?' she asked.

'I don't want you to feel that you must invite me,' he said.

'I don't,' she told him. 'I would like to give you dinner. I'm cooking anyway. Nothing special. I would like you to join us.'

'Thank you,' he said.

'Eight o'clock?'

'Yes,' he said. 'That would be very nice.'

When he turned up that evening, precisely at eight, she was rather touched at the effort he had made to look respectable. It was with a pang almost of affection that she noticed, as he walked into the sitting room and her father rose to shake his hand, that part of the back of his shirt had not been pressed properly and the garment hung off him.

Over dinner, her father asked Richard about his home. 'I was posted briefly to Barrow,' he added.

'That's not far away from us,' Richard said.

'Cumberland and Westmorland are beautiful counties.'

'Yes, sir,' Richard agreed. 'They are.'

'Are you a fell-walker?'

'I was once.'

'Not many mountains here.'

'No.'

Cora's father turned to her. 'We had a competition,' he told her, 'in the Naval Air Squadron. To run up a few peaks. Three in thirty-six hours.' He laughed softly to himself, brandy glass in hand. 'Let me see,' he mused. 'We started at Langdale. The Pikes, if I recall rightly.'

'I've walked them many times,' Richard said.

'Beautiful, quite beautiful,' Cora's father said. 'Bit younger then, of course. Right the way down, over Blea Rigg to High Raise, and back towards the big waterfall...'

'Dungeon Ghyll.'

'That's right,' Cora's father confirmed. 'And what is it that you can see across from the waterfall?'

'Side Pike, Wrynose Fell.'

The two men smiled at each other. 'And you,' Cora's father said, 'Rannerdale, you said.'

'That's where I was born,' Richard replied. 'Under another big mountain, Grasmoor.' He turned to Cora. 'Under a mountain and next to a lake.'

'And brought up there?' Cora asked.

'Until I went to boarding-school.'

Cora's father nodded. 'Never forgot Barrow,' he said. 'Never do forget those things. Cora's mother and I were married there.' There was a pause. 'A navy man yourself?' he asked Richard.

'Army. First Battalion, York and Lancaster Regiment.'

'See service?'

'Richard was wounded in Sicily,' Cora said. Out of the corner of her eye, she saw Richard glance at her. He took his arms off the table and sat back in his seat.

'With the invasion?'

'Yes,' Richard said.

'From North Africa?'

'We had a roundabout journey,' Richard said. 'We came from Bombay to Port Said.'

'By sea?' Cora asked.

'No,' he said, 'across country, through

Pakistan and Persia, down to Palestine and Egypt. We sailed from Port Said in July 1943.'

'Hell of a journey,' Cora's father observed.

'Yes, sir,' Richard replied. 'A long way.'

'Well,' Cora's father said, pushing back his chair, 'I expect we all travelled some distance then.' He stood up. Richard, too, got to his feet. 'No, no,' the older man told him. 'You two stay and chat. I have to go into town and see Edward Miles at the Rotary Club.'

Cora saw how he avoided her gaze, and felt momentarily irritated at his obvious ruse to leave her and Richard alone together. She began to clear the table. 'There's no need to help me,' she told Richard, as he made a move after Cora's father had left the room.

'I'd like to,' he told her.

They carried the dishes into the kitchen. As they went in, they saw, in the darkness, for the light was turned off, the garden's landscape: the last rim of daylight on the hill, the silhouette of the trees.

'It's your light I can see sometimes,' she said, realizing it suddenly. 'Through the trees. My room faces in this direction.' She had seen the square of illumination only occasionally but hadn't wondered what it was or to which house it might belong.

Richard said nothing. She opened the window, and a warm, insistent breeze blew

183

in. They stood in silence, in semi-darkness.

'I can smell the Cussons rose,' he said. 'It must have its first flowers.'

'The what?'

'Don't you have roses?' he asked. 'A new hybrid.'

'I don't know,' she said. 'I don't know the names of anything. Mother planted one last year, I think. Just below the terrace.'

They walked out into the growing dusk. A long way down the garden, they could hear several birds calling. The lawn was damp: she could feel the slight resistance of moisture as they walked. They stopped by the new roses, noticed their luminescence, the heavy density of their scent. Older varieties grew all around them, but the few early cerise flowers dominated the bed, their colour striking and solid against the low wall of the terrace, even in the twilight. Then, after a moment, Richard walked towards the fruit cages at the edge of the grass.

Cora followed him. Then she heard what had drawn him there: the fluttering of wings inside the netting.

'There's a bird caught,' he said.

'There can't be,' she told him. 'How could it get in?'

Richard had opened the netting door, and stepped inside. 'Are these raspberries?' he asked, stretching out his hand in the shadows.

'Loganberries,' she said, and brushed against the slightly serrated edges of the leaves.

'I can smell these too,' he said.

It was true: the leaves had a rich, slightly acidic scent. It was all-pervasive in the small enclosure. When the fruit came, it would be overpowering. She saw Richard move slowly along the flimsy wall. 'It's here,' he said.

She found him kneeling. The netting was moving: a bird was struggling, caught in its folds near the ground.

'What is it?' she asked.

'Something little,' he said. 'A sparrow, I think.'

He stayed where he was for a moment.

'What's the matter?' she asked.

'I can't get it free,' he said.

She knelt down next to him. The bird had encased itself in the rolled border of the net. 'It's stuck,' she murmured.

'Can you feel it?' he asked.

'Yes.' She could feel the rapid, panicked beating of its heart under her fingers. It was no stronger than the scratch of a leaf against glass.

He began to untwine the threads with enormous patience from the bird's feet. It took a minute, two minutes; eventually its heartbeat slowed. She was aware of holding a scrap of life in the arch of her palm.

'Be quick,' she whispered.

'Pass it under the netting,' Richard said. 'That way, when I get it free, it won't fly back into the bushes.'

She did as he asked, kneeling awkwardly with her hands under the net floor, which was pegged down for several feet further along to either side of her. 'I must see to this gap,' she murmured, 'in the morning.'

'I'll do it for you,' he replied. And then, a second later, 'That's it.'

They stood up, heard the tumble of wings, and saw the brief shape of the sparrow spiralling upwards, trying to gain momentum. 'I thought it was dying,' Cora said. 'I thought it had frightened itself to death.'

True dark had descended now; only the sky above showed a vague reflection of light from the west.

When he kissed her, it was with the same fragile lightness that had been in her hand, the same rapid trembling. His mouth was cool. Almost immediately, he stepped away. 'I'm sorry,' he said.

'I'm nothing like you imagine,' she said. 'I'm not good for you. For anyone.'

He put his hand on her waist and, very slowly, drew her to him.

She saw him look away, to one side; above them, the first stars clouded, then were revealed, and hidden again just as swiftly by racing grey ghosts. Richard's eyes were on the ground where the bird had been. Her body ached; her skin became warm where his hand rested. She wanted to close her eyes; she wanted to sleep and be carried away. She was so tired of trying to hold everyone apart from her, of the enormous burden of making herself function. She felt almost exhausted, as if she had made a journey, like the journeys he and her father had discussed.

One night that summer, Richard would tell her about those miles as she sat with his arm around her shoulder: she would hear the litany of names, of places, until they became a kind of song in her memory, until it was almost as if she herself had lived them. As if it had been she, late in 1941, travelling the endless rail to Ranchi from Calcutta, then onwards from Ranchi to Karachi. From the Gulf of Oman to Basra and Abadan, in what was then called Persia, from the camp at Kermanshah, to Qum, and Baghdad. And then across the trans-Jordanian desert to Syria, to be stationed at Ismailia; and across the Mediterranean, in a crowded ship, with the drone of aircraft overhead, to a beach called Cassabili, where dawn was breaking as the boat moved to the shore.

He would say that there had been nothing left of him worth having when it was over, after Sicily, after London and the end of the war; and that he had drifted for a long time afterwards, and tried to go home, and failed at the sight of the heights he had once scaled, and been afraid of everything that moved, even of water breaking on sand, the sound of waves, of planes overhead, even of the waters rushing down the Langdales into Great Langdale Beck.

And that he had gone away, anywhere, without plan, without interest, almost waiting to be obliterated – hoping for it almost – by space and emptiness. How he had gone to Italy again, and come down through France and Spain to Morocco. Despaired of noise and the flat light, the seas flatter and bluer than the light, and come home, one December, to rain and the rolling, uninterrupted green of southern England.

And he had bought a piece of land, built a house and been alone.

And there had been no one, no one at all for him, until he saw her that day at the abbey as she came out.

She put her head on his shoulder, in the dark of the garden.

'Let me look after you,' he said. 'That's all I want to do.'

They were married four months later, in the first week of September.

L'Angelo

I am going to Caltagirone.

It is four months since you were here.

You are not coming back.

Despite all that we promised each other, that I have done everything you wanted, that I have waited for you, I know what perhaps you already knew in your heart as you went back to England. That you would not see me again.

The world has changed for me. My father knows. And now I must do as he tells me, or there is no future for me here. Occasionally, he talks to me, to tell me of the work in Caltagirone, of how to ask my cousin there for my money. He tells me in short sentences, as if I'm a child. Because he says I have disgraced him, that I can no longer be regarded as a man and that I can no longer be trusted.

I can't look him in the face any more, and neither can he look at me.

I am forbidden my friends, who have knocked at the door to see me, to drink with me. They are curious. They want to know if the gossip is true; if I have really done what they have heard. But I am treated like a baby who cannot walk anywhere alone. I am shackled, by my father's will and by what I have told him. He has stood

189

over me and threatened to disown me – as if I cared about that. I don't. I despise him for his money and what he likes to imagine is his influence.

The house is silent. It's as if there has been a death. My mother turns her face away and won't touch me. I think she asked my sisters to do the same, and they keep away, but at least they glance at me. Valeria is sorry, I think. She looks as if she might cry when she sees me. She understands because she is the oldest; because she has fallen in love herself, and is waiting to be married. I think perhaps she is consumed by a little of what consumes me. But no one comes to my room. I have the highest room in the house, and I can see the ocean from the window, and I want to stand on the roof and fly across it. I imagine myself flying at the dead of night, escaping the last conversation with my father.

It began on Sunday. We had gone to the cathedral. I was thinking of what it had been like that Friday when we were first together, may God have mercy on me. I was thinking during communion, during the sacrament, of what my father calls my unforgivable sin.

I was thinking of you, the colour of your skin, your face next to mine, your hands, the sound of you, the way you whispered and the way I took you. I was thinking of that as the blessing was pronounced over me, and I am willing to accept that this was wrong, but I am not willing to accept that I am the first man to have thought of such things, the touch of a woman, the sound of a woman, while the sacrament was in his mouth. Because you are greater than heaven to me, and the thing that is between us has the same holiness, and this is my declaration to God, on the Day of Judgement, even if it confines me to hell for eternity, that to have you in my arms was a blessing.

But Sunday. You know how, in the cathedral, there are the angels that guard each side of the aisle just before the altar? On the day that it happened, this Sunday three weeks ago, I was thinking of how afraid I had been as a child, and I was looking at the angels, because the night before I had dreamed of them.

All my life I have seen those faces. I used to think they were very white, and they had thin features, not like most Italian faces. And they had yellow hair and white robes with a yellow star. They were like princesses, the kind you see in Disney films. Like the princess in Cinderella. *I was in love with them, I think, when I was a little boy. I was going to marry someone like that, not an Italian. I had your picture in my mind even before I met you. Do you see that? I was always going to have a woman like you in my arms. I was going to be her husband. I was going to lie next to a kind of saint like this, a kind of angel, with her white face, long hair and blue eyes, just like yours.*

I had a dream the night before it happened. I dreamed that the angels got down from the walls

191

and came towards me, rising up from the floor, their great wings beating; but as they drifted from the wall and hovered an inch above the floor, their wings unfurling, their faces bore a painful look, a contortion, as if the unfurling wings were agony to them. And sure enough, as the wings spread out to either side of them, the tips of their feathers spilt drops of blood onto the floor, spattering against the feathers and onto the angels' feet too.

And their faces weren't the faces of girls any more, but of old women. I don't know why this was terrible, so terrible, for why should angels not be old, old with wisdom of many years, old faces with kindliness in them? Angels' faces like the face of the Madonna, are always untouched and unmarked, and bear no blemishes, as if they are above the suffering of the world. But an angel would know everything, surely; an angel would be an old man, an old woman with experience scored into their face.

And I don't know if I had ever thought this before, or had been thinking it on the day before, but suddenly in my dream that night the faces were old like that. And then the worst thing of all: they began to burn.

Smoke poured from their backs, mouths and hands, and their robes shrank to black shrouds before they, too, began to smoulder. And they circled, like birds, going higher and higher into the roof, everything about them now burning and blackening. And their wings extended to *their full width and showered ash. And everyone in the church was covered with embers that ignited hair and clothes, and sent people shrieking out of the doors. Only I stayed, and they descended on me.*

When I look back on this dream, I can hardly remember a before time – before you, before the kiss in the doorway in the dark, before I felt you beneath me in that bed, in the room under the eaves of the house, the white wood bed, the folded blanket instead of sheets, the sound of the birds beneath the tiles – before all that, I was like the others.

I was thinking of the next term in Rome. You won't believe what the next most important thing was in my head before I met you. It was to buy the French boy's motorcycle. I can't help laughing when I think about it. Joachim's motorcycle. I wanted it so badly. That, and to win at scopo. *To win at cards.*

I am nineteen years old. I used to be told that I had a future: I would inherit my father's business, step into his shoes and be the rich man driving a Mercedes, like his, with a family of five or six children, like his. Now I don't think anyone would tell me I had a future, because I am the boy with a crack in his character, like a hand-wide crack running down a badly built building. I had a woman and it went to my head.

Worse still, I had the English wife of a kind and honourable man who was nursed by my own grandmother, a man my grandfather and

193

father respect, a brave man. I have taken his wife behind his back and I don't have the wit to understand that such a taking is not love, but theft.

I tried to tell him that we made love to each other, and I began to weep when I remembered, and I think it was this, the weeping, the evidence of weakness, that made my father more furious than what had gone before: the confession outside the church.

We had been at mass, and I don't know what happened to me. I saw the angels and I remembered the dream, and I couldn't breathe suddenly. The air felt full of dust. I went outside, and I saw the arch of the white sky, the impossibility of the distance between us. I knew that I would have to find you.

My father came out of the church after me.

'What is the matter with you?' he asked.

I looked at him. All the consequences of what I wanted to say seemed like nothing. I could only think of the arch of the sky and wanting to get to you, that I hadn't heard from you and that your silence might mean you were ill, or in need of me. I thought I would choke, suffocate, that I would die there on the steps if I couldn't leave.

'I'm going to England,' I said. And I told him why.

He stood very still, almost to attention. He looked like his photograph on the wall of the house, in the passageway to the kitchen, in his uniform. An age seemed to pass. He glanced *back once into the cathedral and then he said, 'Follow me.'*

We went home.

I was ready to tell him all about you, that I wanted to marry you, that I loved you, that you had only gone home with Richard for six months, and that you would come back to me. He listened without a word, and I thought he would understand. I have always been my father's favourite, his only son. He has indulged me, I suppose, and now I thought I would have the indulgence of his understanding. What made me think this, truly, I don't now comprehend.

He hit me with the flat of his hand first, and then he hit me with his fist. That was his answer.

But it's not true what my father says. He tells me that women are one thing, but honour and the family another, that the love of a woman is secondary. It is something that is swept away by time, obligation, work, necessity, duty, boredom and familiarity. That love is a story for the movies, books and songs. It doesn't last the heat of the day. It is a pallid lie that children believe, but not men.

When he had finished beating me that Sunday morning, he told me that I could never go to England. I told him I would. I told him it was necessary because Richard already knew.

I told him that Richard is a good person who would not stop you coming back to me, if is was what you really wanted.

But you have not come back, so I am guessing

in the dark. Anything could have happened. Perhaps none of my letters has reached you because you no longer live there. Or perhaps you left of your own accord, because you felt that was the right thing to do. These two, frankly, I have hoped for, expecting a message from you daily, saying what has happened and where you are, when you are coming back to me.

But there has been no letter and no message, only my own letters returned. So I know. I think that perhaps you and Richard have come to some sort of compromise, that he has persuaded you to stay for good, and that part of the compromise is to return my letters, and never contact me again.

But that isn't an answer, either. Because I can't believe you would be as cruel as that: I believe that even if you had come to such a decision, you would at least write and tell me.

So I have no real answers, Cora. I go round and round in my head until the horrible circularity kills me. We are both imprisoned in our separate lives. Perhaps that is the truth, after all: the truth of us.

I wish you would send me just one line.

I feel the imprint of you in my heart and I think that it will never be whole again, never lie quiet. My father says that I have made my name unclean, but that isn't true.

If I had the choice, I would do it again.

I would choose you, over and over and over again.

Ten

It was a piece of her childhood.

Zeph stood at the fence to the field, with Joshua balanced on one hip. The little boy's face was turned into her shoulder. 'Look, darling,' she cajoled him, 'the horse is coming. See him?'

The gelding was crossing the grass, a chestnut, moving its head from side to side against the cold morning breeze.

'He's exactly the same colour as a horse that Mummy used to ride,' she said. 'He used to be in this field, too. My own horse, a pony. Aren't you going to stroke him? Look, he likes you. He's come to talk to you.'

'No,' Joshua insisted, his voice muffled.

The gelding lowered its head.

'You are beautiful,' Zeph murmured to the animal. She reached out her fingers to touch him.

Her father had taught Zeph to ride. He had brought her to these stables, although they had not been so upmarket then. There had been no expensive horse-boxes parked in the yard, and the place had been virtually run by girls like Zeph, all horse-mad, all coming after school, changing out of their uniform in the tack room, slinging their clothes in untidy heaps, pulling on the jeans and sweatshirts that smelt so alluringly of saddles, feed and ponies. From eight to fourteen, Zeph had lived for those hours. She didn't care what job she did, so long as the day finished with the ride out.

The place was run then by a Miss Grady, whom Zeph had never seen out of her layers of dog-hairy sweaters and padded anoraks. Miss Grady had lived in the comfortable squalor of a run-down cottage next to the stableyard; she had habitually carried a mug of tea in one hand and a rein in the other, as if she had absentmindedly misplaced the horse to which the rein had been attached. She must have been seventy-five or eighty even then, Zeph thought.

Where Miss Grady had gone, she had no idea. It had been quite a shock to drive along the road this morning, turn in at the stables and see the perfectly painted fences, the scrubbed yard and the new row of loose boxes built alongside the old.

'Is Miss Grady still here?' she had asked a girl, who was grooming a little cob pony.

'Chloë's on the phone,' the girl said, 'if that's who you mean.'

Chloë wasn't Miss Grady, or anything like her. Chloë turned out to be a smart woman in her twenties.

'I used to ride here,' Zeph told her, 'fifteen

198

years ago. I would like my son to learn.' And she indicated Josh, who was staring wide-eyed and mistrustfully at the woman.

'Never too young,' Chloë had said.

'He's a little bit wary.'

'That's fine,' Chloë had responded. 'We're used to it. We've got a toddler class on Saturday morning. Bring him to that.'

Zeph turned Joshua's face to hers now with the tip of her finger. 'Going to ride a little pony on Saturday?' she asked. 'Just a little one, with Mummy here holding him for you?'

'Daddy hold him,' Josh replied. And he suddenly tried to scramble up from her hip, throwing his arms round her shoulders, pushing with his heels against her stomach.

'Ouch, Josh,' she remonstrated. 'Don't do that. It hurts.'

He ground his feet into her and she tried to hold him away from her. 'Josh,' she said. 'Stop it.'

'Daddy hold him,' her son muttered. 'He hold him.'

They got home at eleven. As they crossed to the house, Joshua sat down in the yard. 'Come inside,' she told him. 'Please, Josh.'

He didn't reply. He began the complicated private game he had been preoccupied with yesterday: arranging the small rough stones of the driveway in lines, then balancing them on the edges of the puddles.

Zeph watched him for a second. 'Don't get wet,' she said resignedly. 'I can see you from the window so I'll know if you do, OK?'

Joshua didn't answer. His head was bowed. Rejection forming a knot in her throat, Zeph wondered if her son would ever again look her in the eye. 'I didn't choose it,' she whispered, 'if that's what you think.'

She went inside, carrying the shopping she had done for her mother on the way to the stables. 'Where are you?' she called.

'Here,' Cora replied.

There was something odd in her mother's tone. As Zeph came into the kitchen, she saw her closing a drawer in the oak dresser.

'They didn't have wholegrain,' Zeph said, tipping out the shopping on to the table and holding up the bread. 'It's wheatgerm. That's the same thing, isn't it?'

'More or less,' Cora answered.

Zeph paused. 'What's the matter?'

'Nothing,' Cora replied. 'I'm waiting for the man from Chalmers'.' She started to busy herself with the shopping.

Zeph came round the table to Cora's side. 'You've been crying,' she said wonderingly.

'No.'

'You have. You've been crying,' Zeph insisted. She gazed at Cora in disbelief. It was years since she had seen Cora's tears; the last time was when her father died. She touched her mother's arm briefly. 'What is it?' she asked.

Cora picked up the kettle and filled it from the cold tap. 'It's just these bills,' she said, nodding at the table end, where a stack of invoices and the farm accounts were strewn.

Zeph looked at the books, then at the drawer Cora had closed. 'That's all?' she said.

'Isn't that enough?' Cora responded.

'When the Chalmers man has gone, sit down and tell me,' Zeph said.

'I'll find a way round it,' Cora said.

'I want to help.'

Cora glanced at her. Then she bent down with her back to her daughter, taking out plates and cups from the bottom cupboard.

At the same time they heard a car in the lane.

Cora put down the plates and went to the window. 'It's him,' she said. She walked over to the door and took her coat from the hook on the back.

Zeph watched her mother cross the yard and lean down to talk to her grandson. To her surprise, he got to his feet and took his grandmother's hand. Cora spent a moment or two brushing down his coat, then straightened to greet the man who had come from the cider factory in the next county. Last night, she had told Zeph that he would be coming to tell her what was needed in the harvest that year, and what chemicals they would allow to be sprayed, and to give his opinion on the state of the Dabinetts and Yarlington Mill.

'Don't you wish you didn't have all this to do?' Zeph had asked. 'Why don't you give it up?'

Her mother had stared at her. 'Because it's what your father would have wanted,' she had said. 'He planted all those trees.'

It was almost lunchtime when Cora got back to the house. Zeph had been waiting for her to return for almost an hour. Joshua ran in ahead of his grandmother. Zeph could hear her mother calling, 'What would you like to eat?' Joshua's footsteps resounded on the stairs: two up, two down, a familiar game from home.

'Go and get your soldiers,' Zeph heard Cora say, as she took off her coat. 'In the cupboard, here.' There was the sound of the door opening to the understairs cubby-hole, where Cora had put his little bike, his football, his Lego. Zeph heard her son scramble down the stairs as Cora walked into the kitchen.

Zeph was sitting at the table, a cup of cold coffee in front of her.

'Do you think he would eat soup?' Cora asked. 'What shall I make for him?'

When there was no reply, Cora glanced at her daughter. 'Zeph?'

Josh came into the room with a box of plastic figures.

Cora put her head on one side, frowned a little. She changed the subject. 'The rep thinks there might be enough yield,' she said. 'I asked him what the minimum would be this year.'

'How long did it take him?' Zeph asked, in a low voice.

Cora nodded towards the window, in the direction that the Chalmers van had driven away. 'An hour,' she said, puzzled. 'You saw him.'

'I don't mean the Chalmers man,' Zeph said. 'How long did it take Daddy to plant the trees?'

'How long?' Cora echoed.

'He told me months.'

'Yes,' Cora said, wavering. She couldn't read the complicated expression on her daughter's face.

'When you first moved here.'

'Yes,' Cora agreed.

'Did you help him?'

Cora paused. Her gaze ran swiftly over the table, then back to Zeph's face. 'Of course,' she answered.

'Planted them?'

'Brought them on the trailer. Staked them, all kinds of things... Why, darling? You know 'how long it took. You know what we did.'

'Working with him. Weeks and weeks.' Zeph put her head on one side speculatively. 'I don't see why you bothered.'

'Well, he thought that an orchard would be a good business.'

'And all the years after that,' Zeph said. 'All those harvests.'

'Yes...' The two women stared at each other. In the frigid atmosphere, Cora faltered. 'What's happened?' she asked.

'But why bother to help him at all?' Zeph asked. 'Wouldn't you rather have been in Sicily?'

Cora put her hand behind her, and leaned on the edge of the stove. She saw Josh squat down on the floor, and empty the box of his toys on to the flagstones.

'It's you,' Zeph said. 'You're the woman, aren't you?'

Cora couldn't reply. Her eyes rested briefly on the chair six feet away from her, but she couldn't cross the floor to it.

Zeph reached behind her and slowly took out from the dresser drawer the brown-paper parcel with the Italian postmark. She placed it square on the table. 'Do you think I don't know who Pietro Caviezel is?' she asked, in a quiet, even voice.

'That was addressed to me,' Cora told her. Hot colour flooded her face. 'It's private.'

Zeph ignored her. 'The novelist,' she said.

'The poet. Even I know who Pietro Caviezel is. He won some sort of prize, didn't he?' she asked. 'Three or four years ago. He came to this country.'

'That parcel was private,' Cora repeated.

'And you are the woman he wouldn't name in *The Light*.'

'No,' Cora said. 'That's not true.' And she made a move to take the package from the table.

Zeph leaped to her feet. She snatched up the journal. 'Do you think I'm an idiot?' she demanded, in a voice like murder.

'You don't understand,' Cora whispered.

'It's here in black and white!' Zeph cried. She tore open the envelope, scattering the journal and all its contents over the table. She picked up the covering letter from the solicitor, and waved it at Cora. 'This is addressed to you!' she said. 'He's died, and he left instructions. It says it right here. It's for you.'

'But the novel's not about me,' Cora protested.

Zeph shot her a look of unparalleled venom. She snatched up the journal.

'Mummy!' Josh said, frightened by Zeph's shouting.

Neither woman looked at him.

'Don't,' Cora said. 'Please don't.'

'Not about you?' Zeph was leafing rapidly through the journal. She stopped at a page, stabbing the text with her finger. 'What does all this mean, then?'

'You had no right to look at that.' Cora was angry now. 'How dare you?'

'Mummy!' Josh repeated.

Cora looked at him. His mouth was open in a little circle of shock.

Zeph took several deep breaths. 'Is it you, or isn't it, in *The Light?*'

'It's none of your business.' Cora's eyes darted about in a feverish, distracted fashion.

'And did he know?' Zeph asked. 'Did my father know about this man?'

'You don't understand,' Cora said.

Zeph put a hand to her head. 'Well, I'm trying to,' she said. 'First Nick, now you ... *you*, of all people!'

'It was a long time ago,' Cora whispered.

'But that doesn't matter,' Zeph snapped. 'He's left you all this. He sends you this journal–'

'Addressed to *me*,' Cora reiterated. 'To me, not you, Zeph.'

Zeph blushed. 'I was looking for the bills,' she replied hotly. 'I wasn't snooping. I looked in the drawer for the bills that you said were worrying you.'

'So you opened this.'

Zeph turned away, closing her eyes to the journal on the kitchen table.

'I loved your father,' Cora said quietly,

'and he worshipped you.' She made a move to grasp the letter that her daughter was still holding.

Zeph took a sudden step backwards. 'How often did you see him, this Caviezel?'

'I never saw him.'

Zeph laughed disbelievingly. 'Oh, I suppose if I read on, I'll find out that you never went back?' she asked. 'You haven't met up with him somewhere?'

'Never,' Cora said.

Zeph held out the journal. 'This is thirty years right here.'

'But I never saw him again. Never.' She sat down at the table, and put her hands over her face.

Zeph was silent for several seconds. Then she said, 'He was eleven years younger than you. Nineteen! A boy of nineteen. And you were my age,' she added. She looked down at the book and up again. 'You were like me,' she murmured. 'My age exactly.'

'It's not...'

'You were married. You were *married*.'

'It's not what you think at all,' Cora said, in a quavering voice, the voice of an old woman, bereft.

'You're just like Nick,' Zeph whispered in horror. 'The two of you are the same.'

She stopped. She didn't know, didn't recognize this woman. This was the woman in an intimate journal kept by a stranger.

This woman was public property.

She couldn't speak to Cora any longer. She couldn't bear it. She couldn't breathe. She couldn't stay in the room a moment longer.

Josh had backed against the wall, and was sitting crouched there, his knees drawn up, his elbows on his knees and his hands over his ears. He was singing to himself, a song from a television programme he loved, the theme song. 'Carry all the bits and bats,' he mumbled. 'Carry this and carry that.' It came out in a jumble, overlaid with his lisp on the letter *r*.

She put a hand to her mouth. She thought for a moment that she was going to be sick.

She walked over to Joshua. She heard her mother start to cry.

'Carry this, carry bits and bats,' Josh sang to himself uncertainly. His gaze flickered from Cora to his mother.

'Get up, darling,' Zeph told him.

He hesitated.

'Do as you're told!'

'Don't bad shout,' he said. 'Please,' he blurted out, repeating the code that he knew deflected Zeph's disapproval.

Mortification churned through her. What was she doing? What had she already done? Everything was messed up beyond repair. She would never get anything straight again. She would never trust anyone else. She snatched at her son's wrist, as if to pull him back from the distance that might unravel between them.

Josh's eyes filled with tears and he began to wail.

She hauled him to his feet, picked him up and, holding him tightly to her, closing her ears to his cries, she walked out of the house.

Eleven

Richard always said she was a good woman. 'The love of a good woman,' he would joke.

Cora had never expected to be happy, only secure, so happiness, when it came, was the best of surprises.

On the day that she was married, in a simple dove-grey suit – in deference, she told everyone, to her mother's death, and yet, in her heart, because she could not bear the private hypocrisy of wearing white – her father told her she was the loveliest girl on earth. 'You're just like your mother,' he said, full of pride, as he handed her out of the car at the steps to the abbey. She had, in addition to the soft silk suit, a flattering little hat, all froth and feathers, pale grey silk shoes, and she carried a posy of the Cussons rose, whose scent surrounded them as they waited in the porch for the organist to play the Wedding March.

Sun poured into the little space; she saw her foreshortened silhouette on the ground, arm in arm with her father. It was he, rather than she, who was nervous. Instead of passion, she simply hoped. She didn't want to let Richard down; she prayed that no word of her relationship with David Menzies would filter back to him via Jenny or one of the other girls from London, who were in the small congregation. She wanted to work hard and help Richard flourish in whatever he chose to do in the future. It was her job, she knew, to support him. To honour and obey him. She would do so: she had no other expectation.

They had not invited many people to the ceremony, only their immediate neighbours, whom her father and Richard knew far better than she did, a few relatives, her aunt and uncle with their two teenage children, and her three London friends, all of whom arrived alone, even the now-engaged Jenny. Richard's side of the church was empty. He had no family, his parents having died some years before, and he had been an only child. Smiling, and joking afterwards that they had looked like Richard's harem, her friends had stood on Richard's side of the church; their faces, as she entered and the Wedding March struck up, were a picture to see. She, the least likely, was the first to be married.

Richard did not turn to look at her: he stood with his hands clasped, his eyes on the floor, his back rigid. He told her afterwards that he had been afraid she would not come.

'Why would I not come?' she had asked him, astounded.

'Because I don't deserve you,' he had replied.

Everyone approved of him. 'He's an awfully good catch,' Jenny told her at the reception. 'A gentleman-farmer in the making. You'll soon be lady of the manor.'

'He strikes me as more interesting than that,' her aunt opined. 'And a war hero, I gather. Your father tells me he has the DSO.'

'He rarely talks about it,' Cora told her.

'Good,' her aunt replied, nodding in approval. 'Modesty and dignity. Everything you could want in a man. Someone mature and respectable. He will do you very well, dear. A very good choice.'

He had hired a car for the honeymoon, and booked a passage to France. It was an unusual and imaginative idea: no one that Cora knew had ever been to the Mediterranean and, in Jenny's eyes, Richard gained a whole new perspective when she was told where they were going just before Cora and Richard left. 'Oh, that's racy of him,' she had said, smiling broadly over her fifth glass of champagne. 'Is he racy, Cora? How fascinating. You are a dark horse.'

They left Sherborne at four; the September weather was perfect. They drove through the lanes and, after an hour, he pulled into a driveway, and along it, under alternating limes and sweet chestnut that formed a dense green tunnel, into the courtyard of a country house.

'This is an hotel,' he said, turning off the engine. 'Do you like it?'

She looked at the lawns on either side of the L-shaped seventeenth-century house, and at the huge herbaceous borders, still full of colour. 'It's very pretty,' she said.

'We could stay somewhere else, if you'd rather,' he told her. 'One of your father's friends recommended it to me.'

'It looks lovely,' she said.

'And we'll drive on in the morning,' he said. 'It's just two hours to the ferry.'

'That seems perfect,' she told him.

He got out their bags and she followed him to the door.

Inside, the owner was waiting for them: a large woman poured into a vivid floral frock, a broad smile on her face. 'Ah,' she beamed, 'my newlyweds. Lovely.'

Richard signed the register; Cora stared down at the names, Mr and Mrs Richard Ward. It felt comforting. She had ceased to be Cora. She had ceased to be single and alone. I will never make another journey without him, she thought.

Their room was like the owner: a vast sea of chintz hung with frills. The woman opened the windows. 'Now, make yourselves at home,' she was saying, as she fussed with the curtains. 'The bathroom is along the corridor. There's only one other couple staying. Dinner is at eight.' She turned to them. They were standing in the centre of the room 'like two soldiers to attention, and she was clutching her handbag, poor dear! And he looking petrified!' the woman would tell her husband later. 'Now, would you like some tea out in the garden?' she asked.

Richard looked questioningly at Cora.

'Yes, please,' she said.

The owner bustled out, and, when the door was closed behind her, Cora made herself busy unpacking her overnight things. She shook out the nightdress she had bought in town, a modest broderie-anglaise affair that she folded and put under her pillow, smoothing it flat.

When she turned back, Richard hadn't moved. 'I can't believe we're here,' he said.

'It's very nice,' she told him, smiling.

He walked over to her, picked up her hand and looked closely at it. 'You don't think the ring is too narrow?' he asked. He had chosen them himself, and she had been surprised, at the ceremony, that there were two, a matching pair. It was not usually done, and he had

213

not told her beforehand. 'I wanted us to be the same,' he murmured, as if reading her thoughts.

'It's not too narrow,' she said.

'Too plain?'

'Not too plain.' In truth, she didn't mind what it was like.

He brought her hand to his lips and kissed it. His eyes closed as his mouth brushed her skin. 'I want to make you happy,' he said, gazing at her.

'I know, dear,' she replied. 'I know.'

After dinner, they walked along the garden path. There was a lake beyond the trees; they stood at the fence and listened to the water running softly through the weirs further upstream. Occasionally, they heard a faint ripple as a fish surfaced. The country here was really dark, far from any town, and the sky was cloudy.

'No stars,' Richard said. 'No moon.'

'You might have ordered them,' Cora joked.

'I shall complain to the management,' he said.

They walked back to the house, and climbed the stairs. As they reached the first floor and the door to their room, Cora felt numb. She watched Richard's hand as he turned the key in the lock. This is something I must do, she told herself.

They went inside. He walked to the dressing-table, and put down the key.

'Might I use the bathroom first?' she asked him.

'Of course.'

She took her wash-bag and went back along the corridor. Inside the room, she stared down at the roll-top bath, the claw feet, the old Victorian shower above it bordered by a glass screen etched with geometric patterns. She sat down on the side of the bath and waited to see if her heart would stop beating so sickeningly. She wiped her palms on her flannel, then got up, washed her face vigorously and combed her hair. She pulled at her dress: she looked like a schoolteacher in its utilitarian blue. She frowned at herself in the mirror. She ought to have worn something more romantic with a lower neckline for dinner. Not this day dress. A hot wave of embarrassment poured over her. She was no good: she would not know what to do. Or she would betray herself, make it obvious that she had had a man before. The thought appalled her; she experienced a moment of real terror.

He would know.

He would know.

Perhaps she could go. Perhaps she could feign illness. She couldn't even sleep in a different bed because there was only one: the double bed and the double bedroom were reserved for a honeymoon couple.

There was nothing for it. She must go back and she must go in to him and she must do whatever he wanted. He wouldn't be like David, she told herself, eyes closed, heart aching against her ribs. David had been cruel and selfish. Richard wasn't the same.

She opened her eyes and stared at herself in the mirror. 'He isn't the same,' she told her reflection. 'He is not the same.'

When she got back to the room, Richard excused himself, holding his own wash-bag. He had taken off his jacket and tie, and when he had gone, she saw that he had neatly stacked the loose change from his pockets on the table. The car keys and his wallet lay alongside in a perfectly precise row. She got undressed quickly, hanging her dress in the wardrobe, and hiding her underclothes in her case. She got into bed and lay there looking at the open window; after a moment, she turned off the light.

When she heard his hand on the door handle, she closed her eyes.

There were a few seconds of silence as he walked across the room. 'Shall I leave the window open?' he asked softly.

'I don't mind,' she said.

She heard him close it.

She had avoided thinking of what it would

be like to be near him, and when he got into bed next to her, it felt strange to have another body in the space where she lay. She, too, was an only child, and had never shared a bed or a room; she had never gone camping with the Girl Guides and slept in a tent with others, or in a hostel. The invasion of another person was startling.

Richard lay perfectly still for a moment, then turned on to his side, and put his hand on her waist. 'Darling,' he murmured. He kissed her. There was no insistence. He moved back from her. 'Are you comfortable?' he asked.

'Yes,' she replied. She moved into his shoulder, and he put his arm round her. She lifted her face to him. His hand moved to her breast. The material of the nightdress lay thickly under his touch. He was wearing pyjamas; they had a starchy smell, a new smell. There was a slight growth of beard on his face; she tried not to mind it. There was the greasy odour of the cream on his hair. She tried to concentrate on other things: the vows she had made in the church, the flower arrangements on either side of the aisle, the food they had eaten, the journey in the car, the route they would take in the morning.

'Cora,' he said.

She thought that the nightclothes got in the way, the bedding stifled her, the air in the bedroom was close and humid. She tried to breathe evenly, slowly, lying still. She put her hands on his back, in the centre. She neither helped him nor obstructed him. When he had finished he lay for some time with his head in the crook of her shoulder and neck, and she liked that very much, the nearness of him, that he didn't move away from her, and that he seemed to need her.

'I'm sorry,' he murmured.

She had no idea what he meant.

'It will be different another time,' he promised.

She waited until his breathing changed and he was asleep, before she disengaged herself from his embrace.

They reached Bergerac on the third day. They sat in the market square under the wide umbrellas of the café and watched the world go by: women with little dogs, their subtle, neat clothes, their wide-brimmed hats sloping at an angle across their faces, the children at their sides in fusty grey shorts and socks, white shirts, and the girls in white dresses.

'Down from Paris,' Richard observed. 'They'll be on their way home soon, after the summer.'

Cora saw a window open on the far side of the square, and billowing white curtains drawn back to reveal a couch, on which a couple sat. The green doors to the balcony were surrounded by red geraniums; inside, Cora could just see an exotic plant with long grey-green leaves. The woman sat with one arm extended along the back of the couch, and the man was reading a magazine. Idly, the woman looked down into the square, and Cora wondered what she saw.

An English couple sitting at a table in the shade, all dressed up and very polite to each other. She would see Cora stand, and Richard hold back her chair, then take her by the elbow, guiding her between the tables, as a man might guide his mother, full of gentle respect. And all around them the world buzzed: the children kicking their heels, the women gesturing with cigarettes held upright between their fingers, the glare of the market stalls. They moved carefully back to the car while the woman in the window stroked her husband's neck, and he lowered the magazine, and fanned himself with the open pages.

Cora often saw herself like this, as if she were outside herself and an observer, as they moved ever more southwards and eastwards through France in that first week. To Domme, on the medieval walls looking down at the curving river below; to Sarlat, in the shadowy streets at twilight. The English couple, he so attentive, she so patient, each deferring to the other, gazing into shop windows but never buying, sitting at bars to sip tea, eat almond biscuits, peel the ripe peaches with fruit knives, and to be remarked upon, 'She so young,' she imagined them saying, 'and both so quiet.'

It was almost the end of the first week when they reached the coast at Cannes. They had been travelling for ten hours when they came into the town, and the car was trailing smoke.

'What's wrong with it?' Cora had asked.

Richard had got out, checked the engine and got back into the driving seat, angry. 'I've no idea,' he told her.

They spent another hour finding a garage, then a further desultory two hours tramping the streets looking for somewhere to stay. They had not booked anywhere. Richard stopped speaking, stopped apologizing, out of desperation. Finally, Cora insisted that they stop at a café in Le Suquet. By some miracle, it had a room to let, and they found themselves there, exhausted, grimy and irritated. There was a lot of noise from the restaurant below and the narrow lane opposite. They could hear the proprietor bullying the kitchen staff, and the waiters calling out the orders.

'This is not what I wanted,' Richard said. He lay down on the bed, and put an arm over his face.

'It will suit us very well,' Cora said.

'Cannes is all noise,' he murmured.

'They've built so much more since I was here. I'll take you to Îles de Lerins tomorrow. It's just a short boat ride. Or the Old Port. They bring the flowers to the Allée de la Liberté. Hundreds and thousands of them.'

'But this is quite all right,' Cora told him. 'This is a nice part of town, isn't it, on this hill? I don't mind it at all. And look,' she added, trying to cheer him up, 'we have everything we need right here in the room. There's even a bath.' And she showed him where it was hidden in a curtained alcove: tiny, with ornate brass taps, set back in a panelled wall.

'Is there anything you want?' she asked him.

'Only to sleep,' he said, his voice slurred. by fatigue.

She regarded him sympathetically. She had driven for the first two hours, but he had taken the wheel through the heat of the day. He had been determined to get to the coast so that they might spend a few days there before they had to go home. He had complained of a headache for the last few miles.

As she watched him, his arm relaxed and he began to snore. She went to the window, opened the shutters a fraction and gazed down into the crowded street and on to the pavement tables below. She wondered if she ought to go down and ask for a tray of cold drinks.

She turned back into the room, closing the shutters so that only a strip of sunlight lay across the floor where the wood did not quite meet the sill. She took off her shoes, walked back to the bath and looked at it longingly. Then, with a glance at Richard's prone form, she took off her clothes, and drew the curtains. She put her face flannel into the bath and ran the water slowly on to it, so that it wouldn't make too much noise. Then she lowered herself, with relish, into the six inches or so of tepid water. The coolness was bliss; she stretched out, lathering herself with the soap that had been provided and rinsing herself from the same slow-running tap.

She looked down at her body in the half-darkness. French women all seemed so slim; she had never been so. She wondered if she should diet; she had seen women just now in little black pencil skirts, and white shirts with the collar turned up, and scarves knotted at the neck. She was probably too heavy to carry that off. She had never thought about it before; perhaps she could be pretty if she styled her hair differently, rather than letting it hang loose. She had never really desperately cared about clothes. Perhaps she should try again, as she had in London. After all, she was Richard's wife. People might judge him by her. And she lay thinking of what she might buy that would not be too expensive and that he might like.

'Cora,' she heard him call.

She sat up abruptly. 'I'm here,' she said. 'In the bath.'

'Are you?' he replied. He sounded sleepy, and amused. 'Was there any hot water?'

'Not really,' she told him.

'Do you think there might be any left for me?'

'I haven't used much,' she said. 'I should think so.' And she stood up, pulling out the plug. She dried herself off, and stepped out from between the curtains with the towel wrapped round her. Richard had turned on to his side; his eyes were closed.

'Shall I run another bath?' she asked.

There was no reply. She sat on the chair at the side of the bed. Then she stepped out of the towel and into her dressing-gown. She got into bed, under the cool cotton sheet.

When she woke up the sun had left the room. The strip of light on the floor had gone, replaced by a pattern of red, green and yellow, cast up from the lights above the café door, which ran the width of their window. The wood floors, the white curtains, the plain white bed were all decorated with it.

For a moment, she couldn't think where she was, or what had woken her. Then, she heard the noise again.

She turned to Richard.

He was lying flat on his back, his arms at his side, his head tipped back on the pillow. His mouth was open, and he was making a little keening sound, a long, continuous note, like a child's cry.

'Richard,' she whispered.

He didn't move. The sound increased; his body stiffened. The noise was eerie, and the more she listened to it, the more eerie it became. Occasionally, he gasped. She put a hand on his arm, and found it cold and clammy.

'Richard,' she repeated, louder.

He woke; but that was hardly an accurate description. He was catapulted out of sleep, thrown into consciousness. He sat bolt upright and put out his hands as if he were trying to grasp something out of his reach; sweat sprang out on his face. To Cora's amazement, he scrambled forward in pursuit of the phantom, his hands moving in a sideways groping motion. 'They're here,' he said.

He was on his feet before she could restrain him, stumbling, crouching. He collided with the chair, let out another cry, and fell to his knees. He sounded as if he were suffocating.

Cora jumped out of bed and ran to him. He caught her arm and wrenched her to the floor. 'They're here,' he whispered.

'Richard,' she said, 'it's me. You're safe. It's Cora. Wake up...'

He gasped, put a hand to his throat, and looked down at himself in confusion.

'Darling,' she said, 'it's a dream.'

He sank back on his heels.

'What was it?' she asked.

'The boy,' he said. 'The sea.'

With some trouble, she helped him to his feet. He seemed dazed. 'What time is it?' he asked.

'I think it's early evening. Seven or so.'

'Seven,' he repeated. 'Seven in the evening.'

'Yes.'

'Oh, Cora,' he said, and put his arms round her. She could feel his heart beating like a drum. He was shaking.

'What is it?' she asked. 'Which boy? Which sea?'

'It doesn't matter,' he said.

'Come and sit down,' she said.

He stayed where he was, holding her now at arm's length and staring intently at her, as if he hardly believed that she, too, was not a ghost.

'I was asleep,' she said, seeing his glance. She made a move to pull the dressing-gown more tightly round herself.

He stopped her hand.

Below them, in the street, they could hear the buzz of the passing crowds. 'Hey,' someone called, 'come back here.' Several others laughed.

'Would you like to go and eat?' Cora asked tentatively. 'Are you hungry? It seems that everyone is out.'

Richard didn't reply. He untied the knot of the dressing-gown belt. She took a half-step backwards.

'Please,' he murmured. He took the robe from her shoulders.

She stood there trembling. He had not seen her before – she had not allowed him to. It seemed indecent to parade in front of him, or to lie naked in a bed without covering herself. She put a hand defensively to her breast.

'You are so lovely,' he murmured.

He took the robe from her entirely, lifted the hand from her breast, turned it over and kissed her wrist. Moving slowly, he drew her to him along the length of her arm, and when she was within his embrace, he lowered his face to her neck.

'Lie down with me,' he said.

He took off his clothes, walked to the bath and ran cool water over his arms and shoulders. As he stood up, she watched the drops run down his back, his pale skin. He was too thin, she thought. She could see every rib, every muscle delineated. With his back to her, she had time to look at him in a way she had not before. He had slim hips, a small waist; his shoulders were knotted and wiry from the building work he had done, his arms more heavily muscular. When he turned back to her, she felt a shock of need: the first slow beat of desire.

As he moved across the room, the muted light moved over him. In the shadows, she thought, they were like two shadows themselves, two barely imprinted shapes – like watercolours, which hinted at forms on paper rather than revealing them in detail. She saw the line of his body, the line of her own, shapes drifting in a dance.

At first he did not lie down next to her: he ran his hands over her, murmuring her name. She stepped out of herself, out of the person she clung to, out of her fears, out of the necessity that she had felt to be correct, to be subdued. She moved out of the dark she had lived in, out of the subterranean, and into the world. She followed where he led, all the small caresses, the softness and then the urgency of his fingers. Sounds became vibrant, then were silenced altogether. The picture she had carried of the clock, the ugly sunburst clock on the wall, vanished on a rapid stream. As if from a great distance she felt Richard's hands, heard her own voice begging him for something that, when it came, was painted in high colour, married to the gaudy lights spilled on the floor and on the linen of the bed and on their own arms and faces.

She forgot herself and became part of the wave, the hot, humid night rolling down La Croisette, sweeping the palm trees, the casinos, the lazy sea, the sports cars, the bars, the flags, the crowds and voices before it, enveloping them, pressing them into the intense, vibrant indigo blue of the night.

When it was over she clung to him. Loving the sensation of his body pressed to hers. He lifted his face and stroked her hair. She kissed him.

There was nothing else to say.

They already knew every word by heart.

Lapis

When I close my eyes, I see the rail of the boat, painted blue, and the boarding inside, not white, but indigo.

When I was a child I would go out with my uncle every time I stayed in Palermo. The front of the house faced the sea, and the boat would go out at five o'clock in the morning. He put me where I would not be a nuisance, and the sound of the motors, knocking as they went out of harbour, was loud. There was the smell of diesel and salt, and my uncle would shout to everyone who passed, other fishermen, other sailors, and he would have the radio on. In my mind's eye, I see the ocean flat blue to the soundtrack of rock music; French, mostly. His grandmother was French, and he had lived with her all his life; he had learned what he knew of women from this exile, this quiet, dark-haired woman from Bearne, on the French and Spanish borders. French rock music and the battering of the waves out of harbour. I was never sick: I was always too excited.

He had a boy who went with him and taught me to catch sea urchins; there were sea urchins and sardines, anchovies and shrimps. I remember that I told you about that on the first night I saw you. The first time at sea with my uncle, I hated the sight of the catch flailing for its life in the nets. But when my uncle began cooking on the bridge, I forgot it. He would cook the fish with olive oil, salt and pepper. Just that. They tasted like ambrosia.

I cook fish all the time now. I have only myself to look after, and I am easy to please. I'm not the boy you knew, Cora: you would smile at me. I've grown fat, or fatter, at least. I have a good man's figure, so they say. A man who likes his food you might tell me, laughing.

I have changed, as you must have changed, too, darling: it is ten years exactly today since you went away.

I wish I could cook for you. I can make **gamberi** in **crosta,** *a little oil, unsalted butter and garlic, shrimp and white fish, all rolled up* *in pastry. That's one of my favourites. Or* pesce di Ischia, *like the island near Capri. Lots of lemon. Good with salmon or sea bass. Or, when I have been to Genoa, I like to eat the* burrida.

I wish I could have shown you the market in Genoa, as my mother's sister once showed it to me. I must have been seven or eight; I had been sent there when my mother was ill, for a month or so. In la superba *there was a fish market of the most amazing varieties that they brought up out of those waters: the praying-fish, the sea-truffle, the* tartufi di mare, *sea-strawberries, and a mussel called* cozze pelose. *I love the* vongole alla marinara *and I cook it myself, a rough dish that some call fishermen's clams. And, best of all, red mullet with oil, onion, wine and wine vinegar,* triglie alla veneziana.

You see the colour in the fish scales, that iridescent colour? It is so vivid when the fish is lifted from the sea. All kinds of blue and indigo and silver, a hint of silver with a blue-white tinge.

Indigo blue, speedwell blue, violet blue. Every shade.

'Fast-fading violets covered up in leaves...' that phrase comes into my head as I write of the colour. It closes you in its hand, that line, it describes you fading as I touched you. Keats. Writing to a nightingale, and wondering if he was awake or dreaming.

I see myself as a child, between the blue sea

230

and the blue sky.

And I think often, also, of that evening, the first evening when I swam – you, Richard and Alex were sitting in the restaurant, and I went down the beach.

I wanted to be out of sight of you because I was angry, to tell you the truth. Which was unattractive, as truth often is – unpalatable, sour in the mouth. I hated Richard that day, and I hated him returning. I wanted to be out of sight of you so I walked past the rocks, then took off my clothes and went into the water. I think, perhaps, that I even had a moment of hoping I would not come back, and would swim until I drowned, because I knew that the possibility of keeping you close to me was small, and I had a fierce longing to die rather than experience that loss.

I know that you saw me; I think you did. I think your face was turned in my direction. As I looked at you, my heart flew from me. I was dispossessed. I knew it was no longer my own. It never would be again. I had to have you; I wanted you for myself. All the selfishness and cruelty of youth in that moment, all the blazing desire.

And, less than a day later, we were in the same sea on the south coast, and I held you naked in my arms in the water, and the coolness only made your body seem warmer to me. And we stood with the water up to our shoulders and I could feel the whole length of you as you put

231

your arms round my neck, as you had in Enna, but it was more wonderful because I could feel the little curve of your belly, the heaviness of your breasts, the pressure of your thighs.

On the rocks beneath us, your foot brushed mine, and there was something more profound, more erotic in that than there was in the rest of you: as if you were stumbling as you walked, and I were holding you upright and moving you where I moved, guiding you where I wanted to be.

And I was indeed entirely where I wanted to be, because the feeling of you was shattering; it tore my life to pieces. I have put myself back together, and I have a very good life, but it will never be like it was before. It is a carefully constructed building, clever, ingenious, but it is not what I found with you. It does not possess the sensation of living, and being part of the world, part of the blue ocean and blue heaven.

What other colour is heaven but blue? Intensely blue, like lapis-lazuli, the stone that the Egyptians believed gave life, and the colour that they called the colour of truth. Zeus was painted blue. Zeus and Jupiter, Vishnu, Indra and Krishna. We live in a blue planet with blue moons. Romantic. But I look up and I don't see the romance; only the same white face gazing down at me.

I think of you, and I wonder, after all this time, if you look at the moon and the stars as you did once.

I wonder if you look at the sea, or the sky, and think of me, or of swimming in a sea the colour of lapis, the colour of the gods.

Twelve

Zeph was dreaming, and everything was how it used to be.

It was the first Valentine's Day after she and Nick had met. They were in the first flat they had rented. It was morning. She was standing in the kitchen eating toast and shuffling through her handbag for her rail ticket; Nick was sitting at the table in the room next door, staring balefully at a laptop. 'Look at the price of fucking roses!' he had complained earlier. 'Did you see what it said in the paper? Ten times the usual price. What's so special about roses, anyway?'

She had agreed with him. Her mother had always liked roses, especially the heavily scented ones, but Zeph had never been fond of their obvious glamour. Besides, she associated them with the overgrown bushes at her grandfather's house, and the old man meandering between them in his carpet slippers and dressing-gown during the last few months of his life.

Anyway, Nick was right about the rampant

cost: it was preying on people's guilt, couples trying to make up to each other for their lack of attention in the rest of the year. She could think of nothing more tasteless, more cynical, than the men who ignored their partners all year, or cheated on them, offering the ubiquitous bunch of flowers on 14 February.

'I wouldn't object to a meal, though,' Zeph had said, as she gathered up her things and glanced at the clock.

'I'll cook for you.'

'In a restaurant, I meant.'

Nick had leaned sideways in his chair to catch sight of her. 'I can't cook meals in other people's restaurants,' he said. 'That would be rude.'

'You idiot,' she had said, laughing.

'I'll cook you pasta,' he offered. 'Your favourite. *Vongole.*'

'You're not cooking clams,' she told him. 'Think of another way to kill me off. One that involves less throwing up.' She stood at the door, twirling her key-ring.

'That's a very wounding thing to suggest,' he said, pulling a mock-outraged face. He had stood up, walked over to her and gripped her in a bear-hug. 'You,' he had said softly, 'are a very bad woman.'

She had smiled at him as his hands drifted downwards. 'No flowers, then?' she said. 'No meal – nothing, right?'

'Nothing,' he told her. 'In case you hadn't noticed, you're in love with a loser who has not a cent to his name.'

But he had done something, of course. It was Saturday; a cold night, but dry. He met her at the door of the pub after work; it was eleven o'clock. 'We're going somewhere,' he told her.

'Not me,' she had said. 'Only home to bed. I'm shattered.'

'OK,' he said, 'but via the river.'

'The river? That's the opposite direction.'

'Do as you're told.' He was holding a plastic carrier-bag, and his battered holdall.

'What's all this?' she had asked.

'You'll see,' he said.

They got down to the embankment and walked up to Westminster Bridge.

'"The river glideth at its own sweet will,"' she intoned, as they got to the centre, and looked down at the water, the lights reflected in it. Then she glanced up at Nick. 'Sorry,' she said. 'Poems in my head. Mum's fault.'

'Here's another,' he said, fishing in the plastic-carrier. '"My love is like a red, red rose that's newly" et cetera, et cetera and so on.' He had made a rose out of paper.

'Oh,' she said. 'That's ... well, possibly it's nice.'

'OK – so origami's overrated.'

'That's not origami,' she replied, amused,

but trying not to smile. 'In fact, what is it, exactly? It looks like the cereal packet.'

'And what the hell is wrong with that?'

'You might have coloured it. I never saw a rose with "Low-fat Crunchy" printed down the side.'

He took it from her. 'I'm real upset now,' he said. 'But, hey, you'll like the next bit more. Sit down.'

'On what?'

'The *chaise-longue*,' he said, indicating the wooden bench behind them. 'I took all day picking it out. Nice view of Cleopatra's Needle.'

'OK.' She hesitated before she sat down. 'This doesn't involve costumes, by any chance?'

'I hadn't planned them,' he said, 'but it's an option later, if you like. Do you want to be nurse or doctor? Can I choose what kind of restraint?'

She ignored him. 'You're not thinking of miming?' she asked warily. 'Or singing? Not dressing up as Romeo or something?'

His shoulders drooped exaggeratedly. 'Aw, now you've spoiled it.'

'Right,' she said. 'That's it. I'm off. Good-bye.'

'You are not.' He pushed her down on to the bench. 'Watch and marvel.'

Out of the bag, he took a package, which turned out to be a small collapsible seat. On the seat, he laid a cloth. On the cloth he arranged two dishes of strawberries and, next to them, a two-glass bottle of cheap sparkling wine. With a final flourish, he put half a dozen jam-jars on the ground around the 'table' and, inside them, tea-lights. With much cursing and dropping of matches, he lit the candles. Someone in the queue of traffic leaned out of a car window and applauded. He bowed.

'Well,' he asked Zeph, 'what do you think?'

'I think you're nuts,' she said, smiling.

'Thank you,' he replied.

He sat down beside her. 'I'm sorry it's crap,' he remarked cheerfully. She linked his arm and moved close to him. 'One day I'll be wildly successful and buy you the real deal,' he whispered, kissing her neck. 'Suite at the Savoy, bucket of ice, Bollinger, four-poster bed, knickers that tie at the side, a pair of waders and a whip.'

'What?' She laughed.

'Oh, pardon me,' he apologized. 'You don't like the Savoy?'

She looked at him, then at the lights and the table, and back to his face. 'I love you,' she murmured.

'That's good,' he told her softly, stroking her hand. 'It would be so embarrassing to go to that place by myself.'

She had felt his touch so clearly, but she woke up – not to Nick, or the river below the bridge – to the room at the top of her mother's house.

She lay for a while trying to orient herself, then realized that she was far away from Nick, and the sorrow of the last few days descended on her with new freshness. She turned her face into her pillow and cried.

After a while, she sat up slowly and gazed out of the open window. The cold air streaming through it chilled her; she got out of bed and closed it. She saw the cider-apple trees, row by row, on the hillside, a silent army that would soon be green, then full of blossom. Nick and she had come down here before in the spring, and it had been magical; they had walked through those trees when she had been pregnant with Joshua.

Nick had been a nervous prospective father, although Zeph's pregnancy had been relatively uneventful. When she went into labour and was taken to hospital, he had sat with her through a day and a night, never sleeping, walking up and down. At one point he had turned to the bed where she lay and she had spread her hands in exasperation. 'Look at you,' she'd exclaimed. 'You're pacing the floor.'

'You're right,' he said. 'I'm supposed to be creative, and I'm a cliché.'

Remembering now, in the cold in the middle of the night, Zeph wiped her eyes. Everything that had once seemed easy was now fraught with difficulty. She hadn't only left Nick: she had left the construction they had built together: their life, their home. And she was torn between feeling that she had walked away from it, and that Nick had stolen it from her. He had stolen her routines, her security; he had stolen Joshua's friends from him. He had taken away things that were familiar, that she and Joshua had depended on. The theft and the loss pressed down on her like a stone weight, and she tried to block out the small voice in the back of her mind that whispered she had been a player in the game of destruction.

Dimly, she tried to recall the first weeks after Joshua had been born. They were a haze of exhaustion. Nick's good humour and attempts to help had irritated her. She had found it hard to sleep, anxious that something dreadful would happen if she lost sight of her child for a single moment. Sometimes – perhaps most days, she considered now – she had sunk into a kind of claustrophobic despair when Nick had left the house. Those first six or eight months had been shrouded in a kind of shadow.

She shook her head at the memory. It should have been blissful. Why hadn't it?

She would have to live here with her mother now because, until the house was sold, she couldn't afford anywhere else. Even the flats in town were hugely expensive. The thought of it all was agony: clearing the home, deciding who would have which things. The eventual compromises to which she knew, in her heart, she would have to come with Nick. The courtroom, the solicitors, the anger and hopelessness. If she thought that now was bad, it was nothing to what might come next.

She wanted to see suffering on Nick's face; she wanted – many times – to see him put his hand on the window of the car because he couldn't touch his son. She wanted him on his knees. She wanted him in the dust. When she thought of what he had done with that other woman, all reason vanished. He would pay over and over again; she would make him. The weapons were within her reach, the emotional gun in her hand. She would pull the trigger, watch him beg and fall. She would tear a hole in his life, the kind he had torn in hers.

In theirs. She pressed her hands to her eyes. In *their* lives. They would all suffer. And Joshua would be the pawn in the centre, the prize. In fact, she realized with a dawning horror, Joshua was the gun she was holding to Nick's head. He was the avenging angel, a little boy of less than three years old, who didn't understand.

Only last week she had been sitting with him on the floor of the kitchen at home, helping him look through photographs. It had begun with her trying to get the albums in order, and ended in the usual disorganization. Joshua had wanted to see the pictures of himself as a baby: he pressed them close to his face and studied them intently.

'Me,' he had said, holding up a picture in the maternity unit when he had just been born.

'Yes,' she had told him. 'You were this big.' And she showed him, holding her hands apart.

'Me,' he had repeated, delighted, fascinated.

She had looked at the photographs of her and Nick on their wedding day, her in a bar somewhere, holding up a glass, laughing, then asleep in a chair. Nick used to do that, she remembered. He always had a camera on hand and took pictures of her. It used to drive her mad; but when a girlfriend had told her that her own partner had never taken a single photograph of her and complained that he could not be interested, Zeph saw Nick's preoccupation differently. He wanted to keep her, she realized. He wanted to look at her.

She had picked up the wedding-day photograph, and one taken much later, just after Joshua's second birthday. She studied her expression as closely as Joshua had himself. There was a change in her: a closing down. There was a small downward pull at the corner of her mouth, a kind of subdued irritation. What had she been thinking of that day? she wondered. What had annoyed her? She seemed impatient; she wasn't looking directly into the camera.

That meant she hadn't been looking at Nick.

She hadn't wanted to look at Nick.

In another photograph, she had Joshua on her lap, aged perhaps eight or nine months, and he was reaching up to her face. Their gaze was fixed on each other with total absorption. Those times were etched with utter clarity: her adaptation to the weight, the feel, the sensation of caring for a child. Joshua's skin was so smooth, so soft; she remembered the first time that Nick had kissed her after she had come back from hospital, and being mildly shocked that his had been so rough. It seemed an obvious, perhaps idiotic, thing to say. Nick had not changed: he was just the same. But he seemed different. He seemed intrusive, too loud.

She dropped her hands and gazed out into the night. Strange, how relationships changed. It was imperceptible, like the leaving of the last light of day. One moment you were standing in the evening light, everything was clear and you had a sharp memory of the day that had passed and, seemingly in the next second, as if time had compressed inwards, you could no longer see the shapes of your surroundings. You passed from darkness to light, light to darkness.

Only sometimes there was no light.

Sometimes you stayed in the dark, plunged into the netherworld.

She looked away from the window, and back into the room. What could she do? How could she make a pattern, a life, here in the dark? She tried to turn her mind to practicalities. She didn't want to go to another part of the country, somewhere strange, because she wanted – had always wanted – Joshua to know the kind of life she had known as a child. The open spaces, the freedom. She wanted him to run wild in the woods and orchards as she had when she was little.

She had a perfect memory in her head of herself, aged four or five, lying under the trees when they were heavy with apples just before harvest. The trees were small, no more than fifteen feet high, and their branches came right down to the ground. To crawl under them and look up through the red fruit hanging between the leaves to the sky was to own everything: the ground she lay on, the crop weighing down the branches, the light. Everything had been light then: the light streaming in through her window in the summer, the high white light of winter on the hill, the light reflecting from the blossom in the spring and making her eyes ache, such was its intensity as she had walked between the trees. Light and easy: like the effortlessness of running when you were a child. Life ran on like that. A country childhood. The idyll.

Zeph sat down on the window-seat, drawing a cushion beneath her against the slight dampness of the stone. Yet it hadn't been like that at all, she thought. It had been an illusion. A lie. Nothing had been easy; her parents had not been happy. How could they have been, with that man in their lives, the Italian?

Everything was untrue. Her parents' lives, her life with Nick. She didn't know how she would ever be able to think of it more positively. She didn't know how she would ever be able to look at her mother and understand her, let alone respect her. And yet she had to live here. She had to see her every day. She imagined her father, herself and Joshua standing on one side of a gulf with Nick and Cora on the other, an incomprehensible abyss between them.

She let her forehead rest on the cold window-pane. She could see her own cloudy breath.

But there were more than five people in the picture, she thought.

Two others stood behind them, shadowy figures who had set these events in motion. Nick's lover, the girl in the newspaper

244

photograph, and Pietro Caviezel.

She cast her mind back to the events of that morning.

She had truly thought that the package had been something to do with her mother's finances or the farm; her motive had been to help her. Cora was so fond of projecting an image that she could do everything alone, that she could cope, and Zeph had been sure that this was just another business problem that her mother was trying to hide. She had reasoned to herself, opening the dresser drawer, that if she were to live in the same house, she needed to know the exact nature of the difficulties facing them.

It had been full of old mail and newspapers; the brown-paper package lay on top. As Zeph extracted it, she had frowned at the postmarks. Sicily. Syracusa. She had twisted it this way and that in her hands, then looked back into the drawer. There was nothing else remotely like it.

The first thought that came to her was that her mother must be planning a holiday, and that the envelope contained brochures. Her father had been in Italy and Sicily during the war; perhaps Cora was intending to revisit the places he had known. She had applied to somewhere directly, instead of going to a travel agent. Curiosity overcoming her, and touched by the idea that Cora might want to go where Richard had been,

Zeph had opened the package and slid the contents on to the table.

She saw at once that it was a tattered leather journal. She picked up the covering letter and read it once, twice, three times. She had frowned. Caviezel? She had never heard the name mentioned at home. He wasn't a family friend. Guilt touched her: she knew that she shouldn't be looking at a private letter. A warning bell clanged in her mind. Her frown had become deeper, her puzzlement more intense. She didn't remember any phone calls or letters from Sicily. Why would her mother, of all people, be sent this as a dying wish?

She had opened the book. Not at the first page but in the centre.

Caviezel. Pietro Caviezel. There was something distantly familiar about the name. Now the warning bell rang louder. She hesitated. Consumed with curiosity, she looked at the text.

The handwriting was attractive: flowing and clear. The writer was describing a wedding. She turned the page back. There was a photo: a tall, handsome man with a woman on his arm. A man with thick, dark, curly hair, and a slim, lean body. The hand resting against his chest as he linked the woman's arm was long-fingered and artistic. Zeph looked at the couple intently. The woman was rather plain, and older than the man.

She turned the photograph over, but there was no inscription on the reverse. Then she saw the newspaper cutting. There was another photograph, with the man now standing beside a couple. 'Gabriella e Giovanni Cimino,' read the caption.

She put the photograph carefully back into the book, and turned to the first page. The date was 1973. 'You remember there is a road that runs south...'

She read down the page, skipping sentences here and there. Something about building a house. 'You told me how Richard had made a new house on land that no one wanted...'

This person knew about her father, she realized abruptly, and the house he had owned when he married her mother, the first house they had lived in, next door to her grandfather.

Then, as her eye drifted downwards, a single word leaped out at her.

Darling.

She had looked back up the page. She had missed something, surely. Was this a woman? Perhaps the first page had been written by a woman who was her mother's friend. And then...

I have thought of you...

She read the sentence beyond that. Her head spun. She read it again and again, then dropped the journal as if it were on fire. She

247

stared ahead of her without registering a single thing other than that this man had been her mother's lover.

She had got up, walked out of the room, along the hall, to the front door and flung it open. Cold air had rushed in.

I cannot put down on the page what my heart carries.

She had stood on the step and stared in the direction that her mother had gone with Joshua.

It is a poem, just like us.

After a minute or so, she had closed the door, walked back again, and stared down at the journal. It lay on the table, face down.

Just like us.

The journal was made of beautiful soft, worn leather, rubbed to a pale red shine. Other scraps of paper had fallen from it. Slowly, she picked up receipts, tickets, cuttings. There was a table of tides and phases of the moon.

There was a rose-leaf in a small polythene holder for postage stamps.

There was an opera programme.

There was an embossed card, an invitation to an arts event, at the top the two masks of comedy and tragedy. Pietro Caviezel's name was written in gold. The printing at the bottom of the card showed that he was the principal speaker at this black-tie evening in Paris nine years ago.

Zeph had put each item back on the table, exactly where they had fallen. Nine years ago she had been away at college. Her father had been dead for eleven years.

This man had been alive then, and her mother had been alone.

She felt the blood drain from her face. Very slowly, she had replaced all the items in the journal, turned it over, and sat with her chair facing the door, waiting for Cora to return.

Now, in the night, Zeph went back over that morning's conversation. She had run it through her mind so often during the day that it made even less sense now and had merely become a puzzle of unrelated sounds. She felt both angry, and guilty. Unwittingly she had uncovered her mother's past, and she had had no business in reading the journal. But knowing that didn't lessen the impact, the insult, of what she had read. Her father had been betrayed, just as Nick had betrayed her.

She got up from the window-seat and walked back to the other end of the room, where Joshua was lying in a travel cot. She put her hand on its rail and looked down at him, curled on his side with his thumb jammed into his mouth. Traces of tears were still on his face from the tantrum he had thrown earlier. He had not wanted a bath;

he had not wanted her to touch him; he hadn't wanted to eat. He had screamed and struggled in her arms and she couldn't bring herself to be angry with him, because she felt the same rage and frustration.

She had wished she could lie down like him, screaming her head off. Screaming, wailing and crying. Perhaps she should, she thought. Perhaps it would do her good. She got down on her knees, wet the edge of her thumb, and rubbed at the tearstains. Joshua stirred briefly.

He was so like his father.

The same colour hair, the same mouth.

It is a poem, just like us.

Just like his father. Not dark, like her.

Just like us...

'My God,' she murmured. Suddenly she rocked back on her heels and put a hand to her mouth. 'Oh, my God, my God, my God.'

Thirteen

A squall of rain swept along the street as Nick reached the restaurant. He stood inside the door, shaking his coat.

He could see Andy Tyler at the far side of the larger room, sitting at a table near the end of the bar. Nick made his way through the crowd, between tables sandwiched tightly together. The restaurant was in the heart of London's Theatreland, and all round the walls, posters of films and stage shows gazed luridly down at the diners. A waiter stood to one side to let him pass.

'Nick,' Andy said loudly, standing up and shaking his hand. 'Good to see you.'

Everything about Nick's agent was loud: his voice, his clothes. He was known in the business for throwing the rowdiest parties in town, the ones at which, sooner rather than later, Andy would have a knock-down argument with someone. The last few months had seen him draw in his horns a little: at fifty-two, he had been diagnosed with diabetes. Nick saw at once that his friend had not taken the doctor's advice: three bottles of champagne stood on the table in ice-buckets.

'We're expecting somebody?' Nick asked, sitting down.

'Are we ever?' Andy laughed. He sat back in his chair and surveyed his author. 'How're you feeling today?'

Nick paused. He hadn't said anything to anyone about Zeph. 'I've been better.' He glanced again at the bottles. 'What is this? Somebody's birthday?'

Andy suppressed a smile, then sighed dramatically. 'Ought to be a wake,' he said. 'Several wakes. People dropping like flies.'

'Oh? Such as?'

'You remember Bisley?'

Nick frowned. 'Should I?'

'Alex Cowan and Madeleine Crowe's agent. Got to be a big deal in the sixties, big client list after he landed Cowan's first book, that little shitty novella.'

'Uh, maybe.'

'You met him at the book fair last year.'

'The old guy?'

'He was eighty-five,' Andy told him. 'He died on Monday.'

Nick shrugged.

'Your mother-in-law knows him,' Andy said. 'She worked for him once.'

'Oh,' Nick said, dimly remembering. 'That's right.'

'And Caviezel.'

Nick looked up. 'Pietro Caviezel? What about him?'

'He died this week, too. In Sicily. Cancer.'

'Shit,' Nick murmured. 'He was a genius.'

'Nobel winner four years ago.'

'*The Light*,' Nick agreed. 'Quite a book.' He sat back in his chair. 'He couldn't have been that old?'

'Fifty.'

There was a momentary silence.

'How's your new book?' Andy asked.

Nick made a hissing sound. 'Crawling on its hands and knees.'

'How far on with it are you?'

'Not far enough. Half-way.'

Nick closed his eyes briefly. Half-way was worse to him than the beginning: it felt like he had climbed a mountain and wasn't yet at the peak. Fifty thousand words was death. Fifty thousand done and fifty to go. No man's land. Out in the middle of the big, empty ocean.

'You still got the story, though?'

'Yes,' Nick said. But he didn't meet Andy's eye. He had lost track of the book since the beginning of the week; any excitement that he had felt in progressing with it seemed empty now. He didn't trust his judgement. He had looked at what he had written that morning and hadn't been able to get a handle on it, whether it worked, even at the most basic level. The three pages he had done today had been purely mechanical: a response, a routine. The way he normally spent his mornings. But he didn't feel any of it in his heart, where it mattered.

'What's the problem?' Andy asked. 'Is there a problem?'

Nick paused. 'Zeph left me,' he said.

There was a beat of surprise, of shock.

'She what?' Andy raised his hands, then let them drop. 'No! When was this?'

'Three days ago.'

'Where'd she go?'

'To Cora's.'

'Somerset?'

253

'Yes.'

'Jesus,' Andy said. He frowned deeply, his usual good-humour gone. 'What about Josh?'

'She took him with her. She won't let me talk to him or see him.' Nick's voice cracked. 'She won't discuss anything.'

'Jesus,' Andy repeated. 'I'm sorry.' He regarded Nick for some seconds. 'It was the picture,' he guessed.

'Yes.'

'Hell of a thing,' Andy muttered. He looked at Nick sympathetically. Exhaustion and anxiety were written plainly on the younger man's face now. 'But she'll be back, Nick.'

'I don't know,' Nick muttered. 'It doesn't look like it.' He put a hand to his head; it had ached for the last forty-eight hours. He felt numb with fatigue. He could have put his arms on the table, his head on them, and slept now. He had woken up during the night from a fully fledged nightmare. He hadn't had anything like it since he was a child.

He had been dreaming that the house was getting narrower and narrower, the walls bowed in the centre, as if terrible pressure were being exerted from above. He had been walking down the stairs when the treads began to fragment. He had run to the front door, and found it too warped to open; on running to the back of the house, he had heard the crash of splintering glass as the windows shattered. Barefoot, he stepped on to a carpet of shards. The house rocked, in the grip of what felt like an earthquake. Then, far above him, in the bedroom, he had heard Zeph and Joshua crying.

He had woken with a jolt, swung his legs out of bed, then hung his head, realizing suddenly that his wife and son weren't there. Even in the three a.m. gloom, he could see the torn photograph on the bedside table. He picked up the glass of water next to it and drank; it tasted brackish and bitter.

He had gone downstairs, wandered about aimlessly, switched on the television and stared at the picture with the sound down. It was an old comedy programme, a rerun of a once successful series. He looked in blank incomprehension at the images, then flicked channels. Other faces stared back at him: a woman clutching a small girl to her side, talking to soldiers at a checkpoint; a man in a street staring in the direction of an explosion. Each face turned to the camera mirrored his own disorientation.

He had switched off the set and sat on the couch in the dark, head in his hands. He almost wished for the cataclysm, the explosion, the earthquake and the dream: something to wake him and propel him out of the silence. He almost wished he could tear up his whole life and start again somewhere else, assume another identity. He wished he could say to himself that the other life had been erased. But it could never be true. The earthquake, the explosion would never come. There would never be that kind of dramatic release, that incontrovertible shift. Instead, his life with Zeph and Josh would ease away by degrees.

He had gone back to bed, and tried to sleep.

At last, when it was almost light, he had moved to Joshua's room and lain down on his son's small bed. He could smell the child on the covers, on the pillow.

It had been something. Not much, but something.

'Have you seen Bella?' Andy asked.

Nick tore his mind from last night. 'She came to the house,' he said, 'if you can believe that. After the picture in the paper.'

'Did Zeph see her?'

'No. She'd already gone. This was yesterday.'

'Well, thank God for that,' Andy observed. 'Could have been timed worse.'

Nick shook his head. 'It's Bella all over,' he muttered. 'The bare-faced cheek of it, to walk straight up to the house. She just...' He was lost for words.

'So you and she...'

'Nothing,' Nick replied. 'And there never should have been.'

'These things happen.'

'Not to me.' Nick ran a hand through his hair, propped his elbow on the table and supported his head as if he couldn't carry the weight of his thoughts. 'I don't know why,' he murmured, almost to himself. 'That's the fucking stupidity of it. I don't know why I did it.'

'There's such a thing as making a mistake.'

Nick didn't reply.

'Bella is a beautiful girl.'

'Yes, she is.'

'You know, this next film she's doing is a big deal.'

'Is it?' Nick was staring down at the tablecloth, drawing a line with his fingernail on the white linen.

'Didn't she tell you? Huge budget.'

When Nick didn't respond, Andy tapped his arm. 'Hey.'

'What?'

'Want some good news?'

'That would be a novelty.'

Andy smiled broadly. 'You have an offer for film rights.'

'On what?'

'*The Measure.*'

Nick stared at him. *The Measure* was his first book.

Andy reached across the table and patted his arm. 'I told you something would come of doing this latest script.'

'But it's an old book,' Nick objected. 'Five years.'

'So what? It's not old to them. They just read it. They've made an offer.'

'How much?'

'A lot. That's not the best bit.'

'Well, what is?'

Andy's broad smile was back. At that moment, their attention was drawn to the entrance: a man had just come in. He was talking to the waiter when he saw Andy and waved.

'The rest of our party,' Andy told Nick. He stood up.

Nick stood alongside him. The stranger advanced on them, holding out his arms to Andy. About sixty, he was overweight, shaven-headed and dressed in a striped golf shirt and chinos that accentuated his bulk.

'Hey, Mike,' Andy said. He indicated Nick. 'This is our star.'

Nick found his hand vigorously shaken.

'Mike Kovic.'

'Pleased to meet you,' Nick murmured.

They all sat down.

'Well,' Andy said, beaming, 'this gentleman is your biggest fan.'

Nick looked from one to the other. He had no idea who Mike Kovic was, but felt that he should. Andy kept glancing at him, nodding.

'I loved that book,' Kovic said. 'Loved it.'

He leaned forward and tapped Nick's arm. 'You know when some critic says, "I laughed out loud"?' he asked. 'At a film, at a book? In a review?'

'Yes,' Nick said.

'Yeah.' Kovic winked at him. 'But nobody does, right? Never heard anybody laugh out loud, have you? When you see somebody reading a book on a train, on a beach, ever see them laugh out loud?'

'Never,' Andy agreed.

Nick stole a sideways glance at him.

Kovic was smiling broadly. 'Well, I did,' he told them. He spread his hands wide, palms facing upwards, an appeal to heaven. 'Hey! I did!' he said. 'I laughed out loud when I read this book!'

Andy's grin became wider as he looked at Nick. 'Mike is the one making you the offer for *The Measure.*'

'Oh,' Nick said. 'Well, thank you. Thank you very much.'

Kovic smiled. 'We're over here for a couple of weeks,' he said. 'Family and I. Vacation. But meeting a few people. Met someone you know last night.'

'Yes?'

'Went to see Georgina Lyle,' Kovic said, naming the director of the film Nick was currently working on. He turned to Andy and raised an eyebrow.

'I haven't told him,' Andy said. He looked

at Nick. 'Mike here heard good things about the script you're doing now.'

'Not good,' Kovic corrected. 'Brilliant.'

Nick sat back in his seat. He had suddenly experienced a perfectly defined moment of claustrophobia.

'How would you like to work in the States?' Kovic asked.

'The States?' Nick echoed.

Andy put his hand on Nick's shoulder and made a half-slapping, half-massaging motion. 'Come on, Nick,' he said. 'Somebody's got to write *The Measure*.'

'You want me to write the script?'

'That's the idea,' Kovic said.

'But authors don't write scripts,' Nick expostulated. 'Not of their own books. It's like – well, it's like death, isn't it? Nobody wants a novelist to screenwrite their own stuff.'

'You write scripts,' Kovic reminded him.

'Not of my own books.'

'Funny scripts, too.'

'But not of my own books.'

'Why is that?'

'Nobody ever asked me.'

There was a second of silence, then Kovic and Andy laughed together.

Andy signalled to the waiter. The first bottle of champagne was opened.

'You like this stuff?' Kovic asked Nick.

'Actually, I don't,' Nick said. 'Not really.'

'I'm with you,' Kovic said. He called the waiter back. 'Bring us a bottle of single malt,' he said.

Andy looked momentarily crestfallen, but hid it. He put his champagne flute to one side and lined up his whisky tumbler with the rest of them.

'Look, Nick,' Kovic said, 'let's not beat around the bush. I can't stand those industry committees, you know. Talking in circles.'

'OK,' Nick agreed.

'I want to make the film of *The Measure*. I like what you did. I like this kind of humour.' He sat back with his drink. 'We had a hell of a mess last year. I had four sets of writers. They were shit. I wrote half the thing myself. And I can't write.'

Nick smiled.

'That's right,' Kovic said, catching his expression. 'Pretty funny. It showed. Maybe you saw the film.' And he named it.

Nick tried to look noncommittal.

'Well,' said Kovic, 'I appreciate your kindness, I really do.' He took a swallow of his Scotch. 'Look,' he said, 'I got this idea. Maybe it's also shit. But you wrote the book, you write good scripts, I want you to do the script. And I'm willing to pay you three times what you're getting for the script you're doing with Georgina.'

Nick blinked. His current script had been

manna from heaven; it had quadrupled his previous annual earnings. The sum Kovic was talking about was almost eight times what he had earned eighteen months ago, far into six figures. It was a lottery win. Yet, despite Kovic's presence, despite Andy's patent excitement, which, uncharacteristically, he was failing to hide, Nick felt curiously unmoved. The pain in his head was getting worse, like a steel band tightening just above his eyes and running in a circle to the back. He wondered vaguely if he was getting a migraine. His mother had had them. She had described them to him exactly like this. He put a hand to his forehead.

'You OK?' Kovic asked.

'It's shock,' Andy quipped.

'I'm OK,' Nick said.

'You're American,' Kovic said. His gaze had narrowed slightly.

'Yes.'

'From?'

'Maine. Portland.'

Kovic raised his eyebrows in surprise. 'You don't sound it.'

'I went to Stanford. I lived out there for ten years. But I guess I don't sound from anywhere in particular.'

'So,' Kovic mused, 'what brought you to England?'

'My dad persuaded me to come with him. He paid, so … and I wanted to see it.'

'You and your dad close?'

Nick huffed. 'No. It was a big mistake. Our last try to get on. Didn't work.'

'That right?' Kovic commented. There was a pause. 'Ever want to go back to the west coast?'

What was the right answer, Nick wondered. The right answer was what he wanted, not what they wanted. But he had no idea what it was. 'Maybe,' he muttered.

'Perhaps your family would like to live in the sun for a while?'

'Yes,' Nick said. 'I'm sure.' He had tried not to hesitate this time.

'Maybe for a good while ... you never know, right?'

'Right,' Andy said.

Kovic leaned forward, elbows on the table. 'Look, Nick,' he said, 'I'm not in the business of forcing anybody.'

'It's a great offer,' Andy said.

'Sure it's a great offer, but if it doesn't appeal to Nick, it's not such a great offer, am I right?' There was an edge of irritation in Kovic's voice.

Nick had a moment of acute homesickness for Stanford; for the Lawrence Frost, the Hanna House. He used to go and sit in the arena of the Frost amphitheatre and look up at the magnolia and manzanita trees. He was there in '89, when the Loma Prieta struck. He wondered what it would be like to go back there. To live there. To regress to a single life somewhere along the Bay, maybe. He had run there once before, to escape the atmosphere in his family home where nothing had ever run smoothly: he had grown up listening to his father's smug authoritarianism, and when he had gone back for his mother's funeral and had seen his father again, he had assumed that it would be for the last time. Instead, he had allowed himself to be persuaded to come to England, hoping against hope that his father would behave differently in another country. Foolishness.

'No,' he murmured. 'Just ... taking it in.' He looked up at Kovic. 'Thanks for the offer. I appreciate it.'

Kovic seemed to be trying to read him. 'Funny guys are always real serious,' he mused. He nodded, as if to confirm it to himself. Then he got to his feet. He held out his hand to Nick. 'Tight schedule today,' he said. 'But we'll talk again, OK?'

'Yes,' Nick said, standing up, too.

Kovic began to walk to the door. Andy, shooting Nick a sharp look, walked after him. Nick watched them hold a hurried conversation.

Nick dropped back into his seat and flexed his hands. He wondered how many times he would get another offer like that one. It was the sort of thing he used to dream of. Andy would never have gambled on bringing Kovic straight here without consulting Nick first on the figures, the deal, if he hadn't been sure that Nick would be blown away by it.

Kovic was looking at the floor while Andy talked to him.

Nick closed his eyes. Well, this was it. One of life's defining moments. In the space of a week, one chapter had finished and another begun: he was about to inhabit a brave new world, a world that he knew would suit him if he could put his mind to it. Who would turn down what he had just been offered? He was going back to California.

He thought of the manzanitas, the magnolias, the mountain lilac moving in the breeze, the Paoletti window in the church, the sound of the Tournai bells in the top of the tower. All the things that had once soothed him. He could go back and see them again. He could drive along the coast and get himself a house there.

Andy came back to the table alone. He glared at Nick, then sat down with a sigh. 'This is what you used to talk about,' he said.

'Andy...'

'This is what you always talked about, writing screenplays. When I sold your first book, when I sold *The* fucking *Measure,* you said it then. As I recall, you didn't even thank me. You asked if I could sell the film rights.' He screwed a fist to his temple, then pounded it, mid-air, in Nick's direction. 'I thought you'd never be satisfied. I was right.'

'Don't be like this,' Nick said.

'Why shouldn't I?' Andy demanded. 'What's wrong with Kovic?'

'Nothing,' Nick replied. 'What's the matter with you? Didn't I just thank him?'

'I suppose it's not a big enough company?'

'I don't know what the hell company he's got,' Nick retorted. 'I don't even know what he's offered in any detail.'

'Look,' Andy said, 'we'll go back to the office. I'll show you the figures. We'll run through all the clauses. We'll read it backwards. I'll write it out in my own blood.' He shook his head. 'This is a lot of money, Nick,' he said slowly. 'I thought you'd jump for joy, I really did.'

Nick smiled. 'I'm twitching. Jumping comes later.'

'It's Zeph,' Andy said. 'That's your trouble.' He sighed, pushed back his chair, called the waiter and signed the bill. 'Unless you want to eat?' he asked, pen hovering.

'No, thanks.'

'I thought not.'

Nick knew that Andy was right. He couldn't see himself in the fabled sunshine, driving the fabled soft-top car, with the fabled pubescent starlet on his arm. He wanted Zeph. But the odds were that the door had closed on all that. Grief washed over him. He had to let go of the one thing he wanted.

They got up, wove their way back through the tables. At the door, they both put on their coats and opened the door to the rainy street.

'I'll go,' Nick decided. 'I'll take it.'

Andy squinted up through the drizzle at the clouded London skyline.

'You don't believe me,' Nick said. 'I just said I'll go. I'm going. I'm on the plane. I'm knocking back my free drink. I'm waving goodbye to Heathrow. Goodbye, England. Whoosh! I've gone.'

Andy smiled briefly. 'Look, Nick,' he said, 'why don't you talk to Zeph?'

'Because she won't talk to me.'

'Try again,' the older man said, turning up his collar.

'I don't need to. I'm going for it,' Nick said. 'I can do it. You don't believe me.'

'I believe you,' Andy said. 'If you say so.'

'I mean it,' Nick told him. 'I do say so. I'm going to live on the beach. It'll be great. I'll drive a Ferrari.' He glanced from left to right as if taking in a fantastic new panorama. 'Hey, get a load of me there!' he said. 'Writing by the pool. How cool is that? Oh! And here's me at Kovic's Golden Globe party. I'm the buttocks third from the right in the orgy picture.'

'You're crazy.' Andy smiled.

'That's right.' Nick grimaced. 'Oh, looking down the years, I have a shrink. And I'm putting on weight. It was my birthday last week. I just hit fifty. I have indigestion a whole lot.' He straightened his shoulders, and grinned. 'Oh, but I get lucky at fifty-two,' he said. 'I get married to one of Beyoncé's backing singers. I have a toupee. I have my jowls pinned behind my ears. I mainline Viagra.'

Andy shook his head, grinning.

'Here comes seventy,' Nick continued. 'I have trouble peeing. I have a minor procedure. I have a major procedure. I win an Oscar. The shock gives me a minor stroke. But I'm perky. Time goes by, I make tea for my wife's lover when he visits. The bastard. Never mind, hey-ho, here comes eighty. On a pretty Thursday in October I have a heart attack buying Big Butt jeans in Wal-Mart. I'm dead.' He spread his arms wide. 'Hey!' he said. 'That was a great life.'

Andy laughed.

Nick stood with a rigid, determined smile in place, his arms open. All the while the rain pattered on his hair. He turned his face upwards, closed his eyes, screwed them tight, clenched his fists.

At last, he dropped his arms to his sides.

Not in satisfaction, but defeat. He seemed small, standing there in the middle of the narrow street.

'How did I do?' he asked Andy softly.

'You did great,' Andy replied, taking his arm. 'All your life. Just great.'

Verde

There is a house in Enna behind the cathedral. And the day that I am taken to see it, it is hot. Very hot. Much too hot to be standing in my smartest clothes, wondering if I should buy simply because my heart is here.

The garden is so green it is almost unbelievable. But, then, most of Sicily is green here in the spring. I have driven here through the greenest fields on earth up the winding road under the shadow of the towers of Castello di Lombardia, the castle that overlooks the heartland of this island.

I have come for a wedding. One of my nieces is getting married. Her husband is much older than she is, but I think they will do well together.

Jesus, when I knew you, Cora, this girl hadn't been born. Her mother, my elder sister, had only just got married. That's how long ago it was. Nineteen years.

I have been working hard lately. I am back at

the university. This time, I am the lecturer. I have changed places, and now I am the one taking seminars, watching the students come in by ones and twos, bleary-eyed. I have a pupil called Francesco who always comes with his girlfriend, and I can see them through the open door, saying a torrid goodbye to each other before he walks in.

Parted for a whole hour! Such is youth.

I set them Petrarch to teach Francesco a lesson about patience, though I doubt it will work. He's a big, broad, talkative boy who can't wait to get going. He has big plans. He was telling us all about co-operative farming the other day. He has a dream straight out of the sixties, to have a communal operation. Christ, it hardly seems possible. I thought all those dreams were done with. I told him that the commune farms in California had failed because the men sat about talking politics all day while the women were left with the drudgery. I told him that everything comes to an end, and he looked at me pityingly. I could tell that he was thinking, You are an old man. At thirty-eight, I'm old and cynical. Or so this boy supposes.

Maybe he's right. We all sit reading Petrarch, and I think, Three hundred and sixty-five songs to Laura de Noves: what a waste. Petrarch first saw her when she was seventeen and had been married for two years; he watched her at an Easter service. He probably never spoke to her directly, and she died when she was thirty-eight, twenty-one years to the day after Petrarch first saw her. She was someone else's wife, and she ignored him. But he wrote The Song Book for her just the same.

Don't think that the comparison is lost on me.

But I'm not Petrarch. And I want to reach across the desk and tell Francesco so. I'm not tied up with my books. My life is green, not white. It's not dried to parchment yet. It's not an empty sheet of paper. It's not the dead and plain colour of the wedding dresses, veils and white cloth that I'm looking at this weekend. It's not white like my niece's face as she comes up the aisle of the church, nervous because she always thought that she was insignificant and now this imposing man has decided to marry her. It's not white, like roses. Like some roses. I turn my head away from the bridal couple in the church, and I don't think about white roses climbing the wall of a house in Syracusa, and, if I do, I think it was all a long time ago and a wasted enterprise.

Petrarch had a life far outside the page. He had two mistresses and two illegitimate children, and he got married eventually. He travelled to Flanders and Rome, Liège and Verona, and he created his sonnet form, which had come from the ducal courts in Sicily. He was a classical scholar and a diplomatic courier, and he knew people, he understood them. So, I tell my students, don't think that this laureate lived the life of a bleached saint, always yearning and pining in a closed room for the woman he

271

couldn't have.

I, too, have a mistress, a divorced woman who is older than me. I have known her for a few months. I don't write her love songs. She is a cheerful, independent person who makes time for me occasionally, which suits me. She is a good cook. She laughs a lot. She makes fantastic torrone, *and has shown me how to work the butter, cocoa and almonds together. I think I really wanted to take her to bed the first time I saw her make it, and, when I told her this, she kissed me hard. She tastes delicious, just like* ricotta al caffè; *she tastes of chocolate and coffee and cigarettes, smoky and sweet and bitter all at once. The other day, I watched her pour half a litre of cream into a bowl, beat in five eggs with some wine, then pour it over brioche. I started to laugh. 'What is it?' she asked.*

'I love you,' I told her.

'You don't love me,' she retorted, grinning. 'You love your stomach.'

So, there is no Laura. Anyway I'm too busy in middle age to nourish a passion. The students fire me up and rush my life along; I like the public lectures, the ones where they get up and challenge me. I hate the ones who sit there meekly. And I've got into trouble for not behaving like a good faculty professore. *But I don't want to run along the lines someone draws for me.*

I travel. I go to the States a lot, working. I've been to Australia and Japan. I've made a name

272

for myself. They hire me for talking too loudly. I like being a mouthpiece, and I like causing a little trouble. Poets are ignored in every country of the world, or not appreciated enough. So I get other poets to come to my venues, and they heckle me from the audience. It's like cabaret, which is how living verse should be.

And I have written my book.

At last. I have written my book.

And I try not to listen to the little voice when I turn out the light to go to sleep.

I am an academic, a writer, a man of property.

And from this week I shall have another house.

And that's what matters, a full life.

And no Laura and no love songs.

And the small midnight voice in the dark each night whispers, Liar, and tells me how green it was, in the shade of another garden.

Fourteen

Cora and Richard had been married for fourteen years when they went to Sicily. One of the men with whom Richard had served had settled there, and occasionally letters came. Once or twice a year, Richard would receive the bulky white envelopes; alongside the letter there would invariably be photo-graphs of a house where Alex Carlyle lived alone, a beautiful place in Taormina.

'You must come,' the last letter had said. 'This year if no other.'

All that week Richard didn't refer to the letter; he was due to be out of the house for two days, delivering medlar and quince to an estate near the Fowey estuary that had ordered them. Cora helped him load the five-year-old trees into the truck, wrapping each one to protect the branches. It was early March and they had pruned them a week earlier, thinning out the exhausted shoots and fruit spurs. There were forty, ordered two years previously. She had watched Rich-ard drive away, and had gone back to the garden, to the sheds and greenhouses.

It was still too early for the sun, rimming the horizon, to be fully up; there was frost on the ground. As had been her custom every day since they had first built the south-facing walls, Cora walked back along the lines of trained espaliers, fans and trees, admiring the beautiful shapes of the new morellos, flourishing where it would be too cold for anything else at the top of the slope.

She drew her coat close round her. Two dogs, black Labradors, were at her heels. They were nine years old, from a litter at a farm where Richard and she had bought their first rootstock. They followed her now to the top of the garden where she could see the roof of the white van disappearing between the hedges. Richard would be out on the Honiton road within half an hour, and in Cornwall by twelve. For the rest of the day he would be planting at the country house whose owners were trying to re-establish its Victorian garden.

'I'll come back tomorrow,' he had told her. 'I'll be home by six.'

She looked down at the house, with its lean-to extension along one side, and the roofs of the sheds showing in neat red parallel lines to the edge of the field. As she turned in the other direction, she could see smoke curling from her father's chimney. She decided to go down to see him; since his stroke, he had managed well but he could be forgetful. Tearful, too, which was the worst of it. In winter, when it was more difficult for him to get out, Cora would sit with him during the afternoon and listen to the long list of her mother's virtues, delivered in a voice that was not quite her father's any more. He had become a querulous old man, unsure of himself, forgetful of his friends. He never turned Richard away, though: he liked him to stay in the evening sometimes to play gin rummy and whist with him; and Cora, who had never been good at cards, would go home alone, through the garden and out of the lane gate.

Sometimes when she made this journey she would stop where the fruit cages used to be; the bushes inside them had long ago grown too woody to be productive, and the area had been turned over to lawn. She didn't know what she had imagined when she accepted Richard that night: something safe, something good? She was not quite sure. She had received safety, kindness and sweetness.

And yet there were the pauses: the pause by the empty lawn, or by the rose-beds, or in the house when she looked out from cleaning the bedrooms on to the view of her and Richard's house, and the new vista of the market garden, so cleanly laid out in its rows. Then she would think that she was exactly as she had once feared: her mother, married to an older man, keeping his house. Keeping Richard's house and her father's house. She was in her mother's role and her own. Her father was seventy-three that year, Richard was fifty-four, and she was thirty-three. In the pauses, she would feel stranded in another generation, a generation that had been young in the 1940s. She was still young, she would think, and she would open the newspaper and see the 1960s passing. She felt she had lost her twenties and thirties; she felt herself to be Richard's age.

A few years ago, on her twenty-fifth birthday, she had gone up to London. She had found herself longing to see the city and Jenny again. Richard had not wanted to come: he was busy, and happy for her to arrange a day out for herself in town.

'You can talk about old times,' he had joked, as he saw her off at the station. She'd smiled back. She had never told him about David Menzies. She never would.

Jenny had met her at the station: she looked much older in the face but was dressed as if she were sixteen. Cora had taken in the sight of Jenny's dumpy legs, revealed by the mini-dress, and the eyes almost obscured by black liner. Her friend had grown her hair and darkened it; she bore little resemblance to the curly-haired girl Cora had known at school.

They got into a taxi. Jenny sat back and appraised her. 'So,' she said, 'how is life down on the farm?'

'Fine,' Cora replied. 'How's Terry?'

Jenny had shrugged. 'I don't see much of him.' Her husband, she told Cora, was travelling. He had spent three months of the previous year in India and was now importing Indian goods.

'The house is full of bloody incense-burners,' Jenny told her. 'Don't be afraid to kick a few out of the way.'

When they got to the Georgian terrace in Kensington, Cora was astonished by it. It was huge, a shrine in itself. The hallway was hung with silk flags of every imaginable shade; there were mosaic mirrors on the floor. Joss sticks burned in a sitting room that was almost dark, and had no furniture except vast floor cushions.

'We've gone native,' Jenny explained, as they walked through it. 'We have to. Business.'

When they got to the kitchen, Cora saw something of the old Jenny. The table and the chairs round it were just like those in Cora's father's house, hard-polished mahogany that seemed plaintively out of place among the Che Guevara posters.

'He keeps saying he'll throw everything of mine out,' Jenny said derisively.

'And will he? Will you let him?'

'No,' Jenny retorted. 'Anyway, he's never home long enough.'

Cora admired the paintings. There were all sorts of prints and posters, and a few originals. She stood in front of a largely white canvas and read the signature at the bottom: Mark Tobey. 'Did you buy this?' she asked Jenny.

'I don't buy any of it,' her friend replied tersely. 'To tell you the truth, I don't like it. Do you?'

'I've never seen anything like it,' Cora told her. 'I think it's lovely.'

Jenny began to laugh. 'Oh, my God,' she said. 'You're not allowed to say, "It's lovely", darling. You have to stand about in galleries at first nights saying things like "The forms are so meditative."'

'I don't know what that means.'

'Neither do I,' Jenny said. 'Between you and me, Cora, it's all crap, Terry's world.'

Cora frowned to herself as Jenny took cups from a cupboard. She looked around for something else to comment on, and saw the photograph of Jenny and Terry's two sons propped on the dresser. Both, she knew, were away at boarding-school. Jenny had told her some time ago that that had been against her better judgement. The last time Cora had seen her was at the youngest's christening. She picked up the photograph. 'They've grown so handsome,' she said.

Jenny's gaze rested on it. 'They became other people when that school got its hands on them.'

The two women regarded each other across the table, and two cups of strong coffee.

'Let's have cake,' Jenny said. 'Diet be buggered.'

They ate silently for a while. Jenny pressed her fingertips to the plate then licked the crumbs off them. 'I never get the chance to do this,' she said. 'Nobody eats in London. They just do acid.'

'Do you still work at the shop?' Cora asked.

'Now and then.' Jenny grabbed Cora's arm. 'Hey,' she said, 'let's go and look at it. Let's go and look at the whole scene.'

The shop had moved to swinging London's epicentre. It was in a side-street a hundred yards from the King's Road; lanterns hung outside, and above it a picture of an Indian woman, her arms outstretched. When they walked into the gloom, Cora could just make out the salesgirl curled on a rug, lighting a cigarette. She got up when she saw them. She was dressed the same as Jenny: a tiny skirt, with black-and-white patent Courrèges-style boots that ended just under the knee.

'Vinny about?' Jenny asked.

'In the back,' the girl said.

They went through to the office. A man was sitting with his feet up on the desk, sorting through a pile of invoices in his lap. He was a tall, rangy Jamaican.

'Vinny,' Jenny said. 'This is Cora.'

The man looked Cora up and down, and grinned as he got up. 'You two girls ready for lunch?' he asked.

'Take us somewhere,' Jenny told him.

They walked down Elystan Place and out on to the King's Road. Cora glanced across to Radnor Walk.

'Didn't that guy Menzies live down here?' Jenny asked. She had taken Vinny's hand as they waited for a gap in the traffic.

'Yes,' Cora replied.

'Hear anything of him?'

'No.' Cora tried to hide her disgust. 'Have you?'

'He married some Swedish woman,' Vinny said. 'Moved there.'

'You knew him?' Cora asked.

Vinny laughed. 'Everybody knew David,' he said.

'What was wrong with him?' Jenny asked, as they started to cross. 'He seemed all right to me.'

'He seemed all right to most women,' Vinny told her.

'He was vile,' Cora murmured, and ignored Jenny's astonishment.

They stopped at a bar. It was packed. Over the heads of the customers, Vinny ordered sandwiches. They moved to a cramped table in a corner.

Jenny patted Cora's knee. 'How's Richard?' she asked.

'Fine,' Cora said, watching Vinny light a cigarette and pass it to her friend. He offered one to her; she shook her head.

'What're you doing down there?'

'The market garden,' Cora said. 'I wrote to you about it.'

Jenny smiled at Vinny, and cocked her head in her friend's direction. 'Cora is Mother Earth.'

'We cultivate fruit trees,' Cora explained.

'Hard work?' Vinny asked.

'Yes, quite hard. Busy.'

'Got kids?'

'No,' Cora replied. 'Have you?'

'Five,' he said. And he laughed. 'I cultivate them.' He drew out the word lovingly, with a grin.

Jenny gripped Cora's arm. 'I know what we'll do with you this afternoon,' she said. 'We'll buy you some clothes.'

'I don't need any,' Cora said.

'Yes, you do,' Jenny replied. 'Look at you.'

Cora glanced down at herself. 'What's wrong with me?'

'You look like a farmer's wife.'

'But that's what I am.'

'Jesus, Cora,' Jenny said. 'You're not forty.'

The crowd was pressing in to them so they got up and went out on to the street. When Vinny walked ahead, Cora held Jenny back. 'What are you doing?' she said. 'Who is this man?'

Jenny regarded her with surprise. 'He's the office manager. Didn't you see?'

'You're having an affair with him.'

'Darling,' Jenny said, 'everybody does it. What do you think Terry's up to?'

Cora stopped dead.

'Not everyone lives in Cloud Cuckoo Land,' Jenny went on, 'with their hands in the soil and their hearts entwined like the briar, tra-la.'

'You're making fun of me,' Cora said. 'You

always did.'

'No, I'm not,' Jenny said. 'I envy you. You're happy. But, then, I'm having the wildest time.'

'You should be careful.'

'Haven't you heard of the Pill?'

'Of course.'

'But you haven't any children.' She saw Cora's expression. 'Oh, darling,' she said. 'Sorry.'

Cora felt irritated. Not only by Jenny, but by the city around her. It was a cryptic, stifling sensation: half of her envied Jenny's freedom, the other half disapproved. She felt out of place and stupid. She particularly resented the casual mention of families: she wanted children, and so did Richard. They had talked about moving house when she became pregnant. But she never had. Richard's attitude was to let nature take its course, for good or bad. He would not let her see a doctor. And the idea of himself being examined was never discussed. At first he was especially kind to her each month, as if sympathizing because it was her fault. Then, gradually, the subject slipped away. They had only ever argued twice, heatedly, in their marriage, and it had been about that: Richard's acceptance of the unbearable.

It was all part of it, part of the feeling that life was slipping away from her, passing her. She loved Richard; she could not resent him. But sometimes, in the garden alone, or working silently alongside him, watching his absorption in their work, she would feel a helpless sweeping away of herself. Recently it had become worse. She had felt that the garden was full of little ghosts, the children they had not had. It was surreal and strange, and she worried that she might be slipping back to the wasteland she had inhabited after her mother's death. So she had tried to stop herself thinking about children.

Jenny made a visible effort now to lighten the mood. She linked Cora's arm. 'Has he taken you anywhere exotic lately?' she asked. 'France? Further?'

'We've been to Cornwall,' Cora said. 'We like it there.'

'I met Vinny in Lindos,' Jenny said. 'I'm going back this summer.'

'Where's Lindos?'

'Rhodes. Oh, you must go, Cora,' she said. 'Take off your shoes. Take off your clothes. Swim naked in the warm sea.' And she raised her eyebrows, grinned, and nodded in Vinny's direction. 'You'll never look back.'

'We swim in Cornwall,' Cora said.

'In an English summer!' Jenny hooted derision. 'You'll turn permanently blue.'

They had reached the main shops. For the next hour, Cora was hauled into one and then another; eventually she gave in to the silliness, and found herself on the train home with several carrier-bags of skirts and hats, and a pair of white boots. On the station, Jenny had hugged her with just a little too much force.

'Come down and see us,' Cora said. 'Please. Come and stay. Bring the boys.'

Jenny had rolled her eyes. 'I will,' she promised.

But Cora didn't believe her.

When she got home, she showed Richard what she had bought. She put on the skirt and boots and walked up and down.

He sat in the armchair and smiled. 'Very nice,' he had said. 'Very short.'

'I might wear it into town,' she told him.

'Not if I catch you first,' he said.

She had considered him, smiling. 'Everybody wears things like this in London, you know.'

'London is not here,' he replied.

She had put the clothes away in a drawer.

Sometimes she looked at them. But not very often.

Eight years had passed since that day in London. Now, at midday, she heard a car coming into the drive. She was in the greenhouses, potting out pelargonium cuttings. She liked the work: it was slow, fastidious, productive. She liked to stand back and see that she had done two hundred, three hundred, that a morning had turned into afternoon, that the light had changed and the sun had moved to produce a different patch of light, a different patch of shade.

She wiped her hands on a cloth and walked out to see who the customer was.

A man she knew well was standing by a green Ford Zephyr, looking up the garden at the rows of bushes and trees. He glanced round as he heard her footsteps. 'I suppose they all have names, and you know them,' he said. 'In Latin, probably.'

She smiled broadly. 'I do, actually.'

'And you never forget them, with your inhuman encyclopedic brain.'

She began to run, and threw herself into his arms.

He held her tightly. '"In the green grass she loves to lie,"' he murmured, laughing. '"And there with her fair aspect tames the wilder flowers..."'

'"And gives them names."' She stepped back from him. 'Brian,' she said, 'what on earth are you doing here?'

'I came to look at Flora, the goddess, in her field of delight.'

She waved her hand at the garden. 'This is it.'

He took her hand as it fell to her side. 'I was on my way to see an author in Bristol,' he said, 'and it struck me that I was only forty miles from you on the motorway so I turned off. And here you are, looking wonderful,' he said.

They stood apart from each other.

'Six years,' she said. 'You look well.'

'Dear child, I am preserved in alcohol.'

'You met us at Wisley. That was the last time we saw you.'

'That I did. Months it took me to get over the excess of oxygen in that bloody great garden. Months!'

Bisley was older, but looked better than she remembered. 'The high life suits you,' she commented, 'all your success.'

'Better late than never,' he commented wryly. 'And I've been doing outrageous things you won't believe.'

'Such as what?'

'Playing tennis.'

She laughed. 'You? Where?'

'You'd hardly recognize me,' he said. 'I've bought a house in Spain. It has a pool, too. I hold court there, like an ancient guru.' And he laughed at himself. 'So very wise,' he told her, rolling his eyes. 'So *very* astute. So decrepit!'

She smiled back. 'Where exactly is this?'

'A glorious place. Andalucía.'

'I can't imagine you out of London.'

'Neither could I,' he said. 'I bought it from one of my authors.'

'You aren't totally reformed?' she asked. 'You haven't given up smoking?'

'Don't be foolish!' He stood a pace away from her. 'So, where is Richard?'

'You've missed him,' she said, 'but come into the house. Let me give you lunch.'

They sat at the table in the kitchen, Bisley watching her as she warmed some soup. For a while, they ate in silence, Cora feeling herself under his scrutiny.

'Tell me what you do with yourself all day,' he said finally.

'Well, I work here,' she said. 'We have contracts to supply people, and we grow fruit to sell.'

'It sounds like hard labour.'

'Not really,' she replied. 'It was at first – bringing in better soil, improving it year by year, building the walls and terraces, but there's not so much of that now. Everything's established.'

'It must be very pretty when the trees blossom. Will it make you rich?'

'Oh, no,' she said, and laughed. 'I doubt that very much.'

Slowly, he pushed aside his plate. 'Are you happy?' he asked.

She didn't reply immediately.

'With Richard,' he added. He paused. 'After London.'

'Yes,' she answered candidly. 'I never saw that other man again.'

'I hope you understand what a bastard he was.'

'Yes,' she said. 'I know now that it wasn't my fault.'

He nodded, satisfied. 'Well,' he said, letting the subject go, 'do you keep up your reading?'

'Oh, yes,' she replied, enthused. 'I was reading *Alexander's Feast* last night. And I have Robert Graves's book. I like Louis MacNeice. And Yeats. Lots of Yeats.'

'My God,' he said, pretending to look horrified. 'Dryden to Yeats. A whole anthology.' He leaned on the table. 'MacNeice,' he mused. 'A departure for you. A modern poet.'

She mirrored his posture. 'Do you know that poem "Snow"?'

'Yes.'

'About light and dark? About roses?'

'Yes.'

She sat back, smiling. 'I often think about it,' she said. 'The glass between the snow and the pink roses on the windowsill.'

'In what way, particularly?'

'That the world is plural...'

'"The world is crazier and more of it than we think."'

'Yes,' she said. 'There is more than glass between the snow and the roses.'

'You've become a philosopher,' he said.

'I have time to think,' she answered, blushing.

'And you think that the world has its light

289

and shade.'

'Yes,' she said. 'It does.'

'Be careful with him,' Bisley said. 'You know what else he said – "We cannot cage the minute." You have changed,' he said admiringly. 'I rather like you now.'

She laughed and he patted her hand. 'I always thought of you as a kind of daughter,' he said. She squeezed his fingers, touched. 'And what does Richard think of all your reading?'

Cora shrugged. 'He probably thinks it a bit odd,' she admitted. 'He doesn't read. He's not one for poetry, really, but he doesn't object.'

Bisley nodded, and was silent for a moment.

'What is it?' she asked, after she had waited for him to speak. 'There's something. You didn't turn off the motorway just to see how the trees looked.'

He gave her a brief smile. 'I have a letter for you.'

'From whom?'

'The person you used to share a house with, Jennifer.'

Surprised, Cora took the envelope he was holding out to her.

He was smiling. 'Those Saturday parties in your mews house.'

Cora frowned. 'Did I invite you?'

'You did once,' he said. 'But I knew Terry

anyway.'

At the mention of Jenny's husband Cora said, 'They married.'

'Of course they did,' Bisley retorted. 'I'm not a complete recluse, you know.' He shook a cigarette out of a packet, and lit it. 'I've seen them, on and off, at parties for the last ten years. Heard the gossip about them, too.' He squinted at her through the smoke. 'I expect that's what this is about,' he said, nodding at the letter.

'What gossip?'

'Oh, Cora,' he said, 'don't be silly. She told me you went to visit her.'

'Only for a day.'

'Even so, you must know about her darkie.'

Cora frowned again. She didn't like to hear him use such words, but he was from another time, another generation, of the Raj and the empire. Bisley leaned back in his chair. 'Do open it and put me out of my misery,' he said.

The envelope simply had Cora's name on it, nothing else.

'Why didn't she send it to me?'

'She said she'd lost your address,' he replied. 'She came to my house, shoved it into my hands and said I was to give it to you when I saw you.'

Cora opened the letter.

Cora

*I'm afraid I shan't come and see you after all;
and I shan't be in London the next time you
come.*

*You won't think badly of me, will you? I have
left the boys and Terry. If they ask you, you'll be
able to say you don't know where I am.*

*To be honest, Cora, I don't care about the
house or the business, or anything I have here.
Or don't have here. I want to be with Vinny.*

*Don't worry about me is all I wanted to say.
And swim, when you have the chance, sweetie.
Jenny.*

Cora looked up. 'I was thinking about her
this morning,' she said.

'Are you in touch with her?'

'I wrote to her before Christmas,' she said.

'Did she write back?'

'She never does.'

She put the letter on the table. Bisley lifted
it and read it, then looked at Cora over the
paper. 'They were all saying that Terry had
finished her off,' he said. 'It seems not.'

Cora stared at him.

'There was a rumour in town,' he said.
'People said that he was violent to her.' He
touched her hand across the table. 'He put
her in hospital,' he said. 'He fractured her
jaw.'

'When?' she gasped.

'Last year.'

292

She was silent with shock. Then the memory of Terry Ray's hand on Jenny, soon after they had met, rushed back to her. The bullying hand, and the bruises.

'I'm sorry,' Bisley said. 'He confessed it to someone I know. Very remorseful, apparently.'

'She didn't tell me.'

'To my knowledge, she told no one.'

'Oh, my God,' she murmured. 'Poor Jenny. No wonder she left.'

Bisley put the letter down. 'What does she mean, swim?' he asked.

Cora blushed. 'To strike out for oneself... I don't know,' she murmured.

Bisley was smiling. 'To warm before the fire?'

'Yes,' she agreed slowly. 'Perhaps. To live.' And she thought of the photograph of Jenny's two sons propped against the kitchen dresser; and of Vinny's broad, gentle hand in the small of Jenny's back as he and she had crossed the road in front of her.

When Richard came home the next evening, he had made up his mind. Putting his arm round her shoulders as they walked to the house, he said abruptly, 'I think we'll go to Sicily.'

Cora stopped, astonished. 'Sicily?' she repeated. 'When?'

'As soon as we can.'

'But why?' she asked. 'Why now?'

'I'd like to see Alex Carlyle,' he told her. 'He's not well. He asks me every year to go back.' He stroked her hair. 'Would you like to go?'

'Well ... of course. What made you think of it so suddenly?'

'I don't take you out enough,' he said, as if he had finally come to this conclusion. 'We haven't had a proper holiday in two or three years.'

'I'm not here to be entertained,' she pointed out.

'Look after you more, then,' he said. 'I don't do enough of that either.'

'Can we afford it?'

'We could go by train,' he said, 'and stay with Alex. I know he would have us.'

'But we've not been abroad since our honeymoon.'

'All the more reason to go now.'

She looked around herself, at the greenhouses where she had been working yesterday and today. 'But what about the garden?'

'If we go at Easter we can be there and back before the season begins.'

She inspected his face intently. 'Are we running away?' she asked. And the most peculiar feeling went through her.

Jenny's voice echoed in her mind. Since Bisley had left her yesterday, she had been thinking about the hidden expression in

Jenny's face, the one clear picture of happiness. She had been imagining Jenny stepping naked into the sea, her back turned on all she had left behind. And last night, as she drifted into sleep she had felt herself – perhaps even dreamed it – running down the sand after her friend, racing headlong into the water, which was as warm as the day, and the waves closing around them both, the sun beating on their shoulders.

She had woken up this morning and wondered about it.

I want to disappear, she had thought suddenly. *I want to be somewhere else.*

I want to run away, too.

She had felt ashamed of the thought, confused and surprised by it.

'Running away?' Richard had repeated, laughing. 'For two weeks?'

They began to walk again; he held open the door to the house for her.

'Besides,' he said, 'Taormina in the spring – Sicily in the spring. You have never seen anywhere more beautiful.'

Fifteen

It was late in the evening when they reached Taormina.

When they got out of the car at Alex Carlyle's house, they saw that, all the way up the steps from the street, there were candles in metal lanterns, lavender and lemon trees; and Alex had been waiting for them, a man much older than Richard, bent over a walking-cane upon which he leaned.

'Welcome to Taormina,' he had said. 'Welcome to Sicily.'

The two men gripped each other's hands. Thirty years separated their meetings. When Alex turned to her, Cora saw how the sun had lined his face, scored deep white lines where his smile relaxed; she noticed his faint accent, which was explained when he began to talk to the maid in soft, fluent Italian.

'Come in,' he had said, and held out his hand to Cora. 'We're all so excited to see you.'

She caught Richard's eye. He put his hand under her elbow to guide her into the house.

He had been watching her since they first arrived in Italy, seemingly concerned at the length of the journey, the noise of Naples, the stifling confinement of the boat. He had told her he thought it might be too much for her, especially when, in Naples, the weather had turned unseasonably hot, like a blast from the tropics.

'I'm not as fragile as you seem to think,' she had told him, smiling, as they lay in the small hotel room, and he opened the windows to a panorama of roofs crammed together, and the milky blue sky of the morning.

'Anyone would be fragile in this heat,' he had commented.

The closer they got to Italy, the more silent he became. She felt different, energized by the changing scenery. The journey through France had been monochrome, full of endless stops. They had looked out on some stations, disembarked at others, and it had been grey, with rain-heavy skies over the fields and the small anonymous towns. The first night, in the sleeper compartment of the train, she had drifted off wondering where they were, which country was outside the carriage window, trying to assess their speed by the rattle of the wheels on the track.

But the second morning was different. She awoke to sun: they were coming down through northern Italy.

'Where will we stop?' she asked Richard.

'Florence, Pisa...'

'Can we get out?'

'Our tickets are for Naples,' he told her. 'We'll stop there, if you like.'

She had to defer to his arrangements; she could see that it mattered to him. There was some sort of struggle going on inside him: sitting opposite him in the carriage, she could see that he was keeping his impressions, his memories to himself. At one point, she put her hand on his knee. 'You travelled through this part?'

'Not here,' he said.

'Somewhere close?'

He didn't reply. She tried something else. 'Tell me about Taormina,' she said.

'It was very small when we were there,' he told her. 'They say it's grown since.'

'Is it pretty?'

'The prettiest place in the world,' he said. 'There's a wonderful Greek amphitheatre that overlooks the sea, and a piazza half-way down the main street, the Corso Umberto. You'll like it.'

'You were stationed there,' she said. He had told her this much, no more.

'Yes,' he agreed. 'We'll walk down to the piazza and have a drink there one evening,' he said. 'Every evening, if you like. It will be warm. It's already warm in Sicily.'

'Where did you live when you were there?' she asked.

'There was a film unit,' he said, 'a photo-

298

graphic unit attached to the army. After I was injured, I stayed with the officers in a villa until I could be transferred. It was high on the hill overlooking Giardini Naxos. Every night we would watch the sunsets.'

'A photographic unit?'

'They came through with us, every step.'

'Do you have photographs of the time in the villa?'

'No.' He gazed out of the window. The train was drawing into Milan. 'I used to have some of the terrace, of the view. I had one of myself sitting with another officer, in those cane chairs...'

'Like we have at home?'

'Like that.'

'But where are these photos?' she asked. 'I've never seen them.'

'I destroyed them,' he said. 'It seemed indecent to keep them.'

'Why?'

'To enjoy those days when everyone else was at war.'

'But you had been wounded. You were waiting to go back to Egypt. You had earned the sunsets.'

'I earned nothing,' he said. And he had looked out of the window, closing the subject.

Alex's house was lovely. Built in the Moorish style, it resembled two latticed white boxes placed one on top of the other. Each floor had lancet windows; at the very top a roof terrace was edged with a wide black lava frieze inlaid with white stone. Richard and Cora's bedroom adjoined the roof, with a door opening out on to the flat space. When Cora went on to it after her bath, the stones were warm to her bare feet. She had stopped a moment to luxuriate in the feel of it. The night was black, humid, scented; she let her towel drop and stood naked, feeling the air cling to her.

'What on earth are you doing?' Richard had said, coming to the door behind her.

'Come out here,' she whispered. 'It's beautiful.'

'Someone will see you,' he told her irritably. 'Don't stand there like that, Cora. Come inside.'

She did as he asked.

Over dinner, she asked Alex Carlyle about the house. It was ancient, he told her. One of the oldest buildings along the coast. 'All of Sicily is old,' he said. 'It has an old heart, very slow, where Naples and Rome are fast. If you listen hard, you can hear Sicily's heart beating.'

And he raised a finger theatrically, as if they could bear witness to it.

Cora sat back in her chair, gazing at him down the long, pale-wood table. The candles were burning low after their meal; the windows were open. She strained to listen, and heard voices far down in the street, the low drumming of insects.

'You're a romantic,' Richard remarked to her, rather tonelessly.

'One cannot be anything else in this town,' Alex replied. He turned back to Cora. 'Sicily has been at the heart of shifting civilizations for two and a half millennia,' he said. 'In the twelfth century, Palermo was described as the vastest and finest city of the world. The Arabs made the Conca d'Oro a garden. It was they who planted the palms and sugar cane.'

'Sugar?' Cora murmured. 'I've heard of the lemons and oranges.'

The maid returned to the room with coffee, in a little aluminium pot, and three tiny porcelain cups.

'What would Neapolitan coffee be without sugar?' Alex asked. 'Did you know that in Naples the sugar always goes in first?'

'I didn't,' Cora said, beginning to laugh. 'We hardly ever have coffee at home.'

Alex returned her smile. 'And I've forgotten tea,' he said.

'You're an Italian through and through,' she said.

'I'll never be that,' he answered. 'I wish I could be.'

After coffee, they walked out on to the narrow terrace. It was full of flowers: red

pelargonium in large clay pots. The balustrade of the balcony was decorated with
insets of copper, coated with verdigris. Cora
traced the trails of petals in the design
while, far below them, the sea had the same
greenish traces, phosphorus under the low
moon.

'Do you remember the Caviezels?' Alex
asked Richard.

Cora was amazed to feel the current of
electricity that attached itself to the name. It
hung in the air, redolent with its own inner
rhythm. *Caviezel*. It's like the name of one of
those islands, Cora thought, between Sicily
and Italy. The ferry had passed them in the
maddening heat of noon, when the sun had
been too bright to look at the ocean, and all
she had been able to do was listen to the
place names as the captain read them out,
unable to distinguish anything in the blazing
mirror of the water. Lipari, Salina, Alicudi,
Filicudi, Stromboli, Panarea. Names like
poems.

She wondered if this was a place name too.

'I remember,' Richard said.

'They've asked to meet you again,' Alex
continued. 'They have bought a mill site
inland and arranged a party there tomorrow.'

'I see,' Richard said.

Cora gazed at him. He was as rigid and
still as a statue.

302

'If you're not too tired, of course,' Alex added.

When Cora and Richard went to their room, it was slightly cooler than before, enough to close the shutters. Cora sat on the edge of the bed and watched as Richard washed, using the bowl and jug of water.

'Has Alex ever married?' she asked.

'I don't think Alex is the marrying type,' Richard replied.

'You mean he has a string of women?'

He dried himself off. 'You always want to know about people's personal lives,' he remarked.

'I'm interested.'

'Cora,' he said, 'Alex has never married. He has never had an affair with a woman.'

'But why?'

He smiled and shook his head in exasperation.

'Oh,' she said, realizing. 'Well, I didn't know. You didn't tell me.'

'You must always know everything,' he muttered, turning away from her, and sitting on the opposite side of the bed with his back to her.

'Well, I like him,' she said quietly. 'He's a charming man, well-educated.'

'Yes,' Richard agreed, equally softly. 'You should get on together.'

She heard the edge in his voice, leaned

across the bed and touched his back. She stroked the curve of his spine with her fingertips. He straightened, reached behind him and lifted her hand by the wrist.

'What's the matter?' she asked.

'I'm tired,' he said.

He swung his legs into bed, and pulled the sheet over him.

'Who are the Caviezels?' she asked.

One beat of quiet ... two ... three.

'Why does Alex think you know them?'

'I do know them,' Richard said. 'They are a family from Syracusa.'

'You've never mentioned them.'

'I hoped never to see them again,' he told her.

She waited for an explanation.

'Can't you tell me why?' she asked.

'Cora,' he said, 'I'd rather sleep.'

The rebuff was pointed. 'All right,' she said.

Suddenly he looked at her with such violence that she was unnerved. She sat back as if stung.

'Everything's always all right with you, isn't it?' he demanded, in a forced whisper. 'Everything's always fine.'

'What have I done?' she asked.

He turned his face so that the slanted light from the window fell upon it. 'Go to sleep,' he said.

She got up on to the bed on her haunches alongside him. 'I won't go to sleep until you tell me what the matter is,' she said.

'Cora,' he said, 'we've travelled a long way today. Go to sleep, please.'

'It isn't me,' she said. 'It's this place. Why did you come here if you dreaded it so much?'

'I don't dread it.'

She gave a gasp of surprise. 'You've dreaded it in dreams for years,' she told him. He said nothing. She took hold of his arm. 'You've dreamed about men alongside you,' she whispered urgently. 'You've been on your knees hiding from them.' He tried to wrench himself away from her. 'Tell me,' she said. 'Can't you tell me, now we're here? Can't you trust me, Richard? Can't you tell me at all?'

Still with his face turned away, he closed his eyes. She could see the emotion racing under his lids, telegraphed by flickering. She saw the pulse beat hard in his throat.

'Why do you keep it from me?' she asked him. And she put her hand to the pulse. Her heart ached. This was how it had been for such a long time, politeness and withdrawal descending on them. He would never engage in an argument; he would never raise his voice. He would betray his irritation, his disturbance, by some sharp word or phrase. He used silence like a blunt instrument.

He had used it when they talked about children.

305

'Tell me,' she repeated. 'Tell me.'

But he used it again now.

They set out late the following afternoon. It was not as hot as the day before, and clouds occasionally obscured the sun, casting an oppressive shadow.

'Where are we going?' Cora asked Alex, as they went down the steps to the car.

'The Monti Nebrodi,' he told her. 'It's not far, a few miles west of here.'

The road wound upwards, past Randazzo and Cesaro. It reminded her of their honeymoon, travelling inland from the French coast and leaving all the clattering glamour of St Tropez for the foothills of the Mole forest. They had gone through low-lying cloud and endless hairpin bends, deeper and deeper into a blanketed, silent country until, at midday, they had emerged into Collobrières, a pretty little shuttered town recovering, that day, from rainstorms that had washed the square almost yellow, so bright were the saturated sandstone houses. They had sat in a restaurant and looked at the tiers of vines that seemed to rush down the hillside towards the restaurant window, all brilliantly green from the downpour.

Now she leaned forward from the back seat to touch Richard's shoulder. 'It's like the road through the forest,' she said.

'Which one?'

'You know,' she said. 'In France...' And she could see that he was impatient with her interruption. All at once she forgot the names, sat back in her seat, and said no more.

It was almost cold when they reached the mill at nearly six o'clock. They got out of the car in a deserted courtyard, high up in a wooded valley, the condensation of the day collecting in misty pockets between the trees.

'They bought this last year,' Alex explained. 'Giulio has become a man of property, but he wants this as his home.'

'It's vast,' Cora said, peering up at it.

'Medieval,' Alex said. 'It was built to mill grain – you remember what I said about sugar, last night? Well, it was converted to process sugar cane and then, four hundred years later, it went back to grain.'

'It hasn't been used for some time,' Richard said, and kicked a tussock of grass with the tip of his shoe.

'Giulio wants to turn it into a feudal estate,' Alex joked. 'He's a great builder. He has renovated apartments in Syracusa, and built villas on the coast. You'll remember that his father was unstoppable too?'

They waited a minute or so. The place was boarded up, defaced. Cora turned, and saw a tiny stream working its way down the stony hillside.

Then, all at once, the silence was broken. A boy came out of a gate in the wall, stopped and held up his arms in astonishment. He called behind him; other faces appeared. In seconds, half a dozen people were at the mill entrance; the two parties remained where they were, as though assessing each other. Then a yellow dog came barrelling down the hillside, barking for all it was worth. The boy came running after. When he was close, Cora could see that, although he was slight, he was less a boy than a young man with a shock of dark hair.

'Hey, Alex!' he shouted. 'My comrade!' He flew into Alex's arms. Over his friend's shoulder, Cora saw Richard's disapproval. The young man turned to him in the next instant, caught the look and hesitated. Then he held out his hand politely. 'You are Richard Ward,' he said. 'I am Giulio's son. I am Pietro. I am honoured to meet you.'

Richard shook his hand, then indicated Cora. 'This is my wife, Cora,' he said.

Pietro held out his hand; she took it. His grip was firm, unlike Richard's. He beamed at her, his whole face lighting up. She saw how very handsome he was, his looks enhanced by his open smile. 'But that is a very beautiful name,' he told her.

'Thank you,' she said.

'It's a Sicilian name.'

'Oh,' she said, 'I don't think so.'

308

'Yes,' he insisted. 'From Kore. It is another name for our goddess Persephone.' Only then did he drop her hand. As he did so she felt something extraordinary, something that astonished her, something she had never felt in her life with such force: a sudden, electric jolt of desire. A blunt blow, shocking. She took a step back.

'He's right,' Alex said. 'Pietro is always right.'

The young man blushed. 'No,' he murmured. He kept glancing at Cora. Then, 'My father is waiting.'

They followed him up the slope, the dog dancing at their heels. In the space of those few moments, other people had joined the group at the gate. Alex took Cora's elbow to guide her the last few yards. 'Courage,' he muttered. 'The whole tribe is here.' He winked at her secretively. 'But not for us.'

They stopped and Giulio Caviezel walked forward. Cora was astonished to see tears in his eyes. He was immaculately dressed in a dark suit; he held out both hands to Richard, but before Richard could respond, he had placed them on his shoulders and kissed his cheek.

He turned back to the family grouped behind him. Cora's eyes ranged over the women: two older ones, dressed traditionally in black, and four pretty girls in their twenties. Toddlers hung on the hands of the older two; a younger one was heavily pregnant. Three young men stood at their backs, evidently their husbands.

'You remember Galatea,' Giulio said, indicating his wife. 'Her sister ... my daughters...'

Solemnly, Richard bowed to each in turn.

'And this is my son,' Giulio said finally. He brought Pietro to his side and put an arm round his shoulders, 'who could not wait, so that he runs down the hill with the dogs.'

The women laughed softly.

Giulio let his arm drop and spread his hand, once more, in Richard's direction. 'And this,' he said, 'is the man to whom I owe my life.'

The night came in softly across the mountain, in shades of grey and green that darkened until the trees could no longer be distinguished.

In the mill's courtyard, they lit a fire and positioned tables round two sides of the square, against the walls, so that the chairs faced out towards the glow. Sparks rushed up into the darkness; there was a smell of rosemary from the flames. Before long, Cora found herself sitting at one end of the table, a baby balanced in her lap, the women fussing around her, throwing starched cloths over the trestles and bringing bread and olives, water, demijohns of wine, bowls of oranges. Cora split one open, tasted its sweet flavour.

Richard was nowhere to be seen: Giulio had taken him away, leading him through the vast wooden doors to show him his work on the mill. Once, about twenty minutes before, she had glimpsed her husband's face at an upper window, looking down at her in the courtyard. She had raised her hand; he had stepped backwards into the shadow. She had looked up for some time at the pane, hoping he would reappear. She wondered whom he had become, in the last hour – someone unknown to her. It was like seeing a stranger's face emerge in place of something utterly familiar. He hadn't told her a single detail, not about the Caviezels, not about any time after his ship had left Egypt. Only the nightmares about the beaches – that was the only fragment of Sicily. And now he walked out of the past with a different persona. *This is the man to whom I owe my life.*

Eventually Alex came to sit beside her. He brought her a glass of wine. 'Do you know anything at all about this?' he asked. 'Sicily – all this?'

'No,' she told him.

'He's never spoken of it?'

'Not really.'

'This must be a shock to you.'

'It's not a shock to know he's respected.'

'Do you want to know why?'

'Yes,' she said. She smiled gently at him. 'But Richard should tell me.'

He patted her knee. A minute or two later, Richard appeared, the food was brought out and, in the mêlée of eating and drinking and conversation, the subject was lost.

She found herself with Alex on one side and Pietro on the other. Richard was sitting a little way down, next to Giulio, whose wife ladled food on to his plate.

A moment later, a plate was passed to her.

'This is straight from the sea,' Alex murmured. 'Spaghetti with sea-urchins, a little garlic, a little oil. Wonderful.'

She had never eaten anything like it in her life.

'I have fished for sea-urchin,' Pietro said.

'You caught these?' she asked.

'Oh, no. Not these. But I had a friend with a boat, and we fished for urchin and oyster.'

'You dived for them?'

He smiled his brilliant smile. 'I was young,' he told her. A board with a slab of Parmesan came down the table; he took it. 'You would like some?' he asked.

She nodded. He cut a piece, and placed it on the edge of her plate.

'Thank you.'

'*Prego.*' His arm brushed hers as he held out the plate for Alex. She was certain that the pressure was intentional; then, as he turned away, she thought herself very stupid. He was no more than a boy; it had been politeness. She couldn't understand her reaction. She was not the sort of woman who speculated about men. And she tried to listen objectively as, across the table, he began to tell Richard about the summers he had spent, and the colours of the ocean.

She tried the spaghetti, a little at a time.

'There's something else you find here,' Alex said, as the wine was passed back and forth. *'Panelle*. Cheap food, you know. Chick-pea flour fried in slices, cut up and sold at the door of anyone's house. I used to know a place at the Vuccira in Palermo.'

'The Vuccira?'

'A market. Not the same now as it once was.' He smiled. 'When I came back to Sicily, I was very poor. I could only afford a house when my own father died, and he died late in life. Until then, I lived here on *panelle* and bread. I would walk round the Vuccira and look at the fish on the stalls: mackerel and sardines, tuna and swordfish. There was all sorts of meat too. Things I had never seen in England – would never see there now. Horseflesh, goat, and live chickens.' He pushed back his plate and looked sentimental. 'I came back with someone,' he told her, 'and we had no money. We stood in the Vuccira and stared at all the food.' He shook his head. 'There was still rationing in London, and most of Sicily was poor, but that place...' He raised both hands expressively. 'Like a door opening into heaven.'

'When did you buy your house?' she asked.

'In 1960,' he said. 'We lived in a cold-water flat until then, further down the coast, in Catania.'

'And this person?' She didn't know how to phrase the question, or if he would be offended.

'We couldn't live in England. Here it was quite different.'

'Where is he now?' she asked.

'He died three years ago.'

'I'm sorry,' she said.

He looked directly at her. 'Never be sorry for being in love,' he said.

It was almost midnight when the party came to an end. Giulio and his wife walked Richard back to the car in formal ceremony, Pietro behind them; Alex and Cora followed.

'An unusual family,' Alex whispered. 'Academics, builders and a priest among them. Pietro is studying in Rome. The girls are beautiful, and all called after goddesses. They are goddesses, too. Beautiful women in Italy. Beautiful people.'

She could tell that he was more than a little drunk.

Well, she thought, trying to place her own feet steadily one in front of the other along the rocky path, he had a right to be. They all had a right to be drunk on the evening – the fire and the food. Perhaps Richard had a right to be fêted like this; perhaps, after tonight, he would tell her the secret that lay somewhere between him and the man who was shaking his hand again. She saw Pietro turn away from the little group and come towards her. 'My father and Mr Ward are going to Noto the day after tomorrow,' he said.

'I'm sorry,' Cora responded, 'I don't know where Noto is.'

'A place south of here,' he said. He paused. 'The place.'

Alex was looking at the ground.

Pietro made her a deferential bow. 'Perhaps I may come to keep you company,' he said. 'My father has asked if you would like to see Syracusa.'

'With you?' she asked.

'If it would please you.'

She looked at Richard, at his back, his downturned face as he listened to Pietro's father speaking quickly, in a fast, rhythmic voice, at his shoulder. She strained to hear the conversation, but couldn't catch a word. A mixture of smoke, drifting downhill, and mist, rising upwards, moved in the space between them, at their feet, in the darkness, like saturated veils.

She looked back at the boy. 'All right,' she

said. She smiled at his obvious anxiety to entertain her. Her heart beat slowly, heavily. She nodded. 'Yes,' she agreed. 'If that's what they have suggested. Thank you.'

Sixteen

Two days later they drove down from Taormina to Syracusa, and went straight to Ortigia.

Pietro was waiting beside his car close to the Umbertino bridge. He looked, Cora thought, as they pulled in to park close to him, as if he had posed himself directly opposite the terracotta frontage of the first buildings, so that he was dead centre of what already looked like a stage set: the white bridge, the red waterfront houses, the blue of the deep-water channel where tour boats were already drawn up alongside private yachts.

He seemed nervous, Cora noticed, as she got out of the car. When he saw them, he brushed down the sleeves of his jacket. She hid a smile. For a moment he had looked like the kind of man Englishmen mistrusted: any kind of man who was good with women, charming. She pitied Pietro: he had to entertain the wife of one of his father's friends for an interminable day. She wondered what he would prefer to be doing.

'Your guide is already here,' Richard commented.

'Poor chap,' she murmured. 'He looks as if he's waiting for his own execution.'

Richard smiled as he closed the car door.

He had been a little brighter this morning – too bright, even. He had complimented her on her dress, kissed her hand over breakfast. Unlike himself, in so many minor details. He was talking far too much, she realized, as she followed him and Alex to the car. Richard never talked at length. She listened to him, to the inflection of his words, and her mood changed from pleased surprise to apprehension. He was not relaxed, he was the opposite; the talk and brightness were a screen. She had sat in the back of the car and watched the coast go by, seen Etna slip past the windows, and felt rebuffed and excluded.

Richard strode forward now and shook Pietro's hand. 'This is very kind of you,' he said.

'It is my pleasure,' Pietro replied.

The three men talked for a little while about the beauty of the day, the loveliness of the harbour, the island, the town. Cora hung back, grasping her handbag with both hands, feeling awkward, embarrassed.

At last, Richard turned to her. 'We'll be back by six,' he said. 'We'll meet you in the

Piazza Duomo, in front of the cathedral.'

'All right,' she said.

'Do you have some money?'

'Yes,' she told him.

'I've given Pietro enough for lunch,' he said.

She blushed. She was like a child being looked after for the day – so much a dependant that her guardian had to be given money to feed and entertain her. Richard missed the look of disappointment and embarrassment she gave him. He went back to the car and, together, she and Pietro watched the dark blue Bentley thread its way through the traffic to the Via Elorina.

She turned to the boy alongside her. 'I would like to say something,' she told him. 'I would like to say that you're not obliged to stay with me.'

Pietro frowned. 'I'm sorry?'

'You don't have to look after me,' she said, 'if you would rather not. I will understand. I will be perfectly all right.'

He raised his shoulders in a shrug. 'You don't want to be with me?'

'It's not that,' she said. She felt hot with the awkwardness of it. And she was afraid of herself. 'It's just that I shall be quite happy if you would rather do something else.'

'But I wouldn't rather do something else,' he said. 'My father asked me to do this and I will.'

There was a long pause. She knew that she had offended him. She didn't know where to look or what else to say to him. I must stop this, she told herself. It's pitiable.

'Is there anything you would like to see?' he asked formally.

'I don't know the island at all.'

'Well, perhaps the Temple of Apollo? It's not far away.'

'Yes,' she said.

They walked side by side for a minute or two, then crossed the road.

'You've been to Sicily before?' he asked.

'No,' she said.

Another long silence. Beside them, the traffic hooted and swerved. Warmth prickled the back of Cora's neck; the sun was blazing between the buildings.

'Alex told me that you're at the university in Rome,' she said.

'Yes,' he said. 'La Sapienza.'

'What are you studying?'

'Business. Accounting.'

They had come to a road junction. Cora stopped. 'Accounting?'

'Is it surprising?'

'You don't strike me as the type,' she said.

'What type is this?'

'Oh,' she said. 'Like a bank manager. That kind of person.'

'I study so that I can help run my father's business,' Pietro said. 'It is his wish.'

They crossed the road and walked to the railings of a green park. Over the barrier, the temple ruins were in surprisingly good order, with one wall still standing and the bases of vast, fluted columns running on two sides.

'It was discovered in 1860,' Pietro said. 'The temple was built six centuries before Christ. The base is fifty-eight metres by twenty-four.' He still wore a wounded expression.

'Have you learned all this for me?' she asked.

'No,' he said. 'It is something I know.'

'All the facts and figures?'

'It is something I remember.'

'Oh, of course,' she murmured. 'Business and accounting.'

She walked round the side of the site, examining the stones. Pietro followed her. 'Excuse me,' he said suddenly, 'but why am I not the correct person to study business?'

'I didn't mean that,' she said. 'I'm sure you're perfectly capable.'

'But that is not what you think I should do?'

'It's hardly for me to say.' She smiled. 'It doesn't matter what I think, surely.'

'You think I should study something else?' he persisted.

She appraised him. 'If I had been asked to guess...' she said. 'Perhaps art.'

'Art? Why, art?'

'Or literature. Perhaps, even, something very practical.'

'Business is not practical?'

'I meant something creative.'

'I look to you like an artist?' He was staring at her intently.

'Yes,' she said. 'I would have guessed an artist.' She thought of the way he had run down the slope towards them, arms open. 'I can't imagine you in an office,' she said, 'in a suit and tie.'

He fell silent. Wondering if she had upset him again, she tried to explain. 'And it was something you said the other night,' she said, 'about diving, sailing.'

'I seem to you like a fisherman, perhaps?'

She smiled. 'No,' she said. 'It was the way you described it. I heard you explaining to Richard. The colour of the sea.'

'Ah,' he murmured. 'Yes.'

'And you seem...'

He glanced at her, eyebrow raised. 'Yes?'

She didn't reply. She thought she had already said too much to this boy, who seemed to want to please everyone.

'Would you like something to drink?' he asked. 'An espresso?'

They walked down the Corso Giacomo and through another piazza; there were plenty of tourists on the streets, she noticed, even though it was only the beginning of the season. 'It must be full of people here during the summer,' she observed.

'In the summer it is too hot,' he replied, 'even for the beaches, sometimes.'

'Do you come back from Rome during the holidays?'

'Yes,' he said. 'Always home.'

'To be with your family.'

'It is impossible not to,' he said. 'I am my mother's only son. I have to come home.'

'To help with the company?'

'To help with everything.'

They had reached the Piazza Duomo; he took her to a café opposite the cathedral, and they sat down, admiring the elaborate façade: the double height columns, the wide steps. It seemed to glow white in the sun. Pietro ordered the coffee, and indicated the cathedral with a nod. 'You like this?'

'It's wonderful,' she said. 'Don't you have any facts to tell me?'

He looked hard at her, then laughed. 'Now, you are making a joke.'

'Yes,' she admitted. 'I'm sorry.'

He grinned sheepishly. 'I tell you a secret now,' he said. 'I learned those things for you about the temple.'

'Well,' she said, 'I'm flattered that you should take such trouble.'

'I didn't know them myself,' he said. 'What man knows anything about how many stones there are, how wide they may be? He knows only that they are there.'

'I was right,' she declared. 'I knew you weren't really an accountant.'

He sat back, gazing at her with renewed interest.

The coffee arrived, aromatic and dark, in tiny cups, with an accompanying glass of water, and a plate of almond biscuits.

'So,' Pietro said, after a minute or two, 'Mr Ward has gone back to Noto.'

'Apparently so.'

'This is a good journey for him?'

'I don't know,' she said. 'He seemed nervous.'

'That is understandable.'

She stirred her coffee, found grains of sugar in the bottom and lifted the spoon to her lips. 'Oh,' she said, stopping herself, 'Alex told me that one should never do that.'

'Do what?'

'Taste the sugar at the bottom of the cup,' she said. 'Every night at the house he has given me lectures on Italian customs.'

Pietro laughed. 'Perhaps customs should be broken.' He had been watching her.

'But you wouldn't break a custom,' she said, 'a tradition. A family tradition, say?'

'No.' He frowned. 'But, then, all things change. Perhaps I should change them.'

'There's something you want to change?'

He twisted his cup on its saucer.

She leaned towards him. 'Pietro,' she said,

'why would my husband be nervous today?'

'Because of the war,' he said. 'Returning to the place.'

'I know it's because of the war. I know where he landed. I know what day. And I know that Alex was with him, or met him soon afterwards.'

'I think they met in Taormina.'

'OK. Taormina,' she said. 'But where did my husband meet your father?'

'Near Noto,' Pietro said. 'But don't you know all this?'

'I don't know anything,' she told him.

'Not how he met my father?'

'Nothing.'

Pietro pushed his cup aside and leaned almost across the table. 'You do not know why my father talks so much of Richard Ward,' he said, a statement, not a question.

'No.'

'This is very strange,' Pietro said.

'He won't speak of it,' Cora told him, 'and especially not this week.'

'But he is a hero,' Pietro explained, amazed.

She put her hand to her head, pressed the point between her eyes for a second. 'I thought he would tell me,' she murmured. 'I wanted him to tell me. Now ... everyone knows but me. He didn't even want me to go with him today.'

'But there is nothing to hide,' Pietro said,

perplexed. 'This was a very good thing that he did, a very good thing that my father has always talked about, that he told me when I was a child, and many times since.' He looked around himself, as if the answer to the conundrum might suddenly occur to him. 'If someone I loved had done such a thing, I would be very proud of it.'

'All I know is that he landed on a beach,' she said. 'Was there some sort of trouble there?'

'I don't think so,' he said. 'They landed and came straight ashore.'

'There was no trouble, no bombardment?'

'Not much.'

'Was there fighting?'

'Not at first. It came later, at Catania. Then it was bad.'

Cora frowned at him. 'And your father?'

'My father was a boy, ten years old.'

'And something happened with your father and grandfather?' she asked. 'Near here? At Noto?'

Pietro shook his head slowly. 'I cannot believe you don't know,' he said. 'Your husband is a very...' he searched for the word that had deserted him '...*modest* man.'

She sat quietly, waiting.

'My father and grandfather were on the road. My father saw the jeep, he thought it was an American jeep, and he ran from the field to the road...' He smiled. 'Boys do such things, look at cars. They knew the ships were on the coast and my grandfather was hurrying. He was worried. He wanted to be in his own house.'

'And this was Richard's jeep?'

'Yes. Mr Ward and two other men.'

'And what happened?'

'My father ran out into the road, and there was a gun, a place where guns were set up, a ... I don't know what you call it...'

'An emplacement? A dug-out?'

'Yes, a gun emplacement. It had been there for a long time, but no one had been stationed there for weeks. And they thought it was empty. But inside the emplacement there were two soldiers.'

'Two German soldiers.'

'They had a radio, and no machine-gun, just rifles...'

'They were snipers.'

'That is right. And they shoot.'

'They shot your *father?*'

'No, but they shot, and my father began to run to the jeep, to tell them. And my grand-father – you did not know my grandfather. He was a very angry man...'

'Alex called him unstoppable.'

Pietro smiled. 'Yes, unstoppable. He ran to the guns because they had tried to shoot his son, just a boy.'

Cora put her hand to her mouth.

'I think they knew their position was to be

given away.'

'By your father.'

'Yes.'

Cora tried to put herself into the jeep, to see the road ahead through Richard's eyes. A frightened boy careering towards them, and shots from the side of the road.

'I think my father was very frightened, and the men from the jeep were calling for him to lie down in the road, or in the ditch. But he didn't lie down. And they stopped the jeep and Mr Ward got out, and he caught my father and put him inside the car, and he always remembers this, being pulled from the road and lying down in the back of the jeep, among the cans and ammunition and the tarpaulin. And he could hear his own father, and then nothing.'

'What had happened?' Cora asked.

'My grandfather had been shot.'

'Not killed?'

'Injured. He was lying on the ground. And Mr Ward went to carry him, and he, too, was hit by a bullet.'

'Oh, my God,' Cora breathed.

'You see,' Pietro said, 'I think those soldiers were supposed just to look, to report, and they were young boys too. They were not much older than me.'

'They were frightened.'

'Yes, everybody was frightened, maybe.'

'And after that...'

'Mr Ward went to the emplacement. He killed one soldier; they captured the other.'

'But he had been injured?'

'And they had tried to...' Pietro put his hand to his throat and pulled his index finger across it.

'What?' Cora said, not quite believing.

'One of the men, with a knife...'

'He tried to cut Richard's *throat?*'

'Yes,' Pietro said.

Cora sat back in her seat. While they had been talking, the sun had crept round the square and was now blazing full on their table. For a moment, everything became clinically clear to her, all the shapes heavily delineated, as if someone had drawn round the table, the cutlery, the bowl of brown sugar, with a fine black pen. She blinked, and the sharpness of the images dissolved.

'It's very hot now,' Pietro said.

'Yes,' she agreed. 'Very hot.'

'Would you like to go into the cathedral?' he asked. 'That, too, has a secret.'

She looked at him.

'I will show you,' he told her.

She followed him round the cathedral, glad to be out of the heat. Dutifully he showed her the mosaics, the paintings and sculptures. She listened, read the guidebook, and stood in the centre of the aisle at last.

'It feels curious,' she murmured.

'It's been many things,' he told her. 'A temple, a Christian church, a mosque.'

'Where I come from,' she said, 'we have an abbey church. The first kings of Wessex are buried there.'

'You have always lived there?'

'Yes,' she said. 'Except for a few months in London.'

'What is it like, where you live?'

'Green,' she said. 'Like Sicily.'

'Sicily is only green in the spring,' he said. 'In the summer, the fields are burned so pale yellow it is almost white. In the summer, we are on fire.'

'I would like to see that,' she said. 'Something so bright, days so hot.'

'You would suit it here,' he said. 'It would suit you.'

She sat down on a nearby chair and, after a moment, he sat in the row in front, and turned to her. 'There is something the matter,' he said.

She shook her head. For some unaccountable reason, an image had come into her head of the hours and days she spent every year in pruning and training the trees, in making the fans and espaliers along the lines and walls. It was an exact occupation, cutting back the laterals in early summer, shortening the shoots in early autumn. She saw herself counting the leaf shoots from the base, clipping them carefully, tossing them

329

into the basket on the path; carrying summer away and throwing it on to the fire. A shudder went through her.

'I have offended you with something I have said?' he asked.

She pushed herself back in the chair. 'No, no.' She made a concerted effort to erase her thoughts. 'It's nothing.'

'Something to do with today? You are thinking about your husband. You are worried?'

'No,' she said truthfully. Worried was not the word. She was falling. That was what it felt like. And it struck her, with almost unbearable force, that she had been dreaming through her life, marking time, and that it was a kind of retreat, a shadow. She felt a longing to be out in the light, and she hated herself for thinking of Richard in that line of thought, for thinking of him as the dark into which she had strayed.

And in the dark he kept his secrets.

Pietro was staring at her intently. His hands were on the back of his own chair, folded one over the other. She glanced for a second, no more, at the long, slim fingers.

She raised her head. 'Tell me about yourself,' she said. 'What do you like to do?'

'I'm sorry, what do you mean? At university?'

'Here,' she said. 'Tell me about your family.'

'I have four sisters ... you have met them.'

'I didn't get a chance to speak to them. What are they like?'

'Oh, like girls,' he said, and rolled his eyes expressively.

She laughed. 'And they are all called after goddesses.'

Pietro grinned. 'My father,' he said. 'A romantic.'

She thought of Richard using the word of her a few nights before. 'Is that good?' she asked.

'What is better?' Pietro asked.

She looked away, at the dim lights in the sacristy, at the cool stone of the floor. 'And what do you do with your time?' she persisted. 'What sort of things?'

'I read,' he said.

'You do?'

'Too much,' he told her. 'My father says that my head is in the clouds. When I was a little boy, I read all the time. He thinks it is not so good. That is one reason why I study the course. To keep my head here.'

'To fix you in place,' she said.

She had meant it lightheartedly, but he frowned.

'And you always come home,' she said. 'Don't you travel?'

'Not yet,' he said. 'I will one day.'

'You have plans? Where will you go?' she asked.

'I don't know,' he said. 'A long way.'

'To find what?' she asked. 'To see what?'

His gaze lingered on her.

'You haven't told me the secret,' she said. 'You promised me a secret.'

He shifted in his chair. She saw him swallow hard, compress his mouth, as if holding back what he had been going to say. She was intrigued. A sensation raced through her, a constriction of the chest, a tightening in the pit of her stomach.

Moments passed. When he looked up again he was smiling. 'And you, too, are named for a goddess, like my sisters.'

'Yes,' she murmured. 'So you say.'

'I do say,' he insisted, 'and that is how it should be.'

'Oh?' she said. 'Why?'

He gestured to her. His voice brightened. 'This is how she should look, Persephone, Kore, with light hair, the colour of the sun she longed for.'

'The goddess of the underworld can't have blonde hair,' she pointed out. 'She would be dark.'

'No, no,' he persisted. 'She is caught in the dark, but she is the summer.'

'And she was stolen,' Cora said quietly. He had leaned closer to her. 'This is one legend I don't really know,' she said.

'For nine days, her mother Ceres looked for her,' he told her. 'When she couldn't find her, she made the land burn. She took away the water. The crops failed, the earth passed into winter. And it was only when her brother Zeus saw what was happening that he intervened.'

'And he freed her.'

'Only for a while. She was released to spend two-thirds of the year with her mother, when the earth blooms, and a third of the year with Hades.'

'This island is full of gods,' Cora remarked. 'An island of immortals.'

'Oh,' he smiled, agreeing, 'they are everywhere. The sons of Zeus and Thalia were born here; Demeter and Hephaestus fought over it; Charybdis made the whirlpools at Messina; Alpheus followed Arethusa here; Helios owned land here; Heracles laboured here...' He threw up his hands. 'And more. And more. And more.'

'An island of gods and giants,' Cora mused. 'And light.'

'And light,' he agreed.

There was a beat between them: a moment of absolute silence.

'And Persephone,' she asked. Her voice dropped low, almost to a whisper. 'Did she ever leave Hades for good? Did she ever untie the contract? Was she ever freed?'

'Never. The pact was for ever.'

She met his gaze. 'And there she stayed?'

'Always,' Pietro said. 'For eternity.'

Cora got up. Suddenly she felt claustrophobic, smothered, suffocated.

Pietro sprang to his feet.

'Can we go?' she asked.

'What is the matter?' he said.

She almost ran up the aisle to the doors. On the steps, as she emerged, she took a gulp of air. She walked to her right, to the balustrade at the edge of the steps, and put her hands flat on the stone. Then, as Pietro came up behind her, she turned again and went down the steps. The piazza was full of people – it was lunchtime. She turned right again, down the narrower street alongside, and went a few paces, then stopped to lean against the wall of the church.

She felt his hand on the small of her back, then in the centre. 'What is it?' he asked. 'What can I do?'

She didn't look at him: she looked at the stone, and then her gaze travelled upwards. She was standing against a massive column, much wider and taller than those at the front of the church. They were set into the wall – or, rather, the wall had been built round them. She squinted against the sunlight to the top, then looked back at him.

'The temple of Athene,' he murmured. 'This is its secret beginning, here before anything else.' He took his hand from her back, and stood away from her, very still, very upright.

The heat pressed in on her. The light

flexed, refracted as if from a mirror. She put her hand to her face, her eyes. 'Do you think,' she asked, 'that anything is immortal?'

'That lives for ever?'

'Like the gods, for ever.'

'Like this temple, indestructible? Oh, yes,' he told her, with conviction. 'We are immortal, all of us.'

'And what if you do wrong?' she asked. 'Something wrong?' She began to tremble. 'You believe in their retribution? Their bolts of thunder and lightning?'

He stepped into the shadow of the column, took her hand and drew her alongside him.

'Do you believe in the dark?' she whispered. 'Can we be sent to the dark for ever?'

'No,' he said softly, gently. 'There will be no dark for us. No dark at all.'

That night, they met Richard and Alex at six o'clock, as had been arranged. The café opposite the cathedral was rearranging its tables, and there was already a queue. All down the streets, the flags of shops, posters, fluttered in the orange slanted glare from the harbour as the sun began to set.

Both men looked tired.

'What did you do?' Cora asked Richard. 'Where did you go?'

'To Noto,' he said, as if stating the obvious. Then he relented, and gave her an apologetic smile. A contortion of a smile.

335

'Have you had a good day?' he asked, in a perfunctory fashion.

'And you saw anyone?' she persisted. 'What did you see?'

He looked irritated. She only wanted him to tell her. She wanted him to draw her aside, take her away, stop the fall before it began. But he would only glance at her. She felt like grasping him and screaming for him to speak.

'What is it?' she whispered, as the four of them began to walk across the square. She squeezed his hand. 'Won't you tell me everything? Who did you see? Richard...'

Alex turned. 'There's a restaurant up the coast,' he said. 'It's not far and it's quieter. It's on our way.'

They agreed to his suggestion, went to the cars and drove out of Syracusa. They got to the place at seven.

True evening had settled by now, and they sat at tables on a small terrace above a rocky shore, ready to watch the dusk roll across the sea.

They were silent while the olives were placed on the table. They chose their food from the menus, still not speaking. Then, before they ate, Pietro asked if they would mind if he swam. The day had been hot, he said. He often swam in the evening.

The men nodded him away with smiles.

He went back through the restaurant, not

glancing at her or meeting her eye. A minute or two later, Cora saw him go down the lane at the side of the restaurant, on to the stony beach and round an outcrop further down.

Alex had poured the wine. At last, the silence was broken, and he and Richard began to talk about the end of the week, the Easter celebrations in Enna.

Cora saw Pietro walk out into the water, watching carefully where he placed his feet before he struck out from the shoreline. The light was fading, and he moved through the grey-green water, the ripples catching the last of the red in the sky. The reflection fanned out from him as he moved through the sea, copper on grey, copper on green, breaking and changing. She followed his progress, the line of his shoulders, the lithe movement of his body as he turned on his back; and saw him look, just once, towards her.

'What it is to be young,' Richard commented, noticing where she was gazing.

'And foolish,' Alex said. And laughed to himself.

Seventeen

Nick was late as he drove down to the coast. He kept looking at his watch. He had promised Zeph he would be there in good time, but there had been an accident on the motorway and he had been stuck for hours on some godforsaken stretch north of Winchester. By the time he reached the white chalk gash of Twyford Down, he saw why: a sprawl of vehicles across two lanes of the road.

He was supposed to have been at Abbotsbury by two o'clock that afternoon. He had set out early, a kind of miracle for him, with his habitual tardiness, but he had been up since first light, pacing the floor, unable to eat, worrying what she wanted to say to him. Wondering if this would be their last meeting. Frantic that it would be the start of some dark new chapter, whose horrors and farces even he could not have dreamed up.

By the time he had got into the car, he had calmed himself a little. Zeph had called him late yesterday afternoon. She had suggested that they meet each other on neutral ground, somewhere away from Cora and without Joshua. He had leaped at the chance to see her, but had not understood her voice – the strange tone of offhand objectivity, almost as if she were light-hearted or that what she was saying didn't matter. He had tried to unravel it ever since he had put down the phone last night.

It was almost as if she were telling a joke, as if she were reaching a punchline, but it stopped short of humour and dropped away into irrationality. It occurred to him that she had been shocked by something. She sounded like someone who had seen a crisis shear past them and knock down another. He heard unreality in her voice. It worried him.

As he had driven out of London, he had thought that perhaps her mother had persuaded her to do something drastic. Move completely away from him, break off all contact. Leave the country, even. When he had first met her – those centuries ago, before the world turned upside-down and inside-out – she had talked of travelling, going to places like Thailand and Cambodia, India. She had had those dreams then. Within weeks of meeting him, she had stopped mentioning them. She had put them away to be with him, he knew. He had never appreciated it. And he swore to himself, getting through the insanity of the London suburbs, that if she gave him the ghost of a chance, he would rewind all the time they had had together.

He would let her go wherever she wanted, even if she wanted to be without him. He would help her finance it. He would look after Joshua, or he would allow her to take Joshua with her, even if it meant they would be parted for a while. He would encourage her to do whatever it took to make her happy. On one condition: that eventually she would consider coming back to him.

He would give her back her dreams.

And then, thinking about it more calmly, he knew that Cora would never encourage her daughter just to go. Perhaps it was Cora's influence even now that had enabled their meeting today.

Then he nearly drove into the back of a car with a trailer – his concentration had crumbled. 'Jesus,' he muttered to himself. 'Get a grip.'

After Winchester, after Twyford, he pulled off the road at the first opportunity to dial Zeph's number. He got only the answer-phone.

'Can you please wait?' he had asked the dead air at the other end of the line. 'Please. I'll be there as soon as I can.'

Off the motorway, he had put his foot down and driven at a suicidal pace. The New Forest rushed past the windows, the blue-smoke blur of the heathland. An hour later he was running parallel to the little villages of Hardy country, the roofs of

Burleston and Briantspuddle buried in green hills beyond the fast road that ran along the higher ground. Finally, he came down to the coast, places that belonged to his and Zeph's past, places where they had been when they had first visited Cora, the orchards and farm. Places that had always mesmerized him: a secret country of valleys running down to the sea.

As he drew into the car park by the beach, he looked anxiously along the line of cars for Zeph. Then he spotted the red Fiat, and the familiar numberplate.

'Oh, thank you, Jesus,' he breathed. He felt sick. Nerves overwhelmed him. He took one, two deep breaths, unconsciously wringing his hands, then flexing his fists. 'Don't talk to her like this,' he told himself, in a savage whisper. 'Talk to her like you've got a grain of fucking sense.'

He got out of the car.

She was nowhere to be seen. He walked to one end of the parking spaces, then back again, and crossed the little footbridge over the stream behind the shelving bank of pebbles. The track led up over a dune to the crest of the rise. There, about fifty or so yards to the left, Zeph sat on the pebbly shore, with her back to the road, looking at the sea, her arms wrapped round her knees.

He stepped off the boardwalk that led down to the sea, and stumbled across the

341

shifting pebbles. She looked up only when he stood next to her.

'I'm sorry,' he said. 'Did you get my message? There was an accident on the M3. I've driven like a lunatic, Zeph, I promise.'

She gave him the ghost of a smile. 'You always drive like a lunatic,' she said.

He sat down next to her. It was a bright, breezy day; the sea was coming in fast, driven by the offshore current that pulled it westwards, at a slant parallel to the land. Just a few feet from the shoreline, the depth shelved away sharply.

'I've been thinking about when I first brought you down here,' she said, 'that weekend.'

He tried hard to remember. He had known her for about six months, he thought. She had seemed nervous about him meeting Cora. She had spoken ambivalently of her mother, in tones that were occasionally affectionate and occasionally wary.

'Do you get on, the two of you?' he had asked her.

'I'm never quite sure of her,' she had replied. 'I was Daddy's girl.'

'Is she frightening?' he had asked. 'Should I wear a shin guard?'

She had laughed. 'Nothing like that,' she had said.

And he had found Cora charming. A little reserved, maybe, but he understood why any mother would be reserved around him and their daughter. He wasn't the best catch in the world – great for a night, but with a limited shelf life. He had always thought of himself as untrustworthy, the walking-out kind. Until he met Zeph. Then all he had done was try to get as close to her as he could.

Suddenly he realized, with Zeph at his side and the memories of early weekends in his head, that he had proved himself right.

He *was* the untrustworthy kind. One of Joshua's space soldiers sprung to life, a cartoon character. That's all he was, a drawing. An anti-hero. The wicked one coloured black. Not a proper person.

'I was thinking about swimming,' Zeph murmured.

He jolted back to the present. 'Today?' he asked, dismayed.

'Not today, you idiot,' she retorted. 'That weekend.'

'Which one?'

'You don't remember?' she asked.

'I'm sorry,' he said.

She put a hand to her face, then rested her elbow on her knee and kept her eyes shaded.

He watched a little boy, who was playing further down the narrow fringe of sand between the pebbles and the sea. His mother sat a few yards away.

'How's Josh?' he asked.

'A lot better.'

'No temperature?'

'No.' She lifted some pebbles with her free hand, then let them drain, one by one, from the palm. 'What have you been doing?' she asked.

'Not much,' he said. 'Except seeing Andy.'

'How is he?'

'He got me a film deal for *The Measure*.'

Her hand dropped from her eyes and she stared at him. 'You're joking?'

'No,' he said. 'For real.'

'What kind of deal?'

'It's good,' he told her. 'Very good.'

Her eyes ranged over his face. This was what they had talked about ever since they had met, this chance. He saw exactly where he was standing; had seen it clearly over the last few days. He was standing on a piece of ground that, if he shifted his balance one iota, would turn him away from her. A thin peninsula. Or a raft mid-stream, rotating with the current. He had only to make that move, press his weight an inch one way or the other...

'Oh, my God,' she murmured. 'Well...'

'You should have seen Andy with this guy,' he told her. 'I mean, this man comes in in golf pants, you know, like checked knickerbockers. He's got a three-foot-long cigar clamped in his teeth, the regular movie mogul, and he looks like a Technicolor version of Mack Sennet...'

'He did *not* wear knickerbockers,' Zeph said.

'He had the 1920s megaphone, he had a whip, he had a cravat...'

'Oh, right.' She laughed, in an unguarded moment.

'And he has this line-up of bathing beauties, and right in the middle of this restaurant they're singing 'We're In The Money', and this huge fountain comes up, and suddenly Andy's doing synchronized leg splits in a bikini...'

She smiled. 'I missed a hell of a show, then.'

'You missed the best,' he said. 'Andy was on his knees, licking this guy's shoes and worse. It was not a pretty sight.'

'I wish I'd seen it.'

'*I* wish you'd seen it,' he said. 'I wish you'd been there.' And he wished, too, that she would laugh again. He had always been able to make her laugh.

Instead she looked away.

Below them, the little boy was throwing stones into the sea.

'This guy wants me to go to the States,' Nick said.

She didn't respond.

He didn't know what he had expected her to say – to be glad for him, perhaps. Yes, she would be that, even if she disguised it now. She would be pleased. She knew what it had cost to come as far as this, she above all people. After all, she had paid the price.

He remembered her coming in late at night from a job, one of the first she'd had, in a bar that had stayed open until two in the morning. He hated her doing that work; it was a bar in a club, and he had gone once, and seen how hard she worked, and what sort of crap she was expected to accept, with cheerful grace, from the customers, who were smug city suits to a man, and who thought it was all right to shout her name like they were calling a dog to heel. She would walk along the bar – people all down it shouting fucking orders at her, and the music was deafening – and she would smile at someone, and ask what he wanted and, more times than not, he would try to reach across the bar and grab her. The club had had the brilliant idea of making the girls all wear a T-shirt with their names above one breast, and the joke was obvious and constant. 'What's the other one called?' they would yell. And the inevitable: 'What's Zeph? What's it short for?' And those who tried to guess. 'Hey, Stephanie!'

She'd done her time, all right. And more.

'What do you think?' he asked.

'You must do what you need to.'

He leaned forward in an effort to see the

expression on her face. He caught a look of extreme sadness. That was what she had been hiding behind her hand: her desolation.

He put his hand on her arm, and she got to her feet. She started to walk away, and he followed, slipping and sliding as he tried to keep up with her. She got down to the strip of wet sand. They passed the little boy, and went on along the beach. Not many people came down here: it was not family-friendly, with the enormous bank of stones and the terrible current in the water. Yet it was beautiful, startling: the yellow and the blue, more dazzling than any other coastline in the area.

'Zeph,' he said, 'what is it?'

She stopped. Wind blew the hair off her face. She stared at the sea, and he noticed that she had been crying, not just recently but perhaps for some time – days, even. Her eyes were swollen, her face puffy.

'Jesus, Zeph,' he said. 'What's been going on?'

'It's my mother,' she said.

'Cora?' he said. 'What's happened? Is she ill?'

She smiled briefly. 'No,' she said. 'She...' She stopped.

'What?' he demanded. 'What?'

'I'm someone else's daughter,' she said. 'She had an affair. I'm a stranger's daughter.'

It was a full five or ten seconds before he had taken it in. 'An affair?' he echoed.

'Ironic, isn't it?' she said bitterly. 'There's a lot of it about.'

He felt the sting of the remark, closed his eyes for a second. 'But how do you know that you're not Richard's child?'

'I can do simple maths.'

'But you might be mistaken.'

She shook her head. 'The more I think about it... There are details...'

'What details?'

'Well, I don't have my father's ... Richard's colouring, for one thing. One bloody obvious thing, when you come to think of it. I'm dark. And this man was Italian,' she said. 'Sicilian.'

'Sicily?'

'Don't you see it?' she said defiantly.

'Sorry – see what?'

'My name!' she cried. 'Sicily – the island of Persephone!'

'Oh, Jesus,' he murmured. 'But that... Zeph, that doesn't prove it,' he pointed out. 'Not really. It could be that she and Richard loved the place and the name... Persephone's very pretty...'

'Oh, for Christ's sake,' she said, 'It's hardly common, is it?'

'Why were they in Sicily?' he asked.

'They went for a couple of weeks. My father had a friend there, someone he'd known in the war.' She ran a hand across her forehead. 'I've seen this man's photograph. There's a resemblance.'

'Christ,' Nick said, with heavy sarcasm, 'your mother had a holiday romance?'

'He was the son of a friend of my father's,' she said. 'He was nineteen. She was thirty. He wanted her to marry him.'

He was shocked. 'He wanted that, at nineteen? So young?'

'He wanted her to leave England and go and live in Sicily. He wrote to her afterwards. He begged her.'

'How do you know all this? Where did you see his picture?'

'This man kept a diary. At the time he wrote everything down, and he wrote letters to her for years afterwards, and he wrote about her. In fact, he wrote a book about her.'

'A book? What do you mean – he published the diary?'

'A novel,' she said. 'He died just ten days ago, and left the journal to my mother.' She shook her head. 'My mother,' she said softly. 'The love of his life.'

He gazed at her, astounded, trying to match his impression of Cora to the woman Zeph was describing.

Zeph took a huge breath. 'You wouldn't believe the things he says in the book.' She whispered. 'Personal things.'

'Just a minute,' he said. 'He died ten days ago in Sicily? What was his name?'

'You'll know the name,' she told him. 'Pietro Caviezel.'

He gazed at her in astonishment. 'Caviezel?' he repeated. *'Caviezel?* You're his daughter? Holy shit!'

She gave a twisted, wry grimace. 'I thought you'd be impressed.'

'I'm sorry,' he acknowledged. 'I'm sorry, Zeph. But – Jesus Christ! Caviezel himself. Do you know how famous this guy is?'

'Of course.'

'And she actually showed you the journal?'

'No. I found it by mistake. I thought it was something else, something to do with the farm.'

'And you read it ... and you told your mother?'

'Yes.'

'What the hell did she say?'

Zeph raised her gaze to him. 'It doesn't matter what she says,' she replied tonelessly. 'The fact remains that I'm not Richard Ward's daughter. That's all that matters to me. I'm the product of a *lie.*'

'And Caviezel knew about you? That he had a child by your mother?'

'I don't think so. There's nothing in the journal about me.'

'She never *told* him?'

'How should I know?' Zeph asked.

'But haven't you asked her?'

'I don't want to. I don't want to know what I already know, never mind anything else.'

'But you must find out,' he said.

'Why?' she demanded. 'So that she can tell me I've not only lost who I thought was my father but that my biological father never even knew I existed?'

'Oh, my Lord,' he muttered. He knew only too well what her father had meant to her. 'I'm really sorry.' He saw that she had begun to cry and tried to put his arm round her, tried to hold her, but she pulled away.

'Listen,' he said, trying to console her, 'your dad is still your dad, right? He loved you.'

'I don't think he knew.'

'Knew what?'

'I don't think he knew the truth.'

'But surely he must have worked it out.'

'Why?'

'Hadn't they been married – what? – fifteen years when you were born? Had your mother ever been pregnant before, lost a child?'

'No,' she said. 'I don't think so. I don't know. I don't know anything any more.'

'But if there weren't any other children, then surely he put two and two together...'

'But he loved me,' she protested. 'How

could he love a child that wasn't his?' A look of pure childhood terror came over her face, as if to refute this would bring her whole life crashing in pieces around her; as if she truly doubted this once incontrovertible fact.

All kinds of pictures flew through her head: the handles of the cupboards – the wooden animals – which she had stroked for hours after he had died because they reminded her of his care; the warmth of sitting beside him as he read to her; the way he held up his arms for her to swing down out of his truck. And the presents, just little things, bags of sweets, a notebook, a plastic bracelet that poppered together, and songs he made up for her, his patience, his hands on the reins of the pony, and on the girth as he tightened it – *How does that feel? Does it feel safe enough* – and being carried on his shoulders across the field...

The memories nearly asphyxiated her.

Nick put his arms round her, and at last she allowed herself to press her face into his shoulder. 'It was all for nothing,' she said, her voice muffled. 'That's what I keep thinking. It was all untrue.'

'It wasn't untrue,' he told her. 'He loved you, you know he did. You know that for a fact, Zeph.'

Eventually she pulled away, and wiped her face with her handkerchief.

'Is this what you wanted to tell me?' Nick asked her.

'No. Actually I came to say ... about Joshua...' She blew her nose and stowed the handkerchief in her pocket. 'I wanted to tell you that whatever you wanted to do, whenever you wanted to see him, it was all right.'

'Thank you,' he said, surprised.

'I wanted to talk to you about times, how to arrange it.'

'OK.'

'I don't want to fight.'

'Neither do I.'

'He misses you very much.' She paused. 'I don't want to hurt him.'

Nick flushed, and she noticed it – a sign of deep emotion – but she made no comment.

She turned and began to walk back to the car. At the rise to the top of the dune, she waited for him to catch up. They said nothing until they had come down the other side, and were in the car park.

She hesitated by her car. 'Will you tell me something?' she asked.

'Yes.'

'Will you tell me the truth, if I ask a question?'

'Yes,' he said.

'Are you still seeing her?'

'No.'

She appraised him, as if trying to read his thoughts.

'Zeph...'

'And one other thing.'

He waited.

'Did you love her?'

'Oh, Zeph,' he said. Her tone had been so pathetic: it cut him to the quick. Her voice had wavered with grief. He felt a great wave of guilt rise in him. 'Oh, my God,' he said, 'won't you try to forgive me?'

'You didn't answer me,' she said.

'Love her?' he repeated. He tried to find the words to frame his horror. He could see from the way she held herself, closed in, wrapped up against him, her arms across herself, that everything she had once believed of him had been blown away. And he saw in the same moment that if there was to be any future for them it was up to him, and that he would have to start again from the beginning, making it better than before, building it up with more patience than he had ever summoned in his life. 'Don't you know?' he whispered. 'Don't you realize? I never loved her. I never loved her at all. How could I? I love you.'

'Then why?' she asked. 'Why?'

'I don't know. I just don't know.'

'Was it your doing?' she asked. 'Did you come on to her?'

He paused.

She screwed her hands into fists at her side. 'The truth,' she said.

'It was mutual,' he said.

'Mutual,' she repeated softly.

'I spend every minute of every day regretting it, Zeph.'

'Mutual...'

'Don't,' he said.

'And I spend every minute thinking of you with her,' she whispered.

'I'm so sorry,' he said. 'I'm so sorry.'

She began to cry, but the tears were silent. It appalled him to see them roll down her face unchecked.

'I think of you in bed with her,' she said. 'I think of you ... doing the things we did, lying with her afterwards, talking to her...'

'It wasn't like that,' he protested.

'And having little jokes, eating a meal with her...'

'No, no...'

'Naked with her, making her come...'

'No, Zeph. Please, God, don't do this. I saw her half a dozen times – it wasn't–'

Suddenly she caught hold of his jacket. 'What was it, then?' she demanded. 'You mean you didn't fuck her? You didn't do that? Tell me you didn't! How can I get these pictures of you out of my head?'

They were staring at each other, standing close.

'I love you and I missed you,' he said slowly, choosing each word carefully, deliberately. 'It wasn't your fault, it was mine. It always will be mine.'

'You missed me?'

'After Josh was born.'

'You think I neglected you?'

'No...'

'That's what you're saying.' She let go of him. 'You're jealous of your own son.'

He opened his mouth to deny it, then stopped himself. 'It all changed,' he said. 'You were always tired.'

'It was a bloody tiring job on my own,' she said accusingly. 'You only played at helping me. Not the difficult bits. Just the fun things. That was all you did.' But even as she was saying the words another voice spoke in the back of her mind. *You shut him out*, it whispered. *You were ill, you were depressed*, it insisted, *and you shut him out*.

'OK,' Nick was saying. 'But you never wanted to go anywhere with me, get a babysitter...'

'I did my best,' she said. 'I'm sorry if it wasn't good enough.'

'You did brilliantly,' he told her. 'That was it, don't you see? Can you understand? You did everything brilliantly, and the only person Josh seemed to want was you. Even if I held him I was doing it wrong, and I just...'

'Just what?' she prompted.

'I guess I just gave up trying to be good at this thing. I just accepted I was some klutz that you tolerated, a clumsy klutz.'

'Nick, that's not fair.'

He shrugged.

'You don't really think that,' she said.

He looked surprised. 'That's exactly what I think.'

Grief, guilt and horror gripped her in equal measure. 'So you went to somebody else. Just like that.'

'Not for that reason. And not just like that.'

'Well, it must have had something to do with it, as you bring the subject up.' She rubbed her eyes with the back of her hand.

'I felt dispensable,' he said. 'Like I'd done my job, and I wasn't needed, and that was it.'

'That's rubbish.'

'I'm telling you what I felt.'

She was weighing her car keys in her palm. She was thinking clearly, for the first time, of how she had abandoned him, not the other way round. Like her namesake, she had been in the underworld. Now she had a chance to come back to the light.

'What do you want me to do?' he asked.

'Sorry?'

'What do you want me to do?' he repeated. 'Tell me what would make it all right. What is it? You want me to crawl on my hands and knees?'

She raised her chin. 'Don't be stupid.'

'I mean it,' he said. 'I'll scrub out St Paul's with a toothbrush.'

'Oh, for Christ's sake,' she said, 'if you can't take this seriously...'

'I am serious,' he said. 'I'd do anything. Say what it is.'

'I don't want you to do anything, Nick.'

He tried to take her hand, but she pulled away. There was a fumbling of fingers. At the other side of the car park, a family was returning to their car, the children running riot in circles round the parents; the mother carrying a baby, the father pushing a toddler bike.

Zeph gazed at them, envying them.

'We can be them,' he said.

'No,' she murmured. 'It's all ruined ... ruined.'

She started to cry again.

All at once, he remembered.

He remembered what it was that she had been talking about.

Here. On this beach. That first weekend.

They had come to this spot and it had been late at night. They had tried to swim but it had been too cold and, laughing, they had run back up the slippery, shifting bank of pebbles to their clothes. And she had lain on her back, laughing still, and he had made love to her there, under the black sky, with the vast sea as still as a mirror, and no light at all, either on the water or the land.

Now he stepped towards her, took her in his arms, pressed his lips to her hair. 'It's not ruined,' he told her. 'I won't let it be. Give me half a chance, Zeph, and I'll prove it to you. Only give me the chance, Zeph. Please.'

Rosso

I wonder how anyone else would describe this time, and with what colour. I suppose most would call it black. But it is red for me, because I have come back to Enna to lie here in this house and wait for what comes. Red, the colour of celebration, and of warning. The colour of passion and violence.

All those things signify you. I see you standing in the street as the Easter processions pass us; I see you turning your head as the bands come down the street again at midnight. I feel your hand in mine, your mouth on mine. I feel the aftermath, the ending that I should have foreseen, and the violence of the loss. If I had been a little older, if I had had a little more wisdom, I might have avoided that violence and taken the warning seriously.

But then I wonder if I would have liked myself if I had been a man who could override his passion.

This is a house of soft voices. While I lie here, all sorts of women look after me. They think it is appropriate to walk about talking in whispers as if they were in church. I get them to play music, which they do with bad grace. I want the music playing and all the windows open.

Some I have known and others are strangers. The nurse, for instance, until she started to laugh when I told her stories. I tell her all kinds of things. Some are fiction. Some are true. I like to hear her laughing, and I like to see her putting her hand over her face because she thinks it's not right to have fun in a house where a young man is dying.

I say a young man, although I am fifty in two weeks' time.

But I don't feel old, so what am I? I am as young as the day I met you. Younger. I seem to have regressed in this strange interlude to all the things of my childhood. I remember running up and down this street whenever we came to visit family here. And I ask the nurse for the same things to eat: I ask her to go out for pastries, and I want zabaglione *and* zuccotto, *the treats I had when I was a boy.*

She indulges me. I suppose she's heard everything about me, or what the other women suppose to be true about me. If she has, she hasn't told me. I am supposed to have had a hundred mistresses. Other people's daughters, other people's wives. Italian women, Sicilian women, dark women, light women, whores and saints, friends, and friends of friends. I wonder how I ever had time. I don't bother to deny it. How else, they reason, could I know what women think and how they feel? How else could I read them, unless I had known a legion?

But you don't need to bed an army of women to understand them.

You only need to know one.

You don't know this house: I bought it fifteen years ago. It's on one of the streets behind the cathedral. The garden is overgrown; it has a balcony running the length of the first floor, and one of the tenants I rented it to painted it red, the shutters, too.

So I lie in a red shade. I told the nurse it was not good for me, that I wanted someone to come in and paint the shutters yellow, for the sun. Do you know what she told me? She said that the mere perception of a red colour raises the human metabolism by thirteen per cent. She said it in all seriousness, word for word. I asked her where she had found it out, and she said that she reads magazines people leave on trains. So, I am subject to knowledge gleaned from the carelessness of strangers. I listened to what she said, and then I burst out laughing. She laughed too. That's what amuses us: the idiocy and randomness of the world.

Rosso. The colour of bullfighters' capes, even though the bull is colour-blind. Rosso, the colour of Germanic gods. Thor had red hair. And

Wotan, the god of the hunt. And things we distrust, too. The devil, for one.

I wonder if there is a devil.

I wonder where I shall go when I leave behind this treacherous flesh. One of your British philosophers said that the rising to a great place is always by a winding stair; so, I hope to see a winding stair in front of me at the last. I shall run up it. I have run at things all my life, and even if I had it to live again, I would not change a second, or slow to a walk.

Red was supposed once to have magical properties. Vermilion and mercury were supposed to be the first steps to the philosopher's stone, whose owners were thought to have magical powers. So, perhaps I shouldn't wish to change the shutters, and lying here in what looks like a red pool should make me feel that I possess the secrets of the ancients.

I don't think I ever saw you in red; I remember everything you wore and there was a blue dress, and a white one, and a white shirt and jeans. No red. But I close my eyes and see you in the Syracusa house, the little cottage of my father's, and for some strange reason I have red in my mind. Maybe it's because of John Gray's roses, 'the roses, every one, were red'...

Thirty years ago I planted a white rose by the window. Do you know what has happened to it? I wish you could see it. It survived. It grew very tall and now it swamps the side of the house, and everyone remarks on it, a kind of miracle there in the hot sun. Although perhaps it had some-thing to do with the trees that were planted in the same year. Eucalyptus trees that grew taller than the roof, much taller, and now give shade to the English rose.

After I had planted it, after that year had passed, and after I knew that you were never coming back, and that I should not see you again, I went back to my studies in Rome. I finished the course and I qualified, but I never took up the job my father had prepared for me. Because you were still in my mind, and I kept thinking about what you had said that day in Ortigia. You said I would be more suited to being an artist, and you were right. I went travelling, and I told my father I needed to go before I settled down.

But you know what, Cora? I never did settle down. I lived the life you had predicted for me. I kicked off my shoes and lived through the first summer in Cyprus. I crewed on a boat, although I knew nothing about sailing. But I learned. And I took a job at the end of the summer crewing for someone who had another boat in Greece. And I never did come back to my father's business. One of my sister's husbands took on his accounts, and I began to think of a book of my own.

I was wondering the other day if you had seen it.

I was wondering if you had read it.

If you did, I hope you forgave me.

Only three people in the world would have

guessed that it was about you, even though I called my character by a Sicilian name. I hope that you were not offended, and I hope that Richard was not offended, although it was twelve years after I met you that the book was finally published. Richard would have been seventy-three. Did he mind? Did he care? Did you show it to him?

You know, there is something strange about The Light.

When I was in London to speak, a man came up to me at the ceremony. He was an agent called Bisley – not that I knew him: someone told me his name afterwards.

He was an old man; he had a copy of my book in his hand. Not unusual: everyone in that crowded room had it that night. But he was smiling, and he stared at me with such curiosity.

And do you know what he asked me? He asked if I had ever heard of a poem, and it was the poem you taught me, 'I warmed my hands before the fire of life'.

And he put his hand on my arm. 'I'm glad to know,' he said, 'that she met you at last.'

I don't know if he knew you, Cora.

I don't know if that was what he meant.

I have puzzled over it so often since.

I still wonder what went on between you and Richard.

You must have agreed to stay together, or, if you did not, you must have decided not to stay with me. I don't blame you, after all this time.

364

You were in an impossible position. I don't pretend to be proud of my part in the dilemma. But the boy I was could not have got himself out of that situation. To have done so I would have had to take on another personality, one that I did not then, and I suspect I do not now, possess. The kind of personality that does not want to be swept up in the wave.

I wish I had seen you just once more, Cora.

Despite everything, despite all the mistakes.

I wish I could look into your face now and see that you have forgiven me. Forgiven me for loving you, and for writing that I loved you. Forgiven me for being nineteen and irresponsible. Forgiven me for a lifetime of wanting you back.

I think of you, and wonder what you are doing. You will be sixty-four this year, I think. Sixty-four. It does not seem possible. I can't imagine you at sixty-four. Are you well? Are you alone? I wonder if Richard is still alive. Is there anything I could do to help you, if I knew you? Would you want me to come to you?

I would come even now. Get up from this cursed bed. It would be worth doing; it would be worth the last effort to see you finally.

I have come to London, you know, London and Paris. I have been within an hour or two of where you used to live. Do you know that, a few years ago, in Paris, I rang your telephone number? I don't know what was in my mind. Some selfish wish to disrupt you again. It was an impulse.

So I rang the number; I was a little drunk, maybe. I had won a prize that evening. I thought I was a pretty good guy. I thought I was all right to know. So, full of champagne, I rang you. But the number was wrong. The line gave the sound that meant the number was unobtainable.

When I mentioned it to a colleague, he said that the English telephone numbers, their area codes, had changed. But I didn't try to find the new code. Because by then I had decided that it was a sign. I was not, after all, a pretty good guy. I was not, after all, all right for you to know. You had not tried to speak or write to me in all those years. And that was what you wanted. And it was a sign that I should respect it.

It is evening. I am tired with writing all day.

But I will tell you one last thing.

I have left you the house below Syracusa, the cottage on the coast, which my father left to me.

I have asked my lawyer to send this journal and this news to you after my funeral. I hope that you are at the same address or, if you are not, that the package will find you.

And I hope that you might come here, finally.

If you do, please go back to Syracusa. Please go and stand at the Temple of Apollo again, and go back to the cathedral and stand in the street where we stood.

I felt you change as I drew you into the shadow there. I wondered if I should kiss you; I knew it would not be right. Or, at least, I thought I did. But when my mouth was on yours, I knew that there was nothing more right, and I felt you move to me.

There had been other girls. A girl from my village whom I was supposed to marry: we had been childhood friends, and had been together as teenagers, and our families knew each other and it had always been supposed that we would marry. But she went to Verona and I went to Rome, and we decided against it. She was glad, I think.

And there was a girl at college. This was something different; I took her to bed. She was American. She was careless in her lovemaking: it was routine to her, like cleaning her teeth or washing her face. It was nothing special to her, and we enjoyed ourselves, but it was like running a good race, or watching a good film. It was pleasant. But it was not love.

Not until I had you in my arms did I understand that these two things sometimes come together, the heart and the body. And sometimes, once in a lifetime, if we are lucky, it will happen. I opened my eyes and saw myself in another place, the same but different. The same street and the same town, but different. A different world from the one I entered when I kissed you. I discovered what I had always been sceptical about before that kiss, before I had seen you walking towards me that morning; I discovered that love cannot be judged or stopped. It is like a law of physics, where two elements that have been parted inevitably revert to the original unity. I felt that, until then, I had been missing some essential component, and that by touching you I had regained it. The world that had been so imperfect before made perfect sense.

After you there were other women, Cora. I am a man and I could not live all my life alone. There was a woman in Greece who came to work on the boats with me; she was English, like you. She was very pretty and she liked music. She was talented, she could play, and we had a small apartment for a while, part of a larger house, and in the house there was a piano. Sometimes at dusk, before we went out, she would play. I was quite happy with her, but the playing made me feel so bad. She had a little piece – she told me the name: it was Romance from Piano Concerto No. 1 by Chopin – and it struck something inside me, as if the music had reached into me. I would think then, in front of this girl, that I would become insane if I could never see you again. I did not tell her about you, but I think she knew. And I think she was in love with me as I had felt for you, which made it so much worse when we parted.

Cora, I don't know now what possessed you and me, but I have never believed it was wrong. That sounds unreasonable, as if I have indeed lost my mind. But I wonder if you know what I mean. It was not wrong. I was with another man's wife – which I have not done since, I want you to know – but I couldn't feel it was wrong.

I was glad, so glad, to have known you, and I have been glad all my life. I will take the images of you to my grave with a light heart. I will relive our times, few as they were. The time in Ortigia and in Enna, and the days after Easter, when we went away.

We thought we were running away together, but it did not last. We had four days of happiness before you told me that you had to return with Richard. That you had to go back to England with him, to sell the house, to arrange your affairs. And I don't think you were lying to me, Cora. I think you were sincere in every word. But something happened once you were back with him. Something in his reaction made you change your mind. Or something when you got home. I don't know. I will never know. I will die not knowing the answer to that question.

But I have those four days.

I see you standing by the window in the first light of morning. I get up from the bed where we have hardly slept all night. I put my arms round you, and you stand with your back to me, but your head leaning on my shoulder. And I pass my hands down your body, and you turn your head and kiss me. Such intensity in that kiss; such absolute giving.

And I turn you round and drop my hands

369

down your back, feeling every inch of skin, running my fingers over your shoulders, your waist, to the curve of the spine in the small of your back, and I pass my hands between your legs, beginning to kneel as I do so. And I feel you shudder as I touch you. And you give yourself to me, and never before, never since, have I known the ecstasy I felt with you that morning, that night.

And we ate on the terrace, and looked at the sea. It was a run-down house, really, not much more than a peasant's cottage. It is better now: I have reconstructed it. I have employed a very good carpenter and a gardener, and made it nice for you, darling. It's not bigger. The rooms are the same. The bedroom, and the bathroom with the blue floor. You remember. We filled the bath to overflowing by mistake. You remember. We wiped the floor and laughed while we did it, because I had never done a domestic thing before in my life, and was so hopeless. I changed all that, too, Cora. I would surprise you now.

I have two houses. One in Rome and this one in Enna, and I have the cottage on the coast. I live mostly in Rome, and it is a beautiful house. But I didn't want to end my life there, among strangers. I wanted to come here.

I wish that we had lived in any house, anywhere, together. I wish that we had married, and raised a family. I wish we had had children together. Sometimes I allow myself to think of our family because I have never had children. I *think of them, and I can feel them sometimes in the room, or standing silently by the door.*

I wonder if they are really there.

I wonder if part of me lives in you, darling.

I send you all my love with this journal.

All my love, all of my life.

Eighteen

As Cora stood at the top of the hill with Joshua late that afternoon, she saw them coming.

They were walking across the field together, Zeph a little way ahead of Nick. But the smallest movement had caught Cora's eye: just after they had come through the gate to the house, she had seen Zeph turn and glance at her husband, dipping her head a little. And Nick had put his hand on her daughter's shoulder and run his fingers, just briefly, down her arm. Then he called Joshua.

Cora looked back at her grandson. All afternoon, he had been helping her as she worked her way up the long slope of the orchard, deliriously happy to be sitting alongside her on the field mower, oblivious to its rattling age and the cloud of petrol smoke it dragged in its wake. She had rigged

371

up an amateur seatbelt, but there was really no need: he had been as good as gold. It had been only in the last half-hour that he had squirmed round in his seat to watch the rake pull in the cuttings.

Now he saw his father. For a moment he did nothing at all. Then he jammed his fist into his mouth and chewed his knuckles. Cora turned off the engine and got down.

Nick began to walk away from the house, parallel to them, between the lines of apple trees. Cora saw him grin; he cocked his thumb over his shoulder. Cora knew what the gesture meant. 'Want to swing?' she asked.

There was a rope swing in the woods on one of the big chestnuts.

Joshua began to scramble down, bypassing Cora's outheld arms. From a hundred yards apart, mother and grandmother watched as the little boy ran between the Dabinetts planted in their military sequence, two abreast. Cora shaded her eyes against the weak five o'clock sun and saw Nick pick Joshua up and swing him over his shoulders in a fireman's lift. He waved at her. She waved back, then looked at Zeph.

All at once, watching Zeph come towards her, she was struck by Richard's expression on her daughter's face: of determination. She leaned against the mower, taking off her gloves.

Zeph stopped six feet from her. 'What's the matter?' she asked.

'I'm tired,' Cora admitted. 'What's happened? What have you said? What have you agreed?'

'Nothing yet.'

'But is it all right?'

'Yes,' Zeph told her. 'It's all right.'

For a moment Cora couldn't speak. The relief was so great that she could only nod. Then, 'He's done a very stupid and hurtful thing,' she said, 'but, darling, there are worse men in the world.'

'What do you mean?'

'Men who use women,' Cora replied, 'and don't care whom they hurt. Bullies and liars. Nick isn't like that.'

Zeph looked down the length of the trees. 'He's been offered a job in the USA,' she said.

Immediate fear replaced the relief. Cora was aware that she had gasped. 'Will he take it?' she asked.

'I don't know.'

'Will you go with him?'

'I don't know.'

Cora plunged her hands into her pockets. A little prickle of pain threaded its way through her chest and shoulder. Well, if they had to go, they had to go, she told herself. It was a good thing. They had to be together. That was what was important. She watched

Zeph's profile. She wanted to hold her, but her daughter's face was unreadable. Then, a crooked smile came to Zeph's face. 'I liked this best of all,' she said, 'the first mowing. I liked it better than the blossom, to be out here with Dad for the first time in the year.' She looked at her mother. 'It's what I remember most,' she said. 'It was him and me, all the time. Like a private world, out here. Nobody else up on the hill. Just everything green. And us.'

'Yes, all the time.'

'Never you,' Zeph said.

Cora was silent.

'I used to think you didn't care much about being with us,' Zeph glanced back at her mother, 'but that isn't right, is it? It was because of me that you were never together.'

'No,' Cora told her. 'He wanted you. You have to understand that. There was never any question of it.'

'Even though I wasn't his daughter?'

Their eyes met. 'You were his daughter,' Cora said, 'in every way that mattered.'

'He adjusted to me.'

'No,' Cora said. 'He didn't just accept you, he wanted you from the very first. He never blamed me, Zeph, from the first moment he knew about you.'

'He forgave you? He knew?'

'It was more than that,' Cora said. 'Much more.'

374

She had realized she was pregnant four months after they returned from Sicily. It was early September and they had been busy during the summer. It had been rainy and hot so the crops were heavier than usual, and the stock grew like wildfire. In May, Cora had made up pots and baskets of pelargonium, all scarlet, and taken them to the Saturday market along the main street in town.

She had had a little stall by the abbey gatehouse, and from her vantage-point had been able to look back along the path to the church and down Long Street. Traffic had gone back and forth ceaselessly, and every Saturday, standing first with the pelargonium and, latterly, with the fruit, she had wanted to step to the edge of the pavement and ask any driver to take her away.

Momentary madness like that had populated the weeks after they returned. She had felt a deep irritation with everything around her, the house, the weather. Especially the weather. One afternoon in June, when it had poured and she had been sitting in the kitchen watching the rain stream down the windows, she had put her head on her arms on the table and cried for a long time. She kept thinking of how the heat would be settling in Sicily, burning down into the ground, warming the seas.

She kept thinking of him, of Enna, of Easter. How she had got up very early on that Easter Saturday in Enna and gone out of the small hotel, leaving Richard asleep. She had taken her bag and passport and walked quickly across the square, then down the alley that ran beside the hotel. And gone straight into his arms. Pietro was waiting exactly where they had arranged.

He had borrowed a car. They drove across the mountains, down to Caltagirone, through Ragusa and Modica to the coast, then turned east. She remembered the grey backs of the hills, the great boulders broken in some and dragged to the edge to scour a little pasture on the high ground. She remembered narrow roads that raised dust as they passed. She had sat next to him on the bench seat in the front of the car, and they had hardly spoken, his hand on her thigh.

They reached the cottage in late afternoon.

As she got out of the car, she looked at him. The cottage was down a long stony track; it faced out to sea. The garden was merely a pasture of thorny grass. There was no one to be seen, and they had passed no one on the road for the last three or four miles. There were no other buildings in any direction. Pietro walked round the side of the car. The sun beat down. He took her in his arms and pressed her against the door.

She wanted him. There was no subtlety in it. She could not summon the coyness, the holding-back she had been taught all her life that a nice woman should employ. Even with Richard she sometimes felt, still, on the rare occasions that their lovemaking was anything other than perfunctory, that she should not hold him as she did, or ask him to do certain things. She felt as if he merely obeyed her, bemused by her need, without feeling any of his own. She sometimes wondered if he felt for her in any sexual way, if he thought or fantasized about her. She didn't know. He would smile at her the next day with an odd, preoccupied glance, as if he couldn't quite fathom her.

But this was different. This was a fever. Pietro responded with delight to her every touch; the sound of his voice as she put her hands on him was a revelation. And she was ready to indulge her greed, her overwhelming longing. She couldn't do otherwise. She didn't want to do otherwise. She wanted to close her eyes and be consumed by him. In the back of her mind for the last twenty-four hours, she had heard Bisley's voice, 'the fire of life'. And he had been right. She hadn't known until now exactly how right.

Pietro drew back from her. 'Is this real?' he asked.

'I don't know,' she replied, because she had no idea what she had done, how she would live from now on, or what she could tell Richard. She had a sense of dreaming, yet of being more alive than at any other moment of her life. So she couldn't answer Pietro.

She saw disappointment in his face: he had expected her to reassure him of the promise she had made, her promise to come away with him and stay with him.

'I will make it real,' he said.

They walked to the house, and he opened the door. The inside was cool, the floor tiled. It smelt a little damp, because it had not been opened since the winter rains, and she walked round it, opening the shutters and the windows, letting the light stream in. He took her hand and they went upstairs. As she stood by the bedroom door, watching him, he took off his clothes and stood motionless in front of her. He was very beautiful, more beautiful than a man deserved to be, and she thought of the gods making him in their image.

Four days.

Perhaps they strayed over the Styx in those days; perhaps she sold her soul to the devil to be with him. Perhaps what they had done was truly a sin, dark and desperate, and they were exiling themselves to hell, to purgatory, to be damned. All these ideas went through her mind as she loved him. In the early hours of the morning she would watch him sleep, and she would pray, a thin little prayer to a God she was not sure would listen to her, even if He existed, that they might be protected, that they would not be punished.

On the fifth day, early in the afternoon, as they lay on the bed, they heard a car coming down the drive. They had listened for a while, not believing it could be anyone they knew.

'There will be some mistake,' Pietro had whispered. They were lying curled into one another, both on their left side, his arms round her, she clasping his hands over her breasts. As the engine drew nearer, he tightened his hold. Then he lifted himself on to one elbow, kissed her shoulder almost absentmindedly, listening intently.

The car drew up below the window.

They heard a door open and close, then footsteps on the path.

She sat up. 'Who is it, do you think?' she asked.

Pietro went to the shuttered window. He opened it, stood stock still for a second, then turned and picked up his clothes. 'It is Richard,' he said, without looking at her.

She hurried to dress. She heard Pietro go downstairs, the outer door opening, and the blurred cadence of two voices.

When she came downstairs, she saw Richard's glance stray first to her bare feet.

He was dressed in a shirt and tie, trousers and jacket despite the heat; next to him, Pietro stood in his jeans and unbuttoned shirt. Richard walked forward. He didn't look at the house, only into her face.

'It's time to come home,' he said.

'How did you find us?' she asked.

'Alex told me of this address,' he replied. 'He used to come here with his lover.'

There was a slight emphasis on the word *his*, but nothing more. She waited.

'This is Cora's home now,' Pietro said, at their back.

She looked at him, and back at her husband.

'Cora,' Richard said, 'you will have nothing to live on – no money. And no home, either. When Pietro's father finds out about this, he won't allow you to be here.'

'I am not afraid of my father,' Pietro said. He moved alongside them, and touched Cora's arm.

'I can't come back,' she said. 'Not now.'

'I don't mean for ever,' Richard said. 'Only for six months.'

The two of them stared at him.

'Six months?' Pietro repeated. 'She will not come back even for a day.'

'I don't understand,' Cora said.

'Don't listen to him,' Pietro urged.

Richard ignored him. 'Cora, please think about what you are doing.'

'I shall look after her,' Pietro said. 'The decision is made.'

Cora could not speak; gently, she disengaged Pietro's hand.

Finally Richard looked at Pietro. 'Would you allow us to talk alone?' he asked.

Pietro was watching Cora's face. Eventually he nodded. He walked out of the house, and Cora saw him go down the garden and sit on the low wall at the edge of the terrace.

She went to the chairs by the kitchen table; pulled one out and sat down. Richard seated himself opposite her. She studied his face. She couldn't believe that he wasn't angry. She had expected a scene. He would be perfectly justified in losing his temper, to have come here like an avenging angel. But there was no trace of it, only concern.

'Would you like anything to drink?' she asked him. 'It's very hot.'

'No,' he said. 'Thank you.'

His politeness filled her with grief.

'I'm sorry,' she murmured, looking down at her hands on the table top.

'I will never say anything about this,' he told her. 'I will never refer to it.'

'I can't leave him now. You must see that.'

'I can see that he's a boy,' Richard said, 'with a life ahead of him, and a family name to protect. You know that what you have done will disgrace him?'

'He doesn't care about that.'

'He will,' Richard said. His voice was perfectly calm. 'Perhaps not at this moment, but at some point in the near future he will care very much that he has disgraced himself and his family. The concept is very strong here, Cora. It's shameful enough in England, but this is not England.'

'It's not shameful,' she said, equally quietly. 'I'm not ashamed of what I've done.'

There was silence. She was appalled to see that tears had formed in his eyes. She glanced away, unable to bear the expression on his face.

'You're in love with him,' he said.

'Do you think that I would do this if I weren't?'

'No.'

'You must go,' she said. 'I'll be all right.'

'I doubt it.'

'We'll go to another country,' she said. 'We'll go somewhere else.'

'And cut him off from his family for ever?'

She said nothing. Outside, she caught movement: Pietro was pacing up and down. 'We'll work something out,' she said.

'He has studies to finish.'

'He's going to leave the university.'

'And do what?'

'Get a job.'

'But Pietro is gifted, very talented. Or so Alex tells me.'

'He's not interested in the course he's doing.'

'Then he should do some other academic study,' Richard said. 'It would be a waste to do otherwise. Have you any idea what kind of pressure this will put on you both?'

She had no answer for him. They remained where they were, confronting each other across the table while the silence stretched out.

'I can't understand why you've gone to all this trouble,' she said.

He frowned immediately. 'What trouble?'

'Following me.'

'But of course I had to follow you,' he said. He looked utterly perplexed. 'How could you think that I would just abandon you?'

'Because I'm with another man,' she said. 'And because you've been so remote from me.'

'Remote?' he echoed.

'Since we came here.'

'Oh, Cora,' he said. And, all at once, he put his head into his hands.

'You've excluded me,' she said.

'And that's the reason?'

'No,' she said. 'Not only that.'

'You don't understand.'

'You're right,' she told him. 'You've made no effort to allow me to understand. I've felt at arm's length from you for a long time.'

'Cora,' he said softly, 'this past week...'

'I know what these people feel about you,' she said, 'but I don't know why. Pietro had to tell me. You didn't confide in me before we got here at all. You didn't explain.'

'Pietro told you?'

'He told me about you rescuing his father.'

To her amazement, Richard tipped back his head and gasped.

'What's the matter?' she asked.

'I don't know how to bear this any longer,' he said, almost to himself. She heard real despair in his voice. 'All this week ... the celebrations, the kindnesses, these people...'

'What's the matter?' she asked. 'Don't you appreciate it?'

'I can't endure it,' he said.

'But ... why did you come here?'

'Because Alex is ill, and I thought I must face what I had done.'

She tried to take in this last information. He got up from his seat, leaned on the table with both hands. 'I've been dishonest with you,' he said.

'Dishonest?' The idea was absurd.

'I've allowed you to believe a lie about me.'

'What lie?'

'That I did anything honourable in the war.'

'But you fought in Africa ... you were decorated for bravery...'

'It was fraudulent,' he said. 'Do you understand? Fraudulent.'

She stood up opposite him. His face had turned a greyish colour.

'I didn't pick up Pietro's father to save him,' he said. 'I picked him up to quieten him. To stop him worsening the situation.'

'But they had just shot his father...'

'We had passed up and down that road twice that morning,' Richard said. 'They were just two boys in that dug-out. They weren't going to shoot anyone. They were just reporting movements. They panicked and began to shoot.'

'But you went into their position,' Cora said. 'You stopped them.'

'Yes,' he acknowledged. 'I killed them. I shot a boy not very much older than Pietro who couldn't even reload his rifle properly.'

'You couldn't help it,' Cora said. 'What choice did you have?'

'I shot a frightened boy,' Richard repeated.

'But the knife...'

Richard walked to the window, put his hands on the sill. His body was angular and rigid.

'He had a little bit of olive wood,' he replied quietly. 'He had been carving it. Just a little figure, a dog. It was lying on the edge of the slit trench with the knife. I don't think he had any idea of what was happening. I think he'd been surprised by the other boy's shot. I think he was trying to stop him. He was trying to surrender. He put up his hands...'

She walked over, and stood beside him.

His voice had dropped very low, so low that it was a struggle to catch what he was saying. 'They were just two confused children,' he whispered. 'No more than eighteen. Maybe not even that. And I didn't try to take them prisoner. I stumbled on them. They were right at my feet as I ran up from the road. I was injured. I got into the trench. The second boy didn't even have a gun close to him. When he saw that I had drawn mine, he dropped his hands and reached for the knife. As we fell, we both tried to get hold of it. He cut my neck by mistake, I think. I got free from him, and tried to get out of the trench, then saw that he was lying on his knife.'

There was silence. She saw that his hands were shaking. Instinctively, she placed hers on top of his.

'So, you see,' he said, 'I'm not such a great hero. I was only saving my own skin.'

'That's not true,' she replied. 'You saved two lives.'

'It wasn't my intention to save anyone's life,' he said. 'It was my intention to save my own. And even though I was older than those boys, I behaved in the same way. I panicked.'

'You did not,' she objected.

'I know what I did.'

'This is the nightmare,' she said. 'This is

what you see when you come up from the beach. It wasn't the beach at all. It wasn't the waves. It was inland a little way.'

'I see the water,' he said, 'and then the boy. And then it's always the same... I hide.' He bowed his head.

She turned him towards her. 'And this is what you've been afraid of all these years?' she said, wonderingly. 'This is what you've dreaded my knowing?'

'Can't you see? I could never tell anyone. I got home and no one would let it rest. I went travelling, and then Alex started to write to me. He told me what this family thought of me. It's pursued me, and it's all a fabrication. I'm not the man they or you think I am.' And he let out a subdued sound of exhaustion.

She held his hand tightly. 'You're everything that I *know* you are,' she replied softly. 'And so much more. And nothing less.'

She came home with him. She felt she ought not to leave him – at least, not yet. She felt that she should come back, and end their marriage quietly, in a sensible way. That was what he had asked: that she come home and consider for six months. She did not want it to end in rumour and scandal, to have him face the ignominy. And she had to return to tell her father.

Pietro fought her decision every inch of the

way for the rest of the week. They drove back to Taormina together. She met him every morning in the Villa Communale gardens. She went down to him before breakfast, at first light, between the sub-tropical trees. Between them, the light was bright turquoise, and it was hard to tell if it was the colour of the sea or the sky. She would walk forward, between the hibiscus, the tradescantia and the bird-of-paradise flowers, and see him waiting for her.

He would take her hand, and she would see the same fear and longing in his face as she felt. She would put her arms round him as they stood together, watching the sun progress across the hills, the town, the sea.

Eventually, he accepted that she would go home. But only for six months. He made her promise. Six months, in which he would try to arrange his own life.

But something happened on her return to England.

She felt the wrongness of it. She received Pietro's letters, read them over and over again, heard the boy in them. She thought about the disgrace he might suffer. She thought about the future, when she was forty and he was still just in his twenties. She thought about the difficulty and gradually, inch by inch, hour by hour, the need for him faded.

She still thought of the sea, and of walking

into it, just as Jenny had told her she should, the freedom, the pleasure, the sense of infinite possibilities. Jenny, who had vanished and never returned, whose whole life now seemed to have vanished with her.

Yet Cora still dreamed of him. She dreamed of the joy of him.

For a long time she could hardly look Richard in the face. His tolerance and patience were almost too much to bear. She felt she would be betraying him by returning to Sicily, compounding an injury. Richard had done nothing to her. He had always protected her. And this was how she had repaid him. Yet she longed to go: she longed for it with a physical pain.

In a rush of guilt one day, she returned Pietro's letters, dropping them into the post-box on the lane, standing next to it, tears running down her face. Six weeks later, she did it again. The first time, the dogs stood at her side, bedraggled after a summer downpour, wagging their tails in sympathy. She had a moment then, in the middle of the endless wet, grey day, of utter bleakness.

But most of all, in the agony of that summer, as she was caught between the two men she loved, a longer-lasting feeling surfaced. She realized that if she left Richard she would also leave her father, and the destruction that would cause could never be repaired.

Pietro was young. He would rebuild his life. In fact, he had a life ahead of him. Richard had not. Richard had only her.

And then September came.

She told him she was pregnant; she told him miserably, standing in front of him like a child expecting to be punished, waiting for him to pronounce the death sentence on their marriage.

'Have you written to Pietro?' he asked.

'No,' she said.

'You've replied to his letters?'

'No.'

'Is there a reason?'

'I don't know what to do,' she said truthfully, unable to hide the misery in her voice.

They were standing in the garden. It was evening; the unmistakable scent of autumn hung in the air. The light was altering: it no longer shone directly on the paths but lay slanted in oblique rectangles between the trees.

'You must tell me now,' he said. 'You must make a decision.'

'I can't,' she said, and began to cry, hating herself for this final weakness.

'You must.'

She wiped her face clumsily.

'You must choose,' he emphasized. 'If you tell him about this child, you must go back to him.'

'What?' she asked, not yet understanding

his ultimatum.

'If you choose to tell him, you must go back to Sicily. But if you choose to stay with me, you must never tell him.'

She gazed at him.

'You can go back,' he said, drawing out each word to make sure that she grasped his meaning. 'Marry him, or live with him, make a life there.' He was watching her expression. 'Or stay here, and raise the child as our own. But not two lives. Not a life stretched between two countries. Not a child with two fathers. I will never say a word to you, Cora. I will keep my promise. But you must keep yours. You must never speak to him again, or write to him. You must forget him.'

'I can't do that,' she said.

Around them the first shadows lengthened. She closed her eyes and saw the sea at her feet, blue-green near the shore, darker further out. She would never lose the joy of him, she realized. You couldn't lose a thing like that: you couldn't barter it away.

Richard took her hand. He began to walk along the path, guiding her to walk alongside him. When she followed, he pulled her closer to him, so that they continued arm in arm. All the time, the tears rolled down her face.

'I think I would like to buy somewhere else,' he said. He fixed his gaze on the top of the slope, where the driveway divided the thick hedges. The beech leaves in them had the first hint of orange, and of the white-red fragments that would survive the winter.

'I think I would like to buy a bigger place, and have an orchard.'

He stopped suddenly, and looked down, fleetingly, at her body. He hadn't touched her, slept with her, come near her since the spring. Now he took her in his arms and kissed her; not with the fire of Pietro's kisses, but his own gentle gesture.

'I've seen a farmhouse,' he said quietly, 'with two long sloping hills, and a little wood. An orchard would do well there. So would we.'

He put his hand on her face and tilted it towards him so that she looked into his eyes. 'Stay with me,' he said.

Cora looked back now at her daughter. Zeph was regarding her closely and, just as Cora was thinking how like Richard Zeph had become, even to the tone of her voice occasionally and little physical resemblances – the way she was tilting her head now, in concentration – Zeph asked a question: 'Am I like him?' she said. 'Am I like Pietro?'

Cora put her hand, briefly, on Zeph's, felt slight resistance and trailed her fingers away. In that same second's flash, she thought of Pietro's hand on hers, and pain flickered in her throat, her chest. 'Your hair colour is the same,' she said quietly. 'Your eyes.'

'Do I remind you of him?' Zeph asked. Her voice was full of trepidation. 'Did you think of him every time you saw me?'

'Oh, no,' Cora reassured her. 'No, no.' She tried to think how she could explain it. 'I worried about it before you were born,' she said. 'I worried that Richard would be reminded. But in the end it didn't matter. You were Richard's baby, Richard's child. He loved you to distraction. There was nothing he wouldn't have done for you, and he wasn't bitter. He was incapable of that.'

There were so many pictures in her mind: Richard carrying Zeph, newly born, on the day they left hospital, folding the satin-edged blanket carefully so that the baby would not be cold; Richard pacing the floor to soothe his daughter during the night; Richard wheeling her in a pushchair through town, his face alight with pride. He had been Zeph's slave from the first.

Cora frowned a little, then glanced away. 'We never mentioned Pietro,' she said. She noticed Zeph's surprise. 'Although sometimes I thought of him,' she admitted. 'On special days. When you learned to ride. He would have been proud of that, because his family had horses, and I know that he rode as a boy. And when you learned to swim. You were just like him about the sea. Those things...'

'You loved him.' Zeph was watching Cora's face.

Mother and daughter gazed at each other for several seconds.

'Yes,' Cora said. 'And when I read about him later, when I saw what he had become, what talent he had, I was proud of him. But as for the book ... for myself, for Richard, I wished it hadn't been written.'

'It was you,' Zeph whispered. 'So it was true. Your story.'

'Yes,' Cora admitted. She took a long, slow breath and looked away, down the slope of trees, past the farm, the distant thread of the lane to the hills on the far side of the valley, showing as the merest line of green. 'But whatever Pietro wrote about us afterwards, you must understand one thing, darling. You must remember this above anything else. I loved your father more.'

They stood facing each other in the centre of Richard's orchard, under the lines of naked trees, for some time. Then Zeph took her mother's hand and squeezed it.

Together, without a word, they turned and walked up the hill in the direction Nick had taken, towards the woods.

Postscript

She came out of the house at first light and made her way to the sea. This morning, as every morning since she had got there a year ago, she took off her clothes, laying them in a small, neat pile on the smooth stones at the water's edge.

Cora wouldn't swim for long: even in the summer she would feel cold quickly. But she struck out in long, even strokes from the shore, then lay on her back, relishing the sun on her face. From the ocean, she could see the roof of the cottage, and the garden, now terraced after her labours in the winter, planted with fig trees, almonds and lemons. It would be years before they matured enough to bear a heavy crop, but she didn't mind. Zeph and Nick would have the benefit of it and, after them, Joshua and his sister.

The baby had been born in the spring, and the family had come out to see her after Nick had finished his script, travelling by car and taking the ferry from Naples, as she and Richard had so many years ago. It was the first time that Zeph and Nick had seen the house; the first time that Zeph had been able to put a picture to Pietro's country and his passions. The two women had gone alone together to Enna and stood hand in hand on Good Friday on the Via Roma, watching the processions and crossing the square together at midnight.

Nick had helped the last of the contractors to lay the stone paths alongside the terraces, grinning at the achievement when it was done. He was used to it. The orchards at the farm were far more work than this.

On the last day of their visit, Cora had planted another rose, a red one, in the shade at the opposite end of the house. A young rose, which raced in green haste towards the roof in the months afterwards. And they pruned the white, now more of a tree than a single rose, its thick stem twisted, and the roses themselves a mere scattering of petals in the branches.

Cora swam to the shallows now and looked back up the hill.

Sometimes, when the light was brightening, like this, she thought she saw him coming towards her. She thought she heard Pietro's voice, his laughter.

She closed her eyes and heard him reading to her in those lost days, the only days that they had had to themselves.

'Non vo' che da tal nodo Amor mi scioligia,' he had read to her.

Love will not loose this knot.

As she got out of the water, she felt the sun on her back and stopped, luxuriating in the warmth.

He had given her this year: this year in the winter of her life, when the light burned brightest of all.

This Large Print Book, for people
who cannot read normal print,
is published under the auspices of

THE ULVERSCROFT FOUNDATION